Alien Archives

Alien Archives

Eighteen Stories of Extraterrestrial Encounters

BY

Robert Silverberg

THREE ROOMS PRESS
New York, NY

ALIEN ARCHIVES
Eighteen Stories of Extraterrestrial Encounters
by Robert Silverberg

ISBN 978-1-941110-80-5 (trade paperback)
ISBN 978-1-941110-81-2 (ebook)
Library of Congress Control Number: 2019938484

Pub Date: October 29, 2019

BISAC Coding:
FIC028090 Science Fiction Alien Contact
FIC029000 Science Fiction Short Stories (single author)
FIC028000 Science Fiction General

BOOK COVER AND INTERIOR DESIGN:
KG Design International | www.katgeorges.com

DISTRIBUTED BY:
Publishers Group West / Ingram Content Group | www.pgw.com

Visit our website at www.threeroomspress.com or
write us at info@threeroomspress.com

For Peter and Kat,
who showed up late but were worth waiting for.

TABLE OF CONTENTS

INTRODUCTION: A PLURALITY OF WORLDS

BY ROBERT SILVERBERG

HERE IS AN ASSORTMENT OF stories about human interactions with alien beings, some of them in far corners of the universe, some right here on Earth. (One of them, in fact, takes place in a California suburb a fifteen-minute drive from where I live.) I wrote these stories, the oldest one in 1954 and the most recent almost half a century later, with two beliefs held firmly in mind:

1) We are not alone. The universe is full of non-human life-forms.
2) We are never going to encounter any of these alien beings.

It may seem irrational of me to have written a whole book of stories about things that I don't believe are going to happen, but I remind you that these are science fiction stories, and the essence of science fiction is *what if*—which is why some people like to call science fiction "speculative fiction" instead. I do indeed doubt that any of the events depicted in this book, or anything remotely like them, will ever take place. But what if—what if—

* * *

BACK IN FAR-OFF 2004 I wrote an essay for one of the science fiction magazines titled "*Neque Illorum Ad Nos Pervenire Potest,*" which is Latin for "None of us can go to them, and none of them come to us." The phrase was that of the twelfth-century philosopher Guillaume de Conches, writing about the supposed inhabitants of the Antipodes, the lands that lay beyond the fiery sea that was thought to cut Europe off from the as yet unexplored Southern Hemisphere. I used it to express my belief that we are never going to have any close encounters with the inhabitants of other solar systems. They're just too far away. Despite the best efforts of such people as my friends, the brothers Jim and Greg Benford, who even now are working to drum up interest in an interstellar voyage, the distance even to the nearest star is so great that only by magical means (a faster-than-light drive, for instance) are we likely to get to an extrasolar planet and return.

"It's disheartening," I wrote, back then. "I've spent five decades [six, now] writing stories about other worlds and other intelligent lifeforms, and I don't like the idea that I've simply been peddling pipe dreams all this time. I *do* believe . . . that the universe is full of populated worlds. I *do* want to know what those alien races look like, how they think, what kind of cities they live in. I'd love to read alien poetry and look at alien sculptures. I might even want to risk dinner at a five-star alien restaurant. But none of that is going to happen . . . The speed of light is going to remain the limiting velocity not just for us, but for all those lively and interesting people out there in the adjacent galaxies, and that puts the kibosh on the whole concept of a galaxy-spanning civilization."

That there are worlds out there for the finding, plenty of them, if only we could find a way of getting to them, and that those worlds are inhabited, is something I have never doubted. The comic books I read as a small boy, seventy-plus years ago, were full of gaudy tales of "Martians" and "Venusians". Then, in 1948, when I discovered such pioneering collections of science fiction as the great Healy-McComas anthology *Adventures in Time and Space* and Groff Conklin's splendid *A Treasury of Science Fiction*, such stories as Eric Frank Russell's "Symbiotica," A.E. van Vogt's "Black Destroyer," and Arthur C. Clarke's "Rescue Party" lit up my adolescent mind with visions of galaxy upon galaxy filled with an infinite number of intelligent non-human beings. The thought of those infinities still stirs me, so many decades and so many stories later, whenever I look toward the night sky.

In my 2004 essay I calculated just how many inhabited worlds were likely to be out there. I figured there were twelve billion stars in our local galaxy alone that were neither too big nor too small to provide the energy that life-forms of our sort require.

"If half of these have planets," I wrote, "and half of those planets lie at the correct distance to maintain water in its liquid state, and half of those are large enough to retain an atmosphere, that leaves us with a billion and a half potentially habitable worlds in our immediate galactic vicinity. Say that a billion of these must be rejected because they're so large that gravity would be a problem, or because they have no water, or because they're in some other way unsuitable. That still leaves 500 million possible Earths in the Milky Way galaxy. And there are millions of galaxies."

Half a billion possible Earths in our little galaxy alone? That isn't just a hopeful hypothesis any more, and it may be a very conservative one. In January 2013, scientists at Caltech in Pasadena who had been studying the results sent back by NASA's Kepler Space Telescope offered an estimate of at least 100 billion habitable extrasolar planets just in the Milky Way galaxy—and our galaxy is only one of a nearly infinite number in the universe. They based their findings on a view of a five-planet system called Kepler-32, all of them similar in size to Earth and orbiting their star (M-type, smaller and cooler than our own) closely enough to ensure sufficient warmth. Since there are 100 billion M-type stars in the galaxy and the Kepler findings show planets around many of them, the Caltech people believe it's reasonable to think that they average one habitable world apiece—100 billion more or less Earth-type planets, and that's *billion* with a *b*. A billion, remember, is 1,000 million. Somewhere in all those billions and billions, surely, dwell the alien beings I was reading about in the s-f anthologies of the 1940s.

In fact, the whole idea of an inhabited cosmos was anticipated as early as 300 B.C. by the Greek philosopher Metrodoros the Epicurean: "To consider the Earth the only populated world in infinite space is as absurd as to assert that in an entire field sown with millet only one grain will grow." And it was developed most entertainingly in a lively little book *A Plurality of Worlds* (1686) by the French poet and philosopher Bernard de Fontenelle, which I've been reading in the elegant English translation that John Glanville produced the following year.

Fontenelle's book is one of the earliest attempts to make current scientific knowledge accessible to the lay reader, and it achieves that triumphantly. It is cast in the form of dialogs set at a French country estate, one per night for five nights, in which a philosopher who was probably very much like Fontenelle discusses astronomy and the nature of the universe with his hostess, a witty and somewhat flirtatious countess who is eager to understand the motions of the planets and stars.

What he sets forth is essentially a picture of the universe as we understand it today—the Sun at the center of the solar system, the planets in orbit around it, their various moons in orbit around them, and the stars an immense distance away, each one a sun in its own right and very likely having planets of its own. In all this, Fontenelle risked flying in the face of the traditional Christian belief that the creation of life has taken place only once, in the Garden of Eden, on Earth, and that Earth was the center of the universe. For some fifteen hundred years it was deemed heretical, and downright dangerous, to disagree with that position, until the work of the great astronomers Copernicus, Kepler, and Galileo showed the Earth is merely one of many worlds surrounding the Sun. As recently as 1633 Galileo had been called before the Inquisition and forced to declare that Copernicus's "opinion" that the Earth moved around the Sun was false. (There is a story, probably apocryphal that Galileo, after swearing to his denial, turned aside and muttered under his breath, "*Eppur si muove*"—"Even so, it does move!")

In the years immediately following, the Church reluctantly began to accept the notion that Copernicus might have been right and that the Earth was not the center of all creation. Serious speculation about the possibility of life on other worlds became a wide-spread philosophical pastime. But Fontenelle remained cautious. In his preface he apologized in advance for any offense he might give the religious, and asserted that if the Moon were inhabited, as he supposed, its inhabitants must be products of a separate creation, for "none of

Adam's progeny ever traveled so far as the Moon, nor were any colonies ever sent thither; the men then that are in the Moon are not the sons of Adam." The same, he said, was true of the inhabitants of Mars, Venus, and other nearby worlds, all of whom he described in a playful and inventive manner while taking care to say that he was merely speculating, not claiming any special revelation of truth. ("The people of Mercury are so full of fire that they are absolutely mad; I fancy they have no memory at all . . . and what they do is by sudden starts, and perfectly haphazard . . . As for Saturn, it is so cold that a Saturnian brought to Earth would perish from the heat, even at the North Pole.")

In his discussion of the stars, which Fontenelle, like most people of his time, believed were fixed in the heavens and fastened to the sky "like so many nails," he recognized that they were vastly farther away than the familiar planets: "The fixed stars cannot be less distant from the Earth than fifty millions of leagues; nay, if you anger an astronomer, he will set them further. The distance from the Sun to the farthest planet is nothing in comparison of the distance from the Sun, or from the Earth, to the fixed stars; it is almost beyond arithmetic."

And the stars were suns, he said, shining by virtue of their own fires, not by reflection of our Sun's light. "I will not swear that this is true," he said cautiously, "but I hold it for true, because it gives me pleasure to believe it." And around those distant suns were a multitude of other worlds, each held to its own sun by what he called a "vortex," which in an approximate way equates to what we call a gravitational field. Those planets, he thinks, are inhabited, not by humans but by beings of some other creation. In one of his most delightful flights of fancy he says that in some parts of the universe—the Milky Way, for instance—the stars are so close together "that the people in one world may talk, and shake hands, with those of another; at least I believe, the birds of one world may easily fly into another; and that pigeons may be trained up to carry letters, as they do in the Levant."

All this is set forth lightly, as a mere outpouring of the imagination, but Fontenelle leaves no doubt that he is serious. "When the Heavens were a little blue arch, stuck with stars, methought the universe was too strait and close," he wrote. "I was almost stifled for want of air; but now it is enlarged in height and breadth, and a thousand and a thousand vortexes taken in; I begin to breathe with more freedom, and think the Universe to be incomparably more magnificent than it was before."

* * *

AND NOW WE HAVE PROOF, thanks to NASA and the Kepler telescope, that that multitude of worlds that Fontenelle imagined more than three hundred years ago is really out there. The trouble is that we can't reach them, because the speed of light is likely always to be the limiting velocity not just for us, but for all the inhabitants of those other galaxies, and, barring the development of some quasi-magical means of faster-than-light travel, that makes the idea of intergalactic contact improbable.

So, as I said a decade ago and am forced still to believe, there won't be any Galactic Federation; there'll be no Bureau of Interstellar Trade; no alien wines or artifacts will turn up for sale in our boutiques. Nor will we meet the real-life equivalents of George Lucas's Wookiees, Doc Smith's Arisians, Fred Pohl's Heechees, Larry Niven's Kzinti, or—just as well, perhaps—A.E. van Vogt's terrifying Coeurl. The aliens exist, I'm sure, but the sea that separates us from them, and them from us, is just too wide. And as Guillaume de Conches said in a different context, long ago, *Nullus nostrum ad illos, neque illorum ad nos pervenire potest.* None of us can go to them, and none of them come to us. Except, let me quickly add, by way of the tales that science fiction writers tell.

—Robert Silverberg

Alien Archives

THE SILENT COLONY

It's not unusual or particularly disgraceful for a young writer to imitate the work of the writers he admires. That's one way to discover, from the inside, how those writers achieve the effects that the young writer finds so admirable. I'm not talking now of the various reworkings of the themes of Joseph Conrad that I've done over a period of years, or my deliberate pastiche of C.L. Moore, *In Another Country.* Those were the stunts of a mature writer having a little fun. I mean a novice's flat-out imitation of his betters purely for the sake of mastering their stylistic or structural techniques.

When I began my career in the early 1950s there was a group of about a dozen science fiction writers whose work held special meaning for me—Henry Kuttner, Cyril Kornbluth, James Blish, Alfred Bester, etc. (In 1987 I brought my favorite stories by those writers together in the autobiographical anthology, *Robert Silverberg's Worlds of Wonder*, more recently issued under the title, *Science Fiction 101*, which I recommend to any beginning writer who is as hungry to see print as I was sixty-plus years ago.) There was a particular cluster within my group of favorites whose work I paid special attention to: Robert Sheckley, Philip K. Dick, Jack Vance. Their stories seemed to me the epitome of what I wanted my science fiction to be like; and from time to time during the first five or six years of my career I would—consciously and unabashedly—do something in the model of one of those three, so that I could see, word by word, how they went about constructing such splendid stories.

"The Silent Colony" is one of my Sheckley imitations: an attempt at mimicking his cool, lucid style and his ingenious plotting. I wrote it late in the autumn of 1953, while I was a sophomore at Columbia writing science fiction stories in whatever spare time I could steal from my studies. Sheckley, who was then about 25 years old, had begun selling only a year or two earlier. Already his fiction was appearing in leading slick magazines like *Colliers* and *Esquire* as well as in every sci-fi publication: from the top-ranked *Astounding* and *Galaxy* to the wildest and wooliest of pulps. He even had a collection of his stories published in book form by a major publisher. It was a dazzling beginning to a career: I, seven years younger, envied him frantically. If I couldn't be Robert Sheckley, I could at least learn to write like him. "The Silent Colony," it seems to me now, is a creditable try at a Sheckley story, given the difference in our ages and technical skills. The three doomed alien visitors to Earth were, I think, reasonably original creations. It didn't sell to *Esquire*, or even *Galaxy*, but it did sell. On the strength of my contract for my novel *Revolt on Alpha C* my new agent—I had acquired an agent by then, Scott Meredith, who represented such top figures in the field as Vance, Dick, Arthur C. Clarke, and Poul Anderson—had, after nine tries, sold it (for $15) to Robert W. Lowndes, editor of *Future Science Fiction* in June of 1954. Lowndes needed a very short story to fill his October 1954 issue, published in August, and so, most unusually, "The Silent Colony" was in print just a couple of months after it was accepted.

I spent the summer of 1954 editing a mimeographed newspaper in a children's camp a hundred miles north of New York City; and great was my pride when the October *Future* arrived up there and I displayed my story to my fellow campers—three pages tucked away at the end of the issue, with stories by Philip K. Dick, Algis Budrys, and Marion Zimmer Bradley more prominently displayed. I didn't mind its inconspicuous placement. One didn't expect a little snippet of a story like that to be featured prominently. And Dick, Budrys, and Bradley all were older than me. Each of them had been writing professionally for two or three years already, so I didn't begrudge them their names on the cover. What mattered was that I was in the issue too—my first short story to be published in a widely distributed American magazine. Only three pages: but bigger and better things were to come. I was sure of it.

SKRID, EMERAK, AND ULLOWA DRIFTED through the dark night of space, searching the worlds that passed below them for some sign of their own kind. The urge to wander had come over them, as it does inevitably to all inhabitants of the Ninth World. They had been drifting through space for eons; but time is no barrier to immortals, and they were patient searchers.

"I think I feel something," said Emerak. "The Third World is giving off signs of life."

They had visited the thriving cities of the Eighth World, and the struggling colonies of the Seventh, and the experienced Skrid had led them to the little-known settlements on the moons of the giant Fifth World. But now they were far from home.

"You're mistaken, youngster," said Skrid. "There can't be any life on a planet so close to the sun as the Third World—think of how warm it is!"

Emerak turned bright white with rage. "Can't you *feel* the life down there? It's not much, but it's there. Maybe you're too old, Skrid."

Skrid ignored the insult. "I think we should turn back; we're putting ourselves in danger by going so close to the sun. We've seen enough."

"No, Skrid, I detect life below," Emerak blazed angrily. "And just because you're the leader of this triad doesn't mean that you know everything. It's just that your form is more complex than ours, and it'll only be a matter of time until—"

"Quiet, Emerak." It was the calm voice of Ullowa. "Skrid, I think the hothead's right. I'm picking up weak impressions from the Third World myself; there may be some primitive life-forms evolving there. We'll never forgive ourselves if we turn back now."

"But the sun, Ullowa, the sun! If we go too close—" Skrid was silent, and the three drifted on through the void. After a while he said, "All right, let's investigate."

The three accordingly changed their direction and began to head for the Third World. They spiraled slowly down through space until the planet hung before them, a mottled bowl spinning endlessly.

Invisibly they slipped down and into its atmosphere, gently drifting towards the planet below. They strained to pick up signs of life, and as they approached the life-impulses grew stronger. Emerak cried out vindictively that Skrid should listen to him more often. They knew now, without doubt, that their kind of life inhabited the planet.

"Hear that, Skrid? Listen to it, old one."

"All right, Emerak," the elder being said, "you've proved your point. I never claimed to be infallible."

"These are pretty strange thought-impressions coming up, Skrid. Listen to them, they have no minds down there," said Ullowa. "They don't think."

"That's fine," exulted Skrid. "We can teach them the ways of civilization and raise them to our level. It shouldn't be hard, when time is ours."

"Yes," Ullowa agreed, "they're so mindless that they'll be putty in our hands. Skrid's Colony, we'll call the planet. I can just see the way the Council will go for this. A new colony, discovered by the noted adventurer Skrid and two fearless companions—"

"Skrid's Colony, I like the sound of that," said Skrid. "Look, there's a drifting colony of them now, falling to earth. Let's join them and make contact; here's our chance to begin."

They entered the colony and drifted slowly to the ground among the others. Skrid selected a place where a heap of them lay massed together, and made a skilled landing, touching all six of his delicately constructed limbs to the ground and sinking almost thankfully into a position of repose. Ullowa and Emerak followed and landed nearby.

"I can't detect any minds among them," complained Emerak, frantically searching through the beings near him. "They look just like us—that is, as close a resemblance as is possible for one of us to have to another. But they don't think."

Skrid sent a prying beam of thought into the heap on which he was lying. He entered first one, then another, of the inhabitants.

"Very strange," he reported. "I think they've just been born; many of them have vague memories of the liquid state, and some can recall as far back as the vapor state. I think we've stumbled over something important, thanks to Emerak."

"This is wonderful!" Ullowa said. "Here's our opportunity to study newborn entities firsthand."

"It's a relief to find some people younger than myself," Emerak said sardonically. "I'm so used to being the baby of the group that it feels peculiar to have all these infants around."

"It's quite glorious," Ullowa said, as he propelled himself over the ground to where Skrid was examining one of the beings. "It hasn't been for a million ten-years that a newborn has appeared on our world, and here we are with billions of them all around."

"Two million ten-years, Ullowa," Skrid corrected. "Emerak here is of the last generation. And no need for any more, either, not while the mature entities live forever, barring accidents. But this is a big chance for us—we can make a careful study of these newborn ones, and perhaps set up a rudimentary culture here, and report to the Council once these babies have learned to govern themselves. We can start completely from scratch on the Third Planet. This discovery will rank with Kodranik's vapor theory!"

"I'm glad you allowed me to come," said Emerak. "It isn't often that a youngster like me gets a chance to—" Emerak's voice tailed off in a cry of amazement and pain.

"Emerak?" questioned Skrid. There was no reply.

"Where did the youngster go? What happened?" Ullowa said.

"Some fool stunt, I suppose. That little speech of his was too good to be true, Ullowa."

"No, I can't seem to locate him anywhere. Can you? Uh, Skrid! Help me! I'm—I'm—Skrid, it's killing me!"

The sense of pain that burst from Ullowa was very real, and it left Skrid trembling. "Ullowa! Ullowa!"

Skrid felt fear for the first time in more eons than he could remember, and the unfamiliar fright-sensation disturbed his sensitively balanced mind. "Emerak! Ullowa! Why don't you answer?"

Is this the end, Skrid thought, the end of everything? Are we going to perish here after so many years of life? To die alone and unattended, on a dismal planet billions of miles from home? Death was a concept too alien for him to accept.

He called again, his impulses stronger this time. "Emerak! Ullowa! Where are you?"

In panic, he shot beams of thought all around, but the only radiations he picked up were the mindless ones of the newly born.

"Ullowa!"

There was no answer, and Skrid began to feel his fragile body disintegrating. The limbs he had been so proud of—so complex and finely traced—began to blur and twist. He sent out one more frantic cry, feeling the weight of his great age, and sensing the dying thoughts of the newly born around him. Then he melted and trickled away over the heap, while the newborn snowflakes of the Third World watched uncomprehending, even as their own doom was upon them. The sun was beginning to climb over the horizon, and its deadly warmth beat down.

EN ROUTE TO EARTH

This is another early story—I wrote it In March of 1957—but a whole world of professional experience separates "The Silent Colony" from "En Route to Earth." The first story was the work of an eager, hopeful amateur, just setting out on a risky writing career, who had sold only one previous story, to the Scottish magazine *Nebula*. But by the time I had written "En Route to Earth", less than four years later, I was an established writer with some two hundred published stories behind me and editors asking me for new stories almost every day.

One of those editors was Robert. W. Lowndes, who had given me my first sale to an American s-f magazine in 1954 when he bought "The Silent Colony." By 1957 Lowndes and I had become good friends, with shared interests not only in science fiction but in classical music and much else. He frequently used my work in his three s-f titles (*Future*, *Science Fiction Stories*, and *Science Fiction Quarterly*), as well as in his detective-story magazine and even, occasionally, in one of his sports-fiction pulps or his western-story magazine.

Lowndes edited so many magazines that he had their covers printed in batches, four titles at a time, and usually asked some writer to do a story based on a cover illustration that had already been painted, rather than doing it, as was more common, the other way around. In those years I was one of the writers he frequently called upon for such tasks. One day in March of 1957 he showed me a new painting by the prolific Ed

Emshwiller that was going to be the cover for the August 1957 issue of *Science Fiction Quarterly.* It showed the stewardess of a space-liner being beckoned by one of the passengers—but the stewardess had blue skin, the passenger had three heads, and various other alien beings could be seen in the background.

"Easy," I said. "This is going to be fun." And I went home and wrote "En Route to Earth," which Lowndes published a few months later.

BEFORE THE FLIGHT, THE CHIEF stewardess stopped off in the women's lounge to have a few words with Milissa, who was making her first extra-solar hop as stewardess of the warpliner *King Magnus.*

Milissa was in uniform when the chief stewardess appeared. The low cut, clinging plastic trimmed her figure nicely. Gazing in the mirror, she studied her clear blue skin for blemishes. There were none.

"All set?" the chief stewardess asked.

Milissa nodded, a little too eagerly. "Ready, I guess. Blastoff time's in half an hour, isn't it?"

"Yes. Not nervous, are you?"

"Nervous? Who, me?" Somewhat anxiously she added, "Have you seen the passenger list?"

"Yes."

"How's the breakdown? Are there—many strange aliens?" Milissa said. "I mean—"

"A few," the chief stewardess said cheerfully. "You'd better report to the ship now, dear."

The *King Magnus* was standing on its tail, glimmering proudly in the hot Vegan sun, as Milissa appeared on the arching approach-ramp. Two blueskinned Vegan spacemen lounged against the wall of the Administration Center, chatting with a pilot from Earth. All three whistled as she went by. Milissa ignored them, and proceeded to the ship.

She took the lift-plate up to the nose of the ship, smiled politely at the jetman who waited at the entrance, and went in. "I'm the new stewardess," she said.

"Captain Brilon's waiting for you in the fore cabin," the jetman said.

Milissa checked in as per instructions, adjusted her cap at just the proper angle (with Captain Brilon's too-eager assistance) and picked up the passenger list. As she had feared, there were creatures of all sorts aboard. Vega served as a funnel for travelers from all over the galaxy who were heading to Earth.

She looked down the list.

Grigori—James, Josef, Mike. Returning to Earth after extended stay on Alpheraz IV. Seats 21–22.

Brothers vacationing together, she thought. How nice. But three of them in two seats? Peculiar!

Xfooz, Nartoosh. Home world, Sirius VII. First visit to Earth. Seat 23.

Dellamon, Thogral. Home world, Procyon V. Business trip to Earth. Seat 25.

And on down the list. At the bottom, the chief stewardess had penciled a little note:

> Be courteous, cheerful, and polite. Don't let the aliens frighten you—and above all, don't look at them as if they're worms or toads, even if some of them are worms or toads. Worms or not, they're still customers.
>
> Watch out for any Terrans aboard. They don' t have any color-prejudices against pretty Vegans with blue skin. Relax and have a good time. The return trip ought to be a snap.

I hope so, Milissa thought fervently. She took a seat in the corner of the cabin and started counting seconds till blastoff.

The stasis-generators lifted the *King Magnus* off Vega II as lightly as a feather blown by the wind, and Captain Brilon indicated that Milissa should introduce herself to the passengers. She stepped through the bulkhead doors that led to the passenger section, paused a moment to readjust her cap and tug at her uniform, and pushed open the iris-ing sphincter that segregated crew from passengers.

The passenger hold stretched out for perhaps a hundred feet before her. It was lined with huge view windows on both sides, and the passengers—fifty of them, according to the list—turned as one to look at her when she entered.

She suppressed a little gasp. All shapes, all forms—and what was *that* halfway down the row—?

"Hello," she said, forcing it to come out cheery and bright. "My name is Milissa Kleirn, and I'll be your stewardess for this trip. This is the *King Magnus,* fourth ship of the Vegan Line, and we'll be making the trip from Vega II to Sol III in three days, seven hours, and some minutes, under the command of Captain Alib Brilon. The drive-generators have already hurled us from the surface of Vega, and we've entered warp and are well on our way to Earth. I'll be on hand to answer any of your questions—except the very technical ones; you'll have to refer those through me to the captain. And if you want magazines or anything, please press the button at the side of your seat. Thank you very much."

There, she thought. *That wasn't so bad.*

And then the indicator-panel started to flash. She picked a button out at random and pressed it. A voice said, "This is Mike Grigori, Seat 22. How about coming down here to talk to me a minute?"

She debated. The chief stewardess had warned her about rambunctious Earthmen—but yet, this was her first request as stewardess, and besides there was something agreeably pleasant about Mike Grigori's voice. She started down the aisle and reached Seat 22, still smiling.

Mike Grigori was sitting with his two brothers. As she approached, he extended an arm and beckoned to her wolfishly with a crooked forefinger. He winked.

"You're Mr. Grigori?"

"I'm Mike. Like you to meet my brothers, James and Josef. Fellows, this is Miss Kleirn. The stewardess."

"How do you do," Milissa said. The smile started to fade. With an effort, she restored it.

There was a certain family resemblance about the Grigori brothers. And she saw now why they only needed two seats.

They had only one body between them.

"This is Jim, over here," Mike was saying, indicating the head at farthest left. "He's something of a scholar. Aren't you, Jim?"

The head named Jim turned gravely to examine Milissa, doing so with the aid of a magnifying glass it held to its eye monocle-wise. Jim affected an uptilted mustache; Mike, looking much younger and more ebullient, was cleanshaven and wore his hair close-cropped.

"And this is Josef," Mike said, nodding toward the center head. "Make sure you spell that J-O-S-E-F, like so. He's very fussy about that. Used to be plain Joe, but now nothing's fancy enough for him."

Josef was an aristocratic-looking type whose hair was slicked back flat and whose nose inclined slightly upward; he maintained a fixed pose, staring forward as if in intent meditation, and confined his greetings to a muttered *hmph.*

"He's the intellectual sort," Mike confided. "Keeps us up half the night when he wants to read. But we manage. We have to put up with him because he's got the central nervous system, and half the arms."

Milissa noticed that the brothers had four arms—one at each shoulder, presumably for the use of Mike and Jim, and two more below them, whose scornful foldedness indicated they were controlled entirely by the haughty Josef.

"You're—from Earth?" Milissa asked, a little stunned.

"Mutants," said Jim.

"Genetic manipulation," explained Mike.

"Abnormalities. Excrescences on my shoulders," muttered Josef.

"He thinks he got here first," Mike said. "That Jim and I were tacked on to *his* body later."

It looked about to degenerate into a family feud. Milissa wondered what a fight among the brothers would look like. But one of her duties was to keep peace in the passenger lounge. "Is there anything specific you'd like to ask me, Mr. Grigori?" she said to Mike. "If not, I'm afraid the other passengers—"

"Specific? Sure. I'd like to make a date with you when we hit Earth. Never dated a Vegan girl—but that blue skin is really lovely."

"Vetoed," Josef said without turning his head.

Mike whirled. "*Vetoed!* Now look here, brother—you don't have absolute and final say on every—"

"The girl will only refuse," Josef said. "Don't waste our time on dalliance. I'm trying to think, and your chatter disturbs me."

Again tension grew. Quickly Milissa said, "Your brother's right, Mr. Grigori. Vegan Line personnel are not allowed to date passengers. It's an absolute rule."

Dismay registered on two of the three heads. Josef merely looked more smug. Another crisis seemed brewing among the mutant brothers when suddenly a creature several seats behind them tossed a magazine it had been reading into the aisle with a great outcry of rage.

"Excuse me," Milissa said. "I'll have to see what's upsetting him."

Grateful for the interruption, she moved up the aisle. The alien who had thrown the magazine was a small pinkish being, whose eyes, dangling on six-inch eyestalks, now quivered in what she supposed was rage.

Milissa stooped, one hand keeping her neckline from dipping (there was no telling *what* sexual habits these aliens had) and picked up the magazine. *Science Fiction Stories,* she saw, and there was a painting of an alien much like the one before her printed on the glossy cover.

"I think you dropped this, Mr.—Mr.—"

"Dellamon," the alien replied, in a cold, testy, snappish voice. "Thogral Dellamon, of Procyon V. And I *didn't* drop the magazine. I threw it down violently, as you very well saw."

She smiled apologetically. "Of course, Mr. Dellamon. Did you see something you disagreed with in the magazine?"

"Disagreed with? I saw something that was a positive *insult!*" He snatched the magazine from her, riffled through it, found a page, and handed it back.

The magazine was open to page 113. The title of the story was "Slaves of the Pink Beings," bylined J. Eckman Forester. She skimmed the first few lines; it was typical science fiction, full of monsters and bloodshed, and just as dull as every other science fiction story she had tried to read.

"I hope I won't make you angry when I say I don't see anything worth getting angry over in this, Mr. Dellamon."

"That story," he said, "tells of the conquests and sadistic pleasures of a race of evil pink beings—and of their destruction by *Earthmen.* Look at that cover painting! It's an exact image of—well, you see? This is vicious propaganda aimed at my people! And none of it's true! None!"

The cover indeed bore a resemblance to the indignant little alien. But the date under the heading caught Milissa's eye. *June 2114.* Three hundred years old. "Where did you get this magazine?" she asked.

"Bought it. Wanted to read an Earth magazine, as long as I have to go there, so I had a man on my planet get one for me."

"Oh. That explains it, then. Look at the date, Mr. Dellamon! That story's a complete fantasy! It was written more than a hundred years before Earth and Procyon came into contact!"

"But—fantasy—I don't understand—"

The sputtering little alien threatened to become apoplectic. Milissa wished prodigiously that she had never transferred out of local service. These aliens could be so *touchy,* at times!

"Excuse me, please," said a furry purple creature seated across the aisle. "That magazine you have there—mind if I look at it?"

"Here," the angry alien said. He tossed it over.

The purple being examined it, smiled delightedly, said, "Why, it's an issue I need! Will you take five hundred credits for it?"

"Five hundred—" The eyestalks stopped quivering, and drooped in an expression of probable delight. "Make it five-fifty and the book is yours!"

* * *

CRISIS AFTER CRISIS, MILISSA THOUGHT gloomily. They were two days out from Vega, with better than a day yet to go before Earth hove into sight. And if the voyage lasted much longer, she'd go out of her mind.

The three Grigori brothers had finally erupted into violence late the first day; they sprang from their seat and went rolling up the aisle, cursing fluently at each other in a dozen languages. Josef had the upper hand for a while, rearing back and pounding his brothers' heads together, but he was outnumbered and was in dire straits by the time Milissa found two crewmen to put a stop to the brawl.

Then there was the worm-like being from Albireo III who suddenly discovered she was going to sporulate, and did—casting a swarm of her encapsulated progeny all over the lounge. She was very apologetic, and assisted Milissa in finding the spores, but it caused quite a mess.

The Greklan brothers from Deneb Kaitos I caused the next crisis. Greklans, Milissa discovered, had peculiar sexual practices: they spent most of their existence as neuters, but at regular periods about a decade apart suddenly developed sex, at which time the procedure was to mate, and fast. One of the brothers abruptly became a male, the other female, to their great surprise, consternation, and delight. The squeals of a puritanical being from Fomalhaut V attracted Milissa's attention; she managed to hustle the Greklans off to a washroom just in time. They returned, an hour later, to announce they had reverted to neuter status and would name their offspring Milissa, but that scarcely helped her nerves.

Never again, Milissa told herself, surveying the array of life-forms in the lounge. *Back to local service for me. As soon as the return trip is over—*

Eleven hours to Earth. She hoped she could stay sane that long.

Frozen asparagus turned up on the menu the final night. It was a grave tactical mistake; three vegetable-creatures of Mirach IX accused the Vegan Line of fomenting cannibalism, and stalked out of the dining room. Milissa followed them and found them seriously ill of nausea and threatening to sue. She hadn't noticed until then how very much like asparagus stalks the Mirachians looked; no one in the galley had either, apparently.

A family of reptiloids from Algenib became embroiled with a lizardlike inhabitant of Altair II. It took what was left of Milissa's tattered diplomacy to separate the squabblers and persuade them all to retake their seats.

She counted hours. She counted minutes. And, finally, she counted seconds.

"Earth ahead!" came the announcement from Control Cabin.

She went before the passengers to make the traditional final speech. Calmly, almost numbly, she thanked them for their cooperation, hoped they had enjoyed the flight, wished them the best of everything on Earth.

Mike-Jim-Josef Grigori paused to say good-bye on their way out. They looked slightly bruised and battered. For the seventh time, Milissa explained to Mike how regulations prohibited her from dating, and finally they said good-bye. They walked down the ramp snarling and cursing at each other.

She watched them all go—the Greklans, the angry little man from Procyon, the asparaguslike Mirachians. She felt a perverse fondness for them all.

"That's the last," she said, turning to Captain Brilon. "And thank goodness."

"Tired, huh?"

"All you had to do was watch the instruments," she said. "*I* was playing nursemaid to umpteen different life-forms. But the return trip will be a rest. Just Earthmen and Vegans, I hope. No strange nonhumanoid forms. I can't wait!"

* * *

She returned to the ship after the brief leave allotted her, and found herself almost cheerful at the prospect of the return trip. The passengers filed aboard—pleasant, normal Vegans and Earthmen, who whistled at her predictably but who showed no strange and unforeseeable mating habits or other manifestations.

It was going to be a quiet trip, she told herself. A snap.

But then three dark furry shapes entered the lounge and huddled self-consciously in the back. Milissa bit her lip and glanced down at the passenger list.

> *Three spider-men from Arcturus VII. These creatures do not have names. They are extremely sensitive and will require close personal attention.*

Milissa shuddered. Even without a mirror handy, she knew her face was paling to a weak ultramarine. She could get used to Greklans and sporulating worms from Albireo, she thought. She could calm petulant Procyonites and fend off wolfish three-headed Earthmen. But there was nothing in her contract about travelers from Arcturus.

She stared at the hairy, eight-legged creatures. Twenty-four arachnid eyes glinted beadily back at her.

It was asking too much. No woman should be expected to take solicitous care of *spiders*.

Sighing, she realized it was going to be a long, long voyage home.

THE WAY TO SPOOK CITY

Here's a case where the author experienced more thrills and chills than his own protagonist in the course of writing one simple 18,000-word story. It is altogether possible that aliens were at work trying to prevent this one from ever seeing print.

The saga began during the hot, dry summer of 1991, when I proposed to the editors of *Playboy* that I write a story of double the usual length of the stories I had done for them in the past. I was having increasing difficulty confining my *Playboy* stories to their top limit of 7,500 words or so. Long ago, I pointed out, the magazine had regularly run novellas, such stories as George Langelaan's "The Fly," Arthur C. Clarke's "A Meeting with Medusa," and Ray Bradbury's "The Lost City of Mars." What about reviving that custom and letting me write a long one now?

The powers that be mulled over the idea and gave me a qualified go-ahead. I submitted an outline, and on September 10, 1991, we came to an agreement on the deal. Two days later the printer of my loyal computer, which I had been using for nearly a decade, declined to print a document. Somehow I jollied it into going back to work, and blithely got started on the story that was to become "The Way to Spook City" a day or two later, imagining I'd have the piece behind me before settling down to work on the upcoming winter novel. I promised to deliver it by mid-October so that it could be used in the August

1992 issue. But the printer trouble returned, and worsened, and on September 27—when I was forty pages into the story—the printer died completely. I was trying to print out my forty pages at the time, but what came out was this:

"Everyone had been astonished when Nick announced he was going Lla kciN disiruprus oo, that he should be setting himself up for such a crazy LKthguoht eh nruter ot *brawny young man Tom had become but of the soft-eyed LJs'kciN fo lla nehgt dna ,n"* and then blank space, not another garbled word.

No problem, you say. Get a new printer, hook it up, do the printout. But there *was* a problem. I had been something of a pioneer, as writers go, in the use of a computer for word-processing, and the computer I had been using all those years was now obsolete—incompatible, in fact, with any existing brand. The company that had made it was out of business, and no one then alive knew how to connect a modern printer to it. I did, of course, have a backup of my forty pages on a floppy disk; but my computer was a pre-MS-DOS model and its operating system could not communicate with then-modern machines. The texts on my computer were trapped in it forever, all my business records and the first half of "Spook City" among them. They could be brought up onscreen but they were inaccessible for purposes of printing.

I needed to buy one of the newfangled MS-DOS computers and learn how to use it. And I contemplated the gloomy prospect of having to type "Spook City" and hundreds of other documents onto the new computer, one word at a time. It would take forever. What about my mid-October deadline?

It was possible, at least, to rescue the unfinished story. The technician who had been servicing my old computer discovered that he still had one machine of that model in working order (more or less) in his San Francisco office. I gave him my backup disk; he printed out the forty pages of "Spook City" and faxed them to me. Later in the day I began keying the story into the only working computer in the house, which belonged to my wife Karen and was a perfectly standard DOS-based job. I also went out and bought a new computer myself, also, of course, a DOS machine compatible with hers.

For the next ten days or so, while waiting for the new computer to arrive, I continued writing "Spook City" using my prehistoric manual typewriter, and entering each day's typewritten work on Karen's computer after her work-day was over. By October 4th I had 59 pages on disk. I decided to print them out and halt further work until my own new machine arrived.

Karen's computer wouldn't print it.

I didn't know why.

The text looked fine on screen, but when I gave the familiar print command I was told that the document was "corrupted" and couldn't be sent on to the printer.

Again? Was there a curse on this story?

The backup disk was corrupted too. It began to look as though I had lost the nineteen pages I had written since the first computer glitch plus all the rewriting I had done on the original forty pages that the computer pro had rescued.

"I'm pretty much in shellshock now," I wrote Alice Turner of *Playboy*, "but what I suppose I'll do is wait for the new computer to arrive, maybe by Wednesday, and then start putting the whole damn thing in once more, trying to reconstruct (though you never really can) the stuff I had been doing all this past week. I can see that I'm going to wind up earning about five cents an hour on this project even if everything goes perfectly the third time, which is by no means assured."

Enter a second savior that grim evening: our friend and neighbor Carol Carr, who showed up equipped with some program that allowed us to bring up on screen, page by page, the whole corrupted document, and print it. What came out, alas, was mostly babble: a Martian mix, miscellaneous random consonants (not vowels!) and numbers and keyboard symbols with an occasional intelligible phrase glaring out of the welter of nonsense. But that was better than nothing. The next day I told Alice Turner what Carol had achieved: "She spent hours waving magic wands in front of Karen's computer and was able to coax out pages and pages of gibberish printout, which I am now reassembling, jigsaw-puzzle fashion, by locating recognizable passages, putting them into the proper order, and transcribing them by hand onto the old first draft that the last bunch of computer wizards coaxed out of my old computer last week. So far I've reached page 28 of the original 40-page draft and have pretty much reconstructed all the revisions. Unfortunately, a lot of the really good stuff in the climactic scenes didn't emerge yesterday, but at least I have typed rough drafts of that and I ought to be able to put them back together in something approximating the level of yesterday's destroyed version."

The new computer finally arrived. I learned how to use it by entering poor garbled "Spook City" in something like proper form. I rewrote as I went, and cautiously produced a new printout every afternoon. On Friday, October 18th, I finally finished what looked like a complete draft of the story, though it still needed some trimming and polishing. But the evil extraterrestrials who were determined to keep this story from coming into being weren't finished with me. Two days later—a furiously hot summer day—my part of California caught fire and three thousand houses nearby were destroyed. It looked as though our house might go up in flame as well. Karen and I were forced to flee, taking with us our cats, a handful of household treasures, *and a backup disk of the accursed "Spook City."* Whatever else happened, I didn't want to have to write that thing a third time.

We were able to return home after eighteen hours. The fire had stopped a mile north of us. After a couple of shaky days I got back to work and on October 25th, only two weeks beyond deadline, I sent the story to *Playboy*, telling Alice: "Here, thank God, is the goddamn story, and what a weird experience it has been. Written on four different machines—my old computer, Karen's computer, my ancient manual typewriter, and my jazzy new computer—and lost twice by computers and both times recovered with the aid of technical wizardry, and typed over and over from one machine to the other, and interrupted by a natural disaster that makes our earthquake of a few years ago seem trivial—I feel as though I've been writing it forever. I wake up mumbling it to myself. I never dreamed I was embarking on such an epic struggle when I proposed the story; I thought it would simply be a few weeks of the usual tough work, a nice payday, and on to the next job . . . Anyway, here's the story. I hope you like it." She did, and published it in the August 1992 issue of *Playboy*, just as planned.

Thus, with some trepidation, I will herewith instruct my computer to copy its text from my 1991 story file into this present collection. If you don't find it here, you'll know why.

THE AIR WAS SHINING UP ahead, a cold white pulsing glow bursting imperiously out of the hard blue desert sky. That sudden chilly dazzle told Demeris that he was at the border, that he was finally getting his first glimpse of the place where human territory ended and the alien-held lands began.

He halted and stood staring for a moment, half expecting to see monsters flying around overhead on the far side of the line; and right on cue something weird went flapping by, a blotch of darkness against the brilliant icy sheen that was lighting everything up over there in the Occupied Zone. It was a heavy thing the size of a hawk and a half, with a lumpy greenish body and narrow wings like saw-blades and a long snaky back that had a little globular purple head at the end of it. The creature was so awkward that Demeris had to laugh. He couldn't see how it stayed airborne. The bird, if that was what it was, flew on past, heading north, dropping a line of bright turquoise turds behind it. A little burst of flame sprang up in the dry grass where each one fell.

"Thank you kindly for that pretty welcome," Demeris called out after it, sounding jauntier than he felt.

He went a little closer to the barrier. It sprang straight up out of the ground like an actual wall, but one that was intangible and more or less transparent: he could make out vague outlines of what lay beyond that dizzying shield of light, a blurry landscape that should have been basically the same on the Spook side of the line as it was over here, low sandy hills, gray splotches of sagebrush, sprawling clumps of prickly pear, but which was in fact mysteriously touched by strangeness—unfamiliar serrated buttes, angular chasms with metallic blue-green walls, black-trunked leafless trees with rigid branches jutting out like horizontal crossbars. Everything was veiled, though, by the glow of the barrier that separated the Occupied Zone from the fragment of the former United States that lay to the west of it, and he couldn't be sure how much he was actually seeing and how much was simply the product of his expectant imagination.

A shiver of distaste ran through him. Demeris's father, dead now, had always regarded the Spooks as his personal enemy, and that had carried over to him. "They're just biding their time, Nick," his father would say. "One of these days they'll come across the line and grab our land the way they grabbed what they've got already. And there won't be a goddamned thing we can do about it." Demeris had dedicated himself ever since to maintaining the order and prosperity of the little ranch near the eastern border of Free Country that was his family heritage, and he loathed the Spooks, not just for what they had done but simply because they were hateful—unknown, strange, unimaginable, alien. Not us. Others were able to take the aliens and the regime they had imposed on the old U.S.A. for granted: all that had happened long ago, ancient history. In any case there had never been a hint that the elder Demeris's fears were likely to be realized. The Spooks kept to themselves inside the Occupied Zone. In a hundred fifty years they had shown no sign of interest in expanding beyond the territory they had seized right at the beginning.

He took another step forward, and another, and waited for things to come into better focus. But they didn't.

* * *

DEMERIS HAD MADE THE FIRST part of the journey from Albuquerque to Spook Land on muleback, with his brother Bud accompanying him as far as the west bank of the Pecos. But when they reached the river Demeris had sent Bud back with the mules. Bud was five years younger than Demeris, but he had three kids already. Men who had kids had no business going into Spook territory. You were supposed to go across when you were a kid yourself, for a lark, for a stunt.

Demeris had had no time for larks and stunts when he was younger. His parents had died when he was a boy, leaving him to raise his two small sisters and three younger brothers. By the time they were grown he was too old to be very interested in adventures in the Occupied Zone. But then this last June his youngest brother Tom, who had just turned eighteen, an unpredictable kid whose head seemed stuffed with all sorts of incomprehensible fantasies and incoherent yearnings, had gone off to make his Entrada. That was what New Mexicans called someone's first crossing of the border—a sort of rite of passage, the thing you did to show that you had become an adult. Demeris had never seen what was particularly adult about going to Spook Land, but he saw such things differently from most people. So Tom had gone in.

He hadn't come out, though.

The traditional length of time for an Entrada was thirty days. Tom had been gone three months. Worry nagged at Demeris like an aching tooth. Tom was his reckless baby. Always had been, always would be. And so Demeris had decided to go in after him. Someone had to fetch Tom out of that place, and Demeris, the head of the family, the one who had always seemed to seek out responsibilities the way other people looked for shade on a sunny day, had appointed himself the one to do it. His father would have expected that of him. And Demeris was the only member of the family, besides Tom, who had never married, who had no kids, who could afford to take a risk.

What you do, Bud had said, is walk right up to the barrier and keep on going no matter what you may see or feel or think you want to do. "They'll throw all sorts of stuff at you," Bud had told him. "Don't pay it any mind. Just keep on going."

And now he was there, at the barrier zone itself.

You walk right up to it and keep on going, that was what you had to do. No matter what it did, what it threw at you.

Okay. Demeris walked right up to it. He kept on going.

* * *

THE MOMENT HE STEPPED THROUGH the fringes of the field he felt it starting to attack him. It came on in undulating waves, the way he imagined an earthquake would, shaking him unrelentingly and making him slip and slide and struggle to stay upright. The air around him turned thick and yellow and he couldn't see more than a couple of yards in any direction. Just in front of him was a shimmering blood-hued blur that abruptly dissolved into an army of scarlet caterpillars looping swiftly toward him over the ground, millions of them, a blazing carpet. They spread out all around him. Little teeth gnashed in their pop-eyed heads and they made angry, muttering sounds as they approached. There was no avoiding them. He walked in among them and it was like walking on a sea of slime. A kind of growling thunder rose from them as he crushed them under foot. "Bad dreams," Bud was saying, in his ear, in his brain. "All they are is a bunch of bad dreams." Sure. Demeris forged onward. How deep was the boundary strip, anyway? Twenty yards? Fifty? He ached in a dozen places, his eyes were stinging, his teeth seemed to be coming loose. Beyond the caterpillars he found himself at the edge of an abyss of pale quivering jelly, but there was no turning back. He compelled himself into it and its substance rose up around him like a soft blanket, and a wave of pain swept upward through him from the scrotum to the back of his neck: to avoid it he pivoted and twisted, and he felt his backbone bending as if it was going to pop out of his flesh the way the fishbone comes away from the filleted meat. Stinking rain swept horizontally over him, and then hot sleet that raked his forehead and drew howls of rage from him. No wonder you couldn't get a mule to cross this barrier, he thought. Head down, gasping for breath, he pushed himself forward another few steps. Something like a crab with wings came fluttering up out of a steaming mudhole and seized his arm, biting it just below the elbow on the inside. A stream of black blood spurted out. He yelled and flapped his arm until he shook the thing off. The pain lit a track of fire all along his arm, up to the shoulder and doubling back to his twitching fingers. He stared at his hand and saw just a knob of raw meat with blackened sticks jutting from it. Then it flickered and looked whole again.

Demeris felt tears on his cheeks, and that amazed him: the last time he had wept was when his father died, years ago. Suddenly the urge arose in him to give up and turn back while he still could. That surprised him too. It had always been his way to go plunging ahead, doing what needed to be done, even when others were telling him, Demeris, don't be an asshole, Demeris, don't push yourself so hard, Demeris, let someone else do it for once. He had only shrugged. Let others slack off if they liked: he just didn't have the knack for it. Now, here, in this place, when he absolutely *could not* slack off, he felt the temptation to yield and go back. But he knew it was only the barrier playing devil-tricks with him. So he encapsulated the desire to turn back into a hard little shell and hurled it from him and watched it burn up in a puff of flame. And went onward.

Three suns were blazing overhead, a red one, a green one, a blue. The air seemed to be melting. He heard incomprehensible chattering voices coming out of it like demonic static, and then disembodied faces appeared all around him, jittering and shimmering in the soupy murk, the faces of people he knew, his sisters Ellie and Netta, his nieces and nephews, his friends. He cried out to them. But everyone was horridly distorted, blobby—cheeked and bug-eyed, grotesque fun-house images. They were pointing at him and laughing. Then he saw his father and mother pointing and laughing too, which had to be impossible, and he understood. Bud was right: these were nothing but illusions or maybe delusions. The images he saw were things that he carried within him. Part of him. Harmless.

He began to run, plunging on through a tangle of slippery threads, a kind of soft, spongy curtain. It yielded as he ripped at it and he fell face down onto a bank of dry sandy soil that was unremarkable in every way: mere desert dirt, real-world stuff, no fancy colors, no crazy textures. More trickery? No. No, this was real. The extra suns were gone and the one that remained was the yellow one he had always known. A fresh wind blew against his face. He was across. He had made it.

He lay still for a minute or two, catching his breath.

Hot pain came stabbing from his arm, and when he looked down at it he saw a jagged bloody cut high up near the inside of the elbxow, where he had imagined the crab-thing had bitten him. But the crab-thing had been only a dream, only an illusion. Can an illusion bite? he wondered. The pain, at any rate, was no illusion. Demeris felt it all the way up through the back of his throat, his nostrils, his forehead. A nasty pulsation ran through the whole arm, making his hand quiver rhythmically in time with it. The cut was maybe two inches long, and deep enough to see into. Fresh blood came dribbling from it every time his heart pumped. Fine, he thought, I'll bleed to death from an imaginary cut before I'm ten feet inside the Occupied Zone. But after a moment the wound began to clot over and the bleeding stopped, though the pain remained.

Shakily he stood up and glanced about.

Behind him was the vertical column of the barrier field, looking no more menacing than a searchlight beam from this side. Dimly he saw the desert flatlands of Free Country beyond it, the scrubby ordinary place from which he had just come.

On this side, though, everything was a realm of magic and mysteries. He was able more or less to make out the basic raw material of the landscape, the underlying barren dry New Mexico/Texas nowheresville that he had spent his entire life in. But here on the far side of the barrier the invaders had done some serious screwing around with the look of the land. The jagged buttes and blue-green arroyos that Demeris had glimpsed through the barrier field from the other side were no illusions; somebody had taken the trouble to come out here and redesign the empty terrain, sticking in all sorts of bizarre structures and features. He saw strange zones of oddly colored soil, occasional ramshackle metal towers, entire deformed geological formations—twisted cones and spiky spires and uplifted layers—that made his eyes hurt. He saw groves of unknown wire-leaved trees and arroyos crisscrossed by sinister glossy black threads like stitches across a wound. Everything was solid and real, none of it wiggling and shifting about the way things did inside the barrier field. Wherever he looked there was evidence of how the conquerors had put their mark on the land. Some of it was actually almost beautiful, he thought; and then he recoiled, astonished at his own reaction. But there *was* a strange sort of beauty in the alien landscape. It disgusted him and moved him all at once, a response so complex that he scarcely knew how to handle it.

They must have been trying to make the landscape look like the place they had originally come from, he told himself. The idea of a whole world looking that way practically nauseated him. What they had done was a downright affront. Land was something to live on and to use productively, not to turn into a toy. They didn't have any right to take part of ours and make it look like theirs, he thought, and anger rose in him again.

He thought of his ranch, the horses, the turkeys, the barns, the ten acres of good russet soil, the rows of crops ripening in the autumn sun, the fencing that he had made with his own hands running on beyond the line of virtually identical fencing his father had made. All that was a real kind of reality, ordinary, familiar, solid—something he could not only understand but love. It was home, family, good clean hard work, sanity itself. This, though, this—this lunacy, this horror—!

He tore a strip of cloth from one of the shirts in his backpack and tied it around the cut on his arm. And started walking east, toward the place where he hoped his brother Tom would be, toward the big settlement midway between the former site of Amarillo and the former site of Lubbock that was known as Spook City.

He kept alert for alien wildlife, constantly scanning the landscape, sniffing, watching for tracks. The Spooks had brought a bunch of their jungle beasts from their home world and turned them loose in the desert. "It's like Africa out there," Bud had said. "You never know what's going to come up and try to gobble you."

Once a year, Demeris knew, the aliens held a tremendous hunt on the outskirts of Spook City, a huge apocalyptic round-up where they surrounded and killed the strange beasts by the thousands and the streets ran blue and green with rivers of their blood. The rest of the time the animals roamed free in the hinterlands. Some of them occasionally strayed across the border barrier and went wandering around on the Free Country side: while he was preparing himself for his journey Demeris had visited a ranch near Bernalillo where a dozen or so of them were kept on display as a sort of zoo of nightmares, grisly things with red scaly necks and bird-beaks and ears like rubber batwings and tentacles on their heads, huge ferocious animals that seemed to have been put together randomly out of a stock of miscellaneous parts. But so far out here he had encountered nothing more threatening-looking than jackrabbits and lizards. Now and again a bird-that-was-not-a-bird passed overhead—one of the big snake-necked things he had seen earlier, and another the size of an eagle with four transparent veined wings like a dragonfly's but a thick moth-like furry body between them, and a third one that had half a dozen writhing prehensile rat-tails dangling behind it for eight or ten feet, trolling for food. He watched it snatch a shrieking bluejay out of the air as though it were a bug.

When he was about three hours into the Occupied Zone he came to a cluster of bedraggled little adobe houses at the bottom of a bowl-shaped depression that had the look of a dry lake. A thin fringe of scrubby plant growth surrounded the place, ordinary things, creosote bush and mesquite and yucca. Demeris saw some horses standing at a trough, a couple of scrawny black and white cows munching on prickly pears, a few half-naked children running circles in the dust. There was nothing alien about them, or about the buildings or the wagons and storage bins that were scattered all around. Everyone knew that Spooks were shapeshifters, that they could take on human form when the whim suited them, that when the advance guard of infiltrators had first entered the United States to prepare the way for the invasion they were all wearing human guise. But more likely this was a village of genuine humans. Bud had said there were a few little towns between the border and Spook City, inhabited by the descendants of those who had chosen to remain in the Occupied Zone after the conquest. Most people with any sense had moved out when the invaders came, even though the aliens hadn't formally asked anyone to leave. But some had stayed.

The afternoon was well along and the first chill of evening was beginning to creep into the clear dry air. The cut on his arm was still throbbing and he didn't feel much like camping in the open if he didn't have to. Perhaps these people would let him crash for the night.

When he was halfway to the bottom of the dirt road a gnomish little leathery-skinned man who looked to be about ninety years old stepped slowly out from behind a gnarled mesquite bush and took up a watchful position in the middle of the path. A moment later a boy of about sixteen, short and stocky in torn denim pants and a frayed undershirt, emerged from the same place. The boy was carrying what might have been a gun, which at a gesture from the older man he raised and aimed. It was a shiny tube a foot and a half long with a nozzle at one end and a squeeze-bulb at the other. The nozzle pointed squarely at the middle of Demeris's chest. Demeris stopped short and put his hands in the air.

The old man said something in a language that was full of grunts and clicks, and some whistling snorts. The denim boy nodded and replied in the same language.

To Demeris the boy said, "You traveling by yourself?" He was dark-haired, dark-eyed, mostly Indian or Mexican, probably. A ragged red scar ran up along his cheek to his forehead.

Demeris kept his hands up. "By myself, yes. I'm from the other side."

"Well, sure you are. Fool could see that." The boy's tone was thick, his accent unfamiliar, the end of each word clipped off in an odd way. Demeris had to work to understand him. "You making your Entrada? You a little old for that sort of thing, maybe." Laughter sparkled in the boy's eyes, but not anywhere else on his face.

"This is my first time across," Demeris said. "But it isn't exactly an Entrada."

"Your first time, that's an Entrada." The boy spoke again to the old man and got a long reply. Demeris waited patiently. Finally, the boy turned back to him and said, "Okay. Remigio here says we should make it easy for you. You want to stay here your thirty days, we let you do it. You work as a field hand, that's all. We even sell you some Spook things you can take back and show off like all you people do. Okay?"

Demeris's face grew hot. "I told you, this isn't any Entrada. Entradas are fun and games for kids. I'm not a kid."

"Then what are you doing here?"

"Trying to find my brother."

The boy frowned and spat into the dusty ground, not quite in Demeris's direction. "You think we got your brother here?"

"He's in Spook City, I think."

"Spook City. Yeah. I bet that's where he is. They all go there. For the hunt, they go." He put his finger to his head and moved it in a circle. "You do that, you got to be a little crazy, you know? Going there for the hunt. Sheesh! What dumb crazy fuckers." He laughed and said, "Well, come on, I'll show you where you can stay."

* * *

THEY PUT HIM UP IN a tottering weather-beaten shack made of wooden slats with big stripes of sky showing through, off at the edge of town, a hundred yards or so from the nearest building. There was nothing in it but a mildewed bundle of rags tied together for sleeping on. Some of the rags bore faded inscriptions in the curvilinear Spook script, impenetrable to Demeris. A ditch out back served as a latrine. A little stream, hardly more than a rivulet, ran nearby. Demeris crouched over it and washed out his wound, which was still pulsing unpleasantly but didn't look as bad as it had at first. The water seemed reasonably safe. He took a long drink and filled his canteens. Then he sat quietly in the open doorway of the shack for a time, not thinking of anything at all, simply unwinding from his long day's march and the border crossing.

As darkness fell the boy reappeared and led him to the communal eating hall. Fifty or sixty people were sitting at long benches in family groups. A few had an Anglo look, most seemed mixed Mexican and Indian. There was little conversation, and what there was was in the local language, all clicks and snorts and whistles. Almost nobody paid any attention to him. It was as if he was invisible; but a few did stare at him now and then and he could feel the force of their hostility, an almost intangible thing.

He ate quickly and went back to his shack. But sleep was a tough proposition. He lay awake for hours, listening to the wind blowing in out of Texas and wishing he was home, on his own ten acres, in his familiar adobe house, with the houses of his brothers and sisters around him. For a while there was singing—chanting, really—coming up from the village. It was harsh and guttural and choppy, a barrage of stiff angular sounds that didn't follow any musical scale he knew.

Listening to it, he felt a powerful sense of the strangeness of these people who had lived under Spook rule for so long, tainted by Spook ways, governed by Spook ideas. How had they survived? How had they been able to stand it, the changes, the sense of being owned? But somehow they had adapted, by turning themselves into something beyond his understanding.

Later, other sounds drifted to him, the night sounds of the desert, hoots and whines and screeches that might have been coming from owls and coyotes, but probably weren't. He thought he heard noise just outside his shack, people moving around doing something, but he was too groggy to get up and see what was going on. At last he fell into a sort of stupor and lay floating in it until dawn. Just before morning he dreamed he was a boy again, with his mother and father still alive and Dave and Bud and the girls just babies and Tom not yet even born. He and his dad were out on the plains hunting Spooks, vast swarms of gleaming vaporous Spooks that were drifting overhead as thick as mosquitoes, two brave men walking side by side, the big one and the smaller one, killing the thronging aliens with dart guns that popped them like balloons. When they died they gave off a screeching sound like metal on metal and released a smell like rotting eggs and plummeted to the ground, covering it with a glassy scum that quickly melted away and left a scorched and flaking surface behind. It was a very satisfying dream. Then a flood of morning light broke through the slats and woke him.

Emerging from the shack, he discovered a small tent pitched about twenty yards away that hadn't been there the night before. A huge mottled yellow animal was tethered nearby, grazing on weeds; something that might have been a camel except there weren't any camels the size of elephants, camels with three shallow humps and great goggling green eyes the size of saucers, or knees on the backs of their legs as well as in front. As he gaped at it a woman wearing tight khaki slacks and a shirt buttoned up to the collar came out of the tent and said, "Never seen one of those before?"

"You bet I haven't. This is my first time across."

"Is it, now?" she said. She had an accent too. It wasn't as strange to Demeris as the village boy's but there was some other kind of spin to it, a sound like that of a tolling bell beneath the patterns of the words themselves.

She was youngish, slender, not bad-looking: long straight brown hair, high cheekbones, tanned Anglo face. It was hard to guess her age. Somewhere between 25 and 35 was the best he could figure. She had very dark eyes, bright, almost glossy, oddly defiant. It seemed to him that there was a kind of aura around her, a puzzling crackle of simultaneous attraction and repulsion.

She told him what the camel-thing was called. The word was an intricate slurred sound midway between a whistle and a drone, rising sharply at the end. "You do it now," she said. Demeris looked at her blankly. The sound was impossible to imitate. "Go on. Do it."

"I don't speak Spook."

"It's not all that hard." She made the sound again. Her eyes flashed with amusement.

"Never mind. I can't do it."

"You just need some practice."

Her gaze was focused right on his, strong, direct, almost aggressive. At home he didn't know many women who looked at you like that. He was accustomed to having women depend on him, to draw strength or whatever else they needed from him until they were ready to go on their way and let him go on his.

"My name's Jill," she said. "I live in Spook City. I've been in Texas a few weeks and now I'm on my way back."

"Nick Demeris. From Albuquerque. Traveling up that way too."

"What a coincidence."

"I suppose," he said.

A sudden hot fantasy sprang up just then out of nowhere within him: that instant sexual chemistry had stricken her like a thunderbolt and she was going to invite him to travel with her, that they'd ride right off into the desert together, that when they made camp that evening she would turn to him with parted lips and shining eyes and open her arms and beckon him toward her—

The urgency and intensity of the idea surprised him as much as its adolescent foolishness. Had he really let himself get as horny as that? She didn't even seem that interesting to him.

In any case he knew it wasn't going to happen. She looked cool, self-sufficient, self-contained. She wouldn't have any need for his companionship on her trip home and probably not for anything else he might have to offer.

"What brings you over here?" she asked him.

He told her about his missing brother. Her eyes narrowed thoughtfully as he spoke. She was taking a good long look, studying his face with great care, staring at him as though peering right through his skull into his brain. Turning her head this way and that, checking him out.

"I think I may know him, your brother," she said calmly, after a time.

He blinked. "You *do*? Seriously?"

"Not as tall as you and stockier, right? But otherwise he looks pretty much like you, only younger. Face a lot like yours, broader, but the same cheekbones, the same high forehead, the same color eyes, the same blond hair, but his is longer. The same very serious expression all the time, tight as a drum."

"Yes," Demeris said, with growing wonder. "That's him. It has to be."

"Don, that was his name. No, Tom. Don, Tom, one of those short little names."

"Tom."

"Tom, right."

He was amazed. "How do you know him?" he asked.

"Turned up in Spook City a couple of months back. June, July, somewhere back then. It isn't such a big place that you don't notice new people when they come in. Had that Free Country look about him, you know. Kind of big-eyed, raw-boned, can't stop gawking at things. But he seemed a little different from most the other Entrada kids, like there was something coiled up inside him that was likely to pop out any minute, that this trip wasn't just a thing he was doing for the hell of it but that it had some other meaning for him, something deeper that only he could understand. Peculiar sort of guy, actually."

"That was Tom, yes." The side of Demeris's face was starting to twitch. "You think he might still be there?"

"Could be. More likely than not. He was talking about staying quite a while, at least until fall, until hunt time."

"And when is that?"

"It starts late next week."

"Maybe I can still find him, then. If I can get there in time."

"I'm leaving here this afternoon. You can ride with me to Spook City if you want."

"With you?" Demeris said. He was astonished. The good old instant chemistry after all? His whole little adolescent fantasy coming to life? It seemed too neat, too slick. The world didn't work like this. And yet—yet—

"Sure. Plenty of room on those humps. Take you at least a week if you walk there, if you're a good walker. Maybe longer. Riding, it'll be just a couple of days."

What the hell, he thought.

It would be dumb to turn her down. That Spook-mauled landscape was an evil place when you were on your own.

"Sure," he said, after a bit. "Sure, I'd be glad to. If you really mean it."

"Why would I say it if I didn't mean it?"

Abruptly the notion came to him that this woman and Tom might have had something going for a while in Spook City. Of course. Of course. Why else would she remember in such detail some unknown kid who had wandered into her town months before? There had to be something else there. She must have met Tom in some Spook City bar, a couple of drinks, some chatter, a night or two of lively bed games, maybe even a romance lasting a couple of weeks. Tom wouldn't hesitate, even with a woman ten, fifteen years older than he was. And so she was offering him this ride now as a courtesy to a member of the family, so to speak. It wasn't his tremendous masculine appeal that had done it, it was mere politeness. Or curiosity about what Tom's older brother might be like.

Into his long confused silence she said, "The critter here needs a little more time to feed itself up. Then we can take off. Around two o'clock, okay?"

* * *

AFTER BREAKFAST THE BOY WENT over to him in the dining hall and said, "You meet the woman who come in during the night?"

Demeris nodded. "She's offering me a ride to Spook City."

Something that might have been scorn flickered across the boy's face. "That nice. You take it?"

"Better than walking there, isn't it?"

A quick knowing glance. "You crazy if you go with her, man."

Frowning, Demeris said, "Why is that?"

The boy put his hand over his mouth and muffled a laugh. "That woman, she a Spook, man. You mean you don't see that? Only a damn fool go traveling around with a Spook."

Demeris was stunned for a moment, and then angry. "Don't play around with me," he said, irritated.

"Yeah, man. I'm playing. It's a joke. Just a joke." The boy's voice was flat, chilly, bearing its own built-in contradiction. The contempt in his dark hard eyes was unmistakable now. "Look, you go ride with her if you like. Let her do whatever she wants with you once she got you out there in the desert. Isn't none of my goddamn business. Fucking Free Country guys, you all got shit for brains."

Demeris squinted at him, shaken now, not sure what to believe. The kid's cold-eyed certainty carried tremendous force. But it made no sense to him that this Jill could be an alien. Her voice, her bearing, everything about her, were too convincingly real. The Spooks couldn't imitate humans that well, could they?

Had they?

"You know this thing for a fact?" Demeris asked.

"For a fact I don't know shit," the boy said. "I never see her before, not that I can say. She come around and she wants us to put her up for the night, that's okay. We put her up. We don't care what she is if she can pay the price. But anybody with any sense, he can smell Spook on her. That's all I tell you. You do whatever you fucking like, man."

The boy strolled away. Demeris stared after him, shaking his head. He felt a tremor of bewilderment and shock, as though he had abruptly found himself at the edge of an abyss.

Then came another jolt of anger. Jill a Spook? It couldn't be. Everything about her seemed human.

But why would the boy make up something like that? He had no reason for it. And maybe the kid *could* tell. Over on the other side, really paranoid people carried witch-charms around with them to detect Spooks who might be roaming Free Country in disguise, little gadgets that were supposed to sound an alarm when aliens came near you, but Demeris had never taken such things seriously. It stood to reason, though, that people living out here in Spook Land would be sensitive to the presence of a Spook among them, however well disguised it might be. They wouldn't need any witch-charms to tell them. They had had a hundred fifty years to get used to being around Spooks. They'd know the smell of them by now.

The more Demeris thought about it, the more uneasy he got.

He needed to talk to her again.

* * *

HE FOUND HER A LITTLE way upstream from his shack, rubbing down the shaggy yellow flanks of her elephantine pack-animal with a rough sponge. Demeris halted a short distance away and studied her, trying to see her as an alien being in disguise, searching for some clue to otherworldly origin, some gleam of Spookness showing through her human appearance.

He couldn't see it. He couldn't see it at all. But that didn't necessarily mean she was real.

After a moment she noticed him. "You ready to go?" she asked, over her shoulder.

"I'm not sure."

"What?"

He was still staring.

If she *is* a Spook, he thought, why would she want to pretend she was human? What would a Spook have to gain by inveigling a human off into the desert with her?

On the other hand, what motive did the kid have for lying to him?

Suddenly it seemed to him that the simplest and safest thing was to opt out of the entire arrangement and get to Spook City on his own, as he had originally planned. The kid might just be telling the truth. The possibility of traveling with a Spook, of being close to one, of sharing a campsite and a tent with one, sickened and repelled him. And there might be danger in it as well. He had heard wild tales of Spooks who were soul-eaters, who were energy vampires, even worse things. Why take chances?

He drew a deep breath. "Listen, I've changed my mind, okay? I think I'd just as soon travel by myself."

She turned and gave him a startled look. "You serious?"

"Yep."

"You really want to walk all the way to Spook City by yourself rather than ride with me?"

"Yep. That's what I prefer to do."

"Jesus Christ. What the hell *for*?"

Demeris could detect nothing *un*human in her exasperated tone or in the annoyed expression on her face. He began to think he was making a big, big mistake. But it was too late to back off. Uncomfortably he said, "Just the way I am, I guess. I sort of like to go my own way, I guess, and—"

"Bullshit. I know what's really going on in your head."

Demeris shifted about uneasily and remained silent. He wished he had never become entangled with her in the first place.

Angrily she said, "Somebody's been talking to you, right? Telling you a lot of garbage?"

"Well—"

"All right," she said. "You dumb bastard. You want to test me, is that it?"

"Test?"

"With a witch-charm."

"No," he said. "I'm not carrying any charms. I don't have faith in them. Those things aren't worth a damn."

"They'll tell you if I'm a Spook or not."

"They don't work, is what I hear."

"Some do, some don't." She reached into a saddlepack lying near her on the ground and pulled out a small device, wires and black cords intricately wound around and around each other. "Here," she said harshly. "This is one. You point it and push the button and it emits a red glow if you're pointing it at a Spook. Take it. A gift from me to you. Use it to check out the next woman you happen to meet."

She tossed the little gadget toward him. Demeris grabbed it out of the air by reflex and stood watching helplessly as she slapped the elephant-camel's flank to spur it into motion and started off downstream toward her tent.

Shit, he thought.

He felt like six kinds of idiot. The sound of her voice, tingling with contempt for him and his petty little suspicions, still echoed in his ears.

Baffled and annoyed—with her, with himself, with the boy for starting all this up—he flipped the witch-charm into the stream. There was a hissing and a bubbling around it for a moment and then the thing sank out of sight. Then he turned and walked back to his shack to pack up.

She had already begun to take down her tent. She didn't so much as glance at him. But the elephant-camel thing peered somberly around, extended its long purple lower lip, and gave him a sardonic toothy smirk. Demeris glared at the great beast and made a devil-sign with his upraised fingers. From you, at least, I don't have to take any crap, he thought.

He hoisted his pack to his shoulders and started up the steep trail out of town.

* * *

He was somewhere along the old boundary between New Mexico and Texas, he figured, probably just barely on the New Mexico side of the line. The aliens hadn't respected state boundaries when they had carved out their domain in the middle of the United States halfway through the 21st century, and some of New Mexico had landed in alien territory and some hadn't. Spook Land was roughly triangular, running from Montana to the Great Lakes along the Canadian border and tapering southward through what had been Wyoming, Nebraska, and Iowa down to Texas and Louisiana, but they had taken a little piece of eastern New Mexico too. Demeris had learned all that in school long ago. They made you study the map of the United States that once had been: so you wouldn't forget the past, they said, because someday the old United States was going to rise again.

Fat chance. The Spooks had cut the heart right out of the country, both literally and figuratively. They had taken over with scarcely a struggle and every attempt at a counterattack had been brushed aside with astonishing ease: America's weapons had been neutralized, its communications networks were silenced, its army of liberation had disappeared into the Occupied Zone like raindrops into a lake. Now there was not one United States of America but two: the western one, which ran from Washington State and Idaho down to the Mexican border and liked to call itself Free Country, and the other one in the east, along the coast and inland as far as the Mississippi, which still insisted on using the old formal name. Between the two lay the Occupied Zone, and nobody in either United States had much knowledge of what went on in there. Nor did anyone Demeris knew take the notion of a reunited United States very seriously. If America hadn't been able to cope with the aliens at the time of the invasion, it was if anything less capable of defeating them now, with much of its technical capacity eroded away and great chunks of the country having reverted to a pastoral, preindustrial condition.

What he had to do, he calculated, was keep heading more or less east until he saw indications of Spook presence. Right now, though, the country was pretty empty, just barren sandy wastes with a covering of mesquite and sage. He saw more places where the aliens had indulged in their weird remodeling of the landscape, and now and again he was able to make out the traces of some little ancient abandoned human town, a couple of rusty signs or a few crumbling walls. But mainly there was nothing at all.

He was about an hour and a half beyond the village when what looked like a squadron of airborne snakes came by, a dozen of them flying in close formation. Then the sky turned heavy and purplish-yellow, like bruised fruit getting ready to rot, and three immense things with shining red scales and sail-like three-cornered fleshy wings passed overhead, emitting bursts of green gas that had the rank smell of old wet straw. They were almost like dragons. A dozen more of the snake-things followed them. Demeris scowled and waved a clenched fist at them. The air had a tangible pressure. Something bad was about to happen. He waited to see what was coming next. But then, magically, all the ominous effects cleared away and he was in the familiar old Southwest again, untouched by strangers from the far stars, the good old land of dry ravines and big sky that he had lived in all his life. He relaxed a little, but only a little.

Almost at once he heard a familiar snorting sound behind him. He turned and saw the ponderous yellow form of the elephant-camel looming up, with Jill sitting astride it just back of the front hump.

She leaned down and said, "You change your mind yet about wanting that ride?"

"I thought you were sore at me."

"I am. Was. But it still seems crazy for you to be doing this on foot when I've got room up here for you."

He stared up at her. You don't often get second chances in this life, he told himself. But he wasn't sure what to do.

"Oh, Christ," she said, as he hesitated. "Do you want a ride or don't you?"

Still he remained silent.

She shot him a quick wicked grin. "Still worried that I'm a Spook? You can check me out if you like."

"I threw your gadget in the stream. I don't like to have witch-things around me."

"Well, that's all right." She laughed. "It wasn't a charm at all, just an old power core, and a worn out one at that. It wouldn't have told you anything."

"What's a power core?"

"Spook stuff. You could have taken it back with you to prove you were over here. Look, do you want a ride or not?"

It seemed ridiculous to turn her down again.

"What the hell," Demeris said. "Sure."

Jill spoke to the animal in what he took to be Spook language, a hiccupping wheeze and a long indrawn whistling sound, and it knelt for him. Demeris took her hand and she drew him on top of the beast with surprising ease. An openwork construction made of loosely woven cord, half poncho and half saddle, lay across the creature's broad back, with the three humps jutting through. Her tent and other possessions were fastened to it at the rear. "Tie your pack to one of those dangling strings," she said. "You can ride right behind me."

He fitted himself into the valley between the second and third humps and got a secure hold on the weaving, fingers digging down deep into it. She whistled another command and the animal began to move forward.

Its motion was a rolling, thumping, sliding kind of thing, very hard to take. The sway was both lateral and vertical and with every step the ground seemed to rise and plunge around him in lunatic lunges. Demeris had never seen the ocean or any other large body of water, but he had heard about seasickness, and this was what it was like. He gulped, clamped his mouth shut, gripped the saddle even more tightly.

Jill called back to him, "How are you doing?"

"Fine. Fine."

"Takes some getting used to, huh?"

"Some," he said.

His buttocks didn't have much padding on them. He could feel the vast bones of the elephant-camel grinding beneath him like the pistons of some giant machine. He held on tight and dug his heels in as hard as he could.

"You see those delta-winged things go by a little while ago?" she asked, after a while.

"The big dragons that were giving off the green smoke?"

"Right. Herders. On their way to Spook City for the hunt. They'll be used to drive the game toward the killing grounds. Every year this time they get brought in to help in the round-up."

"And the flying snakes?"

"They herd the herders. Herders aren't very smart. About like dogs, maybe. The snake guys are a lot brighter. The snakes tell the herders where to go and the herders make the game animals go there too."

Demeris thought about that. Level upon level of intelligence among these creatures that the Spooks had transported to the planet they had partly conquered. If the herders were as smart as dogs, he wondered how smart the snakes were. Dogs were pretty smart. He wondered how smart the Spooks were, for that matter.

"What's the hunt all about? Why do they do it?"

"For fun," Jill said. "Spook fun."

"Herding thousands of exotic wild animals together and butchering them all at once, so the blood runs deep enough to swim through? That's their idea of fun?"

"Wait and see," she said.

* * *

THEY SAW MORE AND MORE transformation of the landscape: whorls and loops of dazzling fire, great opaque spheres floating just above ground level, silvery blades revolving in the air. Demeris glared and glowered. All that strangeness made him feel vulnerable and out of place, and he spat and murmured bitterly at each intrusive wonder.

"Why are you so angry?" she asked.

"I hate this weird shit that they've strewn all over the place. I hate what they did to our country."

"It was a long time ago. And it wasn't your country they did it to, it was your great-great-grandfather's."

"Even so."

"Your country is over there. It wasn't touched at all."

"Even so," he said again, and spat.

When it was still well before dark they came to a place where bright yellow outcroppings of sulphur, like foamy stone pillows, marked the site of a spring. Jill gave the command to make her beast kneel and hopped deftly to the ground. Demeris got off more warily, feeling the pain in his thighs and butt from his ride.

"Give me a hand with the tent," she said.

It wasn't like any tent he had ever seen. The center-post was nothing more than a little rod that seemed to be made of white wax, but at the touch of a hand it tripled in height and an elaborate strutwork sprang out from it in five directions to provide support for the tent fabric. A Spook tent, he supposed. The tent pegs were made of the same waxy material, and all you had to do was position them where you wanted them around the perimeter of the tent and they burrowed into the ground on their own. Faint pinging sounds came from them as they dug themselves in.

"What's that?" he asked.

"Security check. The pegs are setting up a defensive zone for a hundred yards around us. Don't try to go through it in the night."

"I'm not going anywhere," Demeris said.

The tent was just about big enough for two. He wondered whether she was going to invite him to sleep inside it.

Together they gathered mesquite brush and built a fire, and she produced some packets of powdered vegetables and a slab of dried meat for their dinner. While they waited for things to cook Jill went to the spring, which despite the sulfurous outcroppings gave fresh, pure water, and crouched by it, stripping to the waist to wash herself. Seeing her like that was unsettling. His gaze flicked a quick glance at her as she bathed, but she didn't seem to care, or even to notice. That was unsettling too. Was she being deliberately provocative? Or did she just not give a damn?

He washed himself also, splashing handfuls of the cold water into his face and over his sweaty shoulders. "Dinner's ready," she said a few minutes later.

Darkness descended swiftly. The sky went from deep blue to utter black in minutes. In the clear desert air the stars began quickly to emerge, sharp and bright and unflickering. He looked up at them, trying to guess which of them might be the home star of the Spooks. They had never troubled to reveal that. They had never revealed very much of anything about themselves.

As they ate he asked her whether she made this trip often.

"Often enough," she said. "I do a lot of courier work for my father, out to Texas, Louisiana, sometimes Oklahoma." She paused a moment. "I'm Ben Gorton's daughter," she said, as though she expected him to recognize the name.

"Sorry. Who?"

"Ben Gorton. The mayor of Spook City, actually."

"Spook City's got a human mayor?"

"The human part of it does. The Spooks have their administration and we have ours."

"Ah," Demeris said. "I'm honored, then. The boss's daughter. You should have told me before."

"It didn't seem important," she said.

They were done with their meal. She moved efficiently around the campsite, gathering utensils, burying trash. Demeris was sure now that the village boy had simply been playing with his head. He told himself that if Jill was really a Spook he'd have sensed it somehow by this time.

When the cleanup work was done she lifted the tent flap and stepped halfway inside. He held back, unsure of the right move.

"Well?" she asked. "It's okay to come in. Or would you rather sleep out there?"

Demeris went in. Though the temperature outside was plunging steeply with the onset of night, it was pleasantly warm inside. There was a single bedroll, just barely big enough for two if they didn't mind sleeping very close together. He heard the sounds she made as she undressed, and tried in the absolute darkness to guess how much she was taking off. It wasn't easy to tell. He removed his own shirt and hesitated with his jeans; but then she opened the flap again to call something out to the elephant-camel, which she had tethered just outside, and by starlight he caught a flashing glimpse of bare thigh, bare buttock. He pulled off his trousers and slipped into the bedroll. She joined him a moment later. He lay awkwardly, trying to avoid rubbing up against her. For a time there was a tense expectant silence. Then her hand reached out in the darkness and grazed his shoulder, lightly but clearly not accidentally. Demeris didn't need a second hint. He had never taken any vows of chastity. He reached for her, found the hollow of her clavicle, trailed his hand downward until he was cupping a small, cool breast, resilient and firm. When he ran his thumb lightly across the nipples she made a little purring sound, and he felt the flesh quickly hardening. As was his. She turned to him. Demeris had some difficulty locating her mouth in the darkness, and she had to guide him, chuckling a little, but when his lips met hers he felt the immediate flicker of her tongue coming forth to greet him.

And then almost as though he was willing his own downfall he found himself perversely wondering if he might be embracing a Spook after all; and a wave of nausea swept through him, making him wobble and soften. But she was pressing tight against him, rubbing her breasts from side to side on him, uttering small eager murmuring sounds, and he got himself quickly back on track, losing himself in her fragrance and warmth and banishing completely from his thoughts anything but the sensations of the moment. After that one attack of doubt everything was easy. He located her long smooth thighs with no problem whatever, and when he glided into her he needed no guidance there either, and though their movements together had the usual first-time clumsiness her hot gusts of breath against his shoulder and her soft sharp outcries told him that all was going well.

He lay awake for a time when it was over, listening to the reassuring pinging of the tent pegs and the occasional far-off cry of some desert creature. He imagined he could hear the heavy snuffling breathing of the elephant-camel too, like a huge recirculating device just outside the tent. Jill had curled up against him as if they were old friends and was lost in sleep.

* * *

SHE SAID OUT OF THE blue, after they had been riding a long while in silence the following morning, "You ever been married, Nick?"

The incongruity of the question startled him. Until a moment ago she had seemed to be a million miles away. His attempt to make love to her a second time at dawn had been met with indifference and she had been pure business, remote and cool, all during the job of breaking camp and getting on the road.

"No," he said. "You?"

"Hasn't been on my program," she said. "But I thought everybody in Free Country got married. Nice normal people who settle down early and raise big families." The elephant-camel swayed and bumped beneath them. They were following a wide dirt track festooned on both sides with glittering strands of what looked like clear jelly, hundreds of feet long, mounted on spiny black poles that seemed to be sprouting like saplings from the ground.

"I raised a big family," he said. "My brothers and sisters. Dad got killed in a hunting accident when I was ten. Possibly got mixed up with a Spook animal that was on the wrong side of the line: nobody could quite figure it out. Then my mother came down with Blue Fever. I was fifteen then and five brothers and sisters to look after. Didn't leave me a lot of time to think about finding a wife."

"Blue Fever?"

"Don't you know what that is? Infectious disease. Kills you in three days, no hope at all. Supposed to be something the Spooks brought."

"We don't have it over here," she said. "Not that I ever heard."

"Spooks brought it, I guess they must know how to cure it. We aren't that lucky. Anyway, there were all these little kids to look after. Of course, they're grown by now."

"But you still look after them. Coming over here to try to track down your brother."

"Somebody has to."

"What if he doesn't want to be tracked down, though?"

Demeris felt a tremor of alarm. He knew Tom was restless and troubled, but he didn't think he was actually disturbed. "Have you any reason to think Tom would want to stay over here for good?"

"I didn't say I did. But he might just prefer not to be found. A lot of boys come across and stay across, you know."

"I didn't know. Nobody I ever heard of did that. Why would someone from Free Country want to live on the Spook side?"

"For the excitement?" she suggested. "To run with the Spooks? To play their games? To hunt their animals? There's all sorts of minglings going on these days."

"Is that so," he said uneasily. He stared at the back of her head. She was so damned odd, he thought, such a fucking mystery.

She said, sounding very far away, "I wonder about marrying." Back to that again. "What it's like, waking up next to the same person every day, day after day. Sharing your life, year after year. It sounds very beautiful. But also kind of strange. It isn't easy for me to imagine what it might be like."

"Don't they have marriage in Spook City?"

"Not really. Not the way you people do."

"Well, why don't you try it and see? You don't like it, there are ways to get out of it. Nobody I know thinks that being married is strange. Christ, I bet whatever the Spooks do is five hundred times as strange, and you probably think that it's the most normal thing in the world."

"Spooks don't marry. They don't even have sex, really. What I hear, it's more like the way fishes do it, no direct contact at all."

"That sounds terrifically appealing. I'd really love to try something like that. All I need is a cute Spook to try it with."

He attempted to keep it light. But she glanced around at him.

"Still suspicious, Nick"

He let that go by. "Listen, you could always take a fling at getting married for a while, couldn't you?" he said. "If you're all that curious about finding out what it's like."

"Is that an offer, Nick?"

"No," he said. "Hardly. Just a suggestion."

* * *

An hour after they set out that morning they passed a site where there was a peculiar purple depression about a hundred yards across at its thickest point. It was vaguely turtle-shaped, a long oval with four stubby projections at the corners and one at each end.

"What the devil is that?" Demeris asked. "A Spook graveyard?"

"It's new," she said. "I've never seen it before."

Some vagrant curiosity impelled him. "Can we look?"

Jill halted the elephant-camel and they jumped down. The site might almost have been a lake, deep-hued and dense against the sandy earth, but there was nothing liquid about it: it was like a stain that ran several yards deep into the ground. Together they walked to the edge. Demeris saw something moving beneath the surface out near the middle, a kind of corkscrew effect, and was about to call it to her attention when abruptly the margin of the site started to quiver and a narrow rubbery arm rose up out of the purpleness and wrapped itself around her left leg. It started to pull her forward. She shrieked and made an odd hissing sound.

Demeris yanked his knife from the scabbard at his belt and sliced through the thing that had seized her. There was a momentary twanging sound and he felt a hot zing go up his arm to the shoulder. The energy of it ricocheted around inside his shirt collar; then it ceased and he staggered back. The part of the ropy arm that had been wrapped around Jill fell away; the rest writhed convulsively before them. He caught her by one wrist and pulled her back.

"It's got to be some kind of trap for game," he said. "Or for passing travelers stupid enough to go close. Let's get the hell out of here."

She was pale and shaky. "Thanks," she said simply, as they ran toward the elephant-camel.

Not much of a show of gratitude, he thought.

But at least the incident told him something about her that he needed to know. A Spook trap wouldn't have gone after one of their own, would it?

Would it?

* * *

AT MIDDAY THEY STOPPED FOR lunch in a cottonwood grove that the Spooks had redecorated with huge crystalline mushroom-shaped things. The elephant-camel munched on one and seemed to enjoy it, but Demeris and Jill left them alone. There was a brackish little stream running through the trees, and once again she stripped and cleaned herself. Bathing seemed very important to her and she had no self-consciousness about her nudity. He watched her with cool pleasure from the bank.

Once in a while, during the long hours of the ride, she would break the silence with a quirky sort of question: "What do people like to do at night in Free Country?" or "Are men closer friends with men than women are with women?" or "Have you ever wished you were someone else?" He gave the best answers he could. She was a strange, unpredictable kind of woman, but he was fascinated by the quick darting movements of her mind, so different from that of anyone he knew in Albuquerque. Of course he dealt mainly with ranchers and farmers, and she was a mayor's daughter. And a native of the Occupied Zone besides: no reason why she should be remotely like the kind of people he knew.

They came to places that had been almost incomprehensibly transformed by the aliens. There was an abandoned one-street town that looked as though it had been turned to glass, everything eerily translucent—buildings, furniture, plumbing fixtures. If there had been any people still living there you most likely could see right through them too, Demeris supposed. Then came a sandy tract where a row of decayed rusting automobiles had been arranged in an overlapping series, the front of each humped up on the rear end of the one in front of it, like a string of mating horses. Demeris stared at the automobiles as though they were ghosts ready to return to life. He had never actually seen one in use. The whole technology of internal combustion devices had dropped away before he was born, at least in his part of Free Country, though he had heard they still had cars of some sort in certain privileged enclaves of California.

After the row of cars there was a site where old human appliances, sinks and toilets and chairs and fragments of things Demeris wasn't able even to identify, had been fused together to form a dozen perfect pyramids fifty or sixty feet in height. It was like a museum of antiquity. By now Demeris was growing numb to the effects of seeing all this Spook meddling. It was impossible to sustain anger indefinitely when evidence of the alien presence was such a constant.

There were more frequent traces now of the aliens' living presence, too: glows on the horizon, mysterious whizzing sounds far overhead that Jill said were airborne traffic, shining roadways through the desert parallel to the unpaved track they were following. Demeris expected to see Spooks go riding by next, but there was no sign of that. He wondered what they were like. "Like ghosts," Bud had said. "Long shining ghosts, but solid." That didn't help much.

When they camped that night, Demeris entered the tent with her without hesitation, and waited only a moment or two after lying down to reach for her. Her reaction was noncommittal for the first instant. But then he heard a sort of purring sound and she turned to him, open and ready. There had been nothing remotely like affection between them all afternoon, but now she generated sudden passion out of nothing at all, pulling it up like water from an artesian well; and he rode with her swiftly and expertly toward sweaty, noisy climaxes. He rested a while and went back to her a second time, but she said simply, "No. Let's sleep now," and turned her back to him. A very strange woman, he thought. He lay awake for a time, listening to the rhythm of her breathing just to see if she was asleep, thinking he might nuzzle up to her anyway if she was still conscious and seemed at all receptive. He couldn't tell. She was motionless, limp: for all he knew, dead. Her breathing-sounds were virtually imperceptible. After a time Demeris rolled away. He dreamed of a bright sky streaked with crimson fire, and dragons flying in formations out of the south.

* * *

Now they were nearing Spook City. Instead of following along a dusty unpaved trail they had moved onto an actual road, perhaps some old United States of America highway that the aliens had jazzed up by giving it an internal glow, a cool throbbing green luminance rising in eddying waves from a point deep underground. Other travelers joined them here, some riding wagons drawn by alien beasts of burden, a few floating along on silent flatbed vehicles that had no apparent means of propulsion. The travelers all seemed to be human.

"How do Spooks get around?" Demeris asked.

"Any way they like," said Jill.

A corroded highway sign that looked five thousand years old announced that they had reached a town called Dimmitt. There wasn't any town there, only a sort of checkpoint of light like a benign version of the border barrier: a cheerful shimmering sheen, a dazzling moire pattern dancing in the air. One by one the wagons and flatbeds and carts passed through it and disappeared. "It's the hunt perimeter," Jill explained, while they were waiting their turn to go through. "Like a big pen around Spook City, miles in diameter, to keep the animals in. They won't cross the line. It scares them."

He felt no effect at all as they crossed it. On the other side she told him that she had some formalities to take care of, and walked off toward a battered shed a hundred feet from the road. Demeris waited for her beside the elephant-camel.

A grizzled-looking weather-beaten man of about fifty came limping up and grinned at him.

"Jack Lawson," he announced. He put out his hand. "On my way back from my daughter's wedding, Oklahoma City."

"Nick Demeris."

"Interesting traveling companion you got, Nick. What's it like, traveling with one of those? I've always wondered about that."

"One of what?" Demeris said.

Lawson winked. "Come on, friend. You know what I mean."

"I don't think I do."

"Your pal's a Spook, friend. Surely you aren't going to try to make me believe she's anything else."

"Friend, my ass. And she's as human as you or me."

"Right."

"Believe me," Demeris said flatly. "I know. I've checked her out at very close range."

Lawson's eyebrows rose a little. "That's what I figured. I've heard there are men who go in for that. Some women, too."

"Shit," Demeris said, feeling himself beginning to heat up. He didn't have the time or the inclination for a fight, and Lawson looked about twice his age anyway. As calmly as he could he said, "You're fucking wrong, just the way that Mex kid down south who said she was a Spook was wrong. Neither of you knows shit about her."

"I know one when I see one."

"And I know an asshole when I see one," said Demeris.

"Easy, friend. Easy. I see I'm mistaken, that you simply don't understand what's going on. Okay. A thousand pardons, friend. Ten thousand." Lawson gave him an oily, smarmy smile, a courtly bow, and started to move away.

"Wait," Demeris said. "You really think she's a Spook?"

"Bet your ass I do."

"Prove it, then."

"Don't have any proof. Just intuition."

"Intuition's not worth much where I come from."

"Sometimes you can just tell. There's something about her. I don't know. I couldn't put it into words."

"My father used to say that if you can't put something into words, that's on account of you don't know what you're talking about."

Lawson laughed. It was that same patronizing I-know-better-than-you laugh that the kid in the village had given him. Anger welled up again in Demeris and it was all he could do to keep from swinging on the older man.

But just then Jill returned. She looked human as hell as she came walking up, swinging her hips. Lawson tipped his hat to her with exaggerated courtesy and went sauntering back to his wagon.

"Ready?" Demeris asked her.

"All set." She glanced at him. "You okay, Nick?"

"Sure."

"What was that fellow saying to you?"

"Telling me about his daughter's wedding in Oklahoma."

He clambered up on the elephant-camel, taking up his position on the middle hump.

His anger over what Lawson had said gradually subsided. They all knew so much, these Occupied Zone people. Or thought they did. Always trying to get one up on the greenhorn from Free Country, giving you their knowledgeable looks, hitting you with their sly insinuations.

Some rational part of him told him that if two people over here had said the same thing about Jill, it might just be true. A fair chance of it, in fact. Well, fuck it. She looked human, she smelled human, she felt human when he ran his hands over her body. That was good enough for him. Let these Spook Land people say what they liked. He intended to go on accepting her as human no matter what anyone might try to tell him. It was too late for him to believe anything else.

He had had his mouth to hers; he had been inside her body; he had given himself to her in the most intimate way there was. There was no way he could let himself believe that he had been embracing something from another planet, not now. He absolutely could not permit himself to believe that now.

And then he felt a sudden stab of wild, almost intoxicating temptation: the paradoxical hope that she *was* a Spook after all, that by embracing her he had done something extraordinary and outrageous. A true crossing of borders: his youth restored. He was amazed. It was a stunning moment, a glimpse of what it might be like to step outside the prisons of his soul. But it passed quickly and he was his old sober self again. She is human, he told himself stolidly. Human. Human.

* * *

A LITTLE CLOSER IN, HE saw one of the pens where the hunt animals were being kept. It was like a sheet of lightning rising from the ground, but lightning that stayed and stayed and stayed. Behind it Demeris thought he could make out huge dark moving shapes. Nothing was clear, and after a few moments of staring at that fluid rippling wall of light he started to feel the way he had felt when he was first pushing through the border barrier.

"What kind of things do they have in there?" he asked her.

"Everything," she said. "Wait and see, when they turn them loose."

"When is that?"

"Couple of days from now." She swung around and pointed. "Look there, Nick. There's Spook City."

They were at the crest of a little hill. In the valley below lay a fair-sized sprawling town, not as big as he had expected, a mongrel place made up in part of little boxy houses and in part of tall, tapering, flickering constructions that didn't seem to be of material substance at all, ghost-towers, fairy castles, houses fit for Spooks. The sight of them gave him a jolt, the way everything was mixed together, human and non. A low line of the same immaterial stuff ran around the edge of the city like a miniature border barrier, but softer in hue and dancing like little swamp-fires.

"I don't see any Spooks," he said to her.

"You want to see a Spook? There's a Spook for you."

An alien fluttered up into view right then and there, as though she had conjured it out of empty air. Demeris, caught unprepared, muttered a whispered curse and his fingers moved with desperate urgency through the patterns of protection signs that his mother had taught him more than twenty years before and that he had never had occasion to use. The Spook was incorporeal, elegant, almost blindingly beautiful: a sleek cone of translucence, a node of darkness limned by a dancing core of internal light. He had expected them to be frightening, not beautiful: but this one, at least, was frightening in its beauty. Then a second one appeared, and it was nothing like the first, except that it too had no solidity. It was flat below and almost formless higher up, and drifted a little way above the ground atop a pool of its own luminescence. The first one vanished; the second one revolved and seemed to spawn three more, and then it too was gone; the newest three, which had s-shaped curves and shining blue eye-like features at their upper tips, twined themselves together almost coquettishly and coalesced into a single fleshy spheroid crisscrossed by radiant purple lines. The spheroid folded itself across its own equator, taking on a half-moon configuration, and slipped downward into the earth.

Demeris shivered.

Spooks, yes. Well named. Dream-beings. No wonder there had been no way of defeating them. How could you touch them? How could you injure them in any way, when they mutated and melted and vanished while you were looking at them? It wasn't fair, creatures like that coming to the world and taking a big chunk of it the way they had, simply grabbing, not even bothering to explain why, just moving in, knowing that they were too powerful to be opposed. All his ancient hatred of them sprang into new life. And yet they were beautiful, almost godlike. He feared and loathed them but at the same time he found himself fighting back an impulse to drop to his knees.

He and Jill rode into town without speaking. There was a sweet little tingle when they went through the wall of dancing light, and then they were inside.

"Here we are," Jill said. "Spook City. I'll show you a place where you can stay."

* * *

THE CITY'S STREETS WERE UNPAVED—THE Spooks wouldn't need sidewalks—and most of the human-style buildings had windows of some kind of semi-clear oiled cloth instead of glass. The buildings themselves were of slovenly construction and were set down higgledy-piggledy without much regard for order and logic. Sometimes there was a gap between them out of which a tall Spook structure sprouted like nightmare fungus, but mainly the Spook sectors of the city and the human sectors were separate, however it had seemed when he had been looking down from the hill. All manner of flying creatures gathered for the hunt were in busy circulation overhead: the delta-winged herders, the flying snakes, a whole host of weirdities traversing the air above the city with such demonic intensity that it seemed to sizzle as they passed through it.

Jill conveyed him to a hotel of sorts made out of crudely squared logs held together clumsily by pegs, a gigantic ramshackle three-story cabin that looked as if it had been designed by people who were inventing architecture from scratch, and left him at the door. "I'll see you later," she told him, when he had jumped down. "I've got some business to tend to."

"Wait," he said. "How am I going to find you when—"

Too late. The elephant-camel had already made a massive about-face and was ambling away.

Demeris stood looking after her, feeling puzzled and a little hurt. But he had begun to grow accustomed to her brusqueness and her arbitrary shifts by now. Very likely she'd turn up again in a day or two. Meanwhile, though, he was on his own, just when he had started to count on her help in this place.

He shrugged and went inside.

The place had the same jerry-built look within: a long dark entry hall, exposed rafters, crazily leaning walls. To the left, from behind a tattered curtain of red gauze, came the sounds of barroom chatter and clinking glasses. On the right was a cubicle with a pale, owlish-looking heavyset woman peering out of a lopsided opening.

"I need a room," Demeris told her.

"We just got one left. Busy time, on account of the hunt. It's five labor units a night room and board and a drink or two."

"Labor units?"

"We don't take Free Country money here, chumbo. An hour cleaning out the shithouse, that's one labor unit. Two hours swabbing grease in the kitchen, that's one. Don't worry, we'll find things for you to do. You staying the usual thirty days?"

"I'm not on an Entrada," Demeris said. "I'm here to find my brother." Then, with a sudden rush of hope: "Maybe you've seen him. Looks a lot like me, shorter, around eighteen years old. Tom Demeris."

"Nobody here by that name," she said, and shoved a square metal key toward him. "Second floor on the left, 103. Welcome to Spook City, chumbo."

The room was small, squalid, dim. Hardly any light came through the oilcloth window. A strangely shaped lamp sat on the crooked table next to the bare cot that would be his bed. It turned on when he touched it and an eerie tapering glow rose from it, like a tiny Spook. He saw now that there were hangings on the wall, coarse cloth bearing cryptic inscriptions in Spook script.

Downstairs, he found four men and a parched-looking woman in the bar. They were having some sort of good-natured argument and gave him only the quickest of glances. Sized him up, wrote him off: he could see that. Free Country written all over his face. His nostrils flared and he clamped his lips.

"Whiskey," Demeris told the bartender.

"We got Shagback, Billyhow, Donovan, and Thread."

"Donovan," he said at random. The bartender poured him a shot from a lumpy-looking blue bottle with a garish yellow label. The stuff was inky-dark, vaguely sour-smelling, strong. Demeris felt it hit bottom like a fishhook. The others were looking at him with more interest now. He took that for an opening and turned to them with a forced smile to tell them what they plainly already knew, which was that he was a stranger here, and to ask them the one thing he wanted to know, which was could they help him discover the whereabouts of a kid named Tom Demeris.

"How do you like the whiskey?" the woman asked him, in response.

"It's different from what I'm accustomed to. But not bad." He fought back his anger. "He's my kid brother, that's the thing, and I've come all this way looking for him, because—"

"Tom what?" one of the men said.

"Demeris. We're from Albuquerque."

They began to laugh. "Abblecricky," the woman said.

"Dabblecricky," said one of the other men, sallow-skinned with a livid scar across his cheek.

Demeris looked coldly from one face to another. "Albuquerque," he said with great precision. "It used to be a big city in New Mexico. That's in Free Country. We still got eight, ten thousand people living there, maybe more. My brother was on his Entrada, only he didn't come back. Been gone since June. I think he's got some idea of settling here, and I want to talk to him about that. Tom Demeris is his name. Not quite as tall as I am, a little heavier set, longer hair than mine."

But he could see that he had lost their attention. The woman rolled her eyes and shrugged, and one of the men gestured to the bartender for another round of drinks.

"You want one too?" the bartender asked Demeris.

"A different kind this time."

It wasn't any better. He sipped it morosely. A few moments later the others began to file out of the room. "Abblekirky," the woman said, as she went past Demeris, and laughed again.

He spent a troubled night. The room was musty and dank and made him feel claustrophobic. The little bed offered no comfort. Sounds came from outside, grinding noises, screeches, strange honkings. When he turned the lamp off the darkness was absolute and ominous, and when he turned it on the light bothered him. He lay stiffly, waiting for sleep to take him, and when it failed to arrive he rose and pulled the oilcloth window-cover aside to stare into the night. Attenuated streaks of brightness were floating through the air, ghostly will-o'-the-wisp glowings, and by that faint illumination he saw huge winged things pumping stolidly across the sky, great dragons no more graceful than flying oxen, while in the road below the building three flickering columns of light that surely were Spooks went past, driving a herd of lean little square-headed monsters as though they were sheep.

In the morning, after the grudging breakfast of stale bread and some sort of coffee-like beverage with an undertaste of barley that the hotel bar provided, he went out into Spook City to look for Tom. But where was he supposed to begin? He had no idea.

It was a chaotic, incomprehensible town. The unpaved streets went squiggling off in all directions, no two of them parallel. Wagons and flatbeds of the kind he had seen at the perimeter checkpoint, some of them very ornate and bizarre, swept by constantly, stirring up whirlwinds of gray dust. Ethereal shimmering Spooks drifted in and among them, ignoring the perils of the busy traffic as though they were operating on some other plane of existence entirely, which very likely they were. Now and again came a great bleating of horns and everyone moved to the side of the street to allow a parade of menacing-looking beasts to pass through, a dozen green-scaled things like dinosaurs with high-stepping big-taloned feet or a procession of elephant-camels linked trunk to tail or a string of long slithery serpentine creatures moving on scores of powerful stubby legs.

Demeris felt a curious numbness coming over him as one enormity after another presented itself. These few days across the border were changing him, creating a kind of dreamy tolerance in him. He had absorbed all the new alien sights and experiences he could and he was overloaded now, no room left for reactions of surprise or fear or even of loathing. The crazy superabundance of strangeness in Spook City was quickly starting to appear normal to him. Albuquerque in all its somnolent ordinariness seemed to him now like a static vision, a mere photograph of a city rather than an actual thriving place. There was still the problem of Tom, though. Demeris walked for hours and found no clue, no starting place: no building marked Police Station or City Hall or Questions Answered Here. What he really hoped to come upon was someone who was recognizably a native of Free Country, someone who could give him an inkling of how to go about tracing his brother through the network of kids making Entradas that must exist on this side. But he saw no one like that either. Where the hell was Jill? She was his only ally, and she had left him to cope with this lunacy all by himself, abandoning him as abruptly as she had picked him up in the first place.

But she, at least, could be located. She was the mayor's daughter, after all.

He entered a dark, squalid little building that seemed to be some sort of shop. A small hunched woman who could have been made of old leather gave him a surly look from behind a warped counter. He met it with the best smile he could manage and said to her, "I'm new in town and I'm trying to find Jill Gorton, Ben Gorton's daughter. She's a friend of mine."

"Who?"

"Jill Gorton? Ben Gorton's—"

She shook her head curtly. "Don't know anybody by that name."

"Ben Gorton, then. Where can he be found?"

"Wherever he might happen to be," she said. "How would I know?" And slammed shut on him like a trapdoor. He peered at her in astonishment. She had turned away from him and was moving things around behind her counter as though no one was there.

"Doesn't he have an office?" Demeris asked. "Some kind of headquarters?"

No response. She got up, moving around in the shadows, ignoring him.

"I'm talking to you," Demeris said.

She might just as well have been deaf. He quivered with frustration. It was midday and he had had practically nothing to eat since yesterday afternoon and he hadn't accomplished anything all this day and it had started to dawn on him that he had no idea how he was going to find his way back to his hotel through the maze of the city—he didn't even know its name or address, and the streets bore no signs anyway—and now this old bitch was pretending he was invisible. Furiously he said, "Jesus Christ, what's the matter with you people? Haven't you ever heard of common courtesy here? Have the fucking Spooks drained everything that's human out of you? All I want to know is how to find the goddamned mayor. Can't you tell me that one little thing? Can't you?"

Instead of answering him, she looked back over her shoulder and made a sound in Spook language, a wheezing whistling noise, the kind of sound that Jill might have directed to her elephant-camel. Almost instantly a tall flat-faced man of about thirty with the same sort of dark leathery skin as hers came out of a back room and gave Demeris a black, threatening stare.

"What the hell you think you're doing yelling at my mother?"

"Look," Demeris said, "I just asked her for a little help, that's all." He was still churning with rage. "I need to find the mayor. I'm a friend of his daughter Jill, and she's supposed to help me track down my brother Tom, who came across from Free Country a few months ago, and I don't know one goddamned building from the next in this town, so I stopped in here hoping she could give me some directions and instead—"

"You yelled at her. You cursed at her."

"Yeah. Maybe so. But if you people don't have any decency why the hell should I? All I want to know—"

"You cursed at my mother."

"Yeah," Demeris said. "Yeah, I did." It was all too much. He was tired and hungry and far from home and the streets were full of monsters and nobody would give him the time of day here and he was sick of it. He had no idea who moved first, but suddenly they were both on the same side of the counter and swinging at each other, butting heads and pummeling each other's chests and trying to slam each other against the wall. The other man was bigger and heavier, but Demeris was angrier, and he got his hands to the other man's throat and started to squeeze. Dimly he was aware of sounds all around him, doors slamming, rapid footsteps, people shouting, a thick incoherent babble of sound. Then someone's arm was bent around his chin and throat and hands were clamped on his wrists and he was being pulled to the floor, kicking as he went and struggling to reach the knife at his waist. The confusion grew worse after that: he had no idea how many of them there were, but they were sitting on him, they were holding his arms, they were dragging him out into the daylight. He thought he saw a Spook hovering in the air above him, but perhaps he was wrong about that. There was too much light everywhere around. Nothing was clear. "Listen," he said, "The only thing I want is—" and they hit him in the mouth and kicked him in the side, and there was some raucous laughter and he heard them speaking in the Spook language; and then he came to understand that he was in a wagon, a cart, some kind of moving contrivance. His hands and feet were tied. A flushed sweaty face looked down at him, grinning.

"Where are you taking me?" Demeris asked.

"Ben Gorton. That's who you wanted to see, isn't it? Ben Gorton, right?"

* * *

He was in a basement room somewhere, windowless, lit by three of the little Spook-lamps. It was the next day, he supposed. Certainly a lot of time had gone by, perhaps a whole night. They had given him a little to eat, some sort of bean mush. He was still bound, but two men were holding him anyway.

"Untie him," Gorton said.

He had to be Gorton. He was around six feet seven, wide as a slab, with a big bald head and a great beaky nose, and everything about him spoke of power and authority. Demeris rubbed his wrists where the cord had chafed them and said, "I wasn't interested in a fight. That's not the sort of person I am. But sometimes when it builds up and builds up and builds up, and you can't stand it anymore—"

"Right. You damn near killed Bobby Bridger, you know that?" His eyes were bugging right out of his head. This is hunt season here, mister. The Spooks will be turning the critters loose any minute now and things are going to get *real* lively. It's important for everybody to stay civil so things don't get any more complicated than they usually are when the hunt's going on."

"If Bridger's mother had been a little more civil to me, it would all have been a lot different," Demeris said.

Gorton gave him a weary look. "Who are you and what are you doing here, anyway?"

Taking a deep breath, Demeris said, "My name's Nick Demeris, and I live in Free Country, and I came over here to find my kid brother Tom, who seems to have gotten sidetracked coming back from his Entrada."

"Tom Demeris," Gorton said, raising his eyebrows.

"Yes. Then I met your daughter, Jill, at some little town near the border, and she invited me to travel with her. But when we got to Spook City she dropped me at some hotel and disappeared, so—"

"Wait a second," said Gorton. His eyebrows went even higher. "My daughter Jill?"

"That's right."

"Shit," the big man said. "What daughter? I don't have no fucking daughter."

"No daughter," said Demeris.

"No daughter. None. Must have been some Spook playing games with you."

The words fell on Demeris like stones. "Some Spook," he repeated numbly. "Pretending to be your daughter. You mean that? For Christ's sake, are you serious, or are you playing games with me too?"

Something in Demeris's agonized tone seemed to register sympathetically on Gorton. He squinted, he blinked, he tugged at the tip of his great nose. He said in a much softer voice, "I'm not playing any games with you. I can't say for sure that she was a Spook but she sure as hell wasn't my daughter, because I don't have any daughter. Spooks doing masks will tell you anything they damn please, though. Chances are, she was a Spook."

"Doing masks?"

"Spooks going around playing at being human. It's a big thing with them these days. The latest Spook fad."

Demeris nodded. Doing masks, he thought. He considered it and it began to sink in, and sink and sink and sink.

Then quietly he said, "Maybe you can help me find my brother, at least."

"No. I can't do that and neither can anybody else. Tom Demeris, you said his name is?"

"That's right."

Gorton glanced toward one of his men. "Mack, how long ago was it that the Demeris kid took the Spooks' nickel?"

"Middle of July, I think."

"Right." To Demeris, Gorton said, "What we call 'taking the Spooks' nickel' means selling yourself to them, do you know what I mean? You agree to go with them to their home planet. They've got a kind of plush country club for humans there where you live like a grand emperor for the rest of your life, comfort, luxury, women, anything you damn please, but the deal is that in return you belong to them forever, that they get to run psychological experiments on you to see what makes you tick, like a mouse in a cage. At least that's what the Spooks tell us goes on there, and we might as well believe it. Nobody who's sold himself to the Spooks has ever come back. I'm sorry, man. I wish it wasn't so."

Demeris looked away for a moment. He felt like smashing things, but he held himself perfectly still. My brother, he thought, my baby brother.

"He was just a kid," he said.

"Well, he must have been a damned unhappy kid. Nobody with his head screwed on right would take the nickel. Hardly anybody ever does." Something flashed momentarily in Gorton's eyes, and Demeris sensed that to these people selling yourself to the Spooks was the ultimate surrender, the deepest sort of self-betrayal. They had all sold themselves to the Spooks, in a sense, by choosing to live in the Occupied Zone; but even here there were levels of yielding to the alien conqueror, he realized, and in the eyes of Spook City people the thing that Tom had done was the lowest level of all. He felt the weight of Gorton's contempt for Tom and pity for him, suddenly, and hated it, and tried to throw it back with a furious glare. Gorton watched him quietly, not reacting.

After a little while Demeris said, "All right. There's nothing I can do, is there? I guess I'd better go back to Albuquerque now."

"You'd better go back to your hotel and wait until the hunt is over," said Gorton. "It isn't safe wandering around in the open while the critters are loose."

"No," said Demeris. "I suppose it isn't."

"Take him to wherever he's staying, Mack," Gorton said to his man. He stared for a time at Demeris. The sorrow in his eyes seemed genuine. "I'm sorry," Gorton said again. "I really am."

* * *

MACK HAD NO DIFFICULTY RECOGNIZING Demeris's hotel from the description he gave, and took him to it in a floating wagon that made the trip in less than fifteen minutes. The streets were practically empty now: no Spooks in sight and hardly any humans, and those who were still out were moving quickly.

"You want to stay indoors while the hunt is going on," Mack said. "A lot of dumb idiots don't, but most of them regret it. This is one event that ought to be left strictly to the Spooks."

"How will I know when it starts?"

"You'll know," Mack said.

Demeris got out of the wagon. It turned immediately and headed away. He paused a moment in front of the building, breathing deeply, feeling a little light-headed, thinking of Tom on the Spook planet, Tom living in a Spook palace, Tom sleeping on satin Spook sheets.

"Nick? Over here, Nick! It's me!"

"Oh, Christ," he said. Jill, coming up the street toward him, smiling as blithely as though this were Christmas Eve. He scanned her, searching for traces of some Spook gleam, some alien shimmer. When she reached him she held out her arms to him as though expecting a hug. He stepped back to avoid her grasp.

In a flat tight voice, he said, "I found out about my brother. He's gone off to the Spook world. Took their nickel."

"Oh, Nick. Nick!"

"You knew, didn't you? Everybody in this town must have known about the kid who came from Free Country and sold himself to the Spooks." His tone turned icy. "It was your father the mayor that told me. He also told me that he doesn't have any daughters."

Her cheeks blazed with embarrassment. It was so human a reaction that he was cast into fresh confusion: how could a Spook learn to mimic a human even down to a blush? It didn't seem possible. And it gave him new hope. She had lied to him about being Ben Gorton's daughter, yes, God only knew why; but there was still the possibility that she was human, that she had chosen to put on a false identity but the body he saw was really her own. If only it was so, he thought. His anger with her, his disdain, melted away in a flash. He wanted everything to be all right. He was rocked by a powerful rush of eagerness to be assured that the woman he had embraced those two nights on the desert was indeed a woman; and with it, astonishingly, came a new burst of desire for her, of fresh yearning stronger than anything he had felt for her before.

"What he told me about was that you were a Spook," Demeris said in a guarded tone. He looked at her hopefully, waiting for her to deny it, praying for her to deny it, ready to accept her denial.

"Yes," she said. "I am."

It was like a gate slamming shut in his face.

Serenely she said, "Humans fascinate me. Their emotions, their reactions, their attitudes toward things. I've been studying them at close range for a hundred of your years and I still don't know as much as I'd like to. And finally I thought, the only way I can make that final leap of understanding is to become one myself."

"Doing masks," Demeris said in a hollow voice. Looking at her, he imagined he could see something cold and foreign peering out at him, and it seemed to him that great chilly winds were sweeping through the empty caverns of his soul. He began to see now that somewhere deep within him he must have been making plans for a future that included this woman, that he had wanted her so much that he had stubbornly refused to accept any of the evidence that had been given him that that was unthinkable. And now he had been given the one bit of evidence that was impossible to reject.

"Right," she said. "Doing masks."

He knew he should be feeling fury, or anguish, or something, at this final revelation that he had slept with a Spook. But he hardly felt anything at all. He was like a stone. Perhaps he had already done the anger and pain, on some level below his consciousness. Or else he had somehow transcended it. The Spooks are in charge here. All right. We are their toys. All right. All right. You could go only so far into despair and then you stopped feeling it, he supposed. Or hatred. Hating the Spooks was useless. It was like hating an avalanche, like hating an earthquake.

"Taking human men as your lovers, too: that's part of doing masks, isn't it?" he asked. "Was my brother Tom one of them?"

"No. Never. I saw him only once or twice."

He believed that. He believed everything she was saying, now.

She seemed about to say something else. But then suddenly a flare of lightning burst across the sky, a monstrous forking shaft of flame that looked as though it could split the world in two. It was followed not by thunder but by music, an immense alien chord that fell like an avalanche from the air and swelled up around them with oceanic force. The vault of the sky rippled with colors: red, orange, violet, green.

"What's happening?" Demeris asked.

"The hunt is starting," she said. "That's the signal."

Yes. In the wake of the lightning and the rippling colors came swarming throngs of airborne creatures, seeming thousands of them, the delta-winged dragon-like herders and their snake-like pilots, turning the midday sky dark with their numbers, like a swarm of bees overhead, colossal ones whose wings made a terrible droning sound as they beat the air; and then Demeris heard gigantic roaring, bellowing sounds from nearby, as if monsters were approaching. There were no animals in the streets, not yet, but they couldn't be very far away. Above him, Spooks by the dozens flickered in the air. Then he heard footsteps, and a pack of humans came running frantically toward them out of a narrow street, their eyes wild, their faces weirdly rigid. Did the Spooks hunt humans too? Demeris wondered. Or was one of the monsters chasing after them? The runners came sweeping down on him. "Get out of the way, man!" one of them cried. "Out of the *way*!"

Demeris stepped back, but not fast enough, and the runner on the inside smacked hard into his shoulder, spinning him around a little. For one startling moment Demeris found himself looking straight into the man's eyes, and saw something close to madness there, but no fear at all—only eagerness, impatience, frenzied excitement—and he realized that they must be running not from but *to* the hunt, that they were on their way to witness the crazy slaughter at close range or even to take part in it themselves, that they lived just as did the Spooks for this annual moment of apocalyptic frenzy.

Jill said, "It'll be berserk here now for two or three days. You ought to be very careful if you go outdoors."

"Yes. I will."

"Listen," she said, putting an edge on her voice to make it cut through the roaring coming from overhead, "I've got a proposition for you, now that you know the truth." She leaned close to him. "Let's stay together, you and me. Despite our differences. I like you a lot, Nick."

He peered at her, utterly astounded.

"I really think we can work something out," she went on. Another horde of winged things shot by just above them, making raspy tearing sounds as they flailed the air, and a new gush of color stained the sky. "Seriously, Nick. We can stay in Spook City if you want to, but I don't suppose you do. If you don't I'll go back across the border with you and live with you in Free Country. In my mind I've already crossed over. I don't want just to study you people from the outside. I want to *be* one of you."

"Are you crazy?" Demeris asked.

"No. Not in the least, I swear. Can you believe me? Can you?"

"I've got to go inside," he said. He was trembling. "It isn't smart to be standing out here while the hunt is going on."

"What do you say, Nick? Give me an answer."

"It isn't possible for us to be together. You know it isn't."

"You want to. Some part of you does."

"Maybe so," he said, amazed at what he was saying, but unable to deny it despite himself. "Just maybe. One little fraction of me. But it isn't possible, all the same. I don't want to live here among the Spooks, and if I take you back with me, some bastard with a sharp nose will sniff you out sooner or later and expose you for what you are, and stand up before the whole community and denounce me for what I am. I'm not going to take that risk. I'm just not, Jill."

"That's your absolute decision."

"My absolute decision, yes."

Something was coming down the street now, some vast hopping thing with a head the size of a cow and teeth like spears. A dozen or so humans ran along beside it, practically within reach of the creature's clashing jaws, and a covey of Spooks hovered over it, bombarding it with flashes of light. Demeris took a step or two toward the door of the hotel. Jill did nothing to hold him back.

He turned when he was in the doorway. She was still standing there. The hunters and their prey sped right past her, but she took no notice. She waved to him.

Sure, he thought. He waved back. Goodbye, Jill.

He went inside. There was a clatter on the stairs, people running down, a woman and some men. He recognized them as the ones who had mocked him in the bar when he had first arrived. Two of the men ran past him and out the door, but the woman halted and caught him by the crook of the arm.

"Hey, Abblecricky!"

Demeris stared at her.

She leaned into his face and grinned. She was flushed and wild-looking, like the ones who had been running through the streets. "Come on, man! It's the hunt! The hunt, man! You're heading the wrong way. Don't you want to be there?"

He had no answer for that.

She was tugging at him. "Come *on*! Live it up! Kill yourself a dragon or two!"

"Ella!" one of the men called after her.

She gave Demeris a wink and ran out the door.

He swayed uncertainly, torn between curiosity about what was going on out there and a profound wish to go upstairs and shut the door behind him. But the street had the stronger pull. He took a step or two after the woman, and then another, and then he was outside again. Jill wasn't there. The scene in the street was wilder than ever: people running back and forth yelling incoherently, colliding with each other in their frenzy, and overhead streams of winged creatures still swarming, and Spooks like beams of pure light moving among them, and in the distance the sounds of bellowing animals and thunderous explosions and high keening cries of what he took to be Spook pleasure. Far off to the south he saw a winged something the size of a small hill circling desperately in the sky, surrounded by implacable flaring pinpoints of Spook-light, and suddenly halting and plummeting like a falling moon toward the ground. He could smell the smell of charred flesh in the air, with a salty underflavor of what he suspected was the blood of alien beasts.

At a sleepwalker's dreamy pace Demeris went to the corner and turned left. Abruptly he found himself confronted with a thing so huge and hideous that it was almost funny—a massive long-snouted frog-shaped thing, sloping upward from a squat base, with a moist-looking greenish-black hide pocked with little red craters and a broad, gaping, yellow-rimmed mouth. It had planted itself in the middle of the street with its shoulders practically touching the buildings at either side and was advancing slowly and clumsily toward the intersection.

Demeris drew his knife. What the hell, he thought. He was here at hunt time, he might as well join the fun. The creature was immense but it didn't have any visible fangs or talons and he figured he could move in at an angle and slash upward through the great baggy throat, and then step back fast before the thing fell on him.

And if it turned out to be more dangerous than it looked, he didn't give a damn. Not now.

He moved forward, knife already arcing upward.

"Hey!" someone cried behind him. "You out of your mind, fellow?"

Demeris glanced around. The bartender had come out of the hotel and was staring at him.

"That critter's just a big sack of acid," he said. "You cut it open, it'll pour all over you."

The frog-thing made a sound like a burp, or perhaps a sardonic chuckle. Demeris backed away.

"You want to cut something with that," the bartender said, "you better know what you're cutting."

"Yeah." Demeris said. "I suppose so." He put the knife back in its sheath, and headed back across the street, feeling all the craziness of the moment go from him like air ebbing from a balloon. This hunt was no business of his. Let the people who live here get mixed up in it if they liked. But there was no reason why he should. He'd just be buying trouble, and he had never seen any sense in that.

As he reached the hotel entrance he saw Spook-light shimmering in the air at the corner—hunters, hovering above—and then there was a soft sighing sound and a torrent of bluish fluid came rolling out of the side street. It was foaming and hissing as it edged along the gutter.

Demeris shuddered. He went into the building.

* * *

Quickly he mounted the stairs and entered his room, and sat for a long while on the edge of the cot, gradually growing calm, letting it all finish sinking in while the din of the hunt went on and on.

Tom was gone, that was the basic thing he had to deal with. Neither dead nor really alive, but certainly gone. Okay. He faced that and grappled with it. It was bitter news, but at least it was a resolution of sorts. He'd mourn for a while and then he'd be all right.

And Jill—

Doing masks. Taking humans as lovers. The whole thing went round and round in his mind, all that he and she had done together, had said, everything that had passed between them. And how he had always felt about Spooks and how—somehow, he had no idea how—his time with Jill had changed that a little.

He remembered what she had said. *I don't just want to study you. I want to* be *one of you.*

What did that mean? A tourist in the human race? A sightseer across species lines?

They are softening, then. They are starting to whore after strange amusements. And if that's so, he thought, then we are beginning to win. The aliens had infiltrated Earth; but now Earth was infiltrating them. This yearning to do masks, to look and act like humans, to experience human feelings and human practices and human follies: it meant the end for them. There were too many humans on Earth and not enough Spooks, and the Spooks would eventually be swallowed up. One by one, they would succumb to the temptation of giving up their chilly godliness and trying to imitate the messy, contradictory, troublesome creatures that humans are. And, Demeris thought, over the course of time—five hundred years, a thousand, who could say?—Earth would complete the job of absorbing the invaders and something new would emerge from the mixture of the species. That was an interesting thing to consider.

But then something clicked in his mind and he felt himself flooded by a strange interior light, a light as weird and intense as the Spooklight in the skies over the city now or the glow of the border barrier, and he realized there was another way of looking at these things altogether. Jill dropped suddenly into a new perspective and instead of thinking of her as a mere sightseer looking for forbidden thrills, he saw her for what she really was—a pioneer, an explorer, a border-jumper, a defiant enemy of boundaries and limitations and rules. The same for Tom. They were two of a kind, those two; and he had been slow to recognize it because he simply wasn't of their sort. Demeris recognized now how little he had understood his youngest brother. To him, Tom was a disturbed kid. To Ben Gorton, he was a contemptible sellout. But the real Tom, Tom's own Tom, might be something entirely different: someone looking not just to make a little thirty-day Entrada but to carry out a real penetration into the alien, to jump deep and far into otherness to find out what it was like. The same with this Jill, this alien, this Spook—she was of that kind too, but coming from the other direction.

And she had wanted his help. She had needed it all along, right from the start. She had missed her chance with Tom, but maybe she thought that Tom's brother might be the same sort of person, someone who lived on the edge, who pushed against walls.

Well, well, well. How wrong she was. That was too bad.

For an instant Demeris felt another surge of the strange excitement that had come over him back at the checkpoint, when he had considered the possibility that Jill might be a Spook and had, for a moment, felt exhilarated by the thought. *Could* he take her back with him? *Could* he sneak her into the human community and live happily ever after with her, hiding the astonishing truth like the man in the old story who had married a mermaid? He saw himself, for a moment, lying beside her at night while she told him Spook stories and whispered weird Spook words and showed him sly little Spook shapeshifting tricks as they embraced. It was an astonishing thought. And he began to quiver and sweat as he thought about it.

Then, as it had before, the moment passed.

He couldn't do it. It just wasn't who he was, not really. Tom might have done it, but Tom was gone, and he wasn't Tom or anything like him. Not one of the leapers, one of the soarers, one of the questers. Not one of the adventurous kind at all: just a careful man, a builder, a planner, a preserver, a protector. Nothing wrong with that. But not of any real use to Jill in her quest.

Too bad, he thought. Too damned bad, Jill.

He walked to the window and peered out, past the oilcloth cover. The hunt was reaching some sort of peak. The street was more crowded than ever with frantic monsters. The sky was full of Spooks. Scattered bands of Spook City humans, looking half crazed or more than half, were running back and forth. There was noise everywhere, sharp, percussive, discordant. Jill was nowhere to be seen out there. He let the oilcloth flap drop back in place and lay down on his cot and closed his eyes.

* * *

THREE DAYS LATER, WHEN THE hunt was over and it was safe to go out again, Demeris set out for home. For the first ten blocks or so a glow that might have been a Spook hovered above him, keeping pace as he walked. He wondered if it was Jill.

She had given him a second chance once, he remembered. Maybe she was doing it again.

"Jill?" he called up to it. "That you?"

No answer came.

"Listen," he called to the hovering glow. "Forget it. It isn't going to work out, you and me. I'm sorry, but it isn't. You hear me?"

A little change in the intensity of the flicker overhead, perhaps. Or perhaps not.

He looked upward and said, "And listen, Jill—if that's you, Jill, I want to tell you: thanks for everything, okay?" It was strange, talking to the sky this way. But he didn't care. "And good luck. You hear? Good luck, Jill! I hope you get what you want."

The glow bobbed for a moment, up, down. Then it was gone.

Demeris, shading his eyes, looked upward for a time, but there was nothing to see. He felt a sharp little momentary pang, thinking of the possibilities. But what could he have done? She had wanted something from him that he wasn't able to give. If he had been somebody else, things might have been different. But he was who he was. He could go only so far toward becoming someone else, and then he had to pull back and return to being who he really was, and that was all there was to it.

He moved onward, toward the edge of the city.

No one gave him any trouble at all on his way out, and the return trip through the western fringe of the Occupied Zone was just as smooth. Everything was quiet, all was peaceful, clear on to the border.

The border crossing itself was equally uncomplicated. The fizzing lights and the weird hallucinatory effects of the barrier were visible, but they had no impact from this side. Demeris passed through them as though they were so much smoke, and kept on walking. In hardly any time he was across the border and back in Free Country again.

AMANDA AND THE ALIEN

Some stories seem almost to write themselves. This was one of them. I wish they were all that easy, or that the results were always that pleasing.

"Amanda" was a product of the rainy winter of 1981–1982, when I was having a particularly fertile run of short-story writing. (Here I need to pause for a digression on California weather and my writing habits. California is one of five places in the world that have the so-called "Mediterranean" climate—the others are Chile, Western Australia, the western part of South Africa, and the Mediterranean region itself—in which the winters are mild and rainy and the summers are dry. Where I live, in the San Francisco region, the heaviest rains fall between November and March. Then they taper off, and from mid-April to early November there's normally no rain at all. Rain in summertime here has been known to happen occasionally, but so rarely that it's a front-page news item. My working pattern followed the weather: in the days when I was writing novels—it's been a while since I last wrote one—I tended to write them during the period of maximum rainfall, tapering off to short stories as the season's rains began to diminish in the spring, and doing as little work as my conscience would allow during the dry season. By fall, just as the rains were getting ready to return, I would warm up the machinery with a short story or two and then embark on the new season's novel. But 1981 was an unusual year: instead of a novel, my book for the year was *Majipoor Chronicles*, which is actually a collection of short stories disguised as a novel, and I wrote it in the spring and summer instead of winter. When autumn came, I was out of sequence with my regular writing rhythm, and I decided to keep on doing short stories and get things straightened out later on.)

And so "Amanda." It wasn't the story I had intended to do then. I had promised one to Ellen Datlow, the new fiction editor of *Omni*, and what I had in mind was a sequel to one from the year before called "Dancers in the Time-Flux"—using the same protagonist, the 17th-century Dutch circumnavigator Olivier van Noort, who has been transported to the far future and this time encounters a Parisian woman from the year 1980 who was, like himself, a creature of antiquity, but nevertheless something out of his own future. My long-range plan was to assemble another story cycle along the lines of *Majipoor Chronicles*, set in the Son of Man world that I had invented for a 1969 novel. But something went wrong and the story died on me after about eight pages. I don't know why. Unfinished stories are as rare around here as heavy rainfall in July. So far as I can recall, that's the only story I've left unfinished in the past sixty years.

"The thing seems terribly slow and ponderous and wrong," I told Ellen in a letter of February 20, 1982, "and after a few days of work I called a halt to find out what the trouble was. The trouble was, apparently, that I wanted to do a different sort of story for you, something bouncier and zippier and more contemporary. And before I really knew what was happening, the enclosed lighthearted chiller came galloping out of the typewriter." Ellen bought it by return mail, and Terry Carr chose it for the 1983 volume of his annual *Best Science Fiction of the Year* anthology series.

Instead of setting my story in the remote future world of "Dancers in the Time-Flux," I had put it right here, in the San Francisco Bay Area of just a few years hence. And, though I wrote it in cool rainy February, I picked warm sunny September as the time in which it took place. Perhaps that was why I wrote it with such ease. It had been pouring outside for days, but in my mind our long golden summer had already come. And, with it, the utterly unscrupulous Amanda, an all too familiar California life-form who comes face to face with a very scary alien and holds her own with it.

Ellen Datlow published it in the May, 1983 issue of *Omni*. Some years later the talented young director Jon Kroll made a very funny television movie out of it, and careful observers will note that in it I made my film debut in a role (non-speaking) that had me on camera for approximately seventeen seconds.

AMANDA SPOTTED THE ALIEN LATE Friday afternoon outside the Video Center on South Main. It was trying to look cool and laid-back, but it simply came across as bewildered and uneasy. The alien was disguised as a seventeen-year-old girl, maybe a Chicana, with olive-toned skin and hair so black it seemed almost blue, but Amanda, who was seventeen herself, knew a phony when she saw one. She studied the alien for some moments from the other side of the street to make absolutely certain. Then she walked across.

"You're doing it wrong," Amanda said. "Anybody with half a brain could tell what you really are."

"Bug off," the alien said.

"No. Listen to me. You want to stay out of the detention center or don't you?"

The alien stared coldly at Amanda and said, "I don't know what the crap you're talking about."

"Sure you do. No sense trying to bluff me. Look, I want to help you," Amanda said. "I think you're getting a raw deal. You know what that means, a raw deal? Hey, look, come home with me and I'll teach you a few things about passing for human. I've got the whole friggin' weekend now with nothing else to do anyway."

A flicker of interest came into the other girl's dark chilly eyes. But it went quickly away and she said, "You some kind of lunatic?"

"Suit yourself, O thing from beyond the stars. *Let* them lock you up again. *Let* them stick electrodes up your ass. I tried to help. That's all I can do, is try," Amanda said, shrugging. She began to saunter away. She didn't look back. Three steps, four, five, hands in pockets, slowly heading for her car. Had she been wrong, she wondered? No. No. She could be wrong about some things, like Charley Taylor's interest in spending the weekend with her, maybe. But not this. That crinkly-haired chick was the missing alien for sure. The whole county was buzzing about it—deadly nonhuman life-form has escaped from the detention center out by Tracy, might be anywhere, Walnut Creek, Livermore, even San Francisco, dangerous monster, capable of mimicking human forms, will engulf and digest you and disguise itself in your shape, and there it was, Amanda knew, standing outside the Video Center. Amanda kept walking.

"Wait," the alien said finally

Amanda took another easy step or two. Then she looked back over her shoulder.

"Yeah?"

"How can you tell?"

Amanda grinned. "Easy. You've got a rain slicker on and it's only September. Rainy season doesn't start around here for another month or two. Your pants are the old spandex kind. People like you don't wear that stuff anymore. Your face paint is San Jose colors, but you've got the cheek chevrons put on in the Berkeley pattern. That's just the first three things I noticed. I could find plenty more. Nothing about you fits together with anything else. It's like you did a survey to see how you ought to appear, and tried a little of everything. The closer I study you, the more I see. Look, you're wearing your headphones and the battery light is on, but there's no cassette in the slot. What are you listening to, the music of the spheres? That model doesn't have any FM tuner, you know. You see? You may think you're perfectly camouflaged, but you aren't."

"I could destroy you," the alien said.

"What? Oh, sure. Sure you could. Engulf me right here on the street, all over in thirty seconds, little trail of slime by the door and a new Amanda walks away. But what then? What good's that going to do you? You still won't know which end is up. So there's no logic in destroying me, unless you're a total dummy. I'm on your side. I'm not going to turn you in."

"Why should I trust you?"

"Because I've been talking to you for five minutes and I haven't yelled for the cops yet. Don't you know that half of California is out searching for you? Hey, can you read? Come over here a minute. Here." Amanda tugged the alien toward the newspaper vending box at the curb. The headline on the afternoon *Examiner* was:

BAY AREA ALIEN TERROR

MARINES TO JOIN NINE-COUNTY HUNT
MAYOR, GOVERNOR CAUTION AGAINST PANIC

"You understand that?" Amanda asked. "That's you they're talking about. They're out there with flame guns, tranquilizer darts, web snares, and God knows what else. There's been real hysteria for a day and a half. And you standing around here with the wrong chevrons on! Christ. Christ! What's your plan, anyway? Where are you trying to go?"

"Home," the alien said. "But first I have to rendezvous at the pickup point."

"Where's that?"

"You think I'm stupid?"

"Shit," Amanda said. "If I meant to turn you in, I'd have done it five minutes ago. But okay. I don't give a damn where your rendezvous point is. I tell you, though, you wouldn't make it as far as San Francisco rigged up the way you are. It's a miracle you've avoided getting caught until now."

"And you'll help me?"

"I've been trying to. Come on. Let's get the hell out of here. I'll take you home and fix you up a little. My car's in the lot on the corner."

"Okay."

"Whew!" Amanda shook her head slowly. "Christ, some people are awfully hard to help."

* * *

AS SHE DROVE OUT OF the center of town, Amanda glanced occasionally at the alien sitting tensely to her right. Basically the disguise was very convincing, Amanda thought. Maybe all the small details were wrong, the outer stuff, the anthropological stuff, but the alien *looked* human, it *sounded* human, it even *smelled* human. Possibly it could fool ninety-nine people out of a hundred, or maybe more than that. But Amanda had always had a good eye for detail. And the particular moment she had spotted the alien on South Main she had been unusually alert, sensitive, all raw nerves, every antenna up. Of course, it wasn't aliens she was hunting for, but just a diversion, a little excitement, something to fill the great gaping emptiness that Charley Taylor had left in her weekend.

Amanda had been planning the weekend with Charley all month. Her parents were going to go off to Lake Tahoe for three days, her kid sister had wangled permission to accompany them, and Amanda was going to have the house to herself, just her and Macavity the cat. And Charley. He was going to move in on Friday afternoon and they'd cook dinner together and get blasted on her stash of choice powder and watch five or six of her parents' X-rated cassettes, and Saturday they'd drive over to the city and cruise some of the kinky districts and go to that bathhouse on Folsom where everybody got naked and climbed into the giant Jacuzzi, and then on Sunday—Well, none of that was going to happen. Charley had called on Thursday to cancel. "Something big came up," he said, and Amanda had a pretty good idea what that was, which was his hot little cousin from New Orleans who sometimes came flying out here on no notice at all; but the inconsiderate bastard seemed to be entirely unaware of how much Amanda had been looking forward to this weekend, how much it meant to her, how painful it was to be dumped like this. She had run through the planned events of the weekend in her mind so many times that she almost felt as though she had experienced them: it was that real to her. But overnight it had become unreal. Three whole days on her own, the house to herself, and so early in the semester that there was no homework to think about, and Charley had stood her up! What was she supposed to do now, call desperately around town to scrounge up some old lover as a playmate? Or pick up some stranger downtown? Amanda hated to fool around with strangers. She was half tempted to go over to the city and just let things happen, but they were all weirdos and creeps over there, anyway, and she knew what she could expect. What a waste, not having Charley! She could kill him for robbing her of the weekend.

Now there was the alien, though. A dozen of these star people had come to Earth last year, not in a flying saucer as everybody had expected, but in little capsules that floated like milkweed seeds, and they had landed in a wide arc between San Diego and Salt Lake City. Their natural form, so far as anyone could tell for sure, was something like a huge jellyfish with a row of staring purple eyes down one wavy margin, but their usual tactic was to borrow any local body they found, digesting it and turning themselves into an accurate imitation of it. One of them had made the mistake of turning itself into a brown mountain bear and another into a bobcat—maybe they thought that those were the dominant life-forms on Earth—but the others had taken on human bodies, at the cost of at least ten lives. Then they went looking to make contact with government leaders, and naturally they were rounded up very swiftly and interned, some in mental hospitals and some in county jails, but eventually—as soon as the truth of what they really were sank in—they were all put in a special detention camp in Northern California. Of course, a tremendous fuss was made over them, endless stuff in the papers and on the tube, speculation by this heavy thinker and that about the significance of their mission, the nature of their biochemistry, a little wild talk about the possibility that more of their kind might be waiting undetected out there and plotting to do God knows what, and all sorts of that stuff, and then came a government clamp on the entire subject, no official announcements except that "discussions" with the visitors were continuing; and after a while the whole thing degenerated into dumb alien jokes ("Why did the alien cross the road?") and Halloween invader masks, and then it moved into the background of everyone's attention and was forgotten. And remained forgotten until the announcement that one of the creatures had slipped out of the camp somehow and was loose within a hundred-mile zone around San Francisco. Preoccupied as she was with her anguish over Charley's heartlessness, even Amanda had managed to pick up *that* news item. And now the alien was in her very car. So there'd be some weekend amusement for her after all.

Amanda was entirely unafraid of the alleged deadliness of the star being: whatever else the alien might be, it was surely no dope, not if it had been picked to come halfway across the galaxy on a mission like this, and Amanda knew that the alien could see that harming her was not going to be in its own best interests. The alien had need of her, and the alien realized that. And Amanda, in some way that she was only just beginning to work out, had need of the alien.

* * *

She pulled up outside her house, a compact split-level at the western end of town. "This is the place," she said. Heat shimmers danced in the air, and the hills back of the house, parched in the long dry summer, were the color of lions. Macavity, Amanda's old tabby, sprawled in the shade of the bottlebrush tree on the ragged front lawn. As Amanda and the alien approached, the cat sat up warily, flattened his ears, hissed. The alien immediately moved into a defensive posture, sniffing the air.

"Just a household pet," Amanda said. "You know what that is? He isn't dangerous. He's always a little suspicious of strangers."

Which was untrue. An earthquake couldn't have brought Macavity out of his nap, and a cotillion of mice dancing minuets on his tail wouldn't have drawn a reaction from him. Amanda calmed him with some fur-ruffling, but he wanted nothing to do with the alien, and went slinking sullenly into the underbrush. The alien watched him with care until he was out of sight.

"You have anything like cats on your planet?" Amanda asked as they went inside.

"We had small wild animals once. They were unnecessary."

"Oh," Amanda said. The house had a stuffy, stagnant air. She switched on air-conditioning. "Where is your planet, anyway?"

The alien ignored the question. It padded around the living room, very much like a prowling cat itself, studying the stereo, the television, the couches, the vase of dried flowers.

"Is this a typical Earthian home?"

"More or less," said Amanda. "Typical for around here, at least. This is what we call a suburb. It's half an hour by freeway from here to

San Francisco. That's a city. A lot of people living all close together. I'll take you over there tonight or tomorrow for a look, if you're interested." She got some music going, high volume. The alien didn't seem to mind, so she notched the volume up more. "I'm going to take a shower. You could use one, too, actually."

"Shower? You mean rain?"

"I mean body-cleaning activities. We Earthlings like to wash a lot, to get rid of sweat and dirt and stuff. It's considered bad form to stink. Come on, I'll show you how to do it. You've got to do what I do if you want to keep from getting caught, you know." She led the alien to the bathroom. "Take your clothes off first."

The alien stripped. Underneath its rain slicker it wore a stained T-shirt that said "Fisherman's Wharf" with a picture of the San Francisco skyline, and a pair of unzipped jeans. Under that it was wearing a black brassiere, unfastened and with the cups over its shoulder blades, and a pair of black shiny panty briefs with a red heart on the left buttock. The alien's body was that of a lean, tough-looking girl with a scar running down the inside of one arm.

"Whose body is that?" Amanda asked. "Do you know?"

"She worked at the detention center. In the kitchen."

"You know her name?"

"Flores Concepion."

"The other way around, probably. Concepion Flores. I'll call you Connie, unless you want to give me your real name."

"Connie will do."

"All right, Connie. Pay attention. You turn the water on here, and you adjust the mix of hot and cold until you like it. Then you pull this knob and get underneath the spout here and wet your body, and rub soap over it and wash the soap off. Afterward you dry yourself and put fresh clothes on. You have to clean your clothes from time to time, too, because otherwise they start to smell and it upsets people. Watch me shower, and then you do it."

Amanda washed quickly, while plans hummed in her head. The alien wasn't going to last long out there wearing the body of Concepion Flores. Sooner or later someone was going to notice that one of the kitchen girls was missing, and they'd get an all-points alarm out for her. Amanda wondered whether the alien had figured that out yet. The alien, Amanda thought, needs a different body in a hurry.

But not mine, she told herself. For sure, not mine.

"Your turn," she said, shutting the water off.

The alien, fumbling a little, turned the water back on and got under the spray. Clouds of steam rose and its skin began to look boiled, but it didn't appear troubled. No sense of pain? "Hold it," Amanda said. "Step back." She adjusted the water. "You've got it too hot. You'll damage that body that way. Look, if you can't tell the difference between hot and cold, just take cold showers, okay? It's less dangerous. This is cold, on this side." She left the alien under the shower and went to find some clean clothes. When she came back, the alien was still showering, under icy water. "Enough," Amanda said. "Here. Put these on."

"I had more clothes than this before."

"A T-shirt and jeans are all you need in hot weather like this. With your kind of build you can skip the bra, and anyway I don't think you'll be able to fasten it the right way."

"Do we put the face paint on now?"

"We can skip it while we're home. It's just stupid kid stuff anyway, all that tribal crap. If we go out we'll do it, and we'll give you Walnut Creek colors, I think. Concepcion wore San Jose, but we want to throw people off the track. How about some dope?"

"What?"

"Grass. Marijuana. A drug widely used by local Earthians of our age."

"I don't need no drug."

"I don't either. But I'd *like* some. You ought to learn how, just in case you find yourself in a social situation." Amanda reached for her pack of Filter Golds and pulled out a joint. Expertly she tweaked its lighter tip and took a deep hit. "Here," she said, passing it. "Hold it like I did. Put it to your mouth, breathe in, suck the smoke deep." The alien dragged the joint and began to cough. "Not so deep, maybe," Amanda said. "Take just a little. Hold it. Let it out. There, much better. Now give me back the joint. You've got to keep passing it back and forth. That part's important. You feel anything from it?"

"No."

"It can be subtle. Don't worry about it. Are you hungry?"

"Not yet," the alien said.

"I am. Come into the kitchen." As she assembled a sandwich—peanut butter and avocado on whole wheat, with tomato and onion—she asked, "What sort of things do you eat?"

"Life."

"Life?"

"We never eat dead things. Only things with life."

Amanda fought back a shudder. "I see. *Anything* with life?"

"We prefer animal life. We can absorb plants if necessary."

"Ah. Yes. And when are you going to be hungry again?"

"Maybe tonight," the alien said. "Or tomorrow. The hunger comes very suddenly, when it comes."

"There's not much around here that you could eat live. But I'll work on it."

"The small furry animal?"

"No. My cat is not available for dinner. Get that idea right out of your head. Likewise me. I'm your protector and guide. It wouldn't be sensible of you to eat me. You follow what I'm trying to tell you?"

"I said that I'm not hungry yet."

"Well, you let me know when you start feeling the pangs. I'll find you a meal." Amanda began to construct a second sandwich. The alien prowled the kitchen, examining the appliances. Perhaps making mental records, Amanda thought, of sink and oven design, to copy on its home world. Amanda said, "Why did you people come here in the first place?"

"It was our mission."

"Yes. Sure. But for what purpose? What are you after? You want to take over the world? You want to steal our scientific secrets?" The alien, making no reply, began taking spices out of the spice rack. Delicately it licked its finger, touched it to the oregano, tasted it, tried the cumin. Amanda said, "Or is it that you want to keep us from going into space? That you think we're a dangerous species, so you're going to quarantine us on our own planet? Come on, you can tell me. I'm not a government spy." The alien sampled the tarragon, the basil, the sage. When it reached for the curry powder, its hand suddenly shook so violently that it knocked the open jars of oregano and tarragon over, making a mess. "Hey, are you all right?" Amanda asked.

The alien said, "I think I'm getting hungry. Are these things drugs, too?"

"Spices," Amanda said. "We put them in our foods to make them taste better." The alien was looking very strange, glassy-eyed, flushed, sweaty. "Are you feeling sick?"

"I feel excited. These powders—"

"They're turning you on? Which one?"

"This, I think." It pointed to the oregano. "It was either the first one or the second."

"Yeah," Amanda said. "Oregano. It can really make you fly." She wondered whether the alien might get violent when zonked. Or whether the oregano would stimulate its appetite. She had to watch out for its appetite. There are certain risks, Amanda reflected, in doing what I'm doing. Deftly she cleaned up the spilled oregano and tarragon and put the caps on the spice jars. "You ought to be careful," she said. "Your metabolism isn't used to this stuff. A little can go a long way."

"Give me some more.

"Later," Amanda said. "You don't want to overdo it."

"More!"

"Calm down. I know this planet better than you, and I don't want to see you get in trouble. Trust me: I'll let you have more oregano when it's the right time. Look at the way you're shaking. And you're sweating like crazy." Pocketing the oregano jar, she led the alien back into the living room. "Sit down. Relax."

"More? Please?"

"I appreciate your politeness. But we have important things to talk about, and then I'll give you some. Okay?" Amanda opaqued the window, through which the hot late-afternoon sun was coming.

Six o'clock on Friday, and if everything had gone the right way Charley would have been showing up just about now. Well, she'd found a different diversion. The weekend stretched before her like an open road leading to mysteryland. The alien offered all sorts of possibilities, and she might yet have some fun over the next few days, if she used her head. Amanda turned to the alien and said, "You calmer now? Yes. Good. Okay: first of all, you've got to get yourself another body."

"Why is that?"

"Two reasons. One is that the authorities probably are searching for the girl you absorbed. How you got as far as you did without anybody but me spotting you is hard to understand. Number two, a teenage girl traveling by herself is going to get hassled too much, and you don't know how to handle yourself in a tight situation. You know what I'm saying? You're going to want to hitchhike out to Nevada, Wyoming, Utah, wherever the hell your rendezvous place is, and all along the way people are going to be coming on to you. You don't need any of that. Besides, it's very tricky trying to pass for a girl. You've got to know how to put your face paint on, how to understand challenge codes, and what the way you wear your clothing says, and like that. Boys have a much simpler subculture. You get yourself a male body, a big hunk of a body, and nobody'll bother you much on the way to where you're going. You just keep to yourself, don't make eye contact, don't smile, and everyone will leave you alone."

"Makes sense," said the alien. "All right. The hunger is becoming very bad now. Where do I get a male body?"

"San Francisco. It's full of men. We'll go over there tonight and find a nice brawny one for you. With any luck we might even find one who's not gay, and then we can have a little fun with him first. And then you take his body over—which incidentally solves your food problem for a while, doesn't it?—and we can have some more fun, a whole weekend of fun." Amanda winked. "Okay, Connie?"

"Okay." The alien winked, a clumsy imitation, first one eye, then the other. "You give me more oregano now?"

"Later. And when you wink, just wink *one* eye. Like this. Except I don't think you ought to do a lot of winking at people. It's a very intimate gesture that could get you in trouble. Understand?"

"There's so much to understand."

"You're on a strange planet, kid. Did you expect it to be just like home? Okay, to continue. The next thing I ought to point out is that when you leave here on Sunday you'll have to—"

The telephone rang.

"What's that sound?" the alien asked.

"Communications device. I'll be right back." Amanda went to the hall extension, imagining the worst: her parents, say, calling to announce that they were on their way back from Tahoe tonight, some mixup in the reservations or something. But the voice that greeted her was Charley's. She could hardly believe it, after the casual way he had shafted her this weekend. She could hardly believe what he wanted, either. He had left half a dozen of his best cassettes at her place last week, Golden Age rock, Abbey Road and the Hendrix one and a Joplin and such, and now he was heading off to Monterey for the festival and he wanted to have them for the drive. Did she mind if he stopped off in half an hour to pick them up?

The bastard, she thought. The absolute trashiness of him! First to torpedo her weekend without even an apology, and then to let her know that he and what's-her-name were scooting down to Monterey for some fun, and could he bother her for his cassettes? Didn't he think she had any feelings? She looked at the telephone in her hand as though it was emitting toads and scorpions. It was tempting to hang up on him.

She resisted the temptation. "As it happens," she said, "I'm just on my way out for the weekend myself. But I've got a friend who's here cat-sitting for me. I'll leave the cassettes with her, okay? Her name's Connie."

"Fine," Charley said. "I really appreciate that, Amanda."

"It's nothing," she said.

The alien was back in the kitchen, nosing around the spice rack. But Amanda had the oregano. She said, "I've arranged for delivery of your next body."

"You did?"

"A large healthy adolescent male. Exactly what you're looking for. He's going to be here in a little while. I'm going to go out for a drive, and you take care of him before I get back. How long does it take for you to—engulf—somebody?"

"It's very fast."

"Good." Amanda found Charley's cassettes and stacked them on the living-room table. "He's coming over here to get these six little boxes, which are music-storage devices. When the doorbell rings, you let him in and introduce yourself as Connie and tell him his things are on this table. After that you're on your own. You think you can handle it?"

"Sure," the alien said.

"Tuck in your T-shirt better. When it's tight it makes your boobs stick out, and that'll distract him. Maybe he'll even make a pass at you. What happens to the Connie body after you engulf him?"

"It won't be here. What happens is I merge with him and dissolve all the Connie characteristics and take on the new ones."

"Ah. Very nifty. You're a real nightmare thing, you know? You're a walking horror show. Here, have a little hit of oregano before I go." She put a tiny pinch of spice in the alien's hand. "Just to warm up your engine a little. I'll give you more later, when you've done the job. See you in an hour, okay?"

* * *

SHE LEFT THE HOUSE. MACAVITY was sitting on the porch, scowling, whipping his tail from side to side. Amanda knelt beside him and scratched him behind the ears. The cat made a low rough purring sound, not much like his usual purr.

Amanda said, "You aren't happy, are you, fella? Well, don't worry. I've told the alien to leave you alone, and I guarantee you'll be okay. This is Amanda's fun tonight. You don't mind if Amanda has a little fun, do you?" Macavity made a glum snuffling sound. "Listen, maybe I can get the alien to create a nice little calico cutie for you, okay? Just going into heat and ready to howl. Would you like that, guy? Would you? I'll see what I call do when 1 get back. But I have to clear out of here now, before Charley shows up."

She got into her car and headed for the westbound freeway ramp. Half past six, Friday night, the sun still hanging high above the Bay. Traffic was thick in the eastbound lanes, the late commuters slogging toward home, and it was beginning to build up westbound, too, as people set out for dinner in San Francisco. Amanda drove through the tunnel and turned north into Berkeley to cruise city streets. Ten minutes to seven now. Charley must have arrived. She imagined Connie in her tight T-shirt, all stoned and sweaty on oregano, and Charley giving her the eye, getting ideas, thinking about grabbing a bonus quickie before taking off with his cassettes. And Connie leading him on, Charley making his moves, and then suddenly that electric moment of surprise as the alien struck and Charley found himself turning into dinner. It could be happening right this minute, Amanda thought placidly No more than the bastard deserves, isn't it? She had felt for a long time that Charley was a big mistake in her life, and after what he had pulled yesterday she was sure of it. No more than he deserves. But, she wondered, what if Charley had brought his weekend date along? The thought chilled her. She hadn't considered that possibility at all. It could ruin everything. Connie wasn't able to engulf two at once, was she? And suppose they recognized her as the missing alien and ran out screaming to call the cops?

No, she thought. Not even Charley would be so tacky as to bring his date over to Amanda's house tonight. And Charley never watched the news or read a paper. He wouldn't have a clue as to what Connie really was until it was too late for him to run.

Seven o'clock. Time to head for home.

The sun was sinking behind her as she turned onto the freeway. By quarter past she was approaching her house. Charley's old red Honda was parked outside. Amanda left hers across the street and cautiously let herself in, pausing just inside the front door to listen.

Silence.

"Connie?"

"In here," said Charley's voice.

Amanda entered the living room. Charley was sprawled out comfortably on the couch. There was no sign of Connie.

"Well?" Amanda said. "How did it go?"

"Easiest thing in the world," the alien said. "He was sliding his hands under my T-shirt when I let him have the nullifier jolt."

"Ah. The nullifier jolt."

"And then I completed the engulfment and cleaned up the carpet. God, it feels good not to be hungry again. You can't imagine how tough it was to resist engulfing you, Amanda. For the past hour I kept thinking of food, food, food—"

"Very thoughtful of you to resist."

"I knew you were out to help me. It's logical not to engulf one's allies."

"That goes without saying. So you feel well fed, now? He was good stuff?"

"Robust, healthy, nourishing—yes."

"I'm glad Charley turned out to be good for something. How long before you get hungry again?"

The alien shrugged. "A day or two. Maybe three, on account of he was so big. Give me more oregano, Amanda?"

"Sure," she said. "Sure." She felt a little let down. Not that she was remorseful about Charley, exactly, but it all seemed so casual, so off-handed—there was something anticlimactic about it, in a way. She suspected she should have stayed and watched while it was happening. Too late for that now, though.

She took the oregano from her purse and dangled the jar teasingly. "Here it is, babe. But you've got to earn it first."

"What do you mean?"

"I mean that I was looking forward to a big weekend with Charley, and the weekend is here, and Charley's here too, more or less, and I'm ready for fun. Come show me some fun, big boy."

She slipped Charley's Hendrix cassette into the deck and turned the volume way up.

The alien looked puzzled. Amanda began to peel off her clothes.

"You too," Amanda said. "Come on. You won't have to dig deep into Charley's mind to figure out what to do. You're going to be my Charley for me this weekend, you follow? You and I are going to do all the things that he and I were going to do. Okay? Come on. Come on." She beckoned. The alien shrugged again and slipped out of Charley's clothes, fumbling with the unfamiliarities of his zipper and buttons. Amanda, grinning, drew the alien close against her and down to the living-room floor. She took its hands and put them where she wanted them to be. She whispered instructions. The alien, docile, obedient, did what she wanted.

It felt like Charley. It smelled like Charley. It even moved pretty much the way Charley moved.

But it wasn't Charley, it wasn't Charley at all, and after the first few seconds Amanda knew that she had goofed things up very badly. You couldn't just ring in an imitation like this. Making love with this alien was like making love with a very clever machine, or with her own mirror image. It was empty and meaningless and dumb.

Grimly she went on to the finish. They rolled apart, panting, sweating.

"Well?" the alien said. "Did the earth move for you?"

"Yeah. Yeah. It was wonderful—Charley."

"Oregano?"

"Sure," Amanda said. She handed the spice jar across. "I always keep my promises, babe. Go to it. Have yourself a blast. Just remember that that's strong stuff for guys from your planet, okay? If you pass out, I'm going to leave you right there on the floor."

"Don't worry about me."

"Okay. You have your fun. I'm going to clean up, and then maybe we'll go over to San Francisco for the nightlife. Does that interest you?"

"You bet, Amanda." The alien winked—one eye, then the other—and gulped a huge pinch of oregano. "That sounds terrific."

Amanda gathered up her clothes, went upstairs for a quick shower, and dressed. When she came down the alien was more than half blown away on the oregano, goggle-eyed, loll-headed, propped up against the couch and crooning to itself in a weird atonal way. Fine, Amanda thought. You just get yourself all spiced up, love. She took the portable phone from the kitchen, carried it with her into the bathroom, locked the door, dialed the police emergency number.

She was bored with the alien. The game had worn thin very quickly. And it was crazy, she thought, to spend the whole weekend cooped up with a dangerous extraterrestrial creature when there wasn't going to be any fun in it for her. She knew now that there couldn't be any fun at all. And in a day or two the alien was going to get hungry again.

"I've got your alien," she said. "Sitting in my living room, stoned out of its head on oregano. Yes, I'm absolutely certain. It was disguised as a Chicana girl first, Concepcion Flores, but then it attacked my boyfriend Charley Taylor, and—yes, yes, I'm safe. I'm locked in the john. Just get somebody over here fast—okay, I'll stay on the line—what happened was, I spotted it downtown, it insisted on coming home with me—"

* * *

THE ACTUAL CAPTURE TOOK ONLY a few minutes. But there was no peace for hours after the police tactical squad hauled the alien away, because the media was in on the act right away, first a team from Channel 2 in Oakland, and then some of the network guys, and then the *Chronicle,* and finally a whole army of reporters from as far away as Sacramento, and phone calls from Los Angeles and San Diego and—about three that morning—New York. Amanda told the story again and again until she was sick of it, and just as dawn was breaking she threw the last of them out and barred the door.

She wasn't sleepy at all. She felt wired up, speedy, and depressed all at once. The alien was gone, Charley was gone, and she was all alone. She was going to be famous for the next couple of days, but that wouldn't help. She'd still be alone. For a time she wandered around the house, looking at it the way an alien might, as though she had never seen a stereo cassette before, or a television set, or a rack of spices. The smell of oregano was everywhere. There were little trails of it on the floor.

Amanda switched on the radio and there she was on the six a.m. news. "—the emergency is over, thanks to the courageous Walnut Creek high school girl who trapped and outsmarted the most dangerous life-form in the known universe—"

She shook her head. “You think that’s true?” she asked the cat. “Most dangerous life-form in the universe? I don’t think so, Macavity. I think I know of at least one that’s a lot deadlier. Eh, kid?” She winked. “If they only knew, eh? If they only knew.” She scooped the cat up and hugged it, and it began to purr. Maybe trying to get a little sleep would be a good idea around this time, she told herself. And then she had to figure out what she was going to do about the rest of the weekend.

ONE-WAY JOURNEY

One of the new science fiction magazines that sprang into being in the late 1950s, just in time to help me harness my unexpectedly vast productivity, was *Infinity*, edited by a shrewd, owlish, pipe-smoking guy named Larry T. Shaw, who had been around science fiction for a long time as a reader, an agent, an editor, and even a (very occasional) writer. Shaw didn't have much in the way of an editorial budget to buy stories with, but he loved and understood science fiction, his taste was enlightened and perceptive, and he had close and long-standing friendships with many of the key figures of the New York science fiction world of the 1940s and 1950s; so *Infinity*, for the three or four years it lasted, was a distinguished effort whose contents pages regularly bore the names of such top-level writers as Clifford D. Simak, Robert Sheckley, Isaac Asimov, James Blish, and Damon Knight. (Not to mention that of Harlan Ellison, who made his first sale there in the summer of 1955.)

I was an eager contributor to *Infinity* too, of course; I missed the first issue, but was in virtually every one thereafter. Shaw was willing to look at and often to buy many of the earnest, careful stories that I had written in my college days and had been unable to sell then. The first, in November of 1955, was "Hopper, "which I expanded a decade later into the novel *The Time Hoppers*, and other sales to his magazine followed steadily. "One-Way Journey," which I wrote in October 1956, was the fifth or sixth of them. I tried it first at *Galaxy*, since I believed that editor Horace

Gold was fond of stories verging into psychopathology, but Gold found the story "too damned strong." He returned it with a rejection slip advising me that he wasn't as enthusiastic about psychiatric-case stories as I and a lot of other writers seemed to think, and wished I would turn to something else. "Why in hell compete with more people than you have to?" he asked me. "Leave these themes to them, where story literally battles story, like any other glut product. You've got other ideas. Let's see them." And so I did, with considerable success. But I took "One-Way Journey" over to Larry Shaw, who used it in the November 1957 *Infinity*. In it I handle the theme of interspecies miscegenation for the first time, though I would return to it again and again in the years ahead.

BEHIND THE COMFORTING WALLS OF Terra Import's headquarters on Kollidor, commander Leon Warshow was fumbling nervously with the psych reports on his mirror-bright desk. Commander Warshow was thinking about spaceman Matt Falk, and about himself. Commander Warshow was about to react very predictably.

Personnel Lieutenant Krisch had told him the story about Falk an hour before, and Warshow was doing the one thing expected of him: he was waiting for the boy, having sent for him, after a hasty conference with Cullinan, the *Magyar*'s saturnine psych officer.

An orderly buzzed and said, "Spaceman Falk to see you, sir."

"Have him wait a few minutes," Warshow said, speaking too quickly. "I'll buzz for him."

It was a tactical delay. Wondering why he, an officer, should be so tense before an interview with an enlisted man, Warshow riffled through the sheaf of records on Matt Falk. *Orphaned, 2543 . . . Academy . . . two years commercial service, military contract . . . injury en route to Kollidor . . .*

Appended were comprehensive medical reports on Falk's injury, and Dr. Sigstrom's okay. Also a disciplinary chart, very favorable, and a jaggle-edged psych contour, good.

Warshow depressed the buzzer. "Send in Falk," he said.

The photon beam clicked and the door swung back. Matt Falk entered and faced his commander stonily; Warshow glared back, studying the youngster as if he had never seen him before. Falk was just twenty-five, very tall and very blond, with wide, bunch-muscled shoulders and keen blue eyes. The scar along the left side of his face was almost completely invisible, but not even chemotherapeutic incubation had been able to restore the smooth evenness of the boy's jaw. Falk's face looked oddly lopsided; the unharmed right jaw sloped easily and handsomely up to the condyle, while the left still bore unseen but definitely present echoes of the boy's terrible shipboard accident.

"You want me, commander?"

"We're leaving Kollidor tomorrow, Matt," Warshow said quietly. "Lieutenant Krisch tells me you haven't returned to ship to pack your gear. Why?"

The jaw that had been ruined and rebuilt quivered slightly.

"*You* know, sir. I'm not going back to Earth, sir. I'm staying here . . . with Thetona."

There was a frozen silence. Then, with calculated cruelty, Warshow said, "You're really hipped on that flatface, eh?"

"Maybe so," Falk murmured. "That flatface. That gook. What of it?" His quiet voice was bitterly defiant.

* * *

WARSHOW TENSED. HE WAS TRYING to do the job delicately, without inflicting further psychopersonal damage on young Falk. To leave a psychotic crewman behind on an alien world was impossible—but to extract Falk forcibly from the binding webwork of associations that tied him to Kollidor would leave scars not only on crewman but on captain.

Perspiring, Warshow said, "You're an Earthman, Matt. Don't you—"

"Want to go home? No."

The commander grinned feebly. "You sound mighty permanent about that, son."

"I am," Falk said stiffly. "You know why I want to stay here. I *am* staying here. May I be excused now, sir?"

Warshow drummed on the desktop, hesitating for a moment, then nodded. “Permission granted, Mr. Falk.” There was little point in prolonging what he now saw had been a predeterminedly pointless interview.

He waited a few minutes after Falk had left. Then he switched on the communicator. “Send in Major Cullinan, please.”

The beady-eyed psychman appeared almost instantly. “Well?”

“The boy’s staying,” Warshow said. “Complete and single-minded fixation. Go ahead—break it.”

Cullinan shrugged. “We may have to leave him here, and that’s all there is to it. Have you met the girl?”

“Kollidorian. Alien. Ugly as sin. I’ve seen her picture; he had it over his bunk until he moved out. And we *can’t* leave him here, Major.”

Cullinan raised one bushy eyebrow quizzically. “We can try to bring Falk back, if you insist—but it won’t work. Not without crippling him.”

Warshow whistled idly, avoiding the psychman’s stern gaze. “I insist,” he said finally. “There’s no alternative.”

He snatched at the communicator.

“Lieutenant Krisch, please.” A brief pause, then: “Krisch, Warshow. Tell the men that departure’s been postponed four days. Have Molhaus refigure the orbits. Yes, four days. *Four.*”

Warshow hung up, glanced at the heaped Falk dossier on his desk, and scowled. Psych Officer Cullinan shook his head sadly, rubbing his growing bald spot.

“That’s a drastic step, Leon.”

“I know. But I’m not going to leave Falk behind.” Warshow rose, eyed Cullinan uneasily, and added, “Care to come with me? I’m going down into Kollidor City.”

“What for?”

“I want to talk with the girl,” Warshow said.

* * *

Later, in the crazily twisting network of aimless streets that was the alien city, Warshow began to wish he had ordered Cullinan to come with him. As he made his way through the swarms of the placid, ugly, broad-faced Kollidorians, he regretted very much that he had gone alone.

What would he do, he wondered, when he finally did reach the flat where Falk and his Kollidorian girl were living? Warshow wasn't accustomed to handling himself in ground-borne interpersonal situations of this sort. He didn't know what to say to the girl. He thought he could handle Falk.

The relation of commander to crewman is that of parent to child, the Book said. Warshow grinned self-consciously.

He didn't feel very fatherly just now—more like a Dutch uncle, he thought.

He kept walking. Kollidor City spread out ahead of him like a tangled ball of twine coming unrolled in five directions at once; it seemed to have been laid down almost at random. But Warshow knew the city well. This was his third tour of duty to the Kollidor sector; three times he had brought cargo from Earth, three times waited while his ship was loaded with Kollidorian goods for export.

Overhead, the distant blue-white sun burnt brightly. Kollidor was the thirteenth planet in its system; it swung on a large arc nearly four billion miles from its blazing primary.

Warshow sniffled; it reminded him that he was due for his regular antipollen injection. He was already thoroughly protected, as was his crew, against most forms of alien disease likely to come his way on the trip.

But how do you protect someone like Falk? The commander had no quick answers for that. It wouldn't ordinarily seem necessary to inoculate spacemen against falling in love with bovine alien women, but—

"Good afternoon, Commander Warshow," a dry voice said suddenly.

Warshow glanced around, surprised and annoyed. The man who stood behind him was tall, thin, with hard, knobby cheekbones protruding grotesquely from parchmentlike chalk-white skin. Warshow recognized the genetic pattern, and the man. He was Domnik Kross, a trader from the quondam Terran colony of Rigel IX.

"Hello, Kross," Warshow said sullenly, and halted to let the other catch up.

"What brings you to the city, commander? I thought you were getting ready to pack up and flit away."

"We're—postponing four days," Warshow said.

"Oh? Got any leads worth telling about? Not that I care to—"

"Skip it, Kross." Warshow's voice was weary. "We've finished our trading for the season. You've got a clear field. Now leave me alone, yes?"

He started to walk faster, but the Rigelian, smiling bleakly, kept in step with him.

"You sound disturbed, commander."

Warshow glanced impatiently at the other, wishing he could unburden himself of the Rigelian's company. "I'm on a mission of top security value, Kross. Are you going to insist on accompanying me?"

Thin lips parted slyly in a cold grin. "Not at all, Commander Warshow. I simply thought I'd be civil and walk with you a way, just to swap the news. After all, if you're leaving in four days we're not really rivals any more, and—"

"Exactly," Warshow said.

"What's this about one of your crewmen living with a native?" Kross asked suddenly.

Warshow spun on his heel and glared up tensely. *"Nothing,"* he grated. "You hear that? There's nothing to it!"

Kross chuckled, and Warshow saw that he had decidedly lost a point in the deadly cold rivalry between Terran and Rigelian, between man and son of man. Genetic drift accounted for the Domnik Krosses—a little bit of chromosome looping on a colonized planet, a faint tincture of inbreeding over ten generations, and a new subspecies had appeared: an alien subspecies that bore little love for its progenitors.

They reached a complex fork in the street, and the commander impulsively turned to the left. Gratifyingly, he noticed that Kross was not following him.

"See you next year!" the Rigelian said.

Warshow responded with a noncommittal grunt and kept moving down the dirty street, happy to be rid of Kross so soon. The Rigelians, he thought, were nasty customers. They were forever jealous of the mother world and its people, forever anxious to outrace an Earthman to a profitable deal on a world such as Kollidor.

Because of Kross, Warshow reflected, *I'm going where I'm going now.* Pressure from the Rigelians forced Earthmen to keep up appearances throughout the galaxy. The Earthman's Burden, Terrans termed it unofficially. To leave a deserter behind on Kollidor would endanger Earth's prestige in the eyes of the entire universe—and the shrewd Rigelians would make sure the entire universe knew.

Warshow felt hemmed in. As he approached the flat where Falk said he was living, he felt cascades of perspiration tumbling stickily down his back.

* * *

"Yes, please?"

Warshow now stood at the door, a little appalled by the sight and the smell. A Kollidorian female faced him squarely.

Good God, he thought. *She's sure no beauty.*

"I'm . . . Commander Warshow," he said. "Of the *Magyar.* Matt's ship. May I come in?"

The sphincterlike mouth rippled into what Warshow supposed was a gracious smile. "Of course. I have hoped you would come. Matt has spoken so much of you."

She backed away from the door, and Warshow stepped inside. The pungent rankness of concentrated Kollidorian odor assaulted his nostrils. It was an unpainted two-room flat; beyond the room they were in, Warshow saw another, slightly larger and sloppier, with kitchen facilities. Unwashed dishes lay heaped in the sink. To his surprise, he noticed an unmade bed in the far room . . . and another in the front one. *Single* beds. He frowned and turned to the girl.

She was nearly as tall as he was, and much broader. Her brown skin was drab and thick, looking more like hide than skin; her face was wide and plain, with two flat, unsparkling eyes, a grotesque bubble of a nose, and a many-lipped compound mouth. The girl wore a shapeless black frock that hung to her thick ankles. For all Warshow knew, she might be the pinnacle of Kollidorian beauty—but her charms scarcely seemed likely to arouse much desire in a normal Earthman.

"You're Thetona, is that right?"

"Yes, Commander Warshow." Voice dull and toneless, he noted.

"May I sit down?" he asked.

He was fencing tentatively, hemming around the situation without cutting towards it. He made a great business of taking a seat and crossing his legs fastidiously; the girl stared, cowlike, but remained standing.

An awkward silence followed; then the girl said, "You want Matt to go home with you, don't you?"

Warshow reddened and tightened his jaws angrily. "Yes. Our ship's leaving in four days. I came to get him."

"He isn't here," she said.

"I know. He's back at the base. He'll be home soon."

"You haven't done anything to him?" she asked, suddenly apprehensive.

He shook his head. "He's all right." After a moment Warshow glanced sharply at her and said, "He loves you, doesn't he?"

"Yes." But the answer seemed hesitant.

"And you love him?"

"Oh, yes," Thetona said warmly. "Certainly."

"I see." Warshow wet his lips. This was going to be difficult. "Suppose you tell me how you came to fall in love? I'm curious."

She smiled—at least, he assumed it was a smile. "I met him about two days after you Earthmen came for your visit. I was walking in the streets, and I saw him. He was sitting on the edge of the street, crying."

"What?"

Her flat eyes seemed to go misty. "Sitting there sobbing to himself. It was the first time I ever saw an Earthman like that—crying, I mean. I felt terribly sorry for him. I went over to talk to him. He was like a little lost boy."

Warshow looked up, astonished, and stared at the alien girl's placid face with total disbelief. In ten years of dealing with the Kollidorians, he had never gone too close to them; he had left personal contact mainly to others. But—

Dammit, the girl's almost human! Almost—

"Was he sick?" Warshow asked, his voice hoarse. "Why was he crying?"

"He was lonely," Thetona said serenely. "He was afraid. He was afraid of me, of you, of everyone. So I talked to him, there by the edge of the street, for many minutes. And then he asked to come home with me. I lived by myself, here. He came with me. And—he has been here since three days after that."

"And he plans to stay here permanently?" Warshow asked.

The wide head waggled affirmatively. "We are very fond of each other. He is lonely; he needs someone to—"

"That'll be enough," Falk's voice said suddenly.

Warshow whirled. Falk was standing in the doorway, his face bleak and grim. The scar on his face seemed to be inflamed, though Warshow was sure that was impossible.

"What are you doing here?" Falk asked.

"I came to visit Thetona," Warshow said mildly. "I didn't expect to have you return so soon."

"I know you didn't. I walked out when Cullinan started poking around me. Suppose you get out."

"You're talking to a superior officer," Warshow reminded him. "If I—"

"I resigned ten minutes ago," Falk snapped. "You're no superior of mine! Get out!"

Warshow stiffened. He looked appealingly at the alien girl, who put her thick six-fingered hand on Falk's shoulder and stroked his arm. Falk wriggled away.

"Don't," he said. "Well—are you leaving? Thetona and I want to be alone."

"Please go, Commander Warshow," the girl said softly. "Don't get him excited."

"Excited? Who's excited?" Falk roared. "I—"

Warshow sat impassively, evaluating and analyzing, ignoring for the moment what was happening.

Falk would have to be brought back to the ship for treatment. There was no alternative, Warshow saw. This strange relationship with the Kollidorian would have to be broken.

He stood up and raised one hand for silence. "Mr. Falk, let me speak."

"Go ahead. Speak quick, because I'm going to pitch you out of here in two minutes."

"I won't need two minutes," Warshow said. "I simply want to inform you that you're under arrest and that you're hereby directed to report back to the base at once, in my custody. If you refuse to come it will be necessary—"

The sentence went unfinished. Falk's eyes flared angrily, and he crossed the little room in three quick bounds. Towering over the much smaller Warshow, he grabbed the commander by the shoulders and shook him violently. "Get out!" he shrieked.

Warshow smiled apologetically, took one step backward, and slid his stunner from its place in his tunic. He gave Falk a quick, heavy jolt, and as the big man sagged towards the floor, Warshow grabbed him and eased him into a chair.

Thetona was crying. Great gobbets of amber liquid oozed from her eyes and trickled heartbreakingly down her coarse cheeks.

"Sorry," Warshow said. "It had to be done."

* * *

IT HAD TO BE DONE.

It had to be done.

It *had* to be done.

Warshow paced the cabin, his weak eyes darting nervously from the bright row of rivets across the ceiling to the quiet gray walls to the sleeping form of Matt Falk, and finally to the waiting, glowering visage of Psych Officer Cullinan.

"Do you want to wake him?" Cullinan asked.

"No. Not yet." Warshow kept prowling restlessly, trying to square his actions within himself. A few more minutes passed. Finally Cullinan stepped out from behind the cot on which Falk lay, and took Warshow's arm.

"Leon, tell me what's eating you."

"Don't shrink *my* skull," Warshow burst out. Then, sorry, he shook his head. "I didn't mean that. You know I didn't."

"It's two hours since you brought him aboard the ship," Cullinan said. "Don't you think we ought to do something?"

"What can we do?" Warshow demanded. "Throw him back to that alien girl? Kill him? Maybe that's the best solution—let's stuff him in the converters and blast off."

Falk stirred. "Ray him again," Warshow said hollowly. "The stunning's wearing off."

Cullinan used his stunner, and Falk subsided. "We can't keep him asleep forever," the psychman said.

"No—we can't." Warshow knew time was growing short; in three days the revised departure date would arrive, and he didn't dare risk another postponement.

But if they left Falk behind, and if word got around that a crazy Earthman was loose on Kollidor, or that Earthmen went crazy at all—

And there was no answer to that.

"Therapy," Cullinan said quietly.

"There's no time for an analysis," Warshow pointed out immediately. *"Three days*—that's all."

"I didn't mean a full-scale job. But if we nail him with an amytal-derivative inhibitor drug, filter out his hostility to talking to us, and run him back along his memories, we might hit something that'll help us."

Warshow shuddered. "Mind dredging, eh?"

"Call it that," the psychman said. "But let's dredge whatever it is that's tipped his rocker, or it'll wreck us all. You, me—and that girl."

"You think we can find it?"

"We can try. No Earthman in his right mind would form a sexual relationship of this kind—or *any* sort of emotional bond with an alien creature. If we hit the thing that catapulted him into it, maybe we can break this obviously neurotic fixation and make him go willingly. Unless you're willing to leave him behind. I absolutely forbid dragging him away as he is."

"Of course not," Warshow agreed. He mopped away sweat and glanced over at Falk, who still dreamed away under the effects of the stunbeam. "It's worth a try. If you think you can break it, go ahead. I deliver him into thy hands."

The psychman smiled with surprising warmth. "It's the only way. Let's dig up what happened to him and show it to him. That should crack the shell."

"I hope so," Warshow said. "It's in your hands. Wake him up and get him talking. You know what to do."

* * *

A MURKY CLOUD OF DRUG-LADEN air hung in the cabin as Cullinan concluded his preliminaries. Falk stirred and began to grope towards consciousness. Cullinan handed Warshow an ultrasonic injector filled with a clear, glittering liquid.

Just as Falk seemed to be ready to open his eyes, Cullinan leaned over him and began to talk, quietly, soothingly. Falk's troubled frown vanished, and he subsided.

"Give him the drug," Cullinan whispered. Warshow touched the injector hesitantly to Falk's tanned forearm. The ultrasonic hummed briefly, blurred into the skin. Warshow administered three cc. and retracted.

Falk moaned gently.

"It'll take a few minutes," Cullinan said.

The wall clock circled slowly. After a while, Falk's sleep-heavy eyelids fluttered. He opened his eyes and glanced up without apparent recognition of his surroundings.

"Hello, Matt. We're here to talk to you," Cullinan said. "Or rather, we want you to talk to us."

"Yes," Falk said.

"Let's begin with your mother, shall we? Tell us what you remember about your mother. Go back, now."

"My—mother?" The question seemed to puzzle Falk, and he remained silent for nearly a minute. Then he moistened his lips. "What do you want to know about her?"

"Tell us everything," Cullinan urged.

There was silence. Warshow found himself holding his breath.

Finally, Falk began to speak.

* * *

WARM. CUDDLY. HOLD ME. MAMAMA.

I'm all alone. It's night, and I'm crying. There are pins in my leg where I slept on it, and the night air smells cold. I'm three years old, and I'm all alone.

Hold me, mama?

I hear mama coming up the stairs. We have an old house with stairs, near the spaceport where the big ships go *woosh!* There's the soft smell of mama holding me now. Mama's big and pink and soft. Daddy is pink too but he doesn't smell warm. Uncle is the same way.

Ah, ah, baby, she's saying. She's in the room now, and holding me tight. It's good. I'm getting very drowsy. In a minute or two I'll be asleep. I like my mama very much.

* * *

("IS THAT YOUR EARLIEST RECOLLECTION of your mother?" Cullinan asked.)

("No. I guess there's an earlier one.")

* * *

DARK HERE. DARK AND VERY warm, and wet, and nice. I'm not moving. I'm all alone here, and I don't know where I am. It's like floating in an ocean. A big ocean. The whole world's an ocean.

It's nice here, real nice. I'm not crying.

Now there's blue needles in the black around me. Colors . . . all kinds. Red and green and lemon-yellow, and I'm *moving!* There's pain and pushing, and—God!—it's getting cold. I'm choking! I'm hanging on, but I'm going to drown in the air out there! I'm—

* * *

("THAT'LL BE ENOUGH," CULLINAN SAID hastily. To Warshow he explained, "Birth trauma. Nasty. No need to put him through it all over again." Warshow shivered a little and blotted his forehead.)

("Should I go on?" Falk asked.)

("Yes. Go on.")

* * *

I'M FOUR, AND IT'S RAINING *plunk-a plunk* outside. It looks like the whole world's turned grey. Mama and daddy are away, and I'm alone again. Uncle is downstairs. I don't know uncle really, but he seems to be here all the time. Mama and daddy are away a lot. Being alone is like a cold rainstorm. It rains a lot here.

I'm in my bed, thinking about mama. I want mama. Mama took the jet plane somewhere. When I'm big, I want to take jet planes somewhere too—someplace warm and bright where it doesn't rain.

Downstairs the phone rings, jingle-jingle. Inside my head I can see the screen starting to get bright and full of colors, and I try to picture mama's face in the middle of the screen. But I can't. I hear uncle's voice talking, low and mumbly. I decide I don't like uncle, and I start to cry.

Uncle's here, and he's telling me I'm too big to cry. That I shouldn't cry any more. I tell him I want mama.

Uncle makes a nasty-mouth, and I cry louder.

Hush, he tells me. Quiet, Matt. There, there, Matt boy.

He straightens my blankets, but I scrunch my legs up under me and mess them up again because I know it'll annoy him. I like to annoy him because he isn't mama or daddy. But this time he doesn't seem to get annoyed. He just tidies them up again, and he pats my forehead. There's sweat on his hands, and he gets it on me.

I want mama, I tell him.

He looks down at me for a long time. Then he tells me, mama's not coming back.

Not *ever,* I ask?

No, he says. Not ever.

I don't believe him, but I don't start crying, because I don't want him to know he can scare me. How about daddy, I say. Get him for me.

Daddy's not going to come back either, he tells me.

I don't believe you, I say. I don't like you, uncle. I hate you.

He shakes his head and coughs. You'd better learn to like me, he says. You don't have anybody else any more.

I don't understand him, but I don't like what he's saying. I kick the blankets off the bed, and he picks them up. I kick them off again, and he hits me.

Then he bends over quick and kisses me, but he doesn't smell right and I start to cry. Rain comes. I want mama, I yell, but mama never comes. Never at all.

* * *

(Falk fell silent for a moment and closed his eyes. "Was she dead?" Cullinan prodded.)

("She was dead," Falk said. "She and dad were killed in a fluke jetliner accident, coming back from a holiday in Bangkok. I was four, then. My uncle raised me. We didn't get along, much, and when I was fourteen he put me in the Academy. I stayed there four years, took two years of graduate technique, then joined Terran Imports. Two-year hitch on Denufar, then transferred to Commander Warshow's ship *Magyar* where—where—")

(He stopped abruptly. Cullinan glanced at Warshow and said, "He's warmed up now, and we're ready to strike paydirt, to mangle a metaphor." To Falk, he said, "Tell us how you met Thetona.")

* * *

I'm alone in Kollidor and wandering around alone. It's a big sprawling place with funny-looking conical houses and crazy streets, but deep down underneath I can see it's just like Earth. The people are people. They're pretty bizarre, but they've got one head and two arms and two legs, which makes them more like people than some of the aliens I've seen.

Warshow gave us an afternoon's liberty. I don't know why I've left the ship, but I'm here in the city alone. Alone. Dammit, *alone!*

The streets are paved, but the sidewalks aren't. Suddenly I'm very tired and I feel dizzy. I sit down at the edge of the sidewalk and put my head in my hands. The aliens just walk around me, like people in any big city would.

Mama, I think.

Then I think, *Where did that come from?*

And suddenly a great empty loneliness comes welling up from inside of me and spills out all over me, and I start to cry. I haven't cried—since—not in a long time. But now I cry, hoarse ratchety gasps and tears rolling down my face and dribbling into the corners of my mouth. Tears taste salty, I think. A little like raindrops.

My side starts to hurt where I had the accident aboard ship. It begins up near my ear and races like a blue flame down my body to my thigh, and it hurts like a devil. The doctors told me I wouldn't hurt any more. They lied.

I feel my aloneness like a sealed spacesuit around me, cutting me off from everyone. *Mama,* I think again. Part of me is saying, *act like a grownup,* but that part of me is getting quieter and quieter. I keep crying, and I want desperately to have my mother again. I realize now I never knew my mother at all, except for a few years long ago.

Then there's a musky, slightly sickening smell, and I know one of the aliens is near me. They're going to grab me by the scruff and haul me away like any weepy-eyed drunk in the public streets. Warshow will give me hell.

You're crying, Earthman, a warm voice says.

The Kollidorian language is kind of warm and liquid and easy to learn, but this sounds especially warm. I turn around, and there's this big native dame.

Yeah, I'm crying, I say, and look away. Her big hands clamp down on me and hang on, and I shiver a little. It feels funny to be handled by an alien woman.

She sits down next to me. You look very sad, she says.

I am, I tell her.

Why are you sad?

You'd never understand, I say. I turn my head away and feel tears start creeping out of my eyes, and she grabs me impulsively. I nearly retch from the smell of her, but in a minute or two I see it's sort of sweet and nice in a strange way.

She's wearing an outfit like a potato sack, and it smells pretty high. But she pulls my head against her big warm breasts and leaves it there.

What's your name, unhappy Earthman?

Falk, I say. Matthew Falk.

I'm Thetona, she says. I live alone. Are you lonely?

I don't know, I say. I really don't know.

But how can you not know if you're lonely? she asks.

She pulls my head up out of her bosom and our eyes come together. Real romantic. She's got eyes like tarnished half dollars. We look at each other, and she reaches out and pushes the tears out of my eyes.

She smiles. I think it's a smile. She has about thirty notches arranged in a circle under her nose, and that's a mouth. All the notches pucker. Behind them I see bright needly teeth.

I look up from her mouth to her eyes again, and this time they don't look tarnished so much. They're bright like the teeth, and deep and warm.

Warm. Her odor is warm. Everything about her is warm.

I start to cry again—compulsively, without knowing why, without knowing what the hell is happening to me. She seems to flicker, and I think I see a Terran woman sitting there cradling me. I blink. Nothing there but an ugly alien.

Only she's not ugly any more. She's warm and lovely, in a strange sort of way, and the part of me that disagrees is very tiny and tinny-sounding. I hear it yelling, *No,* and then it stops and winks out.

Something strange is exploding inside me. I let it explode. It bursts like a flower—a rose, or a violet, and that's what I smell instead of *her.*

I put my arms around her.

Do you want to come to my house, she asks.

Yes, yes, I say. Yes!

* * *

ABRUPTLY, FALK STOPPED ON THE ringing affirmative, and his glazed eyes closed. Cullinan fired the stunner once, and the boy's taut body slumped.

"Well?" Warshow asked. His voice was dry and harsh. "I feel unclean after hearing that."

"You should," the psychman said. "It's one of the slimiest things I've uncovered yet. And you don't understand it, do you?"

The commander shook his head slowly. "No. Why'd he do it? He's in love with her—but *why?*"

Cullinan chuckled. "You'll see. But I want a couple of other people here when I yank it out. I want the girl, first of all—and I want Sigstrom."

"The doctor? What the hell for?"

"Because—if I'm right—he'll be very interested in hearing what comes out." Cullinan grinned enigmatically. "Let's give Falk a rest, eh? After all that talking, he needs it."

"So do I," Warshow said.

* * *

(FOUR PEOPLE WATCHED SILENTLY AS Falk slipped into the drug-induced trance a second time. Warshow studied the face of the alien girl Thetona for some sign of the warmth Falk had spoken of. And yes, Warshow saw—it was there. Behind her sat Sigstrom, the *Magyar*'s head medic. To his right, Cullinan. And lying on the cot in the far corner of the cabin, eyes open but unseeing, was Matt Falk.)

("Matt, can you hear me?" Cullinan asked. "I want you to back up a little . . . you're aboard ship now. The time is approximately one month ago. You're working in the converter section, you and Dave Murff, handling hot stuff. Got that?")

("Yes," Falk said. "I know what you mean.")

* * *

I'M IN CONVERTER SECTION AA, getting thorium out of hock to feed to the reactors; we've gotta keep the ship moving. Dave Murff's with me.

We make a good team on the waldoes.

We're running them now, picking up chunks of hot stuff and stowing them in the reactor bank. It's not easy to manipulate the remote-control mechanihands, but I'm not scared. This is my job, and I know how to do it.

I'm thinking about that bastard Warshow, though. Nothing particular against him, but he annoys me. Funny way he has of tensing up every time he has to order someone to do anything. Reminds me of my uncle. Yeah, my uncle. That's who I was trying to compare him with.

Don't much like Warshow. If he came in here now, maybe I'd tap him with the waldo—not much, just enough to sizzle his hide a little. Just for the hell of it: I always wanted to belt my uncle, just for the hell of it.

Hey, Murff yells. Get number two waldo back in alignment.

Don't worry, I say. This isn't the first time I've handled these babies, lunkhead.

I'm shielded pretty well. But the air smells funny, as if the thorium's been ionizing it, and I wonder maybe something's wrong.

I swing number two waldo over and dump the thorium in the reactor. The green light pops on and tells me it's a square-on hit; the hot stuff is tumbling down into the reactor now and pushing out the neutrons like crazy.

Then Murff gives the signal and I dip into the storage and yank out some more hot stuff with number one waldo.

Hey, he yells again, and then number two waldo, the empty one, runs away from me.

The big arm is swinging in the air, and I see the little fingers of delicate jointed metal bones that so few seconds ago were hanging onto a chunk of red-hot Th-233. They seem to be clutching out for me.

I yell. God, I yell. Murff yells too as I lose control altogether, and he tries to get behind the control panel and grab the waldo handle. But I'm in the way, and I'm frozen so he can't do it. He ducks back and flattens himself on the floor as the big mechanical arm crashes through the shielding.

I can't move.

I stay there. The little fingers nick me on the left side of my jaw, and I scream. I'm on fire. The metal hand rakes down the side of my body, hardly touching me, and it's like a razor slicing through my flesh.

It's too painful even to feel. My nerves are canceling out. They won't deliver the messages to my brain.

And now the pain sweeps down on me. *Help! I'm burning! Help!*

* * *

("Stop there," Cullinan said sharply, and Falk's terrible screaming stopped. "Edit out the pain and keep going. What happens when you wake up?")

* * *

Voices. I hear them above me as I start to come out of the shroud of pain.

Radiation burns, a deep crackly voice is saying. It's Doc Sigstrom. The doc says, he's terribly burnt, Leon. I don't think he'll live.

Dammit, says another voice. That's Commander Warshow. He's got to live, Warshow says. I've never lost a man yet. Twenty years without losing anybody.

He took quite a roasting from that remote-control arm, a third voice says. It's Psych Officer Cullinan, I think. He lost control, Cullinan goes on. Very strange.

Yeah, I think. Very strange. I blanked out just a second, and that waldo seemed to come alive.

I feel the pain ripping up and down me. Half my head feels like it's missing, and my arm's being toasted. Where's the brimstone, I wonder.

Then Doc Sigstrom says, We'll try a nutrient bath.

What's that? Warshow asks.

New technique, the doc says. Chemotherapeutic incubation. Immersion in hormone solutions. They're using it on Earth in severe cases of type one radiation burns. I don't think it's ever been tried in space, but it ought to be. He'll be in free fall; gravity won't confuse things.

If it'll save him, Warshow says, I'm for it.

Then things fade. Time goes on—an eternity in hell, with the blazing pain racing up and back down my side. I hear people talking every now and then; feel myself being shifted from one place to another. Tubes are stuck in me to feed me. I wonder what I look like with half my body frizzled.

Suddenly, cool warmth. Yeah, it sounds funny. But it is warm and nourishing, and yet cool too, bathing me and taking the sting out of my body.

I don't try to open my eyes, but I know I'm surrounded by darkness. I'm totally immobile, in the midst of darkness, and yet I know that outside me the ship is racing on towards Kollidor, enclosing me, holding me.

I'm within the ship, rocking gently and securely. I'm within something within the ship. Wheels within wheels; doors inside doors. Chinese puzzle-box with me inside.

Soft fluid comes licking over me, nudging itself in where the tissue is torn and blasted and the flesh bubbled from heat. Caressing each individual cell, bathing my body organ by organ, I'm being repaired.

I float on an ocean and in an ocean. My body is healing rapidly. The pain ceases.

I'm not conscious of the passage of time at all. Minutes blend into minutes without joint; time flows unbreakingly, and I'm being lulled into a soft, unending existence. Happiness, I think. Security. Peace.

I like it here.

Around me, a globe of fluid. Around that, a striated webwork of metal. Around that, a spheroid spaceship, and around that a universe. Around that? I don't know, and I don't care. I'm safe here, where there's no pain, no fear.

Blackness. Total and utter blackness. Security equals blackness and softness and quiet. But then—

What are they doing?

What's happening?

Blue darts of light against the blackness, and now a swirl of colors. Green, red, yellow. Light bursts in and dazzles me. Smells, feels, noises.

The cradle is rocking. I'm moving.

No. They're pulling me. Out!

It's getting cold, and I can't breathe. I'm choking! I try to hang on, but they won't let go! They keep pulling me out, out, out into the world of fire and pain!

I struggle. I won't go. But it doesn't do any good. I'm out, finally.

I look around. Two blurry figures above me. I wipe my eyes and things come clear. Warshow and Sigstrom, that's who they are.

Sigstrom smiles and says, booming, "Well, he's healed wonderfully!"

A miracle, Warshow says. "A miracle."

I wobble. I want to fall, but I'm lying down already. They keep talking, and I start to cry in rage.

But there's no way back. It's over. All, all over. And I'm terribly alone.

* * *

FALK'S VOICE DIED AWAY SUDDENLY. Warshow fought an impulse to get violently sick. His face felt cold and clammy, and he turned to look at the pale, nervous faces of Sigstrom and Cullinan. Behind them sat Thetona, expressionless.

Cullinan broke the long silence. "Leon, you heard the earlier session. Did you recognize what he was just telling us?"

"The birth trauma," Warshow said tonelessly.

"Obviously," Sigstrom said. The medic ran unshaking fingers through his heavy shock of white hair. "The chemotherapy . . . it was a womb for him. We put him back in the womb."

"And then we pulled him out," said Warshow. "We delivered him. And he went looking for a mother."

Cullinan nodded at Thetona. "He found one too."

Warshow licked his lips. "Well, now we have the answer. What do we do about it?"

"We play the whole thing to him on tapes. His conscious intellectual mind sees his relationship with Thetona for what it is—the neurotic grasping of a grown man forced into an artificial womb and searching for a mother. Once we've gotten that out of his basement and into the attic, so to speak, I think he'll be all right."

"But the ship was his mother," Warshow said. "That was where the incubation tank—the *womb*—was."

"The ship cast him out. You were an uncle-image, not a mother-substitute. He said so himself. He went looking elsewhere, and found Thetona. Let's give him the tapes."

* * *

MUCH LATER, MATT FALK FACED the four of them in the cabin. He had heard his own voice rambling back over his lifetime. He *knew,* now.

There was a long silence when the last tape had played out, when Falk's voice had said, *"All, all over. And I'm terribly alone."*

The words seemed to hang in the room. Finally Falk said, "Thanks," in a cold, hard, tight, dead voice.

"Thanks?" Warshow repeated dully.

"Yes. Thanks for opening my eyes, for thoughtfully giving me a peek at what was behind my lid. Sure—*thanks.*" The boy's face was sullen, bitter.

"You understand why it was necessary, of course," Cullinan said. "Why we—"

"Yeah, I know why," Falk said. "And now I can go back to Earth with you, and your consciences are cleared." He glanced at Thetona, who was watching him with perturbed curiosity evident on her broad face. Falk shuddered lightly as his eyes met the alien girl's. Warshow caught the reaction and nodded. The therapy had been a success.

"I was happy," Falk said quietly. "Until you decided you *had* to take me back to Earth with you. So you ran me through a wringer and combed all the psychoses out of me, and—and—"

Thetona took two heavy steps towards him and put her arms on his shoulders. "No," he murmured, and wriggled away. "Can't you see it's over?"

"Matt—" Warshow said.

"Don't Matt me, cap'n! I'm out of my womb now, and back in your crew." He turned sad eyes on Warshow. "Thetona and I had something good and warm and beautiful, and you busted it up. It can't get put together again, either. Okay. I'm ready to go back to Earth, now."

He stalked out of the room without another word. Grey-faced, Warshow stared at Cullinan and at Thetona, and lowered his eyes.

He had fought to keep Matt Falk, and he had won—or had he? In fact, yes. But in spirit? Falk would never forgive him for this.

Warshow shrugged, remembering the book that said, *"The relation of commander to crewman is that of parent to child."*

Warshow would not allow Falk's sullen eyes to upset him any longer; it was only to be expected that the boy would be bitter.

No child ever really forgives the parent who casts him from the womb.

"Come on, Thetona," he said to the big, enigmatically frowning alien girl. "Come with me. I'll take you back down to the city."

GORGON PLANET

All through my adolescence there was very little I wanted as badly as to see a story bearing my name appear in one of the science fiction magazines. I was a passionate s-f fan, and in those days the magazines were the center of the s-f world; any member of the small cult-group that called itself "fandom" who sold a story to one of the professional magazines attained an increment of instant fame and prestige that can barely be comprehended today. (Among the writers who emerged from fandom in the 1940s via those gaudy-looking magazines were such people as Ray Bradbury, Isaac Asimov, Frederik Pohl, and Arthur C. Clarke.) If I could sell a story, I told myself, it would in a single stroke free me from every aspect of teenage insecurity and admit me to the adult world of achievement and community respect.

In some ways, that's very much what happened, since my debut as a professional writer coincided with my transition from awkward, uncertain adolescent to poised and confident adult. But it didn't happen overnight and there were a few ironic complications along the way. For one thing, my first sale (barring a couple of semiprofessional things) was a novel that was to be published in hard covers, which to me meant that it would be far less visible and impressive to my friends in fandom than, say, a short story printed in the awesomely prestigious magazine *Astounding Science Fiction*, which everybody read. So that book sale, significant though it was to my career, failed to transform my self-image in the way I had hoped. And then I *did* sell a story to one of the professional science fiction magazines—in January 1954, while I was still finishing a very ambitious novelette that I called "Road to Nightfall." The story had the title of "Gorgon Planet," and I had written it in September 1953 for the first s-f editor I had come to know personally: Harry Harrison, who had just taken over the editorship of three magazines. That summer Harrison had asked me to write a short article explaining s-f fandom for one of his magazines—my first real professional sale, though because it was nonfiction it didn't really count in my eyes. A few weeks later I brought him "Gorgon Planet," which he said wasn't quite good enough for his top-of-the-line magazine, *Science Fiction Adventures,* but which he was willing to publish in one of its lesser companions, *Rocket Stories* or *Space Science Fiction.* So I had sold a story at last! (But I hadn't exactly *sold* it yet, merely had had it accepted, because *Rocket* and *Space* paid only on publication).

Since Harry would buy only North American rights, I was free to submit my story overseas—and immediately did, to *Nebula Science Fiction*, a pleasant, somewhat old-fashioned magazine that had begun operations in Scotland the year before. Reasoning correctly that *Nebula's* youthful editor, Peter Hamilton, might be having difficulties getting stories from the better-known writers, I had begun sending him mine as soon as I learned of his magazine's existence. He replied with rejection letters containing friendly encouragement: "If you like to go on trying," he told me in July of 1953, "I'll be only too happy to continue to advise you. If you become a big name through *Nebula* it will be as big a thing for me (nearly) as it will be for you." And on January 11, 1954, he wrote to me to say, "You will be pleased to hear that I have accepted 'Gorgon Planet,' and it will appear in the 7th issue of *Nebula* (due out early February)." Through Hamilton's American agent I duly received my payment—$12.60—and, a few weeks later, a copy of the published story itself.

So, this time, I really *had* sold a story to one of the magazines! But where was my instant fame, where was my sudden prestige? Nowhere, as a matter of fact, because *Nebula* was virtually unknown in the United States and gained me no awe whatever from my friends in fandom. I would have to wait until the story appeared in *Rocket Stories* or *Space Science Fiction* for that.

But *Rocket* and *Space* went out of business almost at once, neither publishing my story nor paying me for it. To Peter Hamilton of *Nebula* went the glory, such as it was, of bringing Robert Silverberg's first professionally-published science fiction story into print. And here it is—mainly for the historical record, I suppose. (I finally did sell it to an American magazine, by the way—in 1958, to a short-lived item called *Super-Science Fiction*. The editor retitled it "The Fight with the Gorgon," which didn't strike me as an improvement, but I kept my mouth shut and cashed my check.) The story's something less than a masterpiece, I suppose; but, glancing through it now, I can see that even at the age of eighteen I had mastered the fundamentals of storytelling as it was practiced in the science fiction magazines of the day. Despondent as I often was in those days as story after story came back rejected, I was obviously on the brink of a writing career. All that was missing was an editor willing to say yes, and finally I had found one. Peter Hamilton published seven more stories of mine in the remaining five years of his magazine's life, and he always seemed as delighted to have discovered me as I had been to be discovered by him.

Our troubles started the moment the stiffened corpse of Flaherty was found, standing frozen in a field half a kilometer from the ship. We had all hated the big Irishman's guts, but finding his body, completely unharmed, stock-still and standing alone, was quite a jolt. There was no apparent sign of death—in fact, at first we thought he was sleeping on his feet. Horses do it, and Flaherty wasn't far removed from a horse.

But he wasn't. He was dead, dead as hell. And when the entire human population of a planet consists of eight, and one of those eight dies suddenly of unknown causes, the framework of your existence tends to sag a bit. We were scared.

"We" being the first Earth Exploratory Party (Type A-7) to Bellatrix IV in Orion. Eight men, altogether, bringing back a full report on the whole planet. Eight, of whom one, ox-like Flaherty, was stiff as a board before us.

"What did it, Joel?" asked Tavy Ramirez, our geologist.

"How the blazes do I know?" I snapped. I regretted losing my temper instantly. "Sorry, Tavy. But I know as much as you do about the whole thing. Flaherty is dead, and there's something out there that killed him."

"But there's *nothing* out there," protested Kai Framer, the biologist. "For three days we've hunted up and down and haven't found a sign of animal life."

Jonathan Morro, biologist, unwound his six-feet-eight and stretched. "Maybe an intelligent plant did him in, eh, Kaftan?"

I shook my head. "Doubt it, Jon. No sign of violence, no plants in the vicinity. We found him standing in the middle of a field, on his two big feet, frozen dead. Doesn't figure."

Over in the corner of the cabin, Steeger—medical officer—was puttering around the corpse. Steeger was an older man than most of us, one who had literally rotted in the service. He had contracted frogpox on Fomalhaut 11, and now wore two chrome-jacketed titanium legs. I looked over at him.

"Any report, Doc?"

Steeger turned watery eyes towards me. "No sign of any physical harm, Joel. But his muscles are all tensed, as if—as if—well, I can't phrase it. He seems to have been frozen in his tracks by some strange force. I'm stuck, Joel."

Phil Janus, our chronicler, looked up from the chess game he'd been playing with pilot Curt Holden and laughed. "Maybe he had an overdose of his own joy-juice and it hardened all his arteries."

That was a reference to the crude still Flaherty had rigged the day we landed on Bellatrix IV. His duties as navigator had kept the big fellow pretty busy all trip, but first day down-planet and he spent his first idle hour building the still. He didn't say a word about it to anyone, but had shown up at mess that night pretty high. He never told us where the still was, though we searched all over. The second day Janus had located a liter flask of whisky, home-brewed, and his sampling had cost him a black eye.

"No," said Framer. "Let's be serious a moment. One of our group is dead, and we don't know what killed him. There's something out there that Flaherty crossed. I move we organize a searching party to find out what."

"Seconded," murmured Morro.

I looked at the corpse for a moment, then at the six men around me. Framer was my solid man, I knew, the leader of the group. Morro was strong, too, but usually too bored to bother with the welfare of the group. Young Holden, the pilot, was a follower; he didn't have any thoughts of his own, or at least he didn't express any. Tavy Ramirez I knew: quiet, smiling, unassuming—not very strong a person. Doc Steeger was small, frightened, not at all the sort of man who'd go gallivanting around space as part of an exploratory crew. Janus was like Morro in many ways: he just didn't care. Flaherty, thank the Lord, was dead. The big ox had threatened nasty incidents many times, and had been a constant source of dissension on-ship.

As for me—Joel Kaftan, Lieut. (Spatial)—I was scared. Plenty scared. Visible monsters on a planet are bad enough; invisible ones were hell. I looked out at the port and saw the vast, empty, tree-studded plain that was our chunk of Bellatrix IV, and looked back at the men.

"All in favor of a searching party, say aye."

* * *

Aye it was, and we divided up. There were seven of us, now, and that made things awkward. Steeger was indispensable, as our doctor, and he was of no use outdoors anyway. Holden was theoretically dispensable—in a pinch I could probably have piloted the ship—but I would have hated to try, and so I confined him to quarters too. That left just five men for the search.

It was logical to split into two groups, one of three men and one of two. But I didn't think too clearly for a moment, and announced we'd have *three* groups. I didn't figure that one poor chap would have to go out alone.

I teamed up with Ramirez, and Framer with Morro. That left Janus as a searching party of one.

Janus didn't mind. Phil rarely minded anything. "Looks like I'm lone wolf," he said. "Okay, gentlemen. If you hear a loud silence from my neck of the woods, run like hell."

The airlock was open anyway (Bellatrix IV has an atmosphere roughly that of Earth's, which was a boon) and the five of us left.

I started out with Tavy and we headed towards the site of Flaherty's finish, very much scared. When your life span is 150 or so years, and you've got a hundred of them left, you're not too anxious to die young, even as a hero on an alien planet. Framer and Morro wandered up towards the big ridge behind the spaceship, and Janus headed for the clump of twisted red-leaved trees about two hundred meters away.

Tavy and I moved slowly, casting our eyes in all directions. As usual, there was no sign of any animal life. Bellatrix IV had an abundance of plants (not chlorophyll-based plants, but ones with some sort of iron-compound base), a temperate climate, flowing streams of real H2O water. But no visible animals. Of course, we hadn't covered very much territory yet, maybe two or three square kilometers.

No one dared to make a sound. Then suddenly, in about two seconds flat, we got our first taste of Bellatrician life. Poor Janus came flying out of his copse, and lumbering behind him out of nowhere came a bizarre thing about ten feet high, with non-functional wings, gleaming golden scales, and a headful of writhing, pencil-like tentacles.

We stood transfixed for a moment. I drew my rifle and put a shot into the scales, without any seeming effect. And then Janus turned and stared up at the beast for a fraction of a second as he ran.

The beast stared too, and the frantic pursuit came to an end. They glared at each other for just a moment, and then the monster wheeled and ran off in the other direction. It disappeared over the hill.

But Janus remained where he was, frozen dead.

* * *

WE PLANTED OUR SECOND CORPSE and sat morosely in the cabin. We missed Flaherty just a bit, but not too much. But Janus, though, genial, clever, enormously capable—it was hard to believe he was dead, killed by a gorgon.

For the beast of the forest was unquestionably a gorgon, right out of the old mythology. Doc Steeger gave us the first inkling when he pointed out that death had been caused by a sudden neural blast.

Framer looked up at this. “We didn’t see any physical contact between Phil and the monster, though.”

“No,” broke in Ramirez. “Janus just looked at the thing, and then he froze stiff—”

The thought came to Morro and myself almost instantaneously.

“A gorgon,” I said.

“Gorgon,” he echoed. He stood up—preposterous lanky fellow—and stared outside at the wide plain with its deadly clump of trees at one corner. “A gorgon.”

“Pardon me, sir.” It was Holden. “Just exactly what *is* a gorgon, sir? They said nothing about them in the Academy.”

Framer muttered something under his breath. Kal, I knew, was a man of wide learning, and he had nothing but scorn for modern educational methods, which are highly specialized. Morro spoke.

“A gorgon, Curt, is a mythological beast. It killed by a glance; if you looked at its eyes, you were turned to stone. The thing outside is almost a living version of a gorgon, complete to those tentacles on its head. The original gorgon was supposed to have living snakes instead of hair.”

Holders said nothing, but his eyes widened.

Ramirez scratched his long nose with a thick finger. “Joel, how are we going to fight our friend outside?”

“The same way Perseus did,” I said.

* * *

AND SO OPERATION MEDUSA GOT under way. It took some preliminary discussion. For one thing, Holden, who held most of our technological information behind his freckled forehead, had not the slightest knowledge of the Perseus myth, and we had to bring him up to date.

Morro patiently did most of the explaining.

“A Greek hero named Perseus boasted he could kill Medusa, the gorgon,” the giant said, smothering a yawn. “With the help of the gods he got a pair of magic sandals which enabled him to fly, and a cap of invisibility. Then he polished his shield to mirror brightness and swooped down on the gorgon, watching her in his mirror-shield, and without ever looking her in the face he cut off her head.”

"I see," Curt said. "We have to hunt down this gorgon too, and we can't look at it either, or—" He nodded outside at the two brown mounds of earth.

"Right," Framer said. "But we don't have a mirror. And we can't build one. What now?"

We racked our brains. Morro wondered if we could somehow polish the ship to the proper brightness, but we saw the scheme was impractical.

"Try radar," Tavy offered.

"That's it!" I whooped. "Hunt down the gorgon with radar and blast it without ever looking at the damned thing!"

From there on Medusa's number was up. But she didn't go down without a fight.

* * *

Holden had the radar screen dismantled and set up for gorgon-hunting in no time at all. The boy's horizons were limited, perhaps, but in the fields for which he had been educated he was tops. On a warm, summery day, we set out on our gorgon-hunt.

We always had difficulty adjusting to the red leaves on the trees and especially the carpet of red grass on the ground. Bellatrix IV, as far as we could see, was a huge plain, covered with what seemed to be a bloody carpet. Every time I looked down I felt a twinge, and thought of the two graves near the ship, and of the two explorers who would never get back for another lecture tour on Earth.

Steeger remained behind on ship, peering intently into the radar screen. The five of us fanned out slowly, armed to the teeth and scared stiff. I could see myself that evening being borne back to the ship, frozen, and sharing that impromptu graveyard with Janus and Flaherty.

Steeger had more to worry about than any of us. Hunched over the radar screen, his job was to relay instructions to us. We knew the gorgon was somewhere in the copse, because Framer had seen the great thing go thundering into the clump of trees the day before, and no one had seen or heard it since. But only a fool would go in there after a beast that killed by a glance.

Slowly, painfully, the five of us formed a wide circle around the copse, standing no closer than a hundred meters from the edge. Not one of us dared to look up, of course; our eyes remained fixed on the blood-red grass and Steeger directed us to our positions, step by painful step. It took half an hour to form the circle, as Doc would tell first one, then another of us, to move a couple of steps to right or left. Finally the circle was complete—five Perseuses, frightened green.

Then came the rough part, as we waited for the attack. When the call came over the phones from Steeger, I was going to hurl a Johnson flare into the copse, and, if all went right, the gorgon would come lumbering out. Without looking, we would fire.

As I look back, I see it was a pretty harebrained scheme. So many things could have gone wrong that it's a wonder we ever went ahead with it.

Doc gave the signal, and I drew back my arm and flung the flare, automatically looking up as I did. For one horror-stricken second I feared the gorgon might approach just as I looked up, but there was no sign of it.

Then all hell broke loose in the copse.

A Johnson flare goes off like a lithium bomb—at least it creates enough light to simulate one. That copse lit up bright yellow, and I caught the odd contrast between the red of the leaves and the yellow of the light. And I saw something huge thrashing around in the heart of the copse before I jerked my head down. I stared at my feet.

Try blindfolding yourself some time and walking down a city street, an empty street, at dawn. The terror is something unimaginable, the unreasoning terror of the blind. That's the way I felt, knowing that at any moment a monster might pop out of thc clump of trees and leap at me while I stood studying my boots. An awful ten seconds passed, and seemed like days, and I grew progressively more numb with fear, until I passed the point of fright and seemed almost calm. Nothing happened, though the flare continued to kick up a powerful light. I heard rustling noises in the copse.

And then all at once I heard Steeger's tinny yell in my phones.

"Joel!"

In the same instant I drew with my right hand and flung my left hand behind my neck, forcing my head down. I aimed the blaster up at a 45-degree angle and began sizzling away for all I was worth. Over to my left I could hear Morro doing the same.

There was the sound of thunder, as of a great beast lumbering around near me. I could hear Steeger screaming something in my phones, but I was unable to stop yelling myself. And I didn't dare look up.

For all I knew the gorgon was standing right over me and bending to bite me in two. But I had passed the point of any coherent reasoning. I was still screaming and squeezing the trigger of the burned-out blaster five minutes later, when Morro and Framer came over to me and led me back to the ship.

* * *

We had killed it, then. And I, Lieut. (Spatial) Joel Kaftan, commander of EExP A-7 to Bellatrix IV, was Perseus.

"We thought we'd never get you up," said Morro.

Steeger said, "I saw that gorgon come out, and I yelled to you. You started waving the blaster around, and Morro came over too. But by the time he reached you, you had blasted Medusa in the neck and pretty near cut that head right off."

Ramirez took up the story. "You were still blasting away without looking, even though the gorgon had fallen on its face. Holden came up and cut its head off, but it's still thrashing its wings out there."

"You ruined about three trees with your blaster," Morro added. "Damned careless of you, Joel."

I looked up. The accumulated tension had built up to such a pitch while I was waiting for the thing to come out of its lair that I felt I had been through a wringer and had been squeezed flat. I looked around at the men ranging the couch on which I lay.

I saw great Morro standing at my feet, and old Steeger looking even older after his remote-control chess-game with the gorgon. And there was Holden, and Ramirez. Four. And I made five. Two dead made seven. It took me another second to realize we were not all together.

"Where's Framer?"

"Out there," Ramirez said. "The biologist in him got the upper hand, and he's out there examining our defunct friend."

"But you said the wings were still thrashing," I yelled, leaping from the couch. "That means—"

But the others realized what it meant, too, and we raced through the airlock door in no time at all.

* * *

WE WERE TOO LATE, OF course. We found the biologist bent over the decapitated gorgon, examining the head with interest. And frozen stiff.

Averting our eyes, we carried Kal back to the ship and buried him next to Flaherty and Janus. More than any of us, Kal had been a scientist, and he couldn't resist trying to solve the puzzle of the gorgon. Whether he had or not we would never know—but apparently the gorgon's neural network had been of a low order, low enough to remain functioning for a while after the organism's death. And there had been enough of a charge left in those deadly eyes to give Framer a freezing blast.

I directed operations from the door of the ship, trying hard not to stare at the upturned gorgon-head. Upton and Morro crept up blindfolded and slipped the gorgon's head into a thick plasticanvas bag, and zipped up the top. We stuck a "danger—do not open" sign on it.

Medusa had cost us three men, but we had beaten her. We loaded her headless corpse into the deep freeze for Earth's scientists to puzzle over. It took all five of us to lift the huge thing and stow it away, and we were glad to see the end of it. No more monsters, we thought; the expedition would be restful from here on.

Until the next day, when Ramirez found that Sphinx crouching near the ship—

THE SHADOW OF WINGS

I have often tried, as the stories in this book demonstrate again and again, to depict the *alienness* of alien beings. There doesn't seem to be much point in writing stories in which the aliens are pretty much like the people you might meet next week in Chicago or Minneapolis (although Ray Bradbury did do just that, and brilliantly, in *The Martian Chronicles*—but that was a one-of-a-kind book).

One of my earlier attempts at such a portrayal is offered here, "The Shadow of Wings." I wrote it in the summer of 1962 and Frederik Pohl published it in *If*, one of the three science-fiction magazines he was editing then, in his July 1963 issue.

THE CHILDREN CAME RUNNING TOWARDS him, laughing and shouting, up from the lakeside to the spot on the grassy hill where he lay reading; and as Dr. John Donaldson saw what was clutched in the hand of his youngest son, he felt an involuntary tremor of disgust.

"Look, John! Look what Paul caught!" That was his oldest, Joanne. She was nine, a brunette rapidly growing tan on this vacation trip. Behind her came David, eight, fair-haired and lobster-skinned, and in the rear was Paul, the six-year-old, out of breath and gripping in his still pudgy hand a small green frog.

Donaldson shoved his book—Haley, *Studies in Morphological Linguistics*—to one side and sat up. Paul thrust the frog almost into his face. "I saw it hop, John—and I caught it!" He pantomimed the catch with his free hand.

"I saw him do it," affirmed David.

The frog's head projected between thumb and first finger; two skinny webbed feet dangled free at the other end of Paul's hand, while the middle of the unfortunate batrachian was no doubt being painfully compressed by the small clammy hand. Donaldson felt pleased by Paul's display of coordination, unusual for a six-year-old. But at the same time he wished the boy would take the poor frog back to the lake and let it go.

"Paul," he started to say, "you really ought to—"

The direct-wave phone at the far end of the blanket bleeped, indicating that Martha, back at the bungalow, was calling.

"It's Mommy," Joanne said. Somehow they had never cared to call her by her first name, as they did him. "See what she wants, John."

Donaldson sprawled forward and activated the phone.

"Martha?"

"John, there's a phone call for you from Washington. I told them you were down by the lake, but they say it's important and they'll hold on."

Donaldson frowned. "Who from Washington?"

"Caldwell, he said. Bureau of Extraterrestrial Affairs. Said it was urgent."

Sighing, Donaldson said, "Okay, I'm corning."

He looked at Joanne and said, as if she hadn't heard the conversation at all, "There's a call for me and I have to go to the cottage to take it. Make sure your brothers don't go into the water while I'm gone. And see that Paul lets that confounded frog go."

Picking up his book, he levered himself to his feet and set out for the phone in the bungalow at a brisk trot.

Caldwell's voice was crisp and efficient and not at all apologetic as he said, "I'm sorry to have to interrupt you during your vacation, Dr. Donaldson. But it's an urgent matter and they tell us you're the man who can help us."

"Perhaps I am. Just exactly what is it you want?"

"Check me if I'm wrong on the background. You're professor of Linguistics at Columbia, a student of the Kethlani languages and author of a study of Kethlani linguistics published in 2087."

"Yes, yes, that's all correct. But—"

"Dr. Donaldson, we've captured a live Kethlan. He entered the System in a small ship and one of our patrol vessels grappled him in, ship and all. We've got him here in Washington and we want you to come talk to him."

For an instant Donaldson was too stunned to react. A live Kethlan? That was like saying, We've found a live Sumerian, or, We've found a live Etruscan.

The Kethlani languages were precise, neat, and utterly dead. At one time in the immeasurable past the Kethlani had visited the Solar System. They had left records of their visit on Mars and Venus, in two languages. One of the languages was translatable, because the Martians had translated it into their own, and the Martian language was still spoken as it had been a hundred thousand years before.

Donaldson had obtained his doctorate with what was hailed as a brilliant Rosetta Stone type analysis of the Kethlani language. But a live Kethlan? Why—

After a moment he realized he was staring stupidly at his unevenly tanned face in the mirror above the phone cabinet, and that the man on the other end of the wire was making impatient noises.

Slowly he said, "I can be in Washington this afternoon, I guess. Give me some time to pack up my things. You won't want me for long, will you?"

"Until we're through talking to the Kethlan," Caldwell said.

"All right," Donaldson said. "I can take a vacation any time. Kethlani don't come along that often."

He hung up and peered at his face in the mirror. He had had curly reddish hair once, but fifteen years of the academic life had worn his forehead bare. His eyes were mild, his nose narrow and unemphatic, his lips thin and pale. As he studied himself, he did not think he looked very impressive. He looked professional. That was to be expected.

"Well?" Martha asked.

Donaldson shrugged. "They captured some kind of alien spaceship with a live one aboard. And it seems I'm the only person who can speak the language. They want me right away."

"You're going?"

"Of course. It shouldn't take more than a few days. You can manage with the children by yourself, can't you? I mean—"

She smiled faintly, walked around behind him and kneaded the muscle of his sun-reddened back in an affectionate gesture. "I know better than to argue," she said. "We can take a vacation next year."

He swivelled his left hand behind his back, caught her hand and squeezed it fondly. He knew she would never object. After all, his happiness was her happiness—and he was never happier than when working in his chosen field. The phone call today would probably lead to all sorts of unwanted and unneeded publicity for him. But it would also bring him academic success, and there was no denying the genuine thrill of finding out how accurate his guesses about Kethlani pronunciation were.

"You'd better go down to the lake and get the children," he said. "I'll want to say good-bye before I leave."

* * *

THEY HAD THE SHIP LOCKED in a stasis field in the basement of the Bureau of ET Affairs Building, on Constitution Avenue just across from the National Academy of Sciences. The great room looked like nothing so much as a crypt, Donaldson thought as he entered. Beam projectors were mounted around the walls, focusing a golden glow on the ship. Caught in the field, the ship hovered in midair, a slim, strange-looking torpedolike object about forty feet long and ten feet across the thickest space. A tingle rippled up Donaldson's spine as he saw the Kethlani cursives painted in blue along the hull. He translated them reflexively: Bringer of Friendship.

"That's how we knew it was a Kethlani ship," Caldwell said, at his side. He was a small, intense man who hardly reached Donaldson's shoulder; he was Associate Director of the Bureau, and in his superior's absence he was running the show.

Donaldson indicated the projectors. "How come the gadgetry? Couldn't you just sit the ship on the floor instead of floating it that way?"

"That ship's heavy," Caldwell said. "Might crack the floor. Anyway, it's easier to maneuver this way. We can raise or lower the ship, turn it, float it in or out of the door."

"I see," Donaldson said. "And you say there's a live Kethlan in there?"

Caldwell nodded. He jerked a thumb toward a miniature broadcasting station at the far end of the big room. "We've been in contact with him. He talks to us and we talk to him. But we don't understand a damned bit of it, of course. You want to try?"

Donaldson shook his head up and down in a tense affirmative. Caldwell led him down to the radio set, where an eager-looking young man in military uniform sat making adjustments.

Caldwell said, "This is Dr. Donaldson of Columbia. He wrote the definitive book on Kethlani languages. He wants to talk to our friend in there."

A microphone was thrust into Donaldson's hands. He looked at it blankly, then at the pink face of the uniformed man, then at the ship. The inscription was in Kethlani A language, for which Donaldson was grateful. There were two Kethlani languages, highly dissimilar, which he had labeled A and B. He knew his way around in A well enough, but his mastery of Kethlani B was still exceedingly imperfect.

"How do I use this thing?"

"You push the button on the handle, and talk. That's all. The Kethlan can hear you. Anything he says will be picked up here." He indicated a tape recorder and a speaker on the table.

Donaldson jabbed down on the button, and, feeling a strange sense of disorientation, uttered two words in greeting in Kethlani A.

The pronunciation, of course, was sheer guesswork. Donaldson had worked out what was to him a convincing Kethlani phonetic system, but whether that bore any relation to fact remained to be seen.

He waited a moment. Then the speaker emitted a series of harsh, unfamiliar sounds—and, buried in them like gems in a kitchen midden, Donaldson detected familiar-sounding words.

"Speak slowly," he said in Kethlani A. "I . . . have only a few words."

The reply came about ten seconds later, in more measured accents. "How . . . do . . . you . . . speak our language?"

Donaldson fumbled in his small vocabulary for some way of explaining that he had studied Kethlani documents left behind on Mars centuries earlier, and compared them with their understandable Martian translations until he had pried some sense out of them.

He glimpsed the pale, sweat-beaded faces of the ET men around him; they were mystified, wondering what he was saying to the alien but not daring to interrupt. Donaldson felt a flash of pity for them. Until today the bureau had concerned itself with petty things: import of Martian antiquities, study visas for Venus, and the like. Now, suddenly, they found themselves staring at an extra-solar spaceship, and all the giant problems that entailed.

"Find out why be came to the Solar System," Caldwell whispered.

"I'm trying to," Donaldson murmured with some irritation. He said in Kethlani, "You have made a long journey."

"Yes . . . and alone."

"Why have you come?"

There was a long moment of silence; Donaldson waited, feeling tension of crackling intensity starting to build within him. The unreality of the situation obsessed him. He had been fondly confident that he would never have the opportunity to speak actual Kethlani, and that confidence was being shattered.

Finally: "I . . . have come . . .why?"

The inversion was grammatically correct. "Yes," Donaldson said. "Why?"

Another long pause. Then the alien said something which Donaldson did not immediately understand. He asked for a repeat.

It made little sense—but, of course, his Kethlani vocabulary was a shallow one, and he had additional difficulty in comprehending because he had made some mistakes in interpreting vowel values when constructing his Kethlani phonetics.

But the repeat came sharp and clear, and there was no mistaking it.

"I do . . . do not like to talk in this way. Come inside my ship and we will talk there."

"What's he saying?" Caldwell prodded.

Shaken, Donaldson let the mic dangle from limp fingers. "He—he says he wants me to come inside the ship. He doesn't like long-distance conversations."

Caldwell turned at a right angle and said to a waiting assistant. "All right. Have Matthews reverse the stasis field and lower the ship. We're going to give the Kethlan some company."

Donaldson blinked. "Company? You mean you're sending me in there?"

"I sure as hell do mean that. The Kethlan said it's the only way he'd talk, didn't he? And that's what you're here for. To talk to him. So why shouldn't you go in there, eh?"

"Well—look, Caldwell, suppose it isn't safe?"

"If I thought it was risky, I wouldn't send you in," Caldwell said blandly.

Donaldson shook his head. "But look—I don't want to seem cowardly, but I've got three children to think about. I'm not happy about facing an alien being inside his own ship, if you get me."

"I get you," said Caldwell tiredly. "All right. You want to go home? You want to call the whole business off right here and now?"

"Of course not. But—"

"But then you'll have to go in."

"How will I be able to breathe?"

"The alien air is close enough to our own. He's used to more carbon dioxide and less oxygen, but he can handle our air. There's no problem. And no risk. We had a man in there yesterday when the Kethlan opened the outer lock. You won't be in any physical danger. The alien won't bother you."

"I hope not," Donaldson said. He felt hesitant about it; he hadn't bargained on going inside any extra solar spaceships. But they were clustered impatiently around him, waiting to send him inside, and he didn't seem to have much choice. He sensed a certain contempt for him on their faces already. He didn't want to increase their distaste.

"Will you go in?" Caldwell asked.

"All right. All right. Yes. I'll go in."

Nervously Donaldson picked up the microphone and clamped a cold finger over the control button.

"Open your lock," he said to the alien being. "I'm coming inside."

There was a moment's delay while the stasis field projectors were reversed, lowering the ship gently to floor level. As soon as it touched, a panel in the gleaming golden side of the ship rolled smoothly open, revealing an inner panel.

Donaldson moistened his lips, handed the microphone to Caldwell, and walked uncertainly forward. He reached the lip of the airlock, stepped up over it and into the ship. Immediately the door rolled shut behind him, closing him into a chamber about seven feet high and four feet wide, bordered in front and back by the outer and inner doors of the lock.

He waited. Had he been claustrophobic he would have been hysterical by now. But I never would have come in here in the first place then, he thought.

He waited. More than a minute passed; then, finally, the blank wall before him rolled aside, and the ship was open to him at last. He entered.

At first it seemed to him the interior was totally dark. Gradually, his retinal rods conveyed a little information.

A dim light flickered at one end of the narrow tubular ship. He could make out a few things: rows of reinforcing struts circling the ship at regular spaced distances; a kind of control panel with quite thoroughly alien-looking instruments on it; a large chamber at one end which might be used for storage of food.

But where's the alien? Donaldson wondered.

He turned, slowly, through a three hundred sixty degree rotation, squinting in the dimness. A sort of mist hung before his eyes; the alien's exhalation, perhaps. But he saw no sign of the Kethlan. There was a sweetish, musky odor in the ship, unpleasant though not unbearable.

"Everything okay?" Caldwell's voice said in his earphones.

"So far. But I can't find the alien. It's damnably dark in here."

"Look up," Caldwell advised. "You'll find him. Took our man a while too, yesterday."

Puzzled, Donaldson raised his head and stared into the gloom-shrouded rafters of the ship, wondering what he was supposed to see. In Kethlani he said loudly, "Where are you? I see you not."

"I am here," came the harsh voice, from above.

Donaldson looked. Then he backed away, doubletaking, and looking again.

A great shaggy thing hung head down against the roof of the ship. Staring intently, Donaldson made out a blunt, piggish face with flattened nostrils and huge flaring ears; the eyes, bright yellow but incredibly tiny, glittered with the unmistakable light of intelligence. He saw a body about the size of a man, covered with darkish thick fur and terminating in two short, thick, powerful-looking legs. As he watched the Kethlan shivered and stretched forth its vast leathery wings. In the darkness, Donaldson could see the corded muscular arm in the wing, and the very human looking fingers which sprouted from the uppermost part of the wing.

Violent disgust rose in him, compounded from his own general dislike for animals and from the half remembered Transylvanian folk-tales that formed part of every child's heritage. He felt sick; he controlled himself only by remembering that he was in essence an ambassador, and any sickness would have disastrous consequences for him and for Earth. He dared not offend the Kethlan.

My God, he thought. An intelligent bat!

He managed to stammer out the words for greeting, and the alien responded. Donaldson, looking away, saw the elongated shadow of wings cast across the ship by the faint light at the other end. He felt weak, wobbly-legged; he wanted desperately to dash through the now closed airlock. But he forced himself to recover balance. He had a job to do.

"I did not expect you to know Kethlani," the alien said. "It makes my job much less difficult."

"And your job is—"

"To bring friendship from my people to yours. To link our worlds in brotherhood."

The last concept was a little muddy to Donaldson; the literal translation he made mentally was children-of-onecave, but some questioning eventually brought over the concept of brotherhood.

His eyes were growing more accustomed to the lighting, now, and he could see the Kethlan fairly well. An ugly brute, no doubt of it—but probably I look just as bad to him, he thought. The creature's wingspread was perhaps seven or eight feet. Donaldson tried to picture a world of the beasts, skies thick with leather-winged commuters on their way to work.

Evolution had made numerous modifications in the bat structure, Donaldson saw. The brain, of course; and the extra fingers, aside from the ones from which the wings had sprouted. The eyes looked weak, in typical bat fashion, but probably there was compensation by way of keen auditory senses.

Donaldson said, "Where is your world?"

"Far from here. I—"

The rest of the answer was unintelligible to Donaldson. He felt savage impatience with his own limited vocabulary; he wished he had worked just a little harder on translating the Syrtis Major documents. Well, it was too late for that now, of course.

Caldwell cut in suddenly from outside. "Well? We're picking up all the jabber. What's all the talk about?"

"Can't you wait till I'm finished?" Donaldson snapped. Then, repenting, he said: "Sorry. Guess I'm jumpy. Seems he's an ambassador from his people, trying to establish friendly relations with us. At least, I think so. I'll tell you more when I know something about it."

Slowly, in fits and starts, the story emerged. Frequently Donaldson had to ask the Kethlan to stop and double back while he puzzled over a word. He had no way of recording any of the new words he was learning, but he had always had a good memory, and he simply tucked them away.

The Kethlani had visited the Solar System many years ago. Donaldson was unable to translate the actual figure, but it sounded like a lot. At that time the Martians were at the peak of their civilization, and Earth was just an untamed wilderness populated by naked primates. The Kethlan wryly admitted that they had written off Earth as a potential place of civilization because a study of the bat population of Earth had proved unpromising. They had never expected the primates to evolve this way.

But now they had returned, thousands of years later. Mars was bleak and its civilization decayed, but the third world had unexpectedly attained a high degree of culture and was welcome to embrace the Kethlani worlds in friendship and amity.

"How many 'worlds' do you inhabit?"

The Kethlan counted to fifteen by ones. "There are many others we do not inhabit, but simply maintain friendly relations with. Yours would be one, we hope."

The conversation seemed to dwindle to a halt. Donaldson had run out of questions to ask, and he was exhausted by the hour-long strain of conversing in an alien language, under these conditions, within a cramped ship, talking to a creature whose physical appearance filled him with loathing and fear.

His head throbbed. His stomach was knotted in pain and sweat made his clothes cling clammily to his body. He started to grope for ways to terminate the interview; then an idea struck him.

He quoted a fragment of a document written in pure Kethlani B.

There was an instant of stunned silence; then the alien asked in tones of unmistakable suspicion, "Where did you learn that language?"

"I haven't really learned it. I just know a few words."

He explained that he had found examples of both Kethlani A and Kethlani B along with their Martian equivalents; he had worked fairly comprehensively on the A language, but had only begun to explore the B recently.

The Kethlan seemed to accept that. Then it said: "That is not a Kethlani language."

Surprised, Donaldson uttered the interrogative expletive.

The Kethlan said, "It is the language of our greatest enemies, our rivals, our bitter foes. It is the Thygnor tongue."

"But—why did we find your language and the other side by side, then?"

After a long pause the alien said, "Once Thygnor and Kethlan were friends. Long ago we conducted a joint expedition to this sector of space. Long ago, before the rivalry sprang up. But now"—the alien took on a sorrowful inflection—"now we are enemies."

That explained a great many things, Donaldson realized. The differences between Kethlani A and Kethlani B had been too great for it to seem as if one race spoke both of them. But a joint expedition—that made it understandable.

"Some day, perhaps, the Thygnor will visit your world. But by then you will be on guard against them."

"What do they look like?"

The alien described-them, and Donaldson listened and was revolted. As far as he could understand, they were giant intelligent toads, standing erect, amphibian but warm-blooded, vile-smelling, their bodies exuding a nauseous thick secretion.

Giant toads, bats, the lizards of Mars—evidently the primate monopoly of intelligence was confined solely to Earth, Donaldson realized. It was a humbling thought. His face wrinkled in displeasure at the mental image of the toad people the Kethlan had created for him, as he recalled the harmless little frog Paul had captured by the lake.

He spoke in English, attracting Caldwell's attention, and explained the situation.

"He wants me to swear brotherhood with him. He also says there's another intelligent race with interstellar travel—toads, no less—and that they're likely to pay us a visit some day too. What should I do?"

"Go ahead and swear brotherhood," Caldwell said after a brief pause. "It can't hurt. We can always unswear it later, if we like. Say we had our fingers crossed while we were doing it, or something. Then when the frogs get here we can find out which bunch is better for us to be in league with."

The cynicism of the reply annoyed Donaldson, but it was not his place to raise any objections. He said to the alien, "I am prepared to pledge brotherhood between Earth and the Kethlan worlds."

The Kethlan fluttered suddenly down from its perch with a rustle of great wings, and stood facing Donaldson, tucking its wings around its thick shaggy body. Alarmed, Donaldson stepped back.

The alien said reassuringly, "The way we pledge is by direct physical embrace, symbolizing harmony and friendship across the cosmos." He unfurled his wings. "Come close to me."

No! Donaldson shrieked inwardly, as the mighty wings rose high and wrapped themselves about him. Go away! Don't touch me! He could smell the sweet, musky smell of the alien, feel its furry warmth, hear the mighty heart pounding, pounding in that massive rib cage. . .

Revulsion dizzied him. He forced himself to wrap his arms around the barrel of a body while the wings blanketed him, and they stood that way for a moment, locked in a tight embrace.

At length the alien released him. "Now we are friends. It is only the beginning of a long and fruitful relationship between our peoples. I hope to speak with you again before long."

It was a dismissal. On watery legs Donaldson tottered forward toward the opening airlock, pausing only to mutter a word of farewell before he stumbled through and out into the arms of the waiting men outside.

"Well?" Caldwell demanded. "What happened? Did you swear brotherhood?"

"Yes," Donaldson said wearily. "I swore." The stench of the alien clung to him, sweet in his nostrils. It was as though throbbing wings still enfolded him. "I'm leaving now," he said. "I still have a little of my vacation left. I want to take it."

He gulped a drink that someone handed him. He was shaking and gray-faced, but the effect of the embrace was wearing off. Only an irrational phobia, he told himself. I shouldn't be reacting this way.

But already he was beginning to forget the embrace of the Kethlan, and the rationalization did him no good. A new and more dreadful thought was beginning to develop within him.

He was the only Terrestrial expert on Kethlani B, too—the Thygnor tongue. And some day, perhaps soon, the Thygnor were going to come to Earth, and Caldwell was going to impress him into service as an interpreter again.

He wondered how the toad people pledged eternal brotherhood.

FLIES

It was 1965 and I was writing science fiction again after a considerable intermission in my career, and beginning to edit it, too. An anthology of reprints called *Earthmen and Strangers* was the first one I did, and I chose to include a story by Harlan Ellison in it. Ellison was willing to grant me permission to use his story, but not without a lot of heavy muttering and grumbling about the terms of the contract, to which I replied on October 2, 1965:

> "Dear Harlan: You'll be glad to know that in the course of a long and wearying dream last night I watched you win *two* Hugos at last year's Worldcon. You acted pretty smug about it, too. I'm not sure which categories you led, but one of them was probably Unfounded Bitching. Permit me a brief and fatherly lecture in response to your letter of permission on the anthology . . . "

Whereupon I dealt with his complaints at some length, and then, almost gratuitously, threw in a postscript:

> "Why don't you do an anthology? HARLAN ELLISON PICKS OFF-BEAT CLASSICS OF S-F, or something . . ."

I think that I had already suggested to Harlan that he edit an anthology of controversial s-f—he was running a paperback line then called Regency Books, published out of Chicago—but for some reason he had brushed the idea aside. Now, though, my suggestion kindled something in him. He was back to me right away, by telephone this time, to tell me in some excitement that he *would* do a science-fiction anthology, all right, but for some major publishing house instead of Regency, and instead of putting together a mere compilation of existing material he would solicit previously unpublished stories, the kind of science fiction that no magazine of that era would *dare* to publish. Truly dangerous stories, Harlan said—a book of dangerous visions. "In fact, that's what I'll call it," he told me, really excited now. "*Dangerous Visions.* I want you to write a story for it, too."

And so I unwittingly touched off a publishing revolution.

By the 18th of October Harlan had sold the book to Doubleday and was soliciting stories far and wide. Requests for material—material of the boldest, most uncompromising kind—went out to the likes of Theodore Sturgeon, Frederik Pohl, Poul Anderson, Philip K. Dick, Philip Jose Farmer, Fritz Leiber, J.G. Ballard, Norman Spinrad, Brian Aldiss, Lester del Rey, Larry Niven, R.A. Lafferty, John Brunner, Roger Zelazny, and Samuel R. Delany. Dick, Pohl, Sturgeon, Anderson, del Rey, Farmer, Brunner, Aldiss, and Leiber were well-established authors, but the work of Ballard, Zelazny, Delany, Niven, and Spinrad, believe it or not, was only just beginning to be known in the United States in 1965. Harlan's eye for innovative talent had always been formidably keen.

As the accidental instigator of the whole thing—and the quickest man with an s-f story since Henry Kuttner in his prime—I sat down right away and wrote the very first dangerous vision, "Flies," in November of 1965, just as soon as Harlan told me the deal was set. It was about as dangerous as I could manage: a demonstration of the random viciousness of the universe and the alien beings that might inhabit it, and a little blasphemy on the side. (I would return to both these themes again and again in the years ahead: my novel *Thorns* of 1966 was essentially a recasting of the underlying material of "Flies" at greater length.) Back at once came Harlan's check for $88.

Which was the first of many, for *Dangerous Visions* would turn out to be the most significant s-f anthology of the decade, destined to go through edition after edition. (It is back in print yet again, years after its first publication.) *All* of the extraordinary writers whose names I rattled off above came through with brilliant stories, along with fifteen or twenty others, some well-known at the time but forgotten now, some obscure then and still obscure, but all of them fiercely determined to live up to Harlan's demand for the kind of stories that other s-f editors would consider too hot to handle.

Dangerous Visions appeared in 1967. "An event," said *The New York Times*, "a jubilee of fresh ideas . . .what we mean when we say an important book." Its success led to the publication of an immense companion volume in 1972, *Again, Dangerous Visions*—760 pages of stories by writers who hadn't contributed to the first book (Ursula K. Le Guin, Gene Wolfe, Kurt Vonnegut, Gregory Benford, James Tiptree, Jr. . . .) And ultimately Harlan began to assemble the mammoth third book in the series, *The Last Dangerous Visions*, which he never managed to complete before his death in 2018.

I knew not what I was setting in motion with my casual postscript of October 2, 1965, suggesting that Harlan edit an anthology. Certainly I had no idea that I was nudging him toward one of the great enterprises of his career. Nor did I suspect that my own 4400-word contribution to the book would open a new and darker phase of my own career—in which, ultimately, almost everything I wrote would become a dangerous vision of sorts.

HERE IS CASSIDAY:
transfixed on a table.

There wasn't much left of him. A brain-box; a few ropes of nerves; a limb. The sudden implosion had taken care of the rest. There was enough, though. The golden ones didn't need much to go by. They had found him in the wreckage of the drifting ship as it passed through their zone, back of Iapetus. He was alive. He could be repaired. The others on the ship were beyond hope.

Repair him? Of course. Did one need to be human in order to be humanitarian? Repair, yes. By all means. And change. The golden ones were creative.

What was left of Cassiday lay in drydock on a somewhere table in a golden sphere of force. There was no change of season here; only the sheen of the walls, the unvarying warmth. Neither day nor night, neither yesterday nor tomorrow. Shapes came and went about him. They were regenerating him, stage by stage, as he lay in complete unthinking tranquility. The brain was intact but not functioning. The rest of the man was growing back: tendon and ligament, bone and blood, heart and elbows. Elongated mounds of tissue sprouted tiny buds that enlarged into blobs of flesh. Paste cell to cell together, build a man from his own wreckage—that was no chore for the golden ones. They had their skills. But they had much to learn too, and this Cassiday could help them learn it.

Day by day Cassiday grew toward wholeness. They did not awaken him. He lay cradled in warmth, unmoving, unthinking, drifting on the tide. His new flesh was pink and smooth, like a baby's. The epithelial thickening came a little later. Cassiday served as his own blueprint. The golden ones replicated him from a shred of himself, built him back from his own polynucleotide chains, decoded the proteins and reassembled him from the template. An easy task, for them. Why not? Any blob of protoplasm could do it—for itself. The golden ones, who were not protoplasm, could do it for others.

They made some changes in the template. Of course. They were craftsmen. And there was a good deal they wanted to learn.

* * *

LOOK AT CASSIDAY:

the dossier.

BORN 1 August 2316
PLACE Nyack, New York
PARENTS Various
ECONOMIC LEVEL Low
EDUCATIONAL LEVEL Middle
OCCUPATION Fuel technician
MARITAL STATUS Three legal liaisons, duration eight months, sixteen months, and two months
HEIGHT Two meters

WEIGHT 96 kg
HAIR COLOR Yellow
EYES Blue
BLOOD TYPE A +
INTELLIGENCE LEVEL High
SEXUAL, INCLINATIONS Normal

* * *

WATCH THEM NOW:
changing him.

The complete man lay before them, newly minted, ready for rebirth. Now came the final adjustments. They sought the gray brain within its pink wrapper, and entered it, and traveled through the bays and inlets of the mind, pausing now at this quiet cove, dropping anchor now at the base of that slab-sided cliff. They were operating, but doing it neatly. Here were no submucous resections, no glittering blades carving through gristle and bone, no sizzling lasers at work, no clumsy hammering at the tender meninges. Cold steel did not slash the synapses. The golden ones were subtler; they tuned the circuit that was Cassiday, boosted the gain, damped out the noise, and they did it very gently.

When they were finished with him, he was much more sensitive. He had several new hungers. They had granted him certain abilities.

Now they awakened him.

"You are alive, Cassiday," a feathery voice said. "Your ship was destroyed. Your companions were killed. You alone survived."

"Which hospital is this?"

"Not on Earth. You'll be going back soon. Stand up, Cassiday. Move your right hand. Your left. Flex your knees. Inflate your lungs. Open and close your eyes several times. What's your name, Cassiday?"

"Richard Henry Cassiday."

"How old?"

"Forty-one."

"Look at this reflection. Who do you see?"

"Myself."

"Do you have any further questions?"

"What did you do to me?"

"Repaired you, Cassiday. You were almost entirely destroyed."

"Did you change me any?"

"We made you more sensitive to the feelings of your fellow man."

"Oh," said Cassiday.

* * *

FOLLOW CASSIDAY AS HE JOURNEYS:

back to Earth.

He arrived on a day that had been programmed for snow. Light snow, quickly melting, an esthetic treat rather than a true manifestation of weather. It was good to touch foot on the homeworld again. The golden ones had deftly arranged his return, putting him back aboard his wrecked ship and giving him enough of a push to get him within range of a distress sweep. The monitors had detected him and picked him up. How was it you survived the disaster unscathed, Spaceman Cassiday? Very simple, sir, I was outside the ship when it happened. It just went swoosh, and everybody was killed. And I only am escaped alone to tell thee.

They routed him to Mars and checked him out, and held him awhile in a decontamination lock on Luna, and finally sent him back to Earth. He stepped into the snowstorm, a big man with a rolling gait and careful calluses in all the right places. He had few friends, no relatives, enough cash units to see him through for a while, and a couple of ex-wives he could look up. Under the rules, he was entitled to a year off with full pay as his disaster allotment. He intended to accept the furlough.

He had not yet begun to make use of his new sensitivity. The golden ones had planned it so that his abilities would remain inoperative until he reached the homeworld. Now he had arrived, and it was time to begin using them, and the endlessly curious creatures who lived back of Iapetus waited patiently while Cassiday sought out those who had once loved him.

He began his quest in Chicago Urban District, because that was where the spaceport was, just outside of Rockford. The slidewalk took him quickly to the travertine tower, festooned with radiant inlays of ebony and violet-hued metal, and there, at the local Televector Central, Cassiday checked out the present whereabouts of his former wives. He was patient about it, a bland-faced, mild-eyed tower of flesh, pushing the right buttons and waiting placidly for the silken contacts to close somewhere in the depths of the Earth. Cassiday had never been a violent man. He was calm. He knew how to wait.

The machine told him that Beryl Fraser Cassiday Mellon lived in Boston Urban District. The machine told him that Lureen Holstein Cassiday lived in New York Urban District. The machine told him that Mirabel Gunryk Cassiday Milman Reed lived in San Francisco Urban District.

The names awakened memories: warmth of flesh, scent of hair, touch of hand, sound of voice. Whispers of passion. Snarls of contempt. Gasps of love.

Cassiday, restored to life, went to see his ex-wives.

* * *

WE FIND ONE NOW:

safe and sound.

Beryl's eyes were milky in the pupil, greenish where they should have been white. She had lost weight in the last ten years, and now her face was parchment stretched over bone, an eroded face, the cheekbones pressing from within against the taut skin and likely to snap through at any moment. Cassiday had been married to her for eight months when he was twenty-four. They had separated after she insisted on taking the Sterility pledge. He had not particularly wanted children, but he was offended by her maneuver all the same. Now she lay in a soothing cradle of webfoam, trying to smile at him without cracking her lips.

"They said you'd been killed," she told him.

"I escaped. How have you been, Beryl?"

"You can see that. I'm taking the cure."

"Cure?"

"I was a triline addict. Can't you see? My eyes, my face? It melted me away. But it was peaceful. Like disconnecting your soul. Only it would have killed me, another year of it. Now I'm on the cure. They tapered me off last month. They're building up my system with prosthetics. I'm full of plastic now. But I'll live."

"You've remarried?" Cassiday asked.

"He split long ago. I've been alone five years. Just me and the triline. But now I'm off that stuff." Beryl blinked laboriously. "You look so relaxed, Dick. But you always were. So calm, so sure of yourself. *You'd* never get yourself hooked on triline. Hold my hand, will you?"

He touched the withered claw. He felt the warmth come from her, the need for love. Great throbbing waves came lalloping into him, low-frequency pulses of yearning that filtered through him and went booming onward to the watchers far away.

"You once loved me," Beryl said. "Then we were both silly. Love me again. Help me get back on my feet. I need your strength."

"Of course I'll help you," Cassiday said.

He left her apartment and purchased three cubes of triline. Returning, he activated one of them and pressed it into Beryl's hand. The green-and-milky eyes roiled in terror.

"No," she whimpered.

The pain flooding from her shattered soul was exquisite in its intensity. Cassiday accepted the full flood of it. Then she clenched her fist, and the drug entered her metabolism, and she grew peaceful once more.

* * *

OBSERVE THE NEXT ONE:

with a friend.

The annunciator said, "Mr. Cassiday is here."

"Let him enter," replied Mirabel Gunryk Cassiday Milman Reed.

The door-sphincter irised open and Cassiday stepped through, into onyx and marble splendor. Beams of auburn palisander formed a polished wooden framework on which Mirabel lay, and it was obvious that she reveled in the sensation of hard wood against plump flesh. A cascade of crystal-colored hair tumbled to her shoulders. She had been Cassiday's for sixteen months in 2346 and she had been a slender, timid girl then, but now he could barely detect the outlines of that girl in this pampered mound.

"You've married well," he observed.

"Third time lucky," Mirabel said. "Sit down? Drink? Shall I adjust the environment?"

"It's fine." He remained standing. "You always wanted a mansion, Mirabel. My most intellectual wife, you were, but you had this love of comfort. You're comfortable now."

"Very."

"Happy?"

"I'm comfortable," Mirabel said. "I don't read much any more, but I'm comfortable."

Cassiday noticed what seemed to be a blanket crumpled in her lap—purple with golden threads, soft, idle, clinging close. It had several eyes. Mirabel kept her hands spread over it.

"From Ganymede?" he asked. "A pet?"

"Yes. My husband bought it for me last year. It's very precious to me."

"Very precious to anybody. I understand they're expensive."

"But lovable," said Mirabel. "Almost human. Quite devoted. I suppose you'll think I'm silly, but it's the most important thing in my life now. More than my husband, even. I love it, you see. I'm accustomed to having others love me, but there aren't many things that I've been able to love."

"May I see it?" Cassiday said mildly.

"Be careful."

"Certainly." He gathered up the Ganymedean creature. Its texture was extraordinary, the softest he had ever encountered. Something fluttered apprehensively within the flat body of the animal. Cassiday detected a parallel wariness coming from Mirabel as he handled her pet. He stroked the creature. It throbbed appreciatively. Bands of iridescence shimmered as it contracted in his hands.

She said, "What are you doing now, Dick? Still working for the spaceline?"

He ignored the question. "Tell me the line from Shakespeare, Mirabel. About flies. The flies and wanton boys."

Furrows sprouted in her pale brow. "It's from *Lear,"* she said. "Wait. Yes. *As flies to wanton boys are we to the gods. They kill us for their sport."*

"That's the one," Cassiday said. His big hands knotted quickly about the blanketlike being from Ganymede. It turned a dull gray, and reedy fibers popped from its ruptured surface. Cassiday dropped it to the floor. The surge of horror and pain and loss that welled from Mirabel nearly stunned him, but he accepted it and transmitted it.

"Flies," he explained. "Wanton boys. My sport, Mirabel. I'm a god now, did you know that?" His voice was calm and cheerful. "Goodbye. Thank you."

* * *

One more awaits the visit:
Swelling with new life.

Lureen Holstein Cassiday, who was thirty-one years old, dark-haired, large-eyed, and seven months pregnant, was the only one of his wives who had not remarried. Her room in New York was small and austere. She had been a plump girl when she had been Cassiday's two-month wife five years ago, and she was even more plump now, but how much of the access of new meat was the result of the pregnancy Cassiday did not know.

"Will you marry now?" he asked.

Smiling, she shook her head. "I've got money, and I value my independence. I wouldn't let myself get into another deal like the one we had. Not with anyone."

"And the baby? You'll have it?"

She nodded savagely. "I worked hard to get it! You think it's easy? Two years of inseminations! A fortune in fees! Machines poking around in me—all the fertility boosters—oh no, you've got the picture wrong. This isn't an unwanted baby. This is a baby I sweated to have."

"That's interesting," said Cassiday. "I visited Mirabel and Beryl, too, and they each had their babies, too. Of sorts. Mirabel had a little beast from Ganymede. Beryl had a triline addiction that she was very proud of shaking. And you've had a baby put in you, without any help from a man. All three of you seeking something. Interesting."

"Are you all right, Dick?'

"Fine."

"Your voice is so flat. You're just unrolling a lot of words. It's a little frightening."

"Mmm. Yes. Do you know the kind thing I did for Beryl? I bought her some triline cubes. And I took Mirabel's pet and wrung its—well, not its neck. I did it very calmly. I was never a passionate man."

"I think you've gone crazy, Dick."

"I feel your fear. You think I'm going to do something to your baby. Fear is of no interest, Lureen. But sorrow—yes, that's worth analyzing. Desolation. I want to study it. I want to help *them* study it. I think it's what they want to know about. Don't run from me, Lureen. I don't want to hurt you, not that way."

She was small-bodied and not very strong, and unwieldy in her pregnancy. Cassiday seized her gently by both wrists and drew her toward him. Already he could feel the new emotions coming from her, the self-pity behind the terror, and he had not even done anything to her.

How did you abort a fetus two months from term?

A swift kick in the belly might do it. Too crude, too crude. Yet Cassiday had not come armed with abortifacients, a handy ergot pill, a quick-acting spasmic inducer. So he brought his knee up sharply, deploring the crudity of it. Lureen sagged. He kicked her a second time. He remained completely tranquil as he did it, for it would be wrong to take joy in violence. A third kick seemed desirable. Then he released her.

She was still conscious, but she was writhing. Cassiday made himself receptive to the outflow. The child, he realized, was not yet dead within her. Perhaps it might not die at all. But it would certainly be crippled in some way. What he drained from Lureen was the awareness that she might bring forth a defective. The fetus would have to be destroyed. She would have to begin again. It was all quite sad.

"Why?" she muttered, ". . .why?"

* * *

Among the watchers:
the equivalent of dismay.

Somehow it had not developed as the golden ones had anticipated. Even they could miscalculate, it appeared, and they found that a rewarding insight. Still, something had to be done about Cassiday.

They had given him powers. He could detect and transmit to them the raw emotions of others. That was useful to them, for from the data they could perhaps construct an understanding of human beings. But in rendering him a switching center for the emotions of others they had unavoidably been forced to blank out his own. And that was distorting the data.

He was too destructive now, in his joyless way. That had to be corrected. For now he partook too deeply of the nature of the golden ones themselves. *They* might have their sport with Cassiday, for he owed them a life. But he might not have his sport with others.

They reached down the line of communication to him and gave him his instructions.

"No," Cassiday said. "You're done with me now. There's no need for me to come back."

"`Further adjustments are necessary."

"I disagree."

"You will not disagree for long."

Still disagreeing, Cassiday took ship for Mars, unable to stand aside from their command. On Mars he chartered a vessel that regularly made the Saturn run and persuaded it to come in by way of Iapetus. The golden ones took possession of him once he was within their immediate reach.

"What will you do to me?" Cassiday asked.

"Reverse the flow. You will no longer be sensitive to others. You will report to us on your own emotions. We will restore your conscience, Cassiday."

He protested. It was useless.

Within the glowing sphere of golden light they made their adjustments on him. They entered him and altered him and turned his perceptions inward, so that he might feed on his own misery like a vulture tearing at its entrails. That would be informative. Cassiday objected until he no longer had the power to object, and when his awareness returned it was too late to object.

"No. . . " he murmured. In the yellow gleam he saw the faces of Beryl and Mirabel and Lureen. "You shouldn't have done this to me. You're torturing me . . . like you would a fly . . . "

There was no response. They sent him away, back to Earth. They returned him to the travertine towers and the rumbling slidewalks, to the house of pleasure on 485th Street, to the islands of light that blazed in the sky, to the eleven billion people. They turned him loose to go among them, and suffer, and report on his sufferings. And a time would come when they would release him, but not yet.

* * *

HERE IS CASSIDAY:

nailed to his cross.

SUNDANCE

This story was a product of the dark year of 1968, that year of assassinations, riots, political turbulence, and many another ugly event. It was written for Edward L. Ferman, the editor and publisher of that excellent magazine *Fantasy & Science Fiction,* in late September. I was working at a new level of complexity, then—sure of myself and my technique, willing now to push the boundaries of the short-story form in any direction that seemed worth exploring. I had always been interested, from the beginning of my career, in technical experimentation, when and as the restrictions imposed on me by my pulp-magazine editors allowed any. But now I was in my thirties and approaching the height of my powers as a writer. So I did "Sundance" by way of producing a masterpiece in the medieval sense of the word—that is, a piece of work which is intended to demonstrate to a craftsman's peers that he has ended his apprenticeship and has fully mastered the intricacies of his trade.

Apparently I told Ed Ferman something about the story's nature while I was working on it, and he must have reacted with some degree of apprehensiveness, because the letter I sent him on October 22, 1968, accompanying the submitted manuscript, says, "I quite understand your hesitation to commit yourself in advance to a story when you've been warned it's experimental; but it's not all *that* experimental . . . I felt that the only way I could properly convey the turmoil in the protagonist's mind, the gradual dissolution of his hold on reality, was through the constant changing of persons and tenses; but as I read it through I think everything remains clear despite the frequent derailments of the reader." And I added, "I don't mean to say that I intend to disappear over the deep end of experimentalism. I don't regard myself as a member of any 'school' of s-f, and don't value obscurity for its own sake. Each story is a technical challenge unique unto itself, and I have to go where the spirit moves me. Sometimes it moves me to a relatively conventional strong-narrative item . . . and sometimes to a relatively avant-garde item like this present 'Sundance;' I'm just after the best way of telling my story, in each case."

Ferman responded on Nov 19 with: "You should do more of this sort of thing. 'Sundance' . . . not only works; it works beautifully. The ending—with the trapdoor image and that last line—is perfectly consistent, and just fine." He had only one suggestion: that I simplify the story's structure a little, perhaps by eliminating the occasional use of second-person narrative. But I wasn't about to do that. I replied with an explanation of *why* the story kept switching about between first person narrative, second person, third person present tense, and third person past tense. Each mode had its particular narrative significance in conveying the various reality-levels of the story, I told him: the first-person material was the protagonist's interior monologue, progressively more incoherent and untrustworthy; the second-person passages provided objective description of his actions, showing his breakdown from the outside, but not so far outside as third person would be—and so forth. Ferman was convinced, and ran the story as is.

And it became something of a classic almost immediately after Ed ran it in his June 1969 issue. Though it was certainly a kind of circus stunt, it was a stunt that worked, and it attracted widespread attention, including a place on the ballot for the Nebula award the following year. (But I had "Passengers" on the same ballot, and had no wish to compete with myself. Shrewdly, if somewhat cynically, I calculated that the more accessible "Passengers" had a better chance of winning the award, and had "Sundance" removed from the ballot. And that was how I came to win a Nebula with my second-best story of 1969.) "Sundance" has since been reprinted dozens of times, both in science fiction anthologies and in textbooks of literature. Here it is once more, a tale of the collision of humans and aliens, with the customary catastrophic results for everybody concerned.

TODAY YOU LIQUIDATED ABOUT 50,000 Eaters in Sector A, and now you are spending an uneasy night. You and Herndon flew east at dawn, with the green-gold sunrise at your backs, and sprayed the neural pellets over a thousand hectares along the Forked River. You flew on into the prairie beyond the river, where the Eaters have already been wiped out, and had lunch sprawled on that thick, soft carpet of grass where the first settlement is expected to rise. Herndon picked some juiceflowers, and you enjoyed half an hour of mild hallucinations. Then, as you headed toward the copter to begin an afternoon of further pellet spraying, he said suddenly, "Tom, how would you feel about this if it turned out that the Eaters weren't just animal pests? That they were people, say, with a language and rites and a history and all?"

You thought of how it had been for your own people.

"They aren't," you said.

"Suppose they were. Suppose the Eaters—"

"They aren't. Drop it."

Herndon has this streak of cruelty in him that leads him to ask such questions. He goes for the vulnerabilities; it amuses him. All night now his casual remark has echoed in your mind. Suppose the Eaters . . . suppose the Eaters . . . suppose . . . suppose . . .

You sleep for a while, and dream, and in your dreams you swim through rivers of blood.

Foolishness. A feverish fantasy. You know how important it is to exterminate the Eaters fast, before the settlers get here. They're just animals, and not even harmless animals at that; ecology-wreckers is what they are, devourers of oxygen-liberating plants, and they have to go. A few have been saved for zoological study. The rest must be destroyed. Ritual extirpation of undesirable beings, the old, old story. But let's not complicate our job with moral qualms, you tell yourself. Let's not dream of rivers of blood.

The Eaters don't even *have* blood, none that could flow in rivers, anyway. What they have is, well, a kind of lymph that permeates every tissue and transmits nourishment along the interfaces. Waste products go out the same way, osmotically. In terms of process, it's structurally analogous to your own kind of circulatory system, except there's no network of blood vessels hooked to a master pump. The life-stuff just oozes through their bodies as though they were amoebas or sponges or some other low-phylum form. Yet they're definitely high-phylum in nervous system, digestive setup, limb-and-organ template, etc. Odd, you think. The thing about aliens is that they're alien, you tell yourself, not for the first time.

The beauty of their biology for you and your companions is that it lets you exterminate them so neatly.

You fly over the grazing grounds and drop the neural pellets. The Eaters find and ingest them. Within an hour the poison has reached all sectors of the body. Life ceases; a rapid breakdown of cellular matter follows, the Eater literally falling apart molecule by molecule the instant that nutrition is cut off; the lymph-like stuff works like acid; a universal lysis occurs; flesh and even the bones, which are cartilaginous, dissolve. In two hours, a puddle on the ground. In four, nothing at all left. Considering how many millions of Eaters you've scheduled for extermination here, it's sweet of the bodies to be self-disposing. Otherwise what a charnel house this world would become!

Suppose the Eaters . . .

Damn Herndon. You almost feel like getting a memory-editing in the morning. Scrape his stupid speculations out of your head. If you dared. If you dared.

* * *

In the morning he does not dare. Memory-editing frightens him; he will try to shake free of his newfound guilt without it. The Eaters, he explains to himself, are mindless herbivores, the unfortunate victims of human expansionism, but not really deserving of passionate defense. Their extermination is not tragic; it's just too bad. If Earthmen are to have this world, the Eaters must relinquish it. There's a difference, he tells himself, between the elimination of the Plains Indians from the American prairie in the nineteenth-century and the destruction of the bison on that same prairie. One feels a little wistful about the slaughter of the thundering herds; one regrets the butchering of millions of the noble brown woolly beasts, yes. But one feels outrage, not mere wistful regret, at what was done to the Sioux. There's a difference. Reserve your passions for the proper cause.

He walks from his bubble at the edge of the camp toward the center of things. The flagstone path is moist and glistening. The morning fog has not yet lifted, and every tree is bowed, the long, notched leaves heavy with droplets of water. He pauses, crouching, to observe a spider-analog spinning its asymmetrical web. As he watches, a small amphibian, delicately shaded turquoise, glides as inconspicuously as possible over the mossy ground. Not inconspicuously enough; he gently lifts the little creature and puts it on the back of his hand. The gills flutter in anguish, and the amphibian's sides quiver. Slowly, cunningly, its color changes until it matches the coppery tone of the hand. The camouflage is excellent. He lowers his hand and the amphibian scurries into a puddle. He walks on.

He is forty years old, shorter than most of the other members of the expedition, with wide shoulders, a heavy chest, dark glossy hair, a blunt, spreading nose. He is a biologist. This is his third career, for he has failed as an anthropologist and as a developer of real estate. His name is Tom Two Ribbons. He has been married twice but has had no children. His great-grandfather died of alcoholism; his grandfather was addicted to hallucinogens; his father had compulsively visited cheap memory-editing parlors. Tom Two Ribbons is conscious that he is failing a family tradition, but he has not found his own mode of self-destruction.

In the main building he discovers Herndon, Julia, Ellen, Schwartz, Chang, Michaelson, and Nichols. They are eating breakfast; the others are already at work. Ellen rises and comes to him and kisses him.

Her short soft yellow hair tickles his cheeks. “I love you,” she whispers. She has spent the night in Michaelson’s bubble. “I love you,” he tells her, and draws a quick vertical line of affection between her small pale breasts. He winks at Michaelson, who nods, touches the tops of two fingers to his lips, and blows them a kiss. We are all good friends here, Tom Two Ribbons thinks.

“Who drops pellets today?” he asks.

“Mike and Chang,” says Julia. “Sector C.”

Schwartz says, “Eleven more days and we ought to have the whole peninsula clear. Then we can move inland.”

“If our pellet supply holds up,” Chang points out.

Herndon says, “Did you sleep well, Tom?”

“No,” says Tom. He sits down and taps out his breakfast requisition. In the west, the fog is beginning to burn off the mountains. Something throbs in the back of his neck. He has been on this world nine weeks now, and in that time it has undergone its only change of season, shading from dry weather to foggy. The mists will remain for many months. Before the plains parch again, the Eaters will be gone and the settlers will begin to arrive. His food slides down the chute and he seizes it. Ellen sits beside him. She is a little more than half his age; this is her first voyage; she is their keeper of records, but she is also skilled at editing. “You look troubled,” Ellen tells him. “Can I help you?”

“No. Thank you.”

“I hate it when you get gloomy.”

“°It’s a racial trait,” says Tom Two Ribbons.

“I doubt that very much.”

“The truth is that maybe my personality reconstruct is wearing thin. The trauma level was so close to the surface. I’m just a walking veneer, you know.”

Ellen laughs prettily. She wears only a sprayon half-wrap. Her skin looks damp; she and Michaelson have had a swim at dawn. Tom Two Ribbons is thinking of asking her to marry him, when this job is over. He has not been married since the collapse of the real estate business. The therapist suggested divorce as part of the reconstruct. He sometimes wonders where Terry has gone and whom she lives with now. Ellen says, “You seem pretty stable to me, Tom.”

“Thank you,” he says. She is young. She does not know.

“If it’s just a passing gloom I can edit it out in one quick snip.”

“Thank you,” he says. “No.”

“I forgot. You don’t like editing.”

“My father—”

“Yes?”

“In fifty years he pared himself down to a thread,” Tom Two Ribbons says. “He had his ancestors edited away, his whole heritage, his religion, his wife, his sons, finally his name. Then he sat and smiled all day. Thank you, no editing.”

“Where are you working today?” Ellen asks.

“In the compound, running tests.”

“Want company? I’m off all morning.”

“Thank you, no,” he says, too quickly. She looks hurt. He tries to remedy his unintended cruelty by touching her arm lightly and saying, “Maybe this afternoon, all right? I need to commune a while. Yes?”

“Yes,” she says, and smiles, and shapes a kiss with her lips.

After breakfast he goes to the compound. It covers a thousand hectares east of the base; they have bordered it with neutral-field projectors at intervals of eighty meters, and this is a sufficient fence to keep the captive population of two hundred Eaters from straying. When all the others have been exterminated, this study group will remain. At the southwest corner of the compound stands a lab bubble from which the experiments are run: metabolic, psychological, physiological, ecological. A stream crosses the compound diagonally. There is a low ridge of grassy hills at its eastern edge. Five distinct copses of tightly clustered knifeblade trees are separated by patches of dense savanna. Sheltered beneath the glass are the oxygen-plants, almost completely hidden except for the photosynthetic spikes that jut to heights of three or four meters at regular intervals, and the lemon-colored respiratory bodies, chest high, that make the grassland sweet and dizzying with exhaled gases. Through the fields move the Eaters in a straggling herd, nibbling delicately at the respiratory bodies.

Tom Two Ribbons spies the herd beside the stream and goes toward it. He stumbles over an oxygen-plant hidden in the grass but deftly recovers his balance and, seizing the puckered orifice of the respiratory body, inhales deeply. His despair lifts. He approaches the Eaters. They are spherical, bulky, slow-moving creatures, covered by masses of coarse orange fur. Saucer-like eyes protrude above narrow rubbery lips. Their legs are thin and scaly, like a chicken's, and their arms are short and held close to their bodies. They regard him with bland lack of curiosity. "Good morning, brothers!" is the way he greets them this time, and he wonders why.

* * *

I NOTICED SOMETHING STRANGE TODAY. Perhaps I simply sniffed too much oxygen in the fields; maybe I was succumbing to a suggestion Herndon planted; or possibly it's the family masochism cropping out. But while I was observing the Eaters in the compound, it seemed to me, for the first time, that they were behaving intelligently, that they were functioning in a ritualized way.

I followed them around for three hours. During that time they uncovered half a dozen outcroppings of oxygen-plants. In each case they went through a stylized pattern of action before starting to munch. They:

Formed a straggly circle around the plants.
Looked toward the sun.
Looked toward their neighbors on left and right around the circle.
Made fuzzy neighing sounds only after having done the foregoing.
Looked toward the sun again.
Moved in and ate.

If this wasn't a prayer of thanksgiving, a saying of grace, then what was it? And if they're advanced enough spiritually to say grace, are we not therefore committing genocide here? Do chimpanzees say grace? Christ, we wouldn't even wipe out chimps the way we're cleaning out the Eaters! Of course, chimps don't interfere with human crops, and some kind of coexistence would be possible, whereas Eaters and human agriculturalists simply can't function on the same planet. Nevertheless, there's a moral issue here. The liquidation effort is predicated on the assumption that the intelligence level of the Eaters is about on par with that of oysters, or, at best, sheep. Our consciences stay clear because our poison is quick and painless and because the Eaters thoughtfully dissolve upon dying, sparing us the mess of incinerating millions of corpses. But if they pray—

I won't say anything to the others just yet. I want more evidence, hard, objective. Films, tapes, record cubes. Then we'll see. What if I can show that we're exterminating intelligent beings? My family knows a little about genocide, after all, having been on the receiving end just a few centuries back. I doubt that I could halt what's going on here. But at the very least I could withdraw from the operation. Head back to Earth and stir up public outcries.

I hope I'm imagining this.

* * *

I'M NOT IMAGINING A THING. They gather in circles; they look to the sun; they neigh and pray. They're only balls of jelly on chicken-legs, but they give thanks for their food. Those big round eyes now seem to stare accusingly at me. Our tame herd here knows what's going on: that we have descended from the stars to eradicate their kind, and that they alone will be spared. They have no way of fighting back or even of communicating their displeasure, but they *know.* And hate us. Jesus, we have killed two million of them since we got here, and in a metaphorical sense I'm stained with blood, and what will I do, what can I do?

I must move very carefully, or I'll end up drugged and edited.

I can't let myself seem like a crank, a quack, an agitator. I can't stand up and *denounce*! I have to find allies. Herndon, first. He surely is onto the truth; he's the one who nudged me to it, that day we dropped pellets. And I thought he was merely being vicious in his usual way!

I'll talk to him tonight.

* * *

HE SAYS, "I'VE BEEN THINKING about that suggestion you made. About the Eaters. Perhaps we haven't made sufficiently close psychological studies. I mean, if they really *are* intelligent—"

Herndon blinks. He is a tall man with glossy dark hair, a heavy beard, sharp cheekbones. "Who says they are, Tom?"

"You did. On the far side of the Forked River, you said—"

"It was just a speculative hypothesis. To make conversation."

"No, I think it was more than that. You really believed it."

Herndon looks troubled. "Tom, I don't know what you're trying to start, but don't start it. If I for a moment believed we were killing intelligent creatures, I'd run for an editor so fast I'd start an implosion wave."

"Why did you ask me that thing, then?" Tom Two Ribbons says.

"Idle chatter."

"Amusing yourself by kindling guilts in somebody else? You're a bastard, Herndon. I mean it."

"Well, look, Tom, if I had any idea that you'd get so worked up about a hypothetical suggestion—" Herndon shakes his head. "The Eaters aren't intelligent beings. Obviously. Otherwise we wouldn't be under orders to liquidate them."

"Obviously," says Tom Two Ribbons.

* * *

Ellen said, "No, I don't know what Tom's up to. But I'm pretty sure he needs a rest. It's only a year and a half since his personality reconstruct, and he had a pretty bad breakdown back then."

Michaelson consulted a chart. "He's refused three times in a row to make his pellet-dropping run. Claiming he can't take time away from his research. Hell, we can fill in for him, but it's the idea that he's ducking chores that bothers me."

"What kind of research is he doing?" Nichols wanted to know.

"Not biological," said Julia. "He's with the Eaters in the compound all the time, but I don't see him making any tests on them. He just watches them."

"And talks to them," Chang observed.

"And talks, yes," Julia said.

"About what?" Nichols asked.

"Who knows?"

Everyone looked at Ellen. "You're closest to him," Michaelson said. "Can't you bring him out of it?"

"I've got to know what he's in, first," Ellen said. "He isn't saying a thing."

* * *

You know that you must be very careful, for they outnumber you, and their concern for your welfare can be deadly. Already they realize you are disturbed, and Ellen has begun to probe for the source of the disturbance. Last night you lay in her arms and she questioned you, obliquely, skillfully, and you knew what she is trying to find out. When the moons appeared she suggested that you and she stroll in the compound, among the sleeping Eaters. You declined, but she sees that you have become involved with the creatures.

You have done probing of your own—subtly, you hope. And you are aware that you can do nothing to save the Eaters. An irrevocable commitment has been made. It is 1876 all over again; these are the bison, these are the Sioux, and they must be destroyed, for the railroad is on its way. If you speak out here, your friends will calm you and pacify you and edit you, for they do not see what you see. If you return to Earth to agitate, you will be mocked and recommended for another reconstruct. You can do nothing. You can do nothing.

You cannot save, but perhaps you can record.

Go out into the prairie. Live with the Eaters; make yourself their friend; learn their ways. Set it down, a full account of their culture, so that at least that much will not be lost. You know the techniques of field anthropology. As was done for your people in the old days, do now for the Eaters.

* * *

He finds Michaelson. "Can you spare me for a few weeks?" he asks.

"Spare you, Tom? What do you mean?"

"I've got some field studies to do. I'd like to leave the base and work with Eaters in the wild."

"What's wrong with the ones in the compound?"

"It's the last chance with wild ones, Mike. I've got to go."

"Alone, or with Ellen?"

"Alone."

Michaelson nods slowly. "All right, Tom. Whatever you want. Go. I won't hold you here."

* * *

I DANCE IN THE PRAIRIE under the green-gold sun. About me the Eaters gather. I am stripped; sweat makes my skin glisten; my heart pounds. I talk to them with my feet, and they understand.

They understand.

They have a language of soft sounds. They have a god. They know love and awe and rapture. They have rites. They have names. They have a history. Of all this I am convinced.

I dance on thick grass.

How can I reach them? With my feet, with my hands, with my grunts, with my sweat. They gather by the hundreds, by the thousands, and I dance. I must not stop. They cluster about me and make their sounds. I am a conduit for strange forces. My great-grandfather should see me now! Sitting on his porch in Wyoming, the firewater in his hand, his brain rotting—see me now, old one! See the dance of Tom Two Ribbons! I talk to these strange ones with my feet under a sun that is the wrong color. I dance. I dance.

"Listen to me," I say. "I am your friend, I alone, the only one you can trust. Trust me, talk to me, teach me. Let me preserve your ways, for soon the destruction will come."

I dance, and the sun climbs, and the Eaters murmur.

There is the chief. I dance toward him, back, toward, I bow, I point to the sun, I imagine the being that lives in that ball of flame, I imitate the sounds of these people, I kneel, I rise, I dance. Tom Two Ribbons dances for you.

I summon skills my ancestors forgot. I feel the power flowing in me. As they danced in the days of the bison, I dance now, beyond the Forked River.

I dance, and now the Eaters dance too. Slowly, uncertainly, they move toward me, they shift their weight, lift leg and leg, sway about. "Yes, like that!" I cry. "Dance!"

We dance together as the sun reaches noon height.

Now their eyes are no longer accusing. I see warmth and kinship. I am their brother, their redskinned tribesman, he who dances with them. No longer do they seem clumsy to me. There is a strange ponderous grace in their movements. They dance. They dance. They caper about me. Closer, closer, closer!

We move in holy frenzy.

They sing, now, a blurred hymn of joy. They throw forth their arms, unclench their little claws. In unison they shift weight, left foot forward, right, left, right. Dance, brothers, dance, dance, dance! They press against me. Their flesh quivers; their smell is a sweet one. They gently thrust me across the field, to a part of the meadow where the grass is deep and untrampled. Still dancing, we seek for the oxygen-plants, and find clumps of them beneath the grass, and they make their prayer and seize them with their awkward arms, separating the respiratory bodies from the photosynthetic spikes. The plants, in anguish, release floods of oxygen. My mind reels. I laugh and sing. The Eaters are nibbling the lemon-colored perforated globes, nibbling the stalks as well. They thrust their plants at me. It is a religious ceremony, I see. Take from us, eat with us, join with us, this is the body, this is the blood, take, eat, join. I bend forward and put a lemon-colored globe to my lips. I do not bite; I nibble, as they do, my teeth slicing away the skin of the globe. Juice spurts into my mouth while oxygen drenches my nostrils. The Eaters sing hosannas. I should be in full paint for this, paint of my forefathers, feathers too, meeting their religion in the regalia of what should have been mine. Take, eat, join. The juice of the oxygen-plant flows in my veins. I embrace my brothers. I sing, and as my voice leaves my lips it becomes an arch that glistens like new steel, and I pitch my song lower, and the arch turns to tarnished silver. The Eaters crowd close. The scent of their bodies is fiery red to me. Their soft cries are puffs of steam. The sun is very warm; its rays are tiny jagged pings of puckered sound, close to the top of my range of hearing, plink! plink! plink! The thick grass hums to me, deep and rich, and the wind hurls points of flame along the prairie. I devour another oxygen-plant, and then a third. My brothers laugh and shout. They tell me of their gods, the god of warmth, the god of food, the god of pleasure, the god of death, the god of holiness, the god of wrongness, and the others. They recite for me the names of their kings, and I hear their voices as splashes of green mold on the clean sheet of the sky. They instruct me in their holy rites. I must remember this, I tell myself, for when it is gone it will never come again. I continue to dance. They continue to dance. The color of the hills becomes rough and coarse, like abrasive gas. Take, eat, join. Dance. They are so gentle!

I hear the drone of the copter, suddenly.

It hovers far overhead. I am unable to see who flies in it. "No!" I scream. "Not here! Not these people! Listen to me! This is Tom Ribbons! Can't you hear me? I'm doing a field study here! You've no right—!"

My voice makes spirals of blue moss edged with red sparks. They drift upward and are scattered by the breeze.

I yell, I shout, I bellow. I dance and shake my fists. From the wings of the copter the jointed arms of the pellet-distributors unfold. The gleaming spigots extend and whirl. The neural pellets rain down into the meadow, each tracing a blazing track that lingers in the sky. The sound of the copter becomes a furry carpet stretching to the horizon, and my shrill voice is lost in it.

The Eaters drift away from me, seeking the pellets, scratching at the roots of the grass to find them. Still dancing, I leap into their midst, striking the pellets from their hands, hurling them into the stream, crushing them to powder. The Eaters growl black needles at me. They turn away and search for more pellets. The copter turns and flies off, leaving a trail of dense oily sound. My brothers are gobbling the pellets eagerly.

There is no way to prevent it.

Joy consumes them and they topple and lie still. Occasionally a limb twitches; then even this stops. They begin to dissolve. Thousands of them melt on the prairie, sinking into shapelessness, losing spherical forms, flattening, ebbing into the ground. The bonds of the molecules will no longer hold. It is the twilight of protoplasm. They perish. They vanish. For hours I walk the prairie. Now I inhale oxygen; now I eat a lemon-colored globe. Sunset begins with the ringing of leaden chimes. Black clouds make brazen trumpet calls in the east and the deepening wind is a swirl of coaly bristles. Silence comes. Night falls. I dance. I am alone.

* * *

THE COPTER COMES AGAIN, AND they find you, and you do not resist as they gather you in. You are beyond bitterness. Quietly you explain what you have done and what you have learned, and why it is wrong to exterminate these people. You describe the plant you have eaten and the way it affects your senses, and as you talk of the blessed synesthesia, the texture of the wind and the sound of the clouds and the timbre of the sunlight, they nod and smile and tell you not to worry, that everything will be all right soon, and they touch something cold to your forearm, so cold that it is a whir and a buzz and the deintoxicant sinks into your vein and soon the ecstasy drains away, leaving only the exhaustion and the grief.

* * *

HE SAYS, "WE NEVER LEARN a thing, do we? We export all our horrors to the stars. Wipe out the Armenians, wipe out the Jews, wipe out the Tasmanians, wipe out the Indians, wipe out everyone who's in our way, and do the same damned murderous thing. You weren't with me out there. You didn't dance with them. You didn't see what a rich, complex culture the Eaters have. Let me tell you about their tribal structure. It's dense: seven levels of matrimonial relationships, to begin with, and an exogamy factor that requires—"

Softly Ellen says, "Tom, darling, nobody's going to harm the Eaters."

"And the religion," he goes on. "Nine gods, each one an aspect of *the* god. Holiness and wrongness both worshiped. They have hymns, prayers, a theology. And we, the emissaries of the god of wrongness—"

"We're not exterminating them," Michaelson says. "Won't you understand that, Tom? This is all a fantasy of yours. You've been under the influence of drugs, but now we're clearing you out. You'll be clean in a little while. You'll have perspective again."

"A fantasy?" he says bitterly. "A drug dream? I stood out in the prairie and saw you drop pellets. And I watched them die and melt away. I didn't dream that."

"How can we convince you?" Chang asks earnestly. "What will make you believe? Shall we fly over the Eater country with you and show you how many millions there are?"

"But how many millions have been destroyed?" he demands.

They insist that he is wrong. Ellen tells him again that no one has ever desired to harm the Eaters. "This is a scientific expedition, Tom. We're here to *study* them. It's a violation of all we stand for to injure intelligent lifeforms."

"You admit that they're intelligent?"

"Of course. That's never been in doubt."

"Then why drop the pellets?" he asks. "Why slaughter them?"

"None of that has happened, Tom," Ellen says. She takes his hand between her cool palms. "Believe us. Believe us."

He says bitterly, "If you want me to believe you, why don't you do the job properly? Get out the editing machine and go to work on me. You can't simply *talk* me into rejecting the evidence of my own eyes."

"You were under drugs all the time," Michaelson says.

"I've never taken drugs! Except for what I ate in the meadow, when I danced—and that came after I had watched the massacre going on for weeks and weeks. Are you saying that it's a retroactive delusion?"

"No, Tom," Schwartz says. "You've had this delusion all along. It's part of your therapy, your reconstruct. You came here programmed with it."

"Impossible," he says.

Ellen kisses his fevered forehead. "It was done to reconcile you to mankind, you see. You had this terrible resentment of the displacement of your people in the nineteenth century. You were unable to forgive the industrial society for scattering the Sioux, and you were terribly full of hate. Your therapist thought that if you could be made to participate in an imaginary modern extermination, if you could come to see it as a necessary operation, you'd be purged of your resentment and able to take your place in society as—"

He thrusts her away. "Don't talk idiocy! If you knew the first thing about reconstruct therapy, you'd realize that no reputable therapist could be so shallow. There are no one-to-one correlations in reconstructs. No, don't touch me. Keep away. Keep away."

He will not let them persuade him that this is merely a drug-born dream. It is no fantasy, he tells himself, and it is no therapy. He rises. He goes out. They do not follow him. He takes a copter and seeks his brothers.

* * *

The sun is much hotter today. The Eaters are more numerous. Today I wear paint, today I wear feathers. My body shines with my sweat. They dance with me, and they have a frenzy in them that I have never seen before. We pound the trampled meadow with our feet. We clutch for the sun with our hands. We sing, we shout, we cry. We will dance until we fall.

This is no fantasy. These people are real, and they are intelligent, and they are doomed. This I know.

We dance. Despite the doom, we dance.

My great-grandfather comes and dances with us. He too is real. His nose is like a hawk's, not blunt like mine, and he wears the big headdress, and his muscles are like cords under his brown skin. He sings, he shouts, he cries.

Others of my family join us.

We eat the oxygen-plants together. We embrace the Eaters. We know, all of us, what it is to be hunted.

The clouds make music and the wind takes on texture and the sun's warmth has color.

We dance. We dance. Our limbs know no weariness.

The sun grows and fills the whole sky, and I see no Eaters now, only my own people, my father's fathers across the centuries, thousands of gleaming skins, thousands of hawk's noses, and we eat the plants, and we find sharp sticks and thrust them into our flesh, and the sweet blood flows and dries in the blaze of the sun, and we dance, and we dance, and some of us fall from weariness, and we dance, and the prairie is a sea of bobbing headdresses, an ocean of feathers, and we dance, and my heart makes thunder, and my knees become water, and the sun's fire engulfs me, and I dance, and I fall, and I dance, and I fall, and I fall, and I fall.

* * *

Again they find you and bring you back. They give you the cool snout on your arm to take the oxygen-plant drug from your veins, and then they give you something else so you will rest. You rest and you are very calm. Ellen kisses you and you stroke her soft skin, and then the others come in and they talk to you, saying soothing things, but you do not listen, for you are searching for realities. It is not an easy search. It is like falling through many trapdoors, looking for the one room whose floor is not hinged. Everything that has happened on this planet is your therapy, you tell yourself, designed to reconcile an embittered aborigine to the white man's conquest; nothing is really being exterminated here. You reject that and fall through and realize that this must be the therapy of your friends; they carry the weight of accumulated centuries of guilts and have come here to shed that load, and you are here to ease them of their burden, to draw their sins into yourself and give them forgiveness. Again you fall through, and see that the Eaters are mere animals who threaten the ecology and must be removed; the culture you imagined for them is your hallucination, kindled out of old churnings. You try to withdraw your objections to this necessary extermination, but you fall through again and discover that there is no extermination except in your mind, which is troubled and disordered by your obsession with the crime against your ancestors, and you sit up, for you wish to apologize to these friends of yours, these innocent scientists whom you have called murderers. And you fall through.

BRIDE 91

More galactic miscegenation—a theme that had fascinated me as far back as "One-Way Journey" in the mid-1950s—and Frederik Pohl, the editor for whom I wrote it in March 1967, wasn't very happy with it. Fred had begun not to be happy with much of my stuff, as I took advantage of my newly stretched literary range to delve into ever darker places. A couple of months before he had reacted negatively to my novel *To Live Again*, telling me, "Please, Bob, leave this Existentialist despair to Sartre and Philip K. Dick. It bores the readers stiff, and it doesn't do much for this particular editor, either." And when he had read "Bride 91" he grumbled that "80 percent of s-f writers are devoting 80 percent of their time to sex, homosex, intersex, etc. . . . Jesus Christ, Bob, what a waste. The readers think this sort of thing is tedious crap. They're the people who feed us all, so their opinions must be respected. Apart from the fact that in this they are right." He bought the story anyway, and ran it in the September, 1967 of his magazine *If*; but he asked me to get back to my previous modes of storytelling in the future.

I loved and respected Fred Pohl, but I didn't always agree with him, and we were entering a period when he and I didn't seem to agree about anything. I wrote back to say that I couldn't follow what he was saying—that to me "Bride 91" was "a fast, lively, flip story with lots of plot, glittering prose, bright images, etc." And I cited his own masterly little story, "Day Million"—what was that, I said, if not a story about sex? He replied in a genial though unrelenting way, amplifying his feelings about the story and my work of that time in general, and indicating a general hostility to publishing stories that might offend readers unless they were major works of art, which neither he nor I considered "Bride 91" to be.

It was a sign of trouble ahead. My most sympathetic and supportive magazine editor was turning more conservative in his tastes just as I (and a lot of other science fiction writers with me) was taking off in a radical new direction. Looking back on my correspondence with Fred in this time, I feel now that some of the points he was raising (having to do with the carryover of old pulp-magazine habits into my new writing) were more valid than I cared to admit back then, and some (having to do with my choice of themes) weren't. Fred was going through a spell of personal trouble in that period, and how much of that was connected with his increased editorial testiness is hard to say, but there must have been some relationship. We went on arguing for years. Sometimes things got pretty stormy, though we always remained good friends even when we were yelling at each other. (Through the mail, I mean. Fred didn't raise his voice much in person and neither do I.) I went on writing for him, too. He grumbled about some stories, praised others. One of them—the novella version of "Nightwings"—won a Hugo for me in 1969. But I had a pervasive sense, during the final years of our editorial relationship, that he was growing disappointed with what I was writing. Which made it more and more difficult for me to muster the same enthusiasm for submitting stories for him, and I was less upset than I might otherwise have been when Fred decided to resign his editorship of *Galaxy* and *If* in the spring of 1969. It was his successor, Ejler Jakobsson, who over the next few years would serialize in *Galaxy*, virtually consecutively, the novels of the most fertile period I would ever have: *Downward to the Earth* (1969), *Tower of Glass* (1970), *The World Inside* (1970), *A Time of Changes* (1971), and *Dying Inside* (1972). The only other writer I can think of who ever had such a run of serialized novels at one major science fiction magazine was Robert A. Heinlein, who had four of them published in *Astounding*, in the years between 1940 and 1942.

Fred Pohl and I were *still* good friends to the end of his life, 45 years later. There are certain areas where we agreed to disagree, that's all.

It was a standard six-month marriage contract. I signed it, and Landy signed it and we were man and wife, for the time being. The registrar clicked and chuttered and disgorged our license. My friends grinned and slapped me on the back and bellowed congratulations. Five of Landy's sisters giggled and hummed and went through complete spectral changes. We were all very happy.

"Kiss the bride!" cried my friends and her sisters.

Landy slipped into my arms. It was a good fit; she was pliable and slender, and I engulfed her, and the petals of her ingestion-slot fluttered prettily as I pressed my lips against them. We held the pose for maybe half a minute. Give her credit: she didn't flinch. On Landy's world they don't kiss, not with their mouths, at least, and I doubt that she enjoyed the experience much. But by the terms of our marriage contract we were following Terran mores. That has to be decided in advance, in these interworld marriages. And here we kiss the bride; so I kissed the bride. My pal Jim Owens got carried away and scooped up one of Landy's sisters and kissed *her*. She gave him a shove in the chest that knocked him across the chapel. It wasn't her wedding, after all.

The ceremony was over, and we had our cake and hallucinogens, and about midnight someone said, "We ought to give the honeymooners some privacy."

So they all cleared out and Landy and I started our wedding night.

We waited until they were gone. Then we took the back exit from the chapel and got into a transport capsule for two, very snug, Landy's sweet molasses fragrance pungent in my nostrils, her flexible limbs coiled against mine, and I nudged a stud and we went floating down Harriman Channel at three hundred kilometers an hour. The eddy currents weren't bad, and we loved the ride. She kissed me again; she was learning our ways fast. In fifteen minutes we reached our programmed destination and the capsule took a quick left turn, squirted through an access sphincter, and fastened itself to the puckered skin of our hotel. The nose of the capsule produced the desired degree of irritation; the skin parted and we shot into the building. I opened the capsule and helped Landy out, inside our room. Her soft golden eyes were shimmering with merriment and joy. I slapped a privacy seal on the wall-filters.

"I love you," she said in more-or-less English.

"I love you," I told her in her own language.

She pouted at me. "This is a Terran marriage, remember?"

"So it is. So it is. Champagne and caviar?"

"Of course."

I programmed for it, and the snack came rolling out of the storage unit, ice-cold and inviting. I popped the cork and sprinkled lemon juice on the caviar, and we dined. Fish eggs and overripe grape juice, nothing more, I reminded myself.

After that we activated the periscope stack and stared up through a hundred stories of hotel at the stars. There was a lover's moon in the sky that night, and also one of the cartels had strung a row of beady jewels across about twenty degrees of arc, as though purely for our pleasure. We held hands and watched.

After that we dissolved our wedding clothes.

And after that we consummated our marriage.

You don't think I'm going to tell you about *that,* do you? Some things are still sacred, even now. If you want to find out how to make love to a Suvornese, do as I did and marry one. But I'll give you a few hints about what it's like. Anatomically, it's homologous to the process customary on Terra, so far as the relative roles of male and female go. That is, man gives, woman receives, in essence. But there are differences, pretty major ones, in position, texture, sensation, and response. Of course there are. Why marry an alien, otherwise?

I confess I was nervous, although this was my ninety-first wedding night. I had never married a Suvornese before. I hadn't been to bed with one, either, and if you stop to reflect a little on Suvornese ethical practices you'll see what a damn-fool suggestion that was. I had studied a Suvornese marriage manual, but as any adolescent on any world quickly realizes, translating words and tridim prints into passionate action is trickier than it seems, the first time.

Landy was very helpful, though. She knew no more about Terran males than I did about Suvornese females, of course, but she was eager to learn and eager to see that I did all the right things. So we managed excellently well. There's a knack to it. Some men have it, some don't. I do.

We made love a good deal that night, and in the morning we breakfasted on a sun-washed terrace overlooking a turquoise pool of dancing amoeboids, and later in the day we checked out and capsuled down to the spaceport to begin our wedding journey.

"Happy?" I asked my bride.

"Very," she said. "You're my favorite husband already."

"Were any of the others Terrans?"

"No, of course not."

I smiled. A husband likes to know he's been the first.

At the spaceport, Landy signed the manifest as Mrs. Paul Clay, which gave me great pleasure, and I signed beside her, and they scanned us and let us go aboard. The ship personnel beamed at us in delight. A handsome indigo-skinned girl showed us to our cabin and wished us a good trip so amiably that I tried to tip her. I caught her credit-counter as she passed me, and pushed the dial up a notch. She looked aghast and set it right back again. "Tipping's forbidden, sir!"

"Sorry. I got carried away."

"Your wife's so lovely. Is she Honirangi?"

"Suvornese."

"I hope you're very happy together."

We were alone again. I cuddled Landy up against me. Interworld marriages are all the rage nowadays, of course, but I hadn't married Landy merely because it was a fad. I was genuinely attracted to her, and she to me. All over the galaxy people are contracting the weirdest marriages just to say that they've done it—marrying Sthenics, Gruulers, even Hhinamor. Really grotesque couplings. I don't say that the prime purpose of a marriage is sex, or that you necessarily have to marry a member of a species with which a physical relationship is easy to maintain. But there ought to be some kind of warmth in a marriage. How can you feel real love for a Hhinamor wife who is actually seven pale blue reptiles permanently enclosed in an atmosphere? At least Landy was mammalian and humanoid. A Suvornese-Terran mating would of course be infertile, but I am a conventional sort of person at heart and try to avoid committing abominations; I am quite willing to leave the task of continuing the species to those whose job is reproduction, and you can be sure that even if our chromosomes were mutually congruent I would never have brought the disgusting subject up with Landy. Marriage is marriage, reproduction is reproduction, and what does one have to do with the other, anyway?

During the six subjective weeks of our journey, we amused ourselves in various ways aboard the ship. We made love a good deal, of course. We went gravity-swimming and played paddle-polo in the star lounge. We introduced ourselves to other newlywed couples, and to a newlywed super-couple consisting of three Banamons and a pair of Ghinoi.

And also Landy had her teeth transplanted, as a special surprise for me.

Suvornese have teeth, but they are not like Terran teeth, as why should they be? They are elegant little spiny needles mounted on rotating bases, which a Suvornese uses to impale his food while he rasps at it from the rear with his tongue. In terms of Suvornese needs they are quite functional, and in the context of her species Landy's teeth were remarkably attractive, I thought. I didn't want her to change them. But she must have picked up some subtle hint that I found her teeth anti-erotic, or something. Perhaps I was radiating an underlying dislike for that alien dental arrangement of hers even while I was telling myself on the conscious level that they were lovely. So she went to the ship's surgeon and got herself a mouthful of Terran teeth.

I didn't know where she went. She vanished after breakfast, telling me she had something important to attend to. All in ignorance, I donned gills and went for a swim while Landy surrendered her pretty teeth to the surgeon. He cleaned out the sockets and implanted a rooting layer of analogous gum-tissue. He chiseled new receptor sockets in this synthetic implant. He drill-tailored a set of donor teeth to fit, and slipped them into the periodontal membranes, and bonded them with a quick jab of homografting cement. The entire process took less than two hours. When Landy returned to me, the band of colorvariable skin across her forehead was way up toward the violet, indicating considerable emotional disturbance, and I felt a little edgy about it.

She smiled. She drew back the petals of her ingestion-slot. She showed me her new teeth.

"Landy! What the hell—!"

Before I could check myself, I was registering shock and dismay from every pore. And Landy registered dismay at my dismay. Her forehead shot clear past the visible spectrum, bathing me in a lot of ultraviolet that distressed me even though I couldn't see it, and her petals drooped and her eyes glistened and her nostrils clamped together.

"You don't like them?" she asked.

"I didn't expect—you took me by surprise—"

"I did it for you!"

"But I liked your old teeth," I protested.

"No. Not really. You were afraid of them. I know how a Terran kisses. You never kissed me like that. Now I have beautiful teeth. Kiss me, Paul."

She trembled in my arms. I kissed her.

We were having our first emotional crisis. She had done this crazy thing with her teeth purely to please me, and I wasn't pleased, and now she was upset. I did all the things I could to soothe her, short of telling her to go back and get her old teeth again. Somehow that would have made matters worse.

I had a hard time getting used to Landy with Terran choppers in her dainty little mouth. She had received a flawless set, of course, two gleaming ivory rows, but they looked incongruous in her ingestion slot, and I had to fight to keep from reacting negatively every time she opened her mouth. When a man buys an old Gothic cathedral, he doesn't want an architect to trick it up with wiggling bioplast inserts around the spire. And when a man marries a Suvornese, he doesn't want her to turn herself piecemeal into a Terran. Where would it end? Would Landy now decorate herself with a synthetic navel, and have her breasts shifted about, and get the surgeon to make a genital adjustment so that—

Well, she didn't. She wore her Terran teeth for about ten shipboard days, and neither of us took any overt notice of them, and then very quietly she went back to the surgeon and had him give her a set of Suvornese dentals again. It was only money, I told myself. I didn't make any reference to the switch, hoping to treat the episode as a temporary aberration that now was ended. Somehow I got the feeling that Landy still thought she *ought* to have Terran teeth. But we never discussed it, and I was happy to see her looking Suvornese again.

You see how it is, with marriage? Two people try to please one another, and they don't always succeed, and sometimes they even hurt one another in the very attempt to please. That's how it was with Landy and me. But we were mature enough to survive the great tooth crisis. If this had been, say, my tenth or eleventh marriage, it might have been a disaster. One learns how to avoid the pitfalls as one gains experience.

We mingled a good deal with our fellow passengers. If we needed lessons in how not to conduct a marriage, they were easily available. The cabin next to ours was occupied by another mixed couple, which was excuse enough for us to spend some time with them, but very quickly we realized that we didn't relish their company. They were both playing for a bond forfeiture—a very ugly scene, let me tell you.

The woman was Terran—a big, voluptuous sort with orange hair and speckled eyeballs. Her name was Marje. Her new husband was a Lanamorian, a hulking ox of a humanoid with corrugated blue skin, four telescopic arms, and a tripod deal for legs. At first they seemed likable enough, both on the flighty side, interstellar tourists who had been everywhere and done everything and now were settling down for six months of bliss. But very shortly I noticed that they spoke sharply, even cruelly, to one another in front of strangers. They were out to wound.

You know how it is with the six-month marriage contract, don't you? Each party posts a desertion bond. If the other fails to go the route, and walks out before the legal dissolution date, the bond is forfeited. Now, it's not all that hard to stay married for six months, and the bondsmen rarely have to pay off; we are a mature civilization. Such early abuses of the system as conspiring to have one party desert, and then splitting the forfeiture later, have long since become extinct.

But Marje and her Lanamorian mate were both hard up for cash. Each was hot for the forfeiture, and each was working like a demon to outdo the other in obnoxiousness, hoping to break up the marriage fast. When I saw what was going on, I suggested to Landy that we look for friends elsewhere on the ship.

Which led to our second emotional crisis.

As part of their campaign of mutual repulsion, Marje and hubby decided to enliven their marriage with a spot of infidelity. I take a very old-fashioned view of the marriage vow, you understand. I regard myself as bound to love, honor, and obey for six months, with no fooling around on the side; if a man can't stay monogamous through an entire marriage, he ought to get a spine implant. I assumed that Landy felt the same way. I was wrong.

We were in the ship's lounge, the four of us, getting high on direct jolts of fusel oils and stray esters, when Marje made a pass at me. She was not subtle. She deopaqued her clothes, waved yards of bosom in my face, and said, "There's a nice wide bed in our cabin, sweetheart."

"It isn't bedtime," I told her.

"It could be."

"No."

"Be a friend in need, Paulsie. This monster's been crawling all over me for weeks. I want a Terran to love me."

"The ship is full of available Terrans, Marje."

"I want you."

"I'm not available."

"Cut it out! You mean to say you won't do a fellow Terran a little favor?" She stood up, quivering, bare flesh erupting all over the place. In scabrously explicit terms she described her intimacies with the Lanamorian, and begged me to give her an hour of more conventional pleasure. I was steadfast. Perhaps, she suggested, I would tape a simulacrum and send that to her bed? No, not even that, I said.

At length Marje got angry with me for turning her down. I suppose she could be legitimately annoyed at my lack of chivalry, and if I hadn't happened to be married at the moment I would gladly have obliged her, but as it was I couldn't do a thing for her, and she was boiling. She dumped a drink in my face and stalked out of the lounge, and in a few moments the Lanamorian followed her.

I looked at Landy, whom I had carefully avoided during the whole embarrassing colloquy. Her forehead was sagging close to infra-red, which is to say, in effect, that she was almost in tears.

"You don't love me," she said.

"What?"

"If you loved me you'd have gone with her."

"Is that some kind of Suvornese marriage custom?"

"Of course not," she snuffled. "We're married under Terran mores. It's a *Terran* marriage custom."

"What gives you the idea that—"

"Terran men are unfaithful to their wives. I know. I've read about it. Any husband who cares about his wife at all cheats on her now then. But you—"

"You've got things mixed up," I said.

"I *don't*! I *don't*!" And she neared tantrum stage. Gently I tried to tell her that she had been reading too many historical novels, that adultery was very much out of fashion, that by turning Marje down I was demonstrating the solidity of my love for my wife. Landy wouldn't buy it. She got more and more confused and angry, huddling into herself and quivering in misery. I consoled her in all the ways I could imagine. Gradually she became tranquil again, but she stayed moody. I began to see that marrying an alien had its complexities.

Two days later, Marje's husband made a pass at *her.*

I missed the preliminary phases. A swarm of energy globes had encountered the ship, and I was up at the view-wall with most of the other passengers, watching the graceful gyrations of these denizens of hyperspace. Landy was with me at first, but she had seen energy globes so often that they bored her, and so she told me she was going down to the scintillation tank for a while, as long as everyone was up here. I said I'd meet her there later. Eventually I did. There were about a dozen beings in the tank, making sparkling blue tracks through the radiant greenish-gold fluid. I stood by the edge, looking for Landy, but there was no one of her general physique below me.

And then I saw her. She was nude and dripping polychrome fluid, so she must have come from the tank only a few moments before. The hulking Lanamorian was beside her and clearly trying to molest her. He was pawing her in various ways, and Landy's spectrum was showing obvious distress.

But I wasn't needed.

Do you get from this tale an image of Landy as being frail, doll-like, something of porcelain? She was, you know. Scarcely forty kilograms of woman there, not a bone in her body as we understand bone—merely cartilage. And shy, sensitive, easily set aflutter by an unkind word or a misconstrued nuance. Altogether in need of husbandly protection at all times. Yes? No. Sharks, like Suvornese, have only gristle in place of bone, but forty kilograms of shark do not normally require aid in looking after themselves, and neither did Landy. Suvornese are agile, well coordinated, fast-moving, and stronger than they look, as Jim Owens found out at my wedding when he kissed Landy's sister. The Lanamorian found it out, too. Between the time I spied him bothering Landy and the time I reached her side, she had dislocated three of his arms and flipped him on his massive back, where he lay flexing his tripod supports and groaning. Landy, looking sleek and pleased with herself, kissed me.

"What happened?" I asked.

"He made an obscene proposition."

"You really ruined him, Landy."

"He made me terribly angry," she said, although she no longer looked or sounded very angry.

I said, "Wasn't it just the other day that you were telling me I didn't love you because I turned down Marje's obscene proposition? You aren't consistent, Landy. If you think that infidelity is essential to a Terran-mores marriage, you should have given in to him, yes?"

"Terran *husbands* are unfaithful. Terran wives must be chaste. It is known as the double standard."

"The what?"

"The double standard," she repeated, and she began to explain it to me. I listened for a while, then started to laugh at her sweetly innocent words.

"You're cute," I told her.

"You're terrible. What kind of a woman do you think I am? How dare you encourage me to be unfaithful?"

"Landy, I—"

She didn't listen. She stomped away, and we were having our third emotional crisis. Poor Landy was determined to run a Terran-mores marriage in what she considered the proper fashion, and she took bright cerise umbrage when I demurred. For the rest of the week she was cool to me, and even after we had made up, things never seemed quite the same as before. A gulf was widening between us—or rather, the gulf had been there all along, and it was becoming harder for us to pretend it didn't exist.

After six weeks we landed.

Our destination was Thalia, the honeymoon planet. I had spent half a dozen earlier honeymoons there, but Landy had never seen it, so I had signed up for another visit. Thalia, you know, is a good-sized planet, about one and a half earths in mass, density, and gravitation, with a couple of colorful moons that might almost have been designed for lovers, since they're visible day and night. The sky is light green, the vegetation runs heavily to a high-tannin orange-yellow, and the air is as bracing as nutmeg. The place is owned by a cartel that mines prealloyed metals on the dry northern continent, extracts power cores in the eastern lobe of what once was a tropical forest and is now a giant slab of laterite, and, on a half-sized continent in the western ocean, operates a giant resort for newlyweds. It's more or less of a galactic dude ranch; the staff is largely Terran, the clientele comes from all over the cosmos. You can do wonders with an uninhabited habitable planet, if you grab it with the right kind of lease.

Landy and I were still on the chilly side when we left the starship and were catapulted in a grease-flask to our honeymoon cabin. But she warmed immediately to the charm of the environment. We had been placed in a floating monomolecular balloon, anchored a hundred meters above the main house. It was total isolation, as most honeymooners crave. (I know there are exceptions.)

We worked hard at enjoying our stay on Thalia.

We let ourselves be plugged into a pterodactyl kite that took us on a tour of the entire continent. We sipped radon cocktails at a get-together party. We munched algae steaks over a crackling fire. We swam. We hunted. We fished. We made love. We lolled under the friendly sun until my skin grew copper-colored and Landy's turned the color of fine oxblood porcelain, strictly from Kang-hsi. We had a splendid time, despite the spreading network of tensions that were coming to underlie our relationship like an interweave of metallic filaments.

Until the bronco got loose, everything went well.

It wasn't exactly a bronco. It was a Vesilian quadruped of vast size, blue with orange stripes, a thick murderous tail, a fierce set of teeth—two tons, more or less, of vicious wild animal. They kept it in a corral back of one of the proton wells, and from time to time members of the staff dressed up as cowpokes and staged impromptu rodeos for the guests. It was impossible to break the beast, and no one had stayed aboard it for more than about ten seconds. There had been fatalities, and at least one hand had been mashed so badly that he couldn't be returned to life; they simply didn't have enough tissue to put into the centrifuge.

Landy was fascinated by the animal. Don't ask me why. She hauled me to the corral whenever an exhibition was announced, and stood in rapture while the cowpokes were whirled around. She was right beside the fence the day the beast threw a rider, kicked over the traces, ripped free of its handlers, and headed for the wide open spaces.

"Kill it!" people began to scream.

But no one was armed except the cowpokes, and they were in varying stages of disarray and destruction that left them incapable of doing anything useful. The quadruped cleared the corral in a nicely timed leap, paused to kick over a sapling, bounded a couple of dozen meters and halted, pawing the ground and wondering what to do next. It looked hungry. It looked mean.

Confronting it were some fifty young husbands who, if they wanted a chance to show their brides what great heroes they were, had the opportunity of a lifetime. They merely had to grab a sizzler from one of the fallen hands and drill the creature before it chewed up the whole hotel.

There were no candidates for heroism. All the husbands ran. Some of them grabbed their wives; most did not. I was planning to run, too, but I'll say this in my favor: I intended to take care of Landy. I looked around for her, failed for a moment to find her, and then observed her in the vicinity of the snorting beast. She seized a rope dangling from its haunches and pulled herself up, planting herself behind its mane. The beast reared and stamped. Landy clung, looking like a child on that massive back. She slid forward. She touched her ingestion slot to the animal's skin. I visualized dozens of tiny needles brushing across that impervious hide.

The animal neighed, more or less, relaxed, and meekly trotted back to the corral. Landy persuaded it to jump over the fence. A moment later the startled cowhands, those who were able to function, tethered the thing securely. Landy descended.

"When I was a child I rode such an animal every day," she explained gravely to me. "I know how to handle them. They are less fierce than they look. And, oh, it was so good to be on one again!"

"Landy," I said.

"You look angry."

"Landy, that was a crazy thing to do. You could have been killed!"

"Oh, no, not a chance." Her spectrum began to flicker toward the extremes, though. "There was no risk. It's lucky I had my real teeth, though, or—"

I was close to collapse, a delayed reaction. *"Don't ever do a thing like that again, Landy."*

Softly she said, "Why are you so angry? Oh, yes, I know. Among Terrans, the wife does not do such things. It was the man's role I played, yes? Forgive me? Forgive me?"

I forgave her. But it took three hours of steady talking to work out all the complex moral problems of the situation. We ended up by agreeing that if the same thing ever happened again, Landy would let *me* soothe the beast. Even if it killed me, I was going to be a proper Terran husband, and she a proper Terran bride.

It didn't kill me. I lived through the honeymoon, and happily ever after. The six months elapsed, our posted bonds were redeemed, and our marriage was automatically terminated. Then, the instant we were single again, Landy turned to me and sweetly uttered the most shocking proposal I have ever heard a woman propose.

"Marry me again," she said. "Right now!"

We do not do such things. Six-month liaisons are of their very nature transient, and when they end, they end. I loved Landy dearly, but I was shaken by what she had suggested. However, she explained what she had in mind, and I listened with growing sympathy, and in the end we went before the registrar and executed a new six-month contract.

But this time we agreed to abide by Suvornese and not Terran mores. So the two marriages aren't really consecutive in spirit, though they are in elapsed time. And Suvornese marriage is very different from marriage Terran style.

How?

I'll know more about that a few months from now. Landy and I leave for Suvorna tomorrow. I have had my teeth fixed to please her, and it's quite strange walking around with a mouthful of tiny needles, but I imagine I'll adapt. One has to put up with little inconveniences in the give-and-take of marriage. Landy's five sisters are returning to their native world with us. Eleven more sisters are there already. Under Suvornese custom I'm married to all seventeen of them at once, regardless of any other affiliations they may have contracted. Suvornese find monogamy rather odd and even a little wicked, though Landy tolerated it for six months for my sake. Now it's her turn; we'll do things her way.

So Bride Ninety-one is also Bride Ninety-two for me, and there'll be seventeen of her all at once, dainty, molasses-flavored, golden-eyed, and sleek. I'm in no position right now to predict what this marriage is going to be like.

But I think it'll be worth the bother of wearing Suvornese teeth for a while, don't you?

SOMETHING WILD IS LOOSE

By the late months of 1969, I had shaken off most of the fatigue that the various stresses of the fire that had wrecked my house in New York City in February 1968 had caused, and was hitting my full stride as a writer—pouring forth novel after novel, *Downward to the Earth* and *Tower of Glass* and *Son of Man* all in 1969, *The World Inside* and *A Time of Changes* and *The Second Trip* in 1970 (along with a huge non-fiction work exploring the origins of the Prester John myth). My production of short stories diminished drastically as I concentrated on these demanding books.

But I could be cajoled to do one occasionally. My friend Ben Bova had joined the swiftly growing roster of original-anthology editors with a book that was to be called *The Many Worlds of Science Fiction*, and he insisted that my presence on the contents page was obligatory. Well, so be it: in the final weeks of 1969, just after coming up out of the psychedelic frenzies of *Son of Man*, I wrote the relatively conservative (for that era) "Something Wild is Loose" for Ben's anthology. The *Something Wild* of the title is an alien being, and the story, though it is built around one of science fiction's great formulaic situations, refuses to follow the formula. I've been waiting for half a century for someone to make a movie out of it, but perhaps that's why.

The Vsiir got aboard the Earthbound ship by accident. It had absolutely no plans for taking a holiday on a wet, grimy planet like Earth. But it was in its metamorphic phase, undergoing the period of undisciplined change that began as winter came on, and it had shifted so far up-spectrum that Earthborn eyes couldn't see it. Oh, a really skilled observer might notice a slippery little purple flicker once in a while, a kind of snore, as the Vsiir momentarily dropped down out of the ultraviolet; but he'd have to know where to look, and when. The crewman who was responsible for putting the Vsiir on the ship never even considered the possibility that there might be something invisible sleeping atop one of the crates of cargo being hoisted into the ship's hold. He simply went down the row, slapping a floater-node on each crate and sending it gliding up the gravity wall toward the open hatch. The fifth crate to go inside was the one on which the Vsiir had decided to take its nap. The spaceman didn't know that he had inadvertently given an alien organism a free ride to Earth. The Vsiir didn't know it, either, until the hatch was scaled and an oxygen-nitrogen atmosphere began to hiss from the vents. The Vsiir did not happen to breathe those gases, but, because it was in its time of metamorphosis, it was able to adapt itself quickly and nicely to the sour, prickly vapors seeping into its metabolic cells. The next step was to fashion a set of full-spectrum scanners and learn something about its surroundings. Within a few minutes, the Vsiir was aware—

—that it was in a large, dark place that held a great many boxes containing various mineral and vegetable products of its world, mainly branches of the greenfire tree but also some other things of no comprehensible value to a Vsiir—

—that a double wall of curved metal enclosed this place—

—that just beyond this wall was a null-atmosphere zone, such as is found between one planet and another—

—that this entire closed system was undergoing acceleration—

—that this therefore was a spaceship, heading rapidly away from the world of Vsiirs and in fact already some ten planetary diameters distant, with the gap growing alarmingly moment by moment—

—that it would be impossible, even for a Vsiir in metamorphosis, to escape from the spaceship at this point—

—and that, unless it could persuade the crew of the ship to halt and go back, it would be compelled to undertake a long and dreary voyage to a strange and probably loathsome world, where life would at best be highly inconvenient, and might present great dangers. It would find itself cut off painfully from the rhythm of its own civilization. It would miss the Festival of Changing. It would miss the Holy Eclipse. It would not be able to take part in next spring's Rising of the Sea. It would suffer in a thousand ways.

There were six human beings aboard the ship. Extending its perceptors, the Vsiir tried to reach their minds. Though humans had been coming to its planet for many years, it had never bothered making contact with them before; but it had never been in this much trouble before, either. It sent a foggy tendril of thought, roving the corridors, looking for traces of human intelligence. Here? A glow of electrical activity within a sphere of bone: a mind, a mind! A busy mind. But surrounded by a wall, apparently; the Vsiir rammed up against it and was thrust back. That was startling and disturbing. What kind of beings were these, whose minds were closed to ordinary contact? The Vsiir went on, hunting through the ship. Another mind: again closed. Another. Another. The Vsiir felt panic rising. Its mantle fluttered; its energy radiations dropped far down into the visible spectrum, then shot nervously toward much shorter waves. Even its physical form experienced a series of quick involuntary metamorphoses, to the Vsiir's intense embarrassment. It did not get control of its body until it had passed from spherical to cubical to chaotic, and had become a gridwork of fibrous threads held together only by a pulsing strand of ego. Fiercely it forced itself back to the spherical form and resumed its search of the ship, dismally realizing that by this time its native world was half a stellar unit away. It was without hope now, but it continued to probe the minds of the crew, if only for the sake of thoroughness. Even if it made contact, though, how could it communicate the nature of its plight, and even if it communicated, why would the humans be disposed to help it? Yet it went on through the ship. And—

Here: an open mind. No wall at all. A miracle! The Vsiir rushed into close contact, overcome with joy and surprise, pouring out its predicament. *Please listen. Unfortunate nonhuman organism accidentally transported into this vessel during loading of cargo. Metabolically and psychologically unsuited for prolonged life on Earth. Begs pardon for inconvenience, wishes prompt return to home planet recently left, regrets disturbance in shipping schedule but hopes that this large favor will not prove impossible to grant. Do you comprehend my sending? Unfortunate nonhuman organism accidentally transported—*

* * *

LIEUTENANT FALKIRK HAD DRAWN THE first sleep-shift after floatoff. It was only fair; Falkirk had knocked himself out processing the cargo during the loading stage, slapping the floater-nodes on every crate and feeding the transit manifests to the computer. Now that the ship was spaceborne he could grab some rest while the other crewmen were handling the floatoff chores. So he settled down for six hours in the cradle as soon as they were on their way. Below him, the ship's six gravity-drinkers spun on their axes, gobbling inertia and pushing up the acceleration, and the ship floated Earthward at a velocity that would reach the galactic level before Falkirk woke. He drifted into drowsiness. A good trip: enough greenfire bark in the hold to see Earth through a dozen fits of the molecule plague, and plenty of other potential medicinals besides, along with a load of interesting mineral samples, and—Falkirk slept. For half an hour he enjoyed sweet slumber, his mind disengaged, his body loose.

Until a dark dream bubbled through his skull.

Deep purple sunlight, hot and somber. Something slippery tickling the edges of his brain. He lies on a broad white slab in a scorched desert. Unable to move. Getting harder to breathe. The gravity—a terrible pull, bending and breaking him, ripping his bones apart. Hooded figures moving around him, pointing, laughing, exchanging blurred comments in an unknown language. His skin melting and taking on a new texture: porcupine quills sprouting inside his flesh and forcing their way upward, poking out through every pore. Points of fire all over him. A thin scarlet hand, withered fingers like crab claws, hovering in front of his face. Scratching. Scratching. Scratching. His blood running among the quills, thick and sluggish. He shivers, struggling to sit up—lifts a hand, leaving pieces of quivering flesh stuck to the slab—sits up—

Wakes, trembling, screaming.

Falkirk's shout still sounded in his own ears as his eyes adjusted to the light. Lieutenant Commander Rodriguez was holding his shoulders and shaking him.

"You all right?"

Falkirk tried to reply. Words wouldn't come. Hallucinatory shock, he realized, as part of his mind attempted to convince the other part that the dream was over. He was trained to handle crises; he ran through a quick disciplinary countdown and calmed himself, though he was still badly shaken. "Nightmare," he said hoarsely. "A beauty. Never had a dream with that kind of intensity before."

Rodriguez relaxed. Obviously he couldn't get very upset over a mere nightmare. "You want a pill?"

Falkirk shook his head. "I'll manage, thanks."

But the impact of the dream lingered. It was more than an hour before he got back to sleep, and then he fell into a light, restless doze, as if his mind were on guard against a return of those chilling fantasies. Fifty minutes before his programmed wake-up time, he was awakened by a ghastly shriek from the far side of the cabin.

Lieutenant Commander Rodriguez was having a nightmare.

* * *

When the ship made floatdown on Earth a month later it was, of course, put through the usual decontamination procedures before anyone or anything aboard it was allowed out of the starport. The outer hull got squirted with sealants designed to trap and smother any microorganism that might have hitchhiked from another world; the crewmen emerged through the safety pouch and went straight into a quarantine chamber without being exposed to the air; the ship's atmosphere was cycled into withdrawal chambers, where it underwent a thorough purification, and the entire interior of the vessel received a six-phase sterilization, beginning with fifteen minutes of hard vacuum and ending with an hour of neutron bombardment.

These procedures caused a certain degree of inconvenience for the Vsiir. It was already at the low end of its energy phase, due mainly to the repeated discouragements it had suffered in its attempts to communicate with the six humans. Now it was forced to adapt to a variety of unpleasant environments with no chance to rest between changes. Even the most adaptable of organisms can get tired. By the time the starport's decontamination team was ready to certify that the ship was wholly free of alien life-forms, the Vsiir was very, very tired indeed.

The oxygen-nitrogen atmosphere entered the hold once more. The Vsiir found it quite welcome, at least in contrast to all that had just been thrown at it. The hatch was open; stevedores were muscling the cargo crates into position to be floated across the field to the handling dome. The Vsiir took advantage of this moment to extrude some legs and scramble out of the ship. It found itself on a broad concrete apron, rimmed by massive buildings. A yellow sun was shining in a blue sky; infrared was bouncing all over the place, but the Vsiir speedily made arrangements to deflect the excess. It also compensated immediately for the tinge of ugly hydrocarbons in the atmosphere, for the frightening noise level, and for the leaden feeling of homesickness that suddenly threatened its organic stability at the first sight of this unfamiliar, disheartening world. How to get home again? How to make contact, even? The Vsiir sensed nothing but closed minds—sealed like seeds in their shells. True, from time to time the minds of these humans opened, but even then they seemed unwilling to let the Vsiir's message get through.

Perhaps it would be different here. Perhaps those six were poor communicators, for some reason, and there would be more receptive minds available in this place. Perhaps. Perhaps. Close to despair, the Vsiir hurried across the field and slipped into the first building in which it sensed open minds. There were hundreds of humans in it, occupying many levels, and the open minds were widely scattered. The Vsiir located the nearest one and, worriedly, earnestly, hopefully, touched the tip of its mind to the human's. *Please listen, I mean no harm. Am nonhuman organism arrived on your planet through unhappy circumstances, wishing only quick going back to own world.*

* * *

THE CARDIAC WING OF LONG Island Starport Hospital was on the ground floor, in the rear, where the patients could be given floater therapy without upsetting the gravitational ratios of the rest of the building. As always, the hospital was full—people were always coming in sick off starliners, and most of them were hospitalized right at the starport for their own safety—and the cardiac wing had more than its share. At the moment it held a dozen infarcts awaiting implant, nine postimplant recupes, five coronaries in emergency stasis, three ventricle-regrowth projects, an aortal patch job, and nine or ten assorted other cases. Most of the patients were floating, to keep down the gravitational strain on their damaged tissues—all but the regrowth people, who were under full Earthnorm gravity so that their new hearts would come in with the proper resilience and toughness. The hospital had a fine reputation and one of the lowest mortality rates in the hemisphere.

Losing two patients the same morning was a shock to the entire staff.

At 0917 the monitor flashed the red light for Mrs. Maldonado, 87, postimplant and thus far doing fine. She had developed acute endocarditis coming back from a tour of the Jupiter system; at her age there wasn't enough vitality to sustain her through the slow business of growing a new heart with a genetic prod, but they'd given her a synthetic implant and for two weeks it had worked quite well. Suddenly, though, the hospital's control center was getting a load of grim telemetry from Mrs. Maldonado's bed: valve action zero, blood pressure zero, respiration zero, pulse zero, everything zero, zero, zero. The EEG tape showed a violent lurch—as though she had received some abrupt and intense shock—followed by a minute or two of irregular action, followed by termination of brain activity. Long before any hospital personnel had reached her bedside, automatic revival equipment, both chemical and electrical, had gone to work on the patient, but she was beyond reach: a massive cerebral hemorrhage, coming totally without warning, had done irreversible damage.

At 0928 came the second loss: Mr. Guinness, 51, three days past surgery for a coronary embolism. The same series of events. A severe jolt to the nervous system, an immediate and fatal physiological response. Resuscitation procedures negative. No one on the staff had any plausible explanation for Mr. Guinness' death. Like Mrs. Maldonado, he had been sleeping peacefully, all vital signs good, until the moment of the fatal seizure.

"As though someone had come up and yelled *boo* in their ears," one doctor muttered, puzzling over the charts. He pointed to the wild EEG track. "Or as if they'd had unbearably vivid nightmares and couldn't take the sensory overload. But no one was making noise in the ward. And nightmares aren't contagious."

* * *

Dr. Peter Mookherji, resident in neuropathology, was beginning his morning rounds on the hospital's sixth level when the soft voice of his annunciator, taped behind his left ear, asked him to report to the quarantine building immediately. Dr. Mookherji scowled. "Can't it wait? This is my busiest time of day, and—"

"You are asked to come at once."

"Look, I've got a girl in a coma here, due for her teletherapy session in fifteen minutes, and she's counting on seeing me. I'm her only link to the world. If I'm not there when—"

"You are asked to come at once, Dr. Mookherji."

"Why do the quarantine people need a neuropathologist in such a hurry? Let me take care of the girl, at least, and in forty-five minutes they can have me."

"Dr. Mookherji—"

It didn't pay to argue with a machine. Mookherji forced his temper down. Short tempers ran in his family, along with a fondness for torrid curries and a talent for telepathy. Glowering, he grabbed a data terminal, identified himself, and told the hospital's control center to reprogram his entire morning schedule. "Build in a half-hour postponement somehow," he snapped. "I can't help it—see for yourself. I've been requisitioned by the quarantine staff." The computer was thoughtful enough to have a rollerbuggy waiting for him when he emerged from the hospital. It whisked him across the starport to the quarantine building in three minutes, but he was still angry when he got there. The scanner at the door ticked off his badge and one of the control center's innumerable voice-outputs told him solemnly, "You are expected in Room 403, Dr. Mookherji."

Room 403 turned out to be a two-sector interrogation office. The rear sector of the room was part of the building's central quarantine core, and the front sector belonged to the public-access part of the building, with a thick glass wall in between. Six haggard-looking spacemen were slouched on sofas behind the wall, and three members of the starport's quarantine staff paced about in the front. Mookherji's irritation ebbed when he saw that one of the quarantine men was an old medical-school friend, Lee Nakadai. The slender Japanese was a year older than Mookherji—29 to 28; they met for lunch occasionally at the starport commissary, and they had double-dated a pair of Filipina twins earlier in the year, but the pressure of work had kept them apart for months. Nakadai got down to business quickly now: "Pete, have you ever heard of an epidemic of nightmares?"

"Eh?"

Indicating the men behind the quarantine wall, Nakadai said, "These fellows came in a couple of hours ago from Norton's Star. Brought back a cargo of greenfire bark. Physically they check out to five decimal places, and I'd release them except for one funny thing. They're all in a bad state of nervous exhaustion, which they say is the result of having had practically no sleep during their whole month-long return trip. And the reason for that is that they were having nightmares—every one of them—real mind-wrecking dreams, whenever they tried to sleep. It sounded so peculiar that I thought we'd better run a neuropath checkup, in case they've picked up some kind of cerebral infection."

Mookherji frowned. "For this you get me out of my ward on emergency requisition, Lee?"

"Talk to them," Nakadai said. "Maybe it'll scare you a little."

Mookherji glanced at the spacemen. "All right," he said. "What about these nightmares?"

A tall, bony-looking officer who introduced himself as Lieutenant Falkirk said, "I was the first victim—right after floatoff. I almost flipped. It was like, well, something touching my mind, filling it with weird thoughts. And everything absolutely real while it was going on—I thought I was choking, I thought my body was changing into something alien, I felt my blood running out my pores—" Falkirk shrugged. "Like any sort of bad dream, I guess, only ten times as vivid. Fifty times. A few hours later Lieutenant Commander Rodriguez had the same kind of dream. Different images, same effect. And then, one by one, as the others took their sleep-shifts, they started to wake up screaming. Two of us ended up spending three weeks on happy-pills. We're pretty stable men, doctor—we're trained to take almost anything. But I think a civilian would have cracked up for good with dreams like those. Not so much the images as the intensity, the realness of them."

"And these dreams recurred, throughout the voyage?" Mookherji asked.

"Every shift. It got so we were afraid to doze off, because we knew the devils would start crawling through our heads when we did. Or we'd put ourselves real down on sleeper-tabs. And even so we'd have the dreams, with our minds doped to a level where you wouldn't imagine dreams would happen. A plague of nightmares, doctor. An epidemic."

"When was the last episode?"

'The final sleep-shift before floatdown."

"You haven't gone to sleep, any of you, since leaving ship?"

'No," Falkirk said.

One of the other spacemen said, "Maybe he didn't make it clear to you, doctor. These were killer dreams. They were mind-crackers. We were lucky to get home sane. If we did."

Mookherji drummed his fingertips together, rummaging through his experience for some parallel case. He couldn't find any. He knew of mass hallucinations, plenty of them, episodes in which whole mobs had persuaded themselves they had seen gods, demons, miracles, the dead walking, fiery symbols in the sky. But a series of hallucinations coming in sequence, shift after shift, to an entire crew of tough, pragmatic spacemen? It didn't make sense.

Nakadai said, "Pete, the men had a guess about what might have done it to them. Just a wild idea, but maybe—"

"What is it?"

Falkirk laughed uneasily. "Actually, it's pretty fantastic, doctor."

"Go ahead."

"Well, that something from the planet came aboard the ship with us. Something, well, telepathic. Which fiddled around with our minds whenever we went to sleep. What we felt as nightmares was maybe this thing inside our heads."

"Possibly it rode all the way back to Earth with us," another spaceman said. "It could still be aboard the ship. Or loose in the city by now."

"The Invisible Nightmare Menace?" Mookherji said, with a faint smile. "I doubt that I can buy that."

"There *are* telepathic creatures," Falkirk pointed out.

"I know," Mookherji said sharply. "I happen to be one myself."

"I'm sorry, doctor, if—"

"But that doesn't lead me to look for telepaths under every bush. I'm not ruling out your alien menace, mind you. But I think it's a lot more likely that you picked up some kind of inflammation of the brain out there. A virus disease, a type of encephalitis that shows itself in the form of chronic hallucinations." The spacemen looked troubled. Obviously they would rather be victims of an unknown monster preying on them from outside than of an unknown virus lodged in their brains. Mookherji went on, "I'm not saying that's what it is, either. I'm just tossing around hypotheses. We'll know more after we've run some tests." Checking his watch, he said to Nakadai, "Lee, there's not much more I can find out right now, and I've got to get back to my patients. I want these fellows plugged in for the full series of neuropsychological checkouts. Have the outputs relayed to my office as they come in. Run the tests in staggered series and start letting the men go to sleep, two at a time, after each series—I'll send over a technician to help you rig the telemetry. I want to be notified immediately if there's any nightmare experience."

"Right."

"And get them to sign telepathy releases. I'll give them a preliminary mind-probe this evening after I've had a chance to study the clinical findings. Maintain absolute quarantine, of course. This thing might just be infectious. Play it very safe."

Nakadai nodded. Mookherji flashed a professional smile at the six somber spacemen and went out, brooding. A nightmare virus? Or a mind-meddling alien organism that no one can see? He wasn't sure which notion he liked less. Probably, though, there was some prosaic and unstartling explanation for that month of bad dreams—contaminated food supplies, or something funny in the atmosphere recycler. A simple, mundane explanation.

Probably.

* * *

THE FIRST TIME IT HAPPENED, the Vsiir was not sure what had actually taken place. It had touched a human mind; there had been an immediate vehement reaction; the Vsiir had pulled back, alarmed by the surging fury of the response, and then, a moment later, had been unable to locate the mind at all. Possibly it was some defense mechanism, the Vsiir thought, by which the humans guarded their minds against intruders. But that seemed unlikely since the humans' minds were quite effectively guarded most of the time anyway. Aboard the ship, whenever the Vsiir had managed to slip past the walls that shielded the minds of the crewmen, it had always encountered a great deal of turbulence—plainly these humans did not enjoy mental contact with a Vsiir—but never this complete shutdown, this total cutoff of signal. Puzzled, the Vsiir tried again, reaching toward an open mind situated not far from where the one that had vanished had been. *Kindly attention, a moment of consideration for confused other-worldly individual, victim of unhappy circumstances, who—*

Again the violent response: a sudden tremendous flare of mental energy, a churning blaze of fear and pain and shock. And again, moments later, complete silence, as though the human had retreated behind an impermeable barrier. *Where are you? Where did you go?* The Vsiir, troubled, took the risk of creating an optical receptor that worked in the visible spectrum—and that therefore would itself be visible to humans—and surveyed the scene. It saw a human on a bed, completely surrounded by intricate machinery. Colored lights were flashing. Other humans, looking agitated, were rushing toward the bed. The human on the bed lay quite still, not even moving when a metal arm descended and jabbed a long bright needle into his chest.

Suddenly the Vsiir understood.

The two humans must have experienced termination of existence!

Hastily the Vsiir dissolved its visible-spectrum receptor and retreated to a sheltered corner to consider what had happened. *Datum:* two humans had died. *Datum:* each had undergone termination immediately after receiving a mental transmission from the Vsiir. *Problem:* had the mental transmission brought about the terminations?

The possibility that the Vsiir might have destroyed two lives was shocking and appalling, and such a chill went through its body that it shrank into a tight, hard ball, with all thought-processes snarled. It needed several minutes to return to a fully functional state. If its attempts at communicating with these humans produced such terrible effects, the Vsiir realized, then its prospects of finding help on this planet were slim. How could it dare risk trying to contact other humans, if—

A comforting thought surfaced. The Vsiir realized that it was jumping to a hasty conclusion on the basis of sketchy evidence, while overlooking some powerful arguments against that conclusion. All during the voyage to this world the Vsiir had been making contact with humans, the six crewmen, and none of them had terminated. That was ample evidence that humans could withstand contact with a Vsiir mind. Therefore contact alone could not have caused these two deaths.

Possibly it was only coincidental that the Vsiir had approached two humans in succession that were on the verge of termination. Was this the place where humans were brought when their time of termination was near? Would the terminations have happened even if the Vsiir had not tried to make contact? Was the attempt at contact just enough of a drain on dwindling energies to push the two over the edge into termination? The Vsiir did not know. It was uncomfortably conscious of how many important facts it lacked. Only one thing was certain: its time was running short. If it did not find help soon, metabolic decay was going to set in, followed by metamorphic rigidity, followed by a fatal loss in adaptability, followed by . . . termination.

The Vsiir had no choice. Continuing its quest for contact with a human was its only hope of survival. Cautiously, timidly, the Vsiir again began to send out its probes, looking for a properly receptive mind. This one was walled. So was this. And all these: no entrance, no entrance! The Vsiir wondered if the barriers these humans possessed were designed merely to keep out intruding nonhuman consciousnesses, or actually shielded each human against mental contact of all kinds, including contact with other humans. If any human-to-human contact existed, the Vsiir had not detected it, either in this building or aboard the spaceship. What a strange race!

Perhaps it would be best to try a different level of this building. The Vsiir flowed easily under a closed door and up a service staircase to a higher floor. Once more it sent forth its probes. A closed mind here. And here. And here. And then a receptive one. The Vsiir prepared to send its message. For safety's sake it stepped down the power of its transmission, letting a mere wisp of thought curl forth. *Do you hear? Stranded extraterrestrial being is calling. Seeks aid. Wishes—*

From the human came a sharp, stinging displeasure-response, wordless but unmistakably hostile. The Vsiir at once withdrew. It waited, terrified, fearing that it had caused another termination. No: the human mind continued to function, although it was no longer open, but now surrounded by the sort of barrier humans normally wore. Drooping, dejected, the Vsiir crept away. Failure, again. Not even a moment of meaningful mind-to-mind contact. Was there no way to reach these people? Dismally, the Vsiir resumed its search for a receptive mind. What else could it do?

* * *

THE VISIT TO THE QUARANTINE building had taken forty minutes out of Dr. Mookherji's morning schedule. That bothered him. He couldn't blame the quarantine people for getting upset over the six spacemen's tale of chronic hallucinations, but he didn't think the situation, mysterious as it was, was grave enough to warrant calling him in on an emergency basis. Whatever was troubling the spacemen would eventually come to light; meanwhile they were safely isolated from the rest of the starport. Nakadai should have run more tests before asking him. And he resented having to steal time from his patients.

But as he began his belated morning rounds, Mookherji calmed himself with a deliberate effort: it wouldn't do him or his patients any good if he visited them while still loaded with tensions and irritations. He was supposed to be a healer, not a spreader of anxieties. He spent a moment going through a de-escalation routine, and by the time he entered the first patient's room—that of Satina Ransom—he was convincingly relaxed and amiable.

Satina lay on her left side, eyes closed, a slender girl of sixteen with a fragile-looking face and long, soft straw-colored hair. A spidery network of monitoring systems surrounded her. She had been unconscious for fourteen months, twelve of them here in the starport's neuropathology ward and the last six under Mookherji's care, As a holiday treat, her parents had taken her to one of the resorts on Titan during the best season for viewing Saturn's rings; with great difficulty they succeeded in booking reservations at Galileo Dome, and were there on the grim day when a violent Titanquake ruptured the dome and exposed a thousand tourists to the icy moon's poisonous methane atmosphere. Satina was one of the lucky ones: she got no more than a couple of whiffs of the stuff before a dome guide with whom she'd been talking managed to slap a breathing mask over her face. She survived. Her mother, father, and young brother didn't. But she had never regained consciousness after collapsing at the moment of the disaster. Months of examination on Earth had shown that her brief methane inhalation hadn't caused any major brain damage; organically there seemed to be nothing wrong with her, but she refused to wake up. A shock reaction, Mookherji believed: she would rather go on dreaming forever than return to the living nightmare that consciousness had become. He had been able to reach her mind telepathically, but so far he had been unable to cleanse her of the trauma of that catastrophe and bring her back to the waking world.

Now he prepared to make contact. There was nothing easy or automatic about his telepathy; "reading" minds was strenuous work for him, as difficult and as taxing as running a cross-country race or memorizing a lengthy part in Hamlet. Despite the fears of laymen, he had no way of scanning anyone's intimate thoughts with a casual glance. To enter another mind, he had to go through an elaborate procedure of warming up and reaching out, and even so it was a slow business to tune in on somebody's "wavelength", with little coherent information coming across until the ninth or tenth attempt. The gift had been in the Mookherji family for at least a dozen generations, helped along by shrewdly planned marriages designed to conserve the precious gene; he was more adept than any of his ancestors, yet it might take another century or two of Mookherjis to produce a really potent telepath. At least he was able to make good use of such talent for mind-contact as he had. He knew that many members of his family in earlier times had been forced to hide their gift from those about them, back in India, lest they be classed with vampires and werewolves and cast out of society.

Gently he placed his dark hand on Satina's pale wrist. Physical contact was necessary to attain the mental linkage. He concentrated on reaching her. After months of teletherapy, her mind was sensitized to his; he was able to skip the intermediate steps, and, once he was warmed up, could plunge straight into her troubled soul. His eyes were closed. He saw a swirl of pearly-gray fog before him: Satina's mind. He thrust himself into it, entering easily. Up from the depths of her spirit swam a question mark.

—Who is it? Doctor?

—Me, yes. How are you today, Satina?

—Fine. Just fine.

—Been sleeping well?

—It's so peaceful here, doctor.

—Yes. Yes, I imagine it is. But you ought to see how it is here. A wonderful summer day. The sun in the blue sky. Everything in bloom. A perfect day for swimming, eh? Wouldn't you like a swim? He puts all the force of his concentration into images of swimming: a cold mountain stream, a deep pool at the base of a creamy waterfall, the sudden delightful shock of diving in, the crystal flow tingling against her warm skin, the laughter of her friends, the splashing, the swift powerful strokes carrying her to the far shore—

—I'd rather stay where I am, she tells him.

—Maybe you'd like to go floating instead? He summons the sensations of free flight: a floater-node fastened to her belt, lifting her serenely to an altitude of a hundred feet, and off she goes, drifting over fields and valleys, her friends beside her, her body totally relaxed, weightless, soaring on the updrafts, rising until the ground is a checkerboard of brown and green, looking down on the tiny houses and the comical cars, now crossing a shimmering silvery lake, now hovering over a dark, somber forest of thick-packed spruce, now simply lying on her back, legs crossed, hands clasped behind her head, the sunlight on her cheeks, three hundred feet of nothingness underneath her—

But Satina doesn't take his bait. She prefers to stay where she is. The temptations of floating are not strong enough.

Mookherji does not have enough energy left to try a third attempt at luring her out of her coma. Instead he shifts to a purely medical function and tries to probe for the source of the trauma that has cut her off from the world. The fright, no doubt; and the terrible crack in the dome, spelling the end to all security; and the sight of her parents and brother dying before her eyes; and the swampy reek of Titan's atmosphere hitting her nostrils—all of those things, no doubt. But people have rebounded from worse calamities. Why does she insist on withdrawing from life? Why not come to terms with the dreadful past, and accept existence again?

She fights him. Her defenses are fierce; she does not want him meddling with her mind. All of their sessions have ended this way: Satina clinging to her retreat, Satina blocking any shot at knocking her free of her self-imposed prison. He has gone on hoping that one day she will lower her guard. But this is not to be the day. Wearily, he pulls back from the core of her mind and talks to her on a shallower level.

—*You ought to be getting back to school, Satina.*

—*Not yet. It's been such a short vacation!*

—*Do you know how long?*

—*About three weeks, isn't it?*

—*Fourteen months so far,* he tells her.

—*That's impossible. We just went away to Titan a little while ago—the week before Christmas, wasn't it, and—*

—*Satina, how old are you?*

—*I'll be fifteen in April.*

—*Wrong,* he tells her. *That April's been here and so has the next one. You were sixteen two months ago. Sixteen, Satina.*

—*That can't be true, doctor. A girl's sixteenth birthday is something special, don't you know that? My parents are going to give me a big party. All my friends invited. And a nine piece robot orchestra with synthesizers. And I know that that hasn't happened yet, so how can I be sixteen?*

His reservoir of strength is almost drained. His mental signal is weak. He cannot find the energy to tell her that she is blocking reality again, that her parents are dead, that time is passing while she lies here, that it is too late for a Sweet Sixteen party.

—*We'll talk about it . . . another time, Satina. I'll . . . see . . . you . . . again . . . tomorrow . . . Tomorrow . . . morning . . .*

—*Don't go so soon, doctor!* But he can no longer hold the contact, and lets it break.

Releasing her, Mookherji stood up, shaking his head. A shame, he thought. A damned shame. He went out of the room on trembling legs and paused a moment in the hall, propping himself against a closed door and mopping his sweaty forehead. He was getting nowhere with Satina. After the initial encouraging period of contact, he had failed entirely to lessen the intensity of her coma. She had settled quite comfortably into her delusive world of withdrawal, and, telepathy or no, he could find no way to blast her loose.

He took a deep breath. Fighting back a growing mood of bleak discouragement, he went toward the next patient's room.

* * *

The operation was going smoothly. The dozen third-year medical students occupied the observation deck of the surgical gallery on the starport hospital's third floor, studying Dr. Hammond's expert technique by direct viewing and by simultaneous microamplified relay to their individual desk-screens. The patient, a brain-tumor victim in his late sixties, was visible only as a head and shoulders protruding from a life-support chamber. His scalp had been shaved; blue lines and dark red dots were painted on it to indicate the inner contours of the skull, as previously determined by short-range sonar bounces; the surgeon had finished the job of positioning the lasers that would excise the tumor. The hard part was over. Nothing remained except to bring the lasers to full power and send their fierce, precise bolts of light slicing into the patient's brain. Cranial surgery of this kind was entirely bloodless; there was no need to cut through skin and bone to expose the tumor, for the beams of the lasers, calibrated to a millionth of a millimeter, would penetrate through minute openings and, playing on the tumor from different sides, destroy the malignant growth without harming a bit of the surrounding healthy brain tissue. Planning was everything in an operation like this. Once the exact outlines of the tumor were determined, and the surgical lasers were mounted at the correct angles, any intern could finish the job.

For Dr. Hammond it was a routine procedure. He had performed a hundred operations of this kind in the past year alone. He gave the signal; the warning light glowed on the laser rack; the students in the gallery leaned forth expectantly—

And, just as the lasers' glittering fire leaped toward the operating table, the face of the anesthetized patient contorted weirdly, as though some terrifying dream had come drifting up out of the caverns of the man's drugged mind. His nostrils flared; his lips drew back; his eyes opened wide; he seemed to be trying to scream; he moved convulsively, twisting his head to one side. The lasers bit deep the patient's left temple, far from the indicated zone of the tumor. The right side of his face began to sag, all muscles paralyzed. The medical students looked at each other in bewilderment. Dr. Hammond, stunned, retained enough presence of mind to kill the lasers with a quick swipe of his hand. Then, gripping the operating table with both hands in his agitation, he peered at the dials and meters that told him the details of the botched operation. The tumor remained intact; a vast sector of the patient's brain had been devastated. "Impossible," Hammond muttered. What could goad a patient under anesthesia into jumping around like that? "Impossible. Impossible." He strode to the end of the table and checked the readings on the life-support chamber. The question now was not whether the brain tumor would be successfully removed; the immediate question was whether the patient was going to survive.

* * *

By four that afternoon Mookherji had finished most of his chores. He had seen every patient; he had brought his progress charts up to date; he had fed a prognosis digest to the master computer that was the starport hospital's control center; he had found time for a gulped lunch. Ordinarily, now, he could take the next four hours off, going back to his spartan room in the residents' building at the edge of the starport complex for a nap, or dropping in at the recreation center to have a couple rounds of floater-tennis, or looking in at the latest cube-show, or whatever. His next round of patient-visiting didn't begin until eight in the evening. But he couldn't relax: there was that business of the quarantined spacemen to worry about. Nakadai had been sending test outputs over since two o'clock, and now they were stacked deep in Mookherji's data terminal. Nothing had carried an *urgent* flag, so Mookherji had simply let the reports pile up; but now he felt he ought to have a look. He tapped the keys of the terminal, requesting printouts, and Nakadai's outputs began to slide from the slot.

Mookherji ruffled through the yellow sheets. Reflexes, synapse charge, degree of neural ionization, endocrine balances, visual response, respiratory and circulatory, cerebral molecular exchange, sensory percepts, EEG both enhanced and minimated . . . No, nothing unusual here. It was plain from the tests that the six men who had been to Norton's Star were badly in need of a vacation—frayed nerves, blurred reflexes—but there was no indication of anything more serious than chronic loss of sleep. He couldn't detect signs of brain lesions, infection, nerve damage, or other organic disabilities.

Why the nightmares, then?

He tapped out the phone number of Nakadai's office. "Quarantine," a crisp voice said almost at once, and moments later Nakadai's lean, tawny face appeared on the screen. "Hello, Pete. I was just going to call you."

Mookherji said, "I didn't finish up until a little while ago. But I've been through the outputs you sent over. Lee, there's nothing here."

"As I thought."

"What about the men? You were supposed to call me if any of them went into nightmares."

"None of them have," Nakadai said. "Falkirk and Rodriguez have been sleeping since eleven. Like lambs. Schmidt and Carroll were allowed to conk out at half past one. Webster and Schiavone hit the cots at three. All six are still snoring away, sleeping like they haven't slept in years. I've got them loaded with equipment and everything's reading perfectly normal. You want me to shunt the data to you?"

"Why bother? If they aren't hallucinating, what'll I learn?"

"Does that mean you plan to skip the mind-probes tonight?"

"I don't know," Mookherji said, shrugging. "I suspect there's no point in it, but let's leave that part open. I'll be finishing my evening rounds about eleven, and if there's some reason to get into the heads of those spacemen then, I will." He frowned. "But look—didn't they say that each one of them went into the nightmares on *every single sleep-shift?*"

"Right."

"And here they are, sleeping outside the ship to for the first time since the nightmares started, and none of them having any trouble at all. And no sign of possible hallucinogenic brain lesions. You know something, Lee? I'm starting to come around to a very silly hypothesis that those men proposed this morning."

"That the hallucinations were caused by some unseen alien being?" Nakadai asked.

"Something like that. Lee, what's the status of the ship they came in on?"

"It's been through all the routine purification checks, and now it's sitting in an isolation vector until we have some idea of what's on."

"Would I be able to get aboard it?" Mookherji asked.

"I suppose so, yes, but—why—?"

"On the wild shot that something external caused those nightmares and that that something may still be aboard the ship. And perhaps a lowlevel telepath like myself will be able to detect its presence. Can you set up clearance fast?"

"Within ten minutes," Nakadai said. "I'll pick you up."

Nakadai came by shortly in a rollerbuggy. As they headed toward the landing field, he handed Mookherji a crumpled spacesuit and told him to put it on.

"What for?"

"You may want to breathe inside the ship. Right now it's full of vacuum—we decided it wasn't safe to leave it under atmosphere. Also it's still loaded with radiation from the decontamination process. Okay?"

Mookherji struggled into the suit.

They reached the ship: a standard interstellar null-gravity-drive job, looking small and lonely in its corner of the field. A robot cordon kept it under isolation, but, tipped off by the control center, the robots let the two doctors pass. Nakadai remained outside; Mookherji crawled into the safety pouch and, after the hatch had gone through its admission cycle, entered the ship. He moved cautiously from cabin to cabin, like a man walking in a forest that was said to have a jaguar in every tree. While looking about, he brought himself as quickly as possible up to full telepathic receptivity, and, wide open, awaited telepathic contact with anything that might be lurking in the ship.

—Go on. Do your worst.

Complete silence on all mental wavelengths. Mookherji prowled everywhere: the cargo hold, the crew cabins, the drive compartments. Everything empty, everything still. Surely he would have been able to detect the presence of a telepathic creature in here, no matter how alien; if it was capable of reaching the mind of a sleeping spaceman, it should be able to reach the mind of a waking telepath as well. After fifteen minutes he left the ship, satisfied.

"Nothing there," he told Nakadai. "We're still nowhere."

* * *

THE VSIIR WAS GROWING DESPERATE. It had been roaming this building all day; judging by the quality of the solar radiation coming through the windows, night was beginning to fall now. And, though there were open minds on every level of the structure, the Vsiir had had no luck in making contact. At least there had been no more terminations. But it was the same story here as on the ship: whenever the Vsiir touched a human mind, the reaction was so negative as to make communication impossible. And yet the Vsiir went on and on and on, to mind after mind, unable to believe that this whole planet did not hold a single human to whom it could tell its story. It hoped it was not doing severe damage to these minds it was approaching; but it had its own fate to consider.

Perhaps this mind would be the one. The Vsiir started once more to tell its tale—

* * *

HALF PAST NINE AT NIGHT. Dr. Peter Mookherji, bloodshot, tense, hauled himself through his neuropathological responsibilities. The ward was full: a schizoid collapse, a catatonic freeze, Satina in her coma, half a dozen routine hysterias, a couple of paralysis cases, an aphasic, and plenty more, enough to keep him going for sixteen hours a day and strain his telepathic powers, not to mention his conventional medical skills, to their limits. Some day the ordeal of residency would be over; some day he'd be quit of this hospital, and would set up private practice on some sweet tropical isle, and commute to Bombay on weekends to see his family, and spend his holidays on planets of distant stars, like any prosperous medical specialist . . . Some day. He tried to banish such lavish fantasies from his mind. If you're going to look forward to anything, he told himself, look forward to midnight. To sleep. Beautiful, beautiful sleep. And in the morning it all begins again, Satina and the coma, the schizoid, the catatonic, the aphasic . . .

As he stepped into the hall, going from patient to patient, his annunciator said, "Dr. Mookherji, please report at once to Dr. Bailey's office."

Bailey? The head of the neuropathology department, still hitting the desk this late. What now? But of course there was no ignoring such a summons. Mookherji notified the control center that he had been called off his rounds, and made his way quickly down the corridor to the frosted-glass door marked SAMUEL F. BAILEY, M.D.

He found at least half the neuropath staff there already: four of the other senior residents, most of the interns, even a few of the high-level doctors. Bailey, a puffy-faced, sandy-haired, fiftyish man of formidable professional standing, was thumbing a sheaf of outputs and scowling. He gave Mookherji a faint nod by way of greeting. They were not on the best of terms; Bailey, somewhat old-school in his attitudes, had not made a good adjustment to the advent of telepathy as a tool in the treatment of mental disturbance. "As I was just saying," Bailey began, "these reports have been accumulating all day, and they've all been dumped on me, God knows why. Listen: two cardiac patients under sedation undergo sudden violent shocks, described by one doctor as sensory overloads. One reacts with cardiac arrest, the other with cerebral hemorrhage. Both die. A patient being treated for endocrine restabilization develops a runaway adrenaline flow while asleep, and gets a six-month setback. A patient undergoing brain surgery starts lurching around on the operating table, despite adequate anesthesia, and gets badly carved up by the lasers. Et cetera. Serious problems like this all over the hospital today. Computer check of general EEG patterns shows that fourteen patients, other than those mentioned, have experienced exceptionally severe episodes of nightmare in the last eleven hours, nearly all of them of such impact that the patient has sustained some degree of psychic damage and often actual physiological harm. Control center reports no case histories of previous epidemics of bad dreams. No reason to suspect a widespread dietary imbalance or similar cause for the outbreak. Nevertheless, sleeping patients are continuing to suffer, and those whose condition is particularly critical may be exposed to grave risks. Effective immediately, sedation of critical patients has been interrupted where feasible, and sleep schedules of other patients have been rearranged, but this is obviously not an expedient that is going to do much good if this outbreak continues into tomorrow."

Bailey paused, glanced around the room, let his gaze rest on Mookherji. "Control center has offered one hypothesis: that a psychopathic individual with strong telepathic powers is at large in the hospital, preying on sleeping patients and transmitting images to them that take the form of horrifying nightmares. Mookherji, what do you make of that idea?"

Mookherji said, "It's perfectly feasible, I suppose, although I can't imagine why any telepath would want to go around distributing nightmares. But has control center correlated any of this with the business over at the quarantine building?"

Bailey stared at his output slips. "What business is that?"

"Six spacemen who came in early this morning, reporting that they'd all suffered chronic nightmares on their voyage homeward. Dr. Lee Nakadai's been testing them; he called me in as a consultant, but I couldn't discover anything useful. I imagine there are some late reports from Nakadai in my office, but—"

Bailey said, "Control center seems only to be concerned about events in the hospital, not in the starport complex as a whole. And if your six spacemen had their nightmares during their voyage, there's no chance that their symptoms are going to find their way onto—"

"That's just it!" Mookherji cut in. "They had their nightmares in space. But they've been asleep since morning, and Nakadai says they're resting peacefully. Meanwhile an outbreak of hallucinations has started over here. Which means that whatever was bothering them during their voyage has somehow got loose in the hospital today—some sort of entity capable of stirring up such ghastly dreams that they bring veteran spacemen to the edge of nervous breakdowns and can seriously injure or even kill someone in poor health." He realized that Bailey was looking at him strangely, and that Bailey was not the only one. In a more restrained tone, Mookherji said, "I'm sorry if this sounds fantastic to you. I've been checking it out all day, so I've had some time to get used to the concept. And things began to fit together for me just now. I'm not saying that my idea is necessarily correct. I'm simply saying that it's a reasonable notion, that it links up with the spacemen's own idea of what was bothering them, that it corresponds to the shape of the situation—and that it deserves a decent investigation, if we're going to stop this before we lose some more patients."

"All right, doctor," Bailey said. "How do you propose to conduct the investigation?"

Mookherji was shaken by that. He had been on the go all day; he was ready to fold. Here was Bailey abruptly putting him in charge of this snark-hunt, without even asking! But he saw there was no way to refuse. He was the only telepath on the staff. And, if the supposed creature really was at large in the hospital, how could be tracked except by a telepath?

Fighting back his fatigue, Mookherji said rigidly, "Well, I'd want a chart of all the nightmare cases, to begin with, a chart showing the location of each victim and the approximate time of onset hallucination—"

* * *

They would be preparing for the Festival of Changing, now, the grand climax of the winter. Thousands of Vsiirs in the metamorphic phase would be on their way toward the Valley of Sand, toward that great natural amphitheater where the holiest rituals were performed. By now the firstcomers would already have taken up their positions, facing the west, waiting for the sunrise. Gradually the rows would fill as Vsiirs came in from every part of the planet, until the golden valley was thick with them, Vsiirs that constantly shifted their energy levels, dimensional extensions, and inner resonances, shuttling gloriously through the final joyous moments of the season of metamorphosis, competing with one another in a gentle way to display the great variety of form, the most dynamic cycle of physical changes—and, when the first red rays of the sun crept past the Needle, the celebrants would grow even more frenzied, dancing and leaping and transforming themselves with total abandon, purging themselves of the winter's flam boyance as the season of stability swept across the world. And finally, in the full blaze of sunlight, they would turn to one another in renewed kinship, embracing, and—

The Vsiir tried not to think about it. But it was hard to repress that sense of loss, that pang of nostalgia. The pain grew more intense with every moment. No imaginable miracle would get the Vsiir home in time for the Festival of Changing, it knew, and yet it could not really believe that such a calamity had befallen it.

Trying to touch minds with humans was useless. Perhaps if it assumed a form visible to them, and let itself be noticed, and then tried to open verbal communication—

But the Vsiir was so small, and these humans were so large. The dangers were great. The Vsiir, clinging to a wall and carefully keeping its wavelength well beyond the ultraviolet, weighed one risk against another, and, for the moment, did nothing.

* * *

"ALL RIGHT," MOOKHERJI SAID FOGGILY, a little before midnight. "I think we've got the trail clear now." He sat before a wall-sized screen on which the control center had thrown a three-dimensional schematic plan of the hospital. Bright red dots marked the place of each nightmare incident, yellow dashes the probable path of the unseen alien creature. "It came in the side way, probably, straight off the ship, and went into the cardiac wing first. Mrs. Maldonado's bed here, Mr. Guinness' over here, eh? Then it went up to the second level, coming around to the front wing and impinging on the minds of patients here and here and here between ten and eleven in the morning. There were no reported episodes of hallucination in the next hour and ten minutes, but then came that nasty business in the third-level surgical gallery, and after that—" Mookherji's aching eyes closed a moment; it seemed to him that he could still see the red dots and yellow dashes. He forced himself to go on, tracing the rest of the intruder's route for his audience of doctors and hospital security personnel. At last he said, "That's it. I figure that the thing must be somewhere between the fifth and eighth levels by now. It's moving much more slowly than it did this morning, possibly running out of energy. What we have to do is keep the hospital's wings tightly sealed to prevent its free movement, if that can be done, and attempt to narrow down the number of places whom it might be found."

One of the security men said, a little belligerently, "Doctor, just how are we supposed to find an invisible entity?"

Mookherji struggled to keep impatience out of his voice. "The visible spectrum isn't the only sort of electromagnetic energy in the universe. If this thing is alive, it's got to be radiating *somewhere* along the line. You've got a master computer with a million sensory pickups mounted all over the hospital. Can't you have the sensors scan for a point-source of infrared or ultraviolet moving through a room? Or even X-rays, for God's sake: we don't know where the radiation's likely to be. Maybe it's a gamma emitter, even. Look, something wild is loose in this building, and we can't see it, but the computer can. Make it search."

Dr. Bailey said, "Perhaps the energy we ought to be trying to trace it by is, ah, telepathic energy, doctor."

Mookherji shrugged. "As far as anybody knows, telepathic impulses propagate somewhere outside the electromagnetic spectrum. But of course you're right that I might be able to pick up some kind of output, and I intend to make a floor-by-floor search as soon as this briefing session is over." He turned toward Nakadai. "Lee, what's the word from your quarantined spacemen?"

"All six went through eight-hour sleep periods today without any sign of a nightmare episode: there was some dreaming, but all of it normal. In the past couple of hours I've had them on the phone talking with some of the patients who had the nightmares, and everybody agrees that the kind of dreams people have been having here today are the same in tone, texture, and general level of horror as the ones the men had aboard the ship. Images of bodily destruction and alien landscapes, accompanied by an overwhelming, almost intolerable, feeling of isolation, loneliness, separation from one's own kind."

"Which would fit the hypothesis of an alien being as the cause," said Martinson of the psychology staff. "If it's wandering around trying to communicate with us, trying to tell us it doesn't want to be here, say, and its communications reach human minds only in the form of frightful nightmares—"

"Why does it communicate only with sleeping people?" an intern asked.

"Perhaps those are the only ones it can reach. Maybe a mind that's awake isn't receptive," Martinson suggested.

"Seems to me," a security man said, "that we're making a whole lot of guesses based on no evidence at all. You're all sitting around talking about an invisible telepathic thing that breathes nightmares in people's ears, and it might just as easily be a virus that attacks the brain, or something in yesterday's food, or—"

Mookherji said, "The ideas you're offering now have already been examined and discarded. We're working on this line of inquiry now because it seems to hold together, fantastic though it sounds, and because it's all we have. If you'll excuse me, I'd like to start checking the building for telepathic output, now." He went out, pressing his hands to his throbbing temples.

* * *

SATINA RANSOM STIRRED, STRETCHED, SUBSIDED. She looked up and saw the dazzling blaze of Saturn's rings overhead, glowing through the hotel's domed roof. She had never seen anything more beautiful in her life. This close to them, only about 750,000 miles out, she could clearly make out the different zones of the rings, each revolving about Saturn at its own speed, with the blackness of space visible through the open places. And Saturn itself, gleaming in the heavens, so bright, so huge—

What was that rumbling sound? Thunder? Not here, not on Titan. Again: louder. And the ground swaying. A crack in the dome! Oh, no, no, no, feel the air rushing out, look at that cold greenish mist pouring in—people falling down all over the place—what's happening, what's happening, what's happening? Saturn seems to be falling toward us. That taste in my mouth—oh—oh—oh—

Satina screamed. And screamed. And went on screaming as she slipped down into darkness, and pulled the soft blanket of unconsciousness over her, and shivered, and gave thanks for finding a safe place to hide.

* * *

MOOKHERJI HAD PLODDED THROUGH THE whole building accompanied by three security men and a couple of interns. He had seen whole sectors of the hospital that he didn't know existed. He had toured basements and sub-basements and sub-sub-basements; he had been through laboratories and computer rooms and wards and exercise chambers. He had kept himself in a state of complete telepathic receptivity throughout the trek, but he had detected nothing, not even a fit of mental current anywhere. Somehow that came as no surprise to him. Now, with dawn near, he wanted nothing more than sixteen hours or so of sleep. Even with nightmares. He was tired beyond all comprehension of the meaning of tiredness.

Yet something wild was loose, still, and the nightmares still were going on. Three incidents, ninety minutes apart, had occurred during the night: two patients on the fifth level and one on the sixth awakened in states of terror. It had been possible to calm them quickly, and apparently no lasting harm had been done, but now the stranger was close to Mookherji's neuropathology ward, and he didn't like the thought of exposing a bunch of mentally unstable patients to that kind of stimulus. By this time, the control center had reprogrammed all patient- monitoring systems to watch for the early stages of nightmare—hormone changes, EEG tremors, respiration rate rise, and so forth—in the hope of awakening a victim before the full impact could be felt. Even so, Mookherji wanted to see that thing caught and out of the hospital before it got to any of his own people.

But how?

As he trudged back to his sixth-level office, he considered some of the ideas people had tossed around in that midnight briefing session. *Wandering around trying to communicate with us,* Martinson had said. *Its communications reach human minds only in the form of frightful nightmares. Maybe a mind that's awake isn't receptive.* Even the mind of a human telepath, it seemed, wasn't receptive while awake. Mookherji wondered if he should go to sleep and hope the alien would reach him, and then try to deal with it, lead it into a trap of some kind—but no. He wasn't that different from other people. If he slept, and the alien did open contact, he'd simply have a hell of a nightmare and wake up, and nothing gained. That wasn't the answer. Suppose, though, he managed to make contact with the alien through the mind of a nightmare victim—someone he could use as a kind of telepathic loudspeaker—someone who wasn't likely to wake up while the dream was going on—

Satina.

Perhaps. Perhaps. Of course, he'd have to make sure the girl was shielded from possible harm. She had enough horrors running free in her head as it was. But if he lent her his strength, drained off the poison of the nightmare, took the impact himself via their telepathic link, and was able to stand the strain and still speak to the alien mind—that might just work. Might.

He went to her room. He clasped her hand between his.

—Satina?

—Morning so soon, doctor?

—It's still early, Satina. But things are a little unusual here today. We need your help. You don't have to if you don't want to, but I think you can be of great value to us, and maybe even to yourself. Listen to me very carefully, and think it over before you say yes or no—

God help me if I'm wrong, Mookherji thought, far below the level of telepathic transmission.

* * *

CHILLED, ALONE, GROWING GROGGY WITH dismay and hopelessness, the Vsiir had made no attempts at contact for several hours now. What was the use? The results were always the same when it touched a human mind; it was exhausting itself and apparently bothering the humans, to no purpose. Now the sun had risen. The Vsiir contemplated slipping out of the building and exposing itself to the yellow solar radiation while dropping all defenses; it would be a quick death, an end to all this misery and longing. It was folly to dream of seeing the home planet again. And—

What was that?

A call. Clear, intelligible, unmistakable. *Come to me.* An open mind somewhere on this level, speaking neither the human language nor the Vsiir language, but using the wordless, universally comprehensible communion that occurs when mind speaks directly to mind. *Come to me. Tell me everything. How can I help you?*

In its excitement the Vsiir slid up and down the spectrum, emitting a blast of infrared, a jagged blurt of ultraviolet, a lively blaze of visible light, before getting control. Quickly it took a fix on the direction of the call. Not far away: down this corridor, under this door, through this passage. *Come to me.* Yes. Yes. Extending its mind-probes ahead of it, groping for contact with the beckoning mind, the Vsiir hastened forward.

* * *

MOOKHERJI, HIS MIND LOCKED TO Satina's, felt the sudden crashing shock of the nightmare moving in, and even at second remove the effect was stunning in its power. He perceived a clicking sensation of mind touching mind. And then, into Satina's receptive spirit, there poured—

A wall higher than Everest. Satina trying to climb it, scrambling up a smooth white face, digging fingertips into minute crevices. Slipping back one yard for every two gained. Below, a roiling pit, flames shooting up, foul gases rising, monsters with needle-sharp fangs waiting for her to fall. The wall grows taller. The air is so thin she can barely breathe, her eyes are dimming, a greasy hand is squeezing her heart, she can feel her veins pulling free of her flesh like wires coming out of a broken plaster ceiling, and the gravitational pull is growing constantly—pain, her lungs crumbling, her face sagging hideously—a river of terror surging through her skull—

—None of it is real, Satina. They're just illusions. None of it is really happening.

—Yes, she says, *yes, I know,* but still she resonates with fright, her muscles jerking at random, her face flushed and sweating, her eyes fluttering beneath the lids. The dream continues. How much more can she stand?

—Give it to me, he tells her. *Give me the dream!*

She does not understand. No matter. Mookherji knows how to do it. He is so tired that fatigue is unimportant; somewhere in the realm beyond collapse he finds unexpected strength, and reaches into her numbed soul, and pulls the hallucinations forth as though they were cobwebs. They engulf him. No longer does he experience them indirectly; now all the phantoms are loose in his skull, and, even as he feels Satina relax, he braces himself against the onslaught of unreality that he has summoned into himself. And he copes. He drains the excess of irrationality out of her and winds it about his consciousness, and adapts, learning to live with the appalling flood of images. He and Satina share what is coming forth. Together they can bear the burden; he carries more of it than she does, but she does her part, and now neither of them is overwhelmed by the parade of bogeys. They can laugh at the dream monsters; they can even admire them for being so richly fantastic. That beast with a hundred heads, that bundle of living copper wires, that pit of dragons, that coiling mass of spiky teeth—who can fear what does not exist?

Over the clatter of bizarre images Mookherji sends a coherent thought, pushing it through Satina's mind to the alien.

—Can you turn off the nightmares?

—No, something replies. *They are in you, not in me. I only provide the liberating stimulus. You generate the images.*

—All right. Who are you, and what do you want here?

—I am a Vsiir.

—A what?

—Native life form of the planet where you collect the greenfire branches. Through my own carelessness I was transported to your planet. Accompanying the message is an overriding impulse of sadness, a mixture of pathos, self-pity, discomfort, exhaustion. Above this the nightmares still flow, but they are insignificant now. The Vsiir says, *I wish only to be sent home. I did not want to come here.*

And this is our alien monster? Mookherji thinks. This is our fearsome nightmare-spreading beast from the stars?

—Why do you spread hallucinations?

—This was not my intention. I was merely trying to make mental contact. Some defect in the human receptive system, perhaps—I do not know. I do not know. I am so tired, though. Can you help me?

—We'll send you home, yes, Mookherji promises. *Where are you? Can you show yourself to me? Let me know how to find you, and I'll notify the starport authorities, and they'll arrange for your passage home on the first ship out.*

Hesitation. Silence. Contact wavers and perhaps breaks.

Well? Mookherji says, after a moment. *What's happening? Where are you?*

From the Vsiir an uneasy response:

—How can I trust you? Perhaps you merely wish to destroy me. If I reveal myself—

Mookherji bites his lip in sudden fury. His reserve of strength is almost gone; he can barely sustain the contact at all. And if he now has to find some way of persuading a suspicious alien to surrender itself, he may run out of steam before he can settle things. The situation calls for desperate measures.

—Listen, Vsiir. I'm not strong enough to talk much longer, and neither is this girl I'm using. I invite you into my head. I'll drop all defenses if you can look at who I am, look hard, and decide for yourself whether you can trust me. After that it's up to you. I can help you get home, but only if you produce yourself right away.

He opens his mind wide. He stands mentally naked.

The Vsiir rushes into Mookherji's brain.

* * *

A HAND TOUCHED MOOKHERJI'S SHOULDER. He snapped awake instantly, blinking, trying to get his bearings. Lee Nakadai stood above him. They were in—where?—Satina Ransom's room. The pale light of early morning was coming through the window; he must have dozed only a minute or so. His head was splitting.

"We've been looking all over for you, Pete," Nakadai said.

"It's all right now," Mookherji murmured. "It's all right." He shook his head to clear it. He remembered things. Yes. On the floor, next to Satina's bed, squatted something about the size of a frog, but very different in shape, color, and texture from any frog Mookherji had ever seen. He showed it to Nakadai. "That's the Vsiir," Mookherji said. "The alien terror. Satina and I made friends with it. We talked it into showing itself. Listen, it isn't happy here, so will you get hold of a starport official fast, and explain that we've got an organism here that has to be shipped back to Norton's Star at once, and—"

Satina said, "Are you Dr. Mookherji?"

"That's right. I suppose I should have introduced myself when—*you're awake?*"

"It's morning, isn't it?" The girl sat up, grinning. "You're younger than I thought you were. And so serious-looking. And I *love* that color of skin. I—"

"You're awake?"

"I had a bad dream," she said. "Or maybe a bad dream within a bad dream—I don't know. Whatever it was, it was pretty awful but I felt so much better when it went away—I just felt that if I slept any longer I was going to miss a lot of good things, that I had to get up and see what was happening in the world—do you understand any of this, doctor?"

Mookherji realized his knees were shaking. "Shock therapy," he muttered. "We blasted her loose from the coma—without even knowing what we were doing." He moved toward the bed. "Listen, Satina. I've been up for about a million years, and I'm ready to burn out from overload. And I've got a thousand things to talk about with you, only not now. Is that okay? Not now. I'll send Dr. Bailey in—he's my boss—and after I've had some sleep I'll come back and we'll go over everything together, okay? Say, five, six this evening. All right?"

"Well, of course, all right," Satina said, with a twinkling smile. "If you feel you really have to run off, just when I've—sure. Go. Go. You look awfully tired, doctor."

Mookherji blew her a kiss. Then, taking Nakadai by the elbow, he headed for the door. When he was outside he said, "Get the Vsiir over to your quarantine place pronto and try to put it in an atmosphere it finds comfortable. And arrange for its trip home. And I guess you can let your six spacemen out. I'll go talk to Bailey—and then I'm going to drop."

Nakadai nodded. "You get some rest, Pete. I'll handle things."

Mookherji shuffled slowly down the hall toward Dr. Bailey's office, thinking of the smile on Satina's face, thinking of the sad little Vsiir, thinking of nightmares—

"Pleasant dreams, Pete," Nakadai called.

SCHWARTZ BETWEEN THE GALAXIES

In the two years following the completion of the novel *Dying Inside* in the fall of 1971, I wrote nothing but short stories and the novella "Born with the Dead." Despite the struggle that those stories, and "Born with the Dead" in particular had been, I allowed myself to take on commitments to write two more novels, which would eventually become *The Stochastic Man* and *Shadrach in the Furnace*. I also let two friends talk me into writing short stories for publications they were editing. But, even as I locked myself into these four projects, I felt an increasing certainty that I was going to give up writing science fiction once those jobs were done. My own personal fatigue was only one factor in that decision. Another was my sense of having been on the losing side in a literary revolution.

Among the many revolutions that went on in the era known as the Sixties (which actually ran from about 1967 to 1972) there was one in science fiction. A host of gifted new writers, both in England and the United States, brought all manner of advanced literary techniques to bear on the traditional matter of s-f, producing stories that were more deeply indebted to Joyce, Kafka, Faulkner, Mann, and even e.e. cummings than they were to Heinlein, Asimov, and Clarke. This period of stylistic and structural innovation, which reached its highest pitch of activity between 1966 and 1969, was a heady, exciting time for science-fiction writers, especially newer ones such as Thomas Disch, Samuel R. Delany, R.A. Lafferty, and Barry Malzberg, although some relatively well-established people like John

Brunner, Harlan Ellison, and, yes, Robert Silverberg, joined in the fun. My stories grew more and more experimental in mode—and most of them were published, now, in anthologies of original stories rather than in the conventional s-f magazines.

What was fun for the writers, though, turned out to be not so much fun for the majority of the readers, who quite reasonably complained that if they wanted to read Joyce and Kafka, they'd go and read Joyce and Kafka. They didn't want their s-f to be Joycified and Kafkaized. So they stayed away from the new fiction in droves, and by 1972 the revolution was pretty much over. We were heading into the era of *Star Wars*, the trilogy craze, and the return of literarily conservative action-based science fiction to the center of the stage.

One of the most powerful figures in the commercialization of science fiction at that time was the diminutive Judy-Lynn del Rey, a charming and ferociously determined woman whose private reading tastes inclined toward *Ulysses* but who knew, perhaps better than anyone else ever had, what the majority of s-f readers wanted to buy. As a kind of side enterprise during her dynamic remaking of the field, she started a paperback anthology series called *Stellar*, and—despite my recent identification with the experimental side of science fiction—asked me, in May 1973, to do a story for it.

Her stated policy was to bring back the good old kind of s-f storytelling, as exemplified in the magazines of the 1950s, a golden age for readers like me. "I don't want mood pieces without plots," she warned. "I don't want vignettes; I don't want character sketches; and I don't want obvious extrapolations of current fads and newspaper stories. These yarns should have beginnings, middles, and ends. I want the writers to solve the problems they postulate . . ."

Since most of what I had been writing recently embodied most of the characteristics she thus decried, there was a certain incompatibility between Judy-Lynn's strongly voiced requirements and her equally strong insistence on having a Silverberg story for her first issue. And yet I had no real problem with her stated policy. My own tastes in s-f had been formed largely in the early 1950s, when such writers as C.M. Kornbluth, Alfred Bester, James Blish, Theodore Sturgeon, and Fritz

Leiber had been at the top of their form. I had always felt more comfortable with their kind of fiction than with the wilder stuff of fifteen years later; I thought myself rather a reactionary writer alongside people like Disch, Lafferty, Malzberg, or J.G. Ballard. And I thought "Schwartz Between the Galaxies," which I wrote in October 1973, was a reasonably conservative story, too—definitely a story of the 1970s but not particularly experimental in form or tone.

Judy-Lynn bought it—it would have been discourteous of her not to, after urging me so strenuously to write something for her—but she obviously felt let down, even betrayed. Here she was putting together her theme-setting first issue, and here I was still trying to write literature. To her surprise and chagrin, though, the story was extremely popular—one of the five contenders for the Hugo award for best short story the following year—and was fairly widely anthologized afterward.

I won the skirmish, yes; but Judy-Lynn, bless her, won the war. Our little literary revolution ended in total rout, with the space sagas and fantasy trilogies that she published sweeping the more highbrow kind of science fiction into oblivion, and many of the literary-minded writers left science fiction, never to return.

I was among those who left, although, as you will note, I did come back after a while. But it seemed certain to me as 1974 began that my days as a science-fiction writer were over forever. For one thing, the work had become terribly hard: my work-sheets indicate that "Schwartz Between the Galaxies" took me close to three weeks to write. In happier days I could have written a whole novel, and a good one, in that time. Then, too, despite that Hugo nomination, I felt that the readers were turning away from my work. I was still getting on the awards ballots as frequently as ever, but I wasn't winning anything. That seemed symptomatic. The readers no longer understood me, and I felt I understood them all too well.

So in late 1973 I wrote one more short story—"In the House of Double Minds"—because I had promised it to an editor, and then I swore a mighty oath that I would never write short s-f again. In the spring of 1974 I wrote the first of my two promised novels, *The Stochastic Man*. About six months later I launched into the second one, *Shadrach in the Furnace* and finished it in the spring of 1975 after a horrendous battle to get the words down on paper.

That was it. I had spent two decades as a science-fiction writer, and had emerged out of my early hackwork to win a considerable reputation among connoisseurs, and now it was all over. I would never write again, I told myself. (And told anyone else who would listen, too.)

And I didn't. For a while, anyway.

As for "Schwartz," there are aliens in it, which is why it's in this book, but the aliens may, for all I (or Schwartz) know, may merely be imaginary. I don't think that that disqualifies it from inclusion here. I reveal it here: ALL the aliens anybody has ever written about are imaginary. Reader, we just make them up.

THIS MUCH IS REALITY: SCHWARTZ sits comfortably cocooned—passive, suspended—in a first-class passenger rack aboard a Japan Air Lines rocket, nine kilometers above the Coral Sea. And this much is fantasy: the same Schwartz has passage on a shining starship gliding silkily through the interstellar depths, en route at nine times the velocity of light from Betelgeuse IX to Rigel XXI, or maybe from Andromeda to the Lesser Magellanic.

There are no starships. Probably there never will be any. Here we are, a dozen decades after the flight of Apollo 11, and no human being goes anywhere except back and forth across the face of the little O, the Earth, for the planets are barren and the stars are beyond reach. That little O is too small for Schwartz. Too often it glazes for him; it turns to a nugget of dead porcelain; and lately he has formed the habit, when the world glazes, of taking refuge aboard that interstellar ship. So what JAL Flight 411 holds is merely his physical self, his shell, occupying a costly private cubicle on a slender 200-passenger vessel which, leaving Buenos Aires shortly after breakfast, has sliced westward along the Tropic of Capricorn for a couple of hours and will soon be landing at Papua's Torres Skyport. But his consciousness, his *anima,* the essential Schwartzness of him, soars between the galaxies.

What a starship it is! How marvelous its myriad passengers! Down its crowded corridors swarms a vast gaudy heterogeny of galactic creatures, natives of the worlds of Capella, Arcturus, Altair, Canopus, Polaris, Antares, beings both intelligent and articulate, methane-breathing or nitrogen-breathing or argon breathing, spiny-skinned or skinless, many-armed or many-headed or altogether incorporeal, each a product of a distinct and distinctly unique and alien cultural heritage. Among these varied folk moves Schwartz, that superstar of anthropologists, that true heir to Kroeber and Morgan and Malinowski and Mead, delightedly devouring their delicious diversity. Whereas aboard this prosaic rocket, this planet-locked stratosphere needle, one cannot tell the Canadians from the Portuguese, the Portuguese from the Romanians, the Romanians from the Irish, unless they open their mouths, and sometimes not always then.

In his reveries he confers with creatures from the Fomalhaut system about digital circumcision; he tapes the melodies of the Achernarnian eye-flute; he learns of the sneeze-magic of Acrux, the sleep-ecstasies of Aldebaran, the asteroid-sculptors of Thuban. Then a smiling JAL stewardess parts the curtain of his cubicle and peers in at him, jolting him from one reality to another. She is blue-eyed, frizzy-haired, straight-nosed, thin-lipped, bronze-skinned, a genetic mishmash, your standard twenty-first-century- model mongrel human, perhaps Melanesian-Swedish-Turkish-Bolivian, perhaps Polish-Berber-Tatar-Welsh. Cheap intercontinental transit has done its deadly work: all Earth is a crucible, all the gene pools have melted into one indistinguishable fluid. Schwartz wonders about the recessivity of those blue eyes and arrives at no satisfactory solution. She is beautiful, at any rate. Her name is Dawn—O sweet neutral nonculture-bound cognomen!—and they have played at a flirtation, he and she, Dawn and Schwartz, at occasional moments of this short flight.

Twinkling, she says softly, "We're getting ready for our landing, Dr. Schwartz. Are your restrictors in polarity?"

"I never unfastened them."

"Good." The blue eyes, warm, interested, meet his. "I have a layover in Papua tonight," she says.

"That's nice."

"Let's have a drink while we're waiting for them to unload the baggage," she suggests with cheerful bluntness. "All right?"

"I suppose," he says casually. "Why not?" Her availability bores him: somehow he enjoys the obsolete pleasures of the chase. Once such easiness in a woman like this would have excited him, but no longer. Schwartz is forty years old, tall, square-shouldered, sturdy, a showcase for the peasant genes of his rugged Irish mother. His close-cropped black hair is flecked with gray; many women find that interesting. One rarely sees gray hair now. He dresses simply but well, in sandals and Socratic tunic. Predictably, his physical attractiveness, both within his domestic sixness and without, has increased with his professional success. He is confident, sure of his powers, and he radiates an infectious assurance. This month alone eighty million people have heard his lectures.

She picks up the faint weariness in his voice. "You don't sound eager. Not interested?"

"Hardly that."

"What's wrong, then? Feeling sub, Professor?"

Schwartz shrugs. "Dreadfully sub. Body like dry bone. Mind like dead ashes." He smiles, full force depriving his words of all their weight.

She registers mock anguish. "That sounds bad," she says. "That sounds awful!"

"I'm only quoting Chuang Tzu. Pay no attention to me. Actually, I feel fine, just a little stale."

"Too many skyports?"

He nods. "Too much of a sameness wherever I go." He thinks of a star-bright, top-deck bubble dome where three boneless Spicans do a twining dance of propitiation to while away the slow hours of nine-light travel. "I'll be all right," he tells her. "It's a date."

Her hybrid face flows with relief and anticipation. "See you in Papua," she tells him, and winks, and moves jauntily down the aisle.

Papua. By cocktail time Schwartz will be in Port Moresby. Tonight he lectures at the University of Papua; yesterday it was Montevideo; the day after tomorrow it will be Bangkok. He is making the grand academic circuit. This is his year: he is very big, suddenly, in anthropological circles, since the publication of *The Mask Beneath the Skin.* From continent to continent he flashes, sharing his wisdom, Monday in Montreal, Tuesday Veracruz, Wednesday Montevideo, Thursday—Thursday? He crossed the international date line this morning, and he does not remember whether he has entered Thursday or Tuesday, though yesterday was surely Wednesday. Schwartz is certain only that this is July and the year is 2083, and there are moments when he is not even sure of that.

The JAL rocket enters the final phase of its landward plunge. Papua waits, sleek, vitrescent. The world has a glassy sheen again. He lets his spirit drift happily back to the gleaming starship making its swift way across the whirling constellations.

* * *

He found himself in the starship's busy lower-deck lounge, having a drink with his traveling companion, Pitkin, the Yale economist. Why Pitkin, that coarse, florid little man? With all of real and imaginary humanity to choose from, why had his unconscious elected to make him share this fantasy with such a boor?

"Look," Pitkin said, winking and leering. "There's your girlfriend."

The entry-iris had opened and the Antarean not-male had come in.

"Quit it," Schwartz snapped. "You know there's no such thing going on."

"Haven't you been chasing her for days?"

"She's not a 'her'," Schwartz said.

Pitkin guffawed. "Such precision! Such scholarship! *She's* not a *her,* he says!" He gave Schwartz a broad nudge. "To you she's a she, friend, and don't try to kid me."

Schwartz had to admit there was some justice to Pitkin's vulgar innuendos. He did find the Antarean—a slim yellow-eyed ebony-skinned upright humanoid, sinuous and glossy, with tapering elongated limbs and a seal's fluid grace—powerfully attractive. Nor could he help thinking of the Antarean as feminine. That attitude was hopelessly culture-bound and species-bound, he knew; in fact the alien had cautioned him that terrestrial sexual distinctions were irrelevant in the Antares system, that if Schwartz insisted on thinking of "her" in genders, "she" could be considered only the negative of male, with no implication of biological femaleness.

He said patiently, "I've told you. The Antarean's neither male nor female as we understand those concepts. If we happen to perceive the Antarean as feminine, that's the result of our own cultural conditioning. If you want to believe that my interest in this being is sexual, go ahead, but I assure you that it's purely professional."

"Sure. You're only studying her."

"In a sense I am. And she's studying me. On her native world she has the status-frame of 'watcher-of-life,' which seems to translate into the Antarean equivalent of an anthropologist."

"How lovely for you both. She's your first alien and you're her first Jew."

"Stop calling her *her*," Schwartz hissed.

"But you've been doing it!"

Schwartz closed his eyes. "My grandmother told me never to get mixed up with economists. Their thinking is muddy and their breath is bad, she said. She also warned me against Yale men. Perverts of the intellect, she called them. So here I am cooped up on an interstellar ship with five hundred alien creatures and one fellow human, and he has to be an economist from Yale."

"Next trip travel with your grandmother instead."

"Go away," Schwartz said. "Stop lousing up my fantasies. Go peddle your dismal science somewhere else. You see those Delta Aurigans over there? Climb into their bottle and tell them all about the Gross Global Product." Schwartz smiled at the Antarean, who had purchased a drink, something that glittered an iridescent blue, and was approaching them. "Go *on*," Schwartz murmured.

“Don’t worry,” Pitkin said. “I wouldn’t want to crowd you.” He vanished into the motley crowd.

* * *

THE ANTAREAN SAID, “THE CAPELLANS are dancing, Schwartz.”

“I’d like to see that. Too damned noisy in here anyway.” Schwartz stared into the alien’s vertical-slitted citreous eyes. Cat’s eyes, he thought. Panther’s eyes. The Antarean’s gaze was focused, as usual, on Schwartz’s mouth: other worlds, other customs. He felt a strange, unsettling tremor of desire. Desire for what, though? It was a sensation of pure need, nonspecific, certainly nonsexual. “I think I’ll take a look. Will you come with me?”

* * *

THE PAPUA ROCKET HAS LANDED. Schwartz, leaning across the narrow table in the skyport’s lounge, says to the stewardess in a low, intense tone, “My life was in crisis. All my values were becoming meaningless. I was discovering that my chosen profession was empty, foolish, as useless as—playing chess.”

“How awful,” Dawn whispers gently.

“You can see why. You go all over the world, you see a thousand skyports a year. Everything the same everywhere. The same clothes, the same slang, the same magazines, the same styles of architecture and décor.”

“Yes.”

“International homogeneity. Worldwide uniformity. Can you understand what it’s like to be an anthropologist in a world where there are no primitives left, Dawn? Here we sit on the island of Papua—you know, headhunters, animism, body-paint, the drums at sunset, the bone through the nose—and look at the Papuans in their business robes all around us. Listen to them exchanging stock-market tips, talking baseball, recommending restaurants in Paris and barbers in Johannesburg. It’s no different anywhere else. In a single century we’ve transformed the planet into one huge sophisticated plastic western industrial state. The TV relay satellites, the two-hour intercontinental rockets, the breakdown of religious exclusivism and genetic taboo have mongrelized every culture, don't you see? You visit the Zuni and they have plastic African masks on the wall. You visit the Bushmen and they have Japanese-made Hopi-motif ashtrays. It's all just so much interior decoration, and underneath the carefully selected primitive motifs there's the same universal pseudo-American sensibility, whether you're in the Kalahari or the Amazon rain forest. Do you comprehend what's happened, Dawn?"

"It's such a terrible loss," she says sadly. She is trying very hard to be sympathetic, but he senses she is waiting for him to finish his sermon and invite her to share his hotel room. He will invite her, but there is no stopping him once he has launched into his one great theme.

"Cultural diversity is gone from the world," he says. "Religion is dead; true poetry is dead; inventiveness is dead; individuality is dead. Poetry. Listen to this." In a high monotone he chants:

In beauty I walk
With beauty before me I walk
With beauty behind me I walk
With beauty above me I walk
With beauty above and about me I walk
It is finished in beauty
It is finished in beauty.

He has begun to perspire heavily. His chanting has created an odd sphere of silence in his immediate vicinity; heads are turning, eyes are squinting. "Navaho," he says. "The Night Way, a nine-day chant, a vision, a spell. Where are the Navaho now? Go to Arizona and they'll chant for you, yes, for a price, but they don't know what the words mean, and chances are the singers are only one-fourth Navaho, or one-eighth, or maybe just Hopi hired to dress in Navaho costumes, because the real Navaho, if any are left, are off in Mexico City hired to be Aztecs. So much is gone. Listen." He chants again, more piercingly even than before:

The animal runs, it passes, it dies. And it is the great cold.
It is the great cold of the night, it is the dark.
The bird flies, it passes, it dies. And it is—

"JAL Flight 411 Baggage Is Now Unloading On Concourse Four," a mighty mechanical voice cries.

—the great cold.
It is the great cold of the night, it is the dark.

"JAL Flight 411 Baggage . . . "

The fish flees, it passes, it dies. And—

"People are staring," Dawn says uncomfortably.

"—On Concourse Four."

"Let them stare. Do them some good. That's a Pygmy chant, from Gabon, in equatorial Africa. Pygmies? There are no more Pygmies. Everybody's two meters tall. And what do we sing? Listen. Listen." He gestures fiercely at the cloud of tiny golden loudspeakers floating near the ceiling. A mush of music comes from them: the current popular favorite. Savagely he mouths words: *"Star . . . far . . . here . . . near.* Playing in every skyport right now, all over the world." She smiles thinly. Her hand reaches toward his, covers it, presses against the knuckles. He is dizzy. The crowd, the eyes, the music, the drink. The plastic. Everything shines. Porcelain. Porcelain. The planet vitrifies. "Tom?" she asks uneasily. "Is anything the matter?" He laughs, blinks, coughs, shivers. He hears her calling for help, and then he feels his soul swooping outward, toward the galactic blackness.

* * *

With the Antarean not-male beside him, Schwartz peered through the viewport, staring in awe and fascination at the seductive vision of the Capellans coiling and recoiling outside the ship. Not all the passengers on this voyage had cozy staterooms like his. The Capellans were too big to come on board, and in any case they preferred never to let themselves be enclosed inside metal walls. They traveled just alongside the starship, basking like slippery whales in the piquant radiations of space.

So long as they kept within twenty meters of the hull they would be inside the effective field of the Rabinowitz Drive, which swept ship and contents and associated fellow travellers toward Rigel, or the Lesser Magellanic, or was it one of the Pleiades toward which they were bound at a cool nine lights?

He watched the Capellans moving beyond the shadow of the ship in tracks of shining white. Blue, glossy green, and velvet black, they coiled and swam, and every track was a flash of golden fire. "They have a dangerous beauty," Schwartz whispered. "Do you hear them calling? I do."

"What do they say?"

"They say, *'Come to me, come to me, come to me!'*"

"Go to them, then," said the Antarean simply. "Step through the hatch."

"And perish?"

"And enter into your next transition. Poor Schwartz! Do you love your present body so?"

"My present body isn't so bad. Do you think I'm likely to get another one some day?"

"No?"

"No," Schwartz said. "This one is all I get. Isn't it that way with you?"

"At the Time of Openings I receive my next housing. That will be fifty years from now. What you see is the fifth form I have been given to wear."

"Will the next be as beautiful as this?"

"All forms are beautiful," the Antarean said. "You find me attractive?"

"Of course."

A slitted wink. A bobbing nod toward the viewport. "As attractive as *those*?"

Schwartz laughed. "Yes. In a different way."

Coquettishly the Antarean said, "If I were out there, you would walk through the hatch into space?"

"I might. If they gave me a spacesuit and taught me how to use it."

"But not otherwise? Suppose I were out there right now. I could live in space five, ten, maybe fifteen minutes. I am there and I say, *'Come to me, Schwartz, come to me!'* What do you do?"

"I don't think I'm all that much self-destructive."

"To die for love, though! To make a transition for the sake of beauty."

"No. Sorry."

The Antarean pointed toward the undulating Capellans. "If they asked you, you would go."

"They are asking me," he said.

"And you refuse the invitation?"

"So far. So far."

The Antarean laughed an Antarean laugh, a thick silvery snort. "Our voyage will last many weeks more. One of these days, I think, you will go to them."

* * *

"YOU WERE UNCONSCIOUS AT LEAST five minutes," Dawn says. "You gave everyone a scare. Are you sure you ought to go through with tonight's lecture?"

Nodding, Schwartz says, "I'll be all right. I'm a little tired, is all. Too many time zones this week." They stand on the terrace of his hotel room. Night is coming on, already, here in late afternoon: it is midwinter in the Southern Hemisphere, though the fragrance of tropic blossoms perfumes the air. The first few stars have appeared. He has never really known which star is which. That bright one, he thinks, could be Rigel, and that one Sirius, and perhaps this is Deneb over there. And this? Can this be red Antares, in the heart of the Scorpion, or is it only Mars? Because of his collapse at the skyport he has been able to beg off the customary faculty reception and the formal dinner; pleading the need for rest, he has arranged to have a simple snack at his hotel room, *a deux*. In two hours they will come for him and take him to the university to speak. Dawn watches him closely. Perhaps she is worried about his health, perhaps she is only waiting for him to make his move toward her. There's time for all that later, he figures. He would rather talk now. Warming up for the audience he seizes his earlier thread:

"For a long time I didn't understand what had taken place. I grew up insular, cut off from reality, a New York boy, bright mind and a library card. I read all the anthropological classics, *Patterns of Culture* and *Coming of Age in Samoa* and *Life of a South African Tribe* and the rest, and I dreamed of field trips, collecting myths and grammars and folkways and artefacts and all that, until when I was twenty-five I finally got out into the field and started to discover I had gone into a dead science. We have only one worldwide culture now, with local variants but no basic divergences—there's nothing primitive left on Earth, *and there are no other planets.* Not inhabited ones. I can't go to Mars or Venus or Saturn and study the natives. What natives? And we can't reach the stars. All I have to work with is Earth. I was thirty years old when the whole thing clicked together for me and I knew I had wasted my life."

She says, "But surely there was something for you to study on Earth."

"One culture, rootless and homogeneous. That's work for a sociologist, not for me. I'm a romantic, I'm an exotic, I want strangeness, difference. Look, we can never have any real perspective on our own time and lives. The sociologists try to attain it, but all they get is a mound of raw indigestible data. Insight comes later—two, five, ten generations later. But one way we've always been able to learn about ourselves is by studying alien cultures, studying them *completely,* and defining ourselves by measuring what they are that we aren't. The cultures have to be isolated, though. The anthropologist himself corrupts that isolation in the Heisenberg sense when he comes around with his camera and scanners and starts asking questions, but we can compensate more or less, for the inevitable damage a lone observer causes. We can't compensate when our whole culture collides with another and absorbs and obliterates it. Which we technological-mechanical people now have done everywhere. One day I woke up and saw there were no alien cultures left. Hah! Crushing revelation! Schwartz's occupation is gone!"

"What did you do?"

"For years I was in an absolute funk. I taught, I studied, I went through the motions, knowing it was all meaningless. All I was doing was looking at records of vanished cultures left by earlier observers and trying to cudgel new meanings. Secondary sources, stale findings: I was an evaluator of dry bones, not a gatherer of evidence. Paleontology. Dinosaurs are interesting, but what do they tell you about the contemporary world and the meaning of its patterns? Dry bones, Dawn, dry bones. Despair. And then a clue. I had this Nigerian student, this Ibo—well, basically an Ibo, but she's got some Israeli in her and I think Chinese—and we grew very close, she was as close to me as anybody in my own sixness, and I told her my troubles. I'm going to give it all up, I said, because it isn't what I expected it to be. She laughed at me and said, What right do you have to be upset because the world doesn't live up to your expectations? Reshape your life, Tom; you can't reshape the world. I said, But how? And she said, Look inward, find the primitive in yourself, see what made you what you are, what made today's culture what it is, see how these alien streams have flowed together. Nothing's been lost here, only merged. Which made me think. Which gave me a new way of looking at things. Which sent me on an inward quest. It took me three years to grasp the patterns, to come to an understanding of what our planet has become, and only after I accepted the planet—"

It seems to him that he has been talking forever. Talking. Talking. But he can no longer hear his own voice. There is only a distant buzz.

"After I accepted—"

A distant buzz.

"What was I saying?" he asks.

"After you accepted the planet—"

"After I accepted the planet," he says, "that I could begin—" *Buzz. Buzz.* "That I could begin to accept myself."

* * *

He was drawn toward the Spicans too, not so much for themselves—they were oblique, elliptical characters, self-contained and self-satisfied, hard to approach—as for the apparently psychedelic drug they took in some sacramental way before the beginning of each of their interminable ritual dances. Each time he had watched them take the drug, they had seemingly made a point of extending it toward him, as if inviting him, as if tempting him, before popping it into their mouths. He felt baited; he felt pulled.

There were three Spicans on board, slender creatures two and a half meters long, with flexible cylindrical bodies and small stubby limbs. Their skins were reptilian, dry and smooth, deep green with yellow bands, but their eyes were weirdly human, large liquid-brown eyes, sad Levantine eyes, the eyes of unfortunate medieval travelers transformed by enchantment into serpents. Schwartz had spoken with them several times. They understood English well enough—all galactic races did; Schwartz imagined it would become the interstellar *lingua franca* as it had on Earth—but the construction of their vocal organs was such that they had no way of speaking it, and they relied instead on small translating machines hung around their necks that converted their soft whispered hisses into amber words pulsing across a screen.

Cautiously, the third or fourth time he spoke with them, he expressed polite interest in their drug. They told him it enabled them to make contact with the central forces of the universe. He replied that there were such drugs on Earth, too, and that he used them frequently, that they gave him great insight into the workings of the cosmos. They showed some curiosity, perhaps even intense curiosity: reading their eyes was difficult and the tone of their voices gave no clues. He took his elegant leather-bound drug case from his pouch and showed them what he had: learitonin, psilocerebrin, siddharthin, and acid-57. He described the effects of each and suggested an exchange, any of his for an equivalent dose of the shriveled orange fungoid they nibbled.

They conferred. Yes, they said, we will do this. But not now. Not until the proper moment.

Schwartz knew better than to ask them when that would be. He thanked them and put his drugs away.

Pitkin, who had watched the interchange from the far side of the lounge, came striding fiercely toward him as the Spicans glided off. "What are you up to now?" he demanded.

"How about minding your own business?" Schwartz said amiably.

"You're trading pills with those snakes, aren't you?"

"Let's call it field research."

"Research? Research? What are you going to do, trip on that orange stuff of theirs?"

"I might," Schwartz said.

"How do you know what its effects on the human metabolism might be? You could end up blind or paralyzed or crazy or—"

"—or illuminated," Schwartz said. "Those are the risks one takes in the field. The early anthropologists who unhesitatingly sampled peyote and yage and ololiuqui accepted those risks, and—"

"But those were drugs that *humans* were using. You have no way of telling how—oh, what's the use, Schwartz? Research, he calls it. Research." Pitkin sneered. *"Junkie!"*

Schwartz matched him sneer for sneer. *"Economist!"*

* * *

THE HOUSE IS A DECENT one tonight, close to three thousand, every seat in the University's great horseshoe-shaped auditorium taken, and a video relay besides, beaming his lecture to all Papua and half of Indonesia. Schwartz stands on the dais like a demigod under a brilliant no-glare spotlight. Despite his earlier weariness he is in good form now, gestures broad and forceful, eyes commanding, voice deep and resonant, words flowing freely. "Only one planet," he says, "one small and crowded planet, on which all cultures converge to a drab and depressing sameness. How sad that is! How tiny we make ourselves, when we make ourselves to resemble one another!" He flings his arms upward. "Look to the stars, the unattainable stars! Imagine, if you can, the millions of worlds that orbit those blazing suns beyond the night's darkness! Speculate with me on other peoples, other ways, other gods. Beings of every imaginable form, alien in appearance but not grotesque, not hideous, for all life is beautiful—beings that breathe gases strange to us, beings of immense size, beings of many limbs or of none, beings to whom death is a divine culmination of existence, beings who never die, beings who bring forth their young a thousand at a time, beings who do not reproduce—all the infinite possibilities of the infinite universe!

"Perhaps on each of those worlds it is as it has become here. One intelligent species, one culture, the eternal convergence. But the many worlds together offer a vast spectrum of variety. And now, share this vision with me! I see a ship voyaging from star to star, a spaceliner of the future, and aboard that ship is a sampling of many species, many cultures, a random scoop out of the galaxy's fantastic diversity. That ship is like a little cosmos, a small world, enclosed, sealed. How exciting to be aboard it, to encounter in that little compass such richness of cultural variation! Now our own world was once like that starship, a little cosmos, bearing with it all the thousands of Earthborn cultures. Hopi and Eskimo and Aztec and Kwakiutl and Arapesh and Orokolo and all the rest. In the course of our voyage we have come to resemble one another too much, and it has impoverished the lives of all of us, because—" He falters suddenly. He feels faint, and grasps the sides of the lectern. "Because—" The spotlight, he thinks. In my eyes. Not supposed to glare like that, but it's blinding. Got to have them move it. "In the course—the course of our voyage—" What's happening? Breaking into a sweat, now. Pain in my chest. My heart? Wait, slow up, catch your breath. That light in my eyes—

* * *

"Tell me," Schwartz said earnestly, "what it's like to know you'll have ten successive bodies and live more than a thousand years."

"First tell me," said the Antarean, "what it's like to know you'll live ninety years or less and perish forever."

* * *

Somehow he continues. The pain in his chest grows more intense, he cannot focus his eyes; he believes he will lose consciousness at any moment and may even have lost it already at least once, and yet he continues. Clinging to the lectern, he outlines the program he developed in *The Mask Beneath the Skin.* A rebirth of tribalism without a revival of ugly nationalism. The quest for a renewed sense of kinship with the past. A sharp reduction in nonessential travel, especially tourism. Heavy taxation of exported artefacts, including films and video shows. An attempt to create independent cultural units on Earth once again while maintaining present levels of economic and political interdependence. Relinquishment of materialistic technological-industrial values. New searches for fundamental meanings. An ethnic revival, before it is too late, among those cultures of mankind that have only recently shed their traditional folkways. (He repeats and embellishes this point particularly, for the benefit of the Papuans before him, the great-grandchildren of cannibals.)

The discomfort and confusion come and go as he unreels his themes. He builds and builds, crying out passionately for an end to the homogenization of Earth, and gradually the physical symptoms leave him, all but a faint vertigo. But a different malaise seizes him as he nears his peroration. His voice becomes, to him, a far-off quacking, meaningless and foolish. He has said all this a thousand times, always to great ovations, but who listens? Who listens? Everything seems hollow tonight, mechanical, absurd. An ethnic revival? Shall these people before him revert to their loincloths and their pig roasts? His starship is a fantasy; his dream of a diverse Earth is mere silliness. What is, will be. And yet he pushes on toward his conclusion. He takes his audience back to that starship, he creates a horde of fanciful beings for them. He completes the metaphor by sketching the structures of half a dozen vanished "primitive" cultures of Earth, he chants the chants of the Navaho, the Gabon Pygmies, the Ashanti, the Mundugumor. It is over. Cascades of applause engulf him. He holds his place until members of the sponsoring committee come to him and help him down: they have perceived his distress. "It's nothing," he gasps. "The lights—too bright—" Dawn is at his side. She hands him a drink, something cool. Two of the sponsors begin to speak of a reception for him in the Green Room. "Fine," Schwartz says. "Glad to." Dawn murmurs a protest. He shakes her off. "My obligation," he tells her. "Meet community leaders. Faculty people. I'm feeling better now. Honestly." Swaying, trembling, he lets them lead him away.

* * *

"A JEW," THE ANTAREAN SAID. "You call yourself a Jew, but what is this exactly? A clan, a sept, a moiety, a tribe, a nation, what? Can you explain?"

"You understand what a religion is?"

"Of course."

"Judaism—Jewishness—it's one of Earth's major religions."

"You are therefore a priest?"

"Not at all. I don't even practice Judaism. But my ancestors did, and therefore I consider myself Jewish, even though—"

"It is a hereditary religion, then," the Antarean said, "that does not require its members to observe its rites?"

"In a sense," said Schwartz desperately. "More a hereditary cultural subgroup, actually, evolving out of a common religious outlook no longer relevant."

"Ah. And the cultural traits of Jewishness that define it and separate you from the majority of humankind are—?"

"Well—" Schwartz hesitated. "There's a complicated dietary code, a rite of circumcision for newborn males, a rite of passage for male adolescents, a language of scripture, a vernacular language that Jews all around the world more or less understand, and plenty more, including a certain intangible sense of clannishness and certain attitudes, such as a peculiar self-deprecating style of humor—"

"You observe the dietary code? You understand the language of scripture?"

"Not exactly," Schwartz admitted. "In fact I don't do anything that's specifically Jewish except think of myself as a Jew and adopt many of the characteristically Jewish personality modes, which however are not uniquely Jewish any longer—they can be traced among Italians, for example, and to some extent among Greeks. I'm speaking of Italians and Greeks of the late twentieth century, of course. Nowadays—" It was all becoming a terrible muddle. "Nowadays—"

"It would seem," said the Antarean, "that you are a Jew only because your maternal and paternal gene-givers were Jews, and they—"

"No, not quite. Not my mother, just my father, and he was Jewish only on his father's side, but even my grandfather never observed the customs, and—"

"I think this has grown too confusing," said the Antarean. "I withdraw the entire inquiry. Let us speak instead of my own traditions. The Time of Openings, for example, may be understood as—"

* * *

In the Green Room some eighty or a hundred distinguished Papuans press toward him, offering congratulations. "Absolutely right," they say. "A global catastrophe." "Our last chance to save our culture." Their skins are chocolate-tinted but their faces betray the genetic mishmash that is their ancestry: perhaps they call themselves Arapesh, Mundugumor, Tchambuli, Mafulu, in the way that he calls himself a Jew, but they have been liberally larded with chromosomes contributed by Chinese, Japanese, Europeans, Africans, everything. They dress in International Contemporary. They speak slangy, lively English. Schwartz feels seasick. "You look dazed," Dawn whispers. He smiles bravely. Body like dry bone. Mind like dead ashes. He is introduced to a tribal chieftain, tall, gray-haired, who looks and speaks like a professor, a lawyer, a banker. What, will these people return to the hills for the ceremony of the yam harvest? Will newborn girl-children be abandoned, cords uncut, skins unwashed, if their fathers do not need more girls? Will boys entering manhood submit to the expensive services of the initiator who scarifies them with the teeth of crocodiles? The crocodiles are gone. The shamans have become stockbrokers.

Suddenly he cannot breathe.

"Get me out of here," Schwartz mutters hoarsely, choking.

Dawn, with stewardess efficiency, chops a path for him through the mob. The sponsors, concerned, rush to his aid. He is floated swiftly back to the hotel in a glistening little bubble-car. Dawn helps him to bed. Reviving, he reaches for her.

"You don't have to," she says. "You've had a rough day."

He persists. He embraces her and takes her, quickly, fiercely, and they move together for a few minutes and it ends and he sinks back, exhausted, stupefied. She gets a cool cloth and pats his forehead and urges him to rest. "Bring me my drugs," he says. He wants siddharthin, but she misunderstands, probably deliberately, and offers him something blue and bulky, a sleeping pill, and, too weary to object, he takes it. Even so, it seems to be hours before sleep comes.

He dreams he is at the skyport, boarding the rocket for Bangkok, and instantly he is debarking at Bangkok—just like Port Moresby, only more humid—and he delivers his speech to a horde of enthusiastic Thais, while rockets flicker about him carrying him to skyport after skyport, and the Thais blur and become Japanese, who are transformed into Mongols, who become Uighurs, who become Iranians, who become Sudanese, who become Zambians, who become Chileans, and all look alike, all look alike, all look alike.

* * *

THE SPICANS HOVERED ABOVE HIM, weaving, bobbing, swaying like cobras about to strike. But their eyes, warm and liquid, were sympathetic: loving, even. He felt the flow of their compassion. If they had had the sort of musculature that enabled them to smile, they would be smiling tenderly, he knew.

One of the aliens leaned close. The little translating device dangled toward Schwartz like a holy medallion. He narrowed his eyes, concentrating as intently as he could on the amber words flashing quickly across the screen.

". . . has come. We shall . . ."

"Again, please," Schwartz said. "I missed some of what you were saying."

"The moment . . . has come. We shall . . . make the exchange of sacraments now."

"Sacraments?"

"Drugs."

"Drugs, yes. Yes. Of course." Schwartz groped in his pouch. He felt the cool, smooth leather skin of his drug case. Leather? Snakeskin, maybe. Anyway. He drew it forth. "Here," he said. "Siddharthin, learitonin, psilocerebrin, acid-57. Take your pick." The Spicans selected three small blue siddharthins. "Very good," Schwartz said. "The most transcendental of all. And now—"

The longest of the aliens proffered a ball of dried orange fungus the size of Schwartz's thumbnail.

"It is an equivalent dose. We give it to you."

"Equivalent to all three of my tablets, or to one?"

"Equivalent. It will give you peace."

Schwartz smiled. There was a time for asking questions and a time for unhesitating action. He took the fungus and reached for a glass of water.

"Wait!" Pitkin cried, appearing suddenly. "What are you—"

"Too late," Schwartz said serenely, and swallowed the Spican drug in one joyous gulp.

* * *

THE NIGHTMARES GO ON AND on. He circles the Earth like the Flying Dutchman, like the Wandering Jew, skyport to skyport to skyport, an unending voyage from nowhere to nowhere. Obliging committees meet him and convey him to his hotel. Sometimes the committee members are contemporary types, indistinguishable from one another, with standard faces, standard clothing, the all-purpose new-model hybrid unihuman, and sometimes they are consciously ethnic, elaborately decked out in feathers and paint and tribal emblems, but their faces, too, are standard behind the gaudy regalia, their slang is the slang of Uganda and Tierra del Fuego and Nepal, and it seems to Schwartz that these masqueraders are, if anything, less authentic, less honest, than the other sort, who at least are true representatives of their era. So it is hopeless either way. He lashes at his pillow, he groans, he wakens. Instantly Dawn's arms enfold him. He sobs incoherent phrases into her clavicle and she murmurs soothing sounds against his forehead. He is having some sort of breakdown, he realizes: a new crisis of values, a shattering of the philosophical synthesis that has allowed him to get through the last few years. He is bound to the wheel; he spins, he spins, he spins, traversing the continents, getting nowhere. There is no place to go. No. There is one, just one, a place where he will find peace, where the universe will be as he needs it to be. Go there, Schwartz. Go and stay as long as you can. "Is there anything I can *do*?" Dawn asks. He shivers and shakes his head. "Take this," she says, and gives him some sort of pill. Another tranquilizer. All right. All right. The world has turned to porcelain. His skin feels like a plastic coating. Away, away, to the ship. To the ship! "So long," Schwartz says.

* * *

OUTSIDE THE SHIP THE CAPELLANS twist and spin in their ritual dance as, weightless and without mass, they are swept toward the rim of the galaxy at nine times the velocity of light. They move with a grace that is astonishing for creatures of such tremendous bulk. A dazzling light that emanates from the center of the universe strikes their glossy skin and, rebounding, resonates all up and down the spectrum, splintering into brilliant streamers of ultra red, infraviolet, exoyellow. All the cosmos glows and shimmers. A single perfect note of music comes out of the remote distance and, growing closer, swells in an infinite crescendo. Schwartz trembles at the beauty of all he perceives.

Beside him stands the seal-slick Antarean. She—definitely *she,* no doubt of it, *she*—plucks at his arm and whispers, "Will you go to them?"

"Yes. Yes, of course."

"So will I. Wherever you go."

"Now," Schwartz says. He reaches for the lever that opens the hatch. He pulls down. The side of the starship swings open.

The Antarean looks deep into his eyes and says blissfully, "I never told you my name. My name is Dawn."

Together they float through the hatch into space.

The blackness receives them gently. There is no chill, no pressure at the lungs, no discomfort at all. He is surrounded by luminous surges, by throbbing mantles of pure color, as though he has entered the heart of an aurora. He and Dawn swim toward the Capellans, and the huge beings welcome them with deep, glad, booming cries. Dawn joins the dance at once, moving her sinuous limbs with extravagant ease; Schwartz will do the same in a moment, but first he turns to face the starship, hanging in space close by him like a vast coppery needle, and in a voice that could shake universes he calls, "Come, friends! Come, all of you! Come dance with us!" And they come, pouring through the hatch, the Spicans first, then all the rest, the infinite multitude of beings, the travelers from Fomalhaut and Achernar and Acrux and Aldebaran, from Thuban and Arcturus and Altair, from Polaris and Canopus and Sirius and Rigel, hundreds of star-creatures spilling happily out of the vessel, bursting forth, all of them, even Pitkin, poor little Pitkin, everyone joining hands and tentacles and tendrils and whatever, forming a great ring of light across space, everyone locked in a cosmic harmony, everyone dancing. Dancing. Dancing.

DIANA OF THE HUNDRED BREASTS

I visited Turkey in April 1994—Turkey is a country that has exerted continued fascination on me since my first trip there in 1967, which produced my Byzantine time-travel novel *Up the Line*—and this time I went down the Aegean coast, which is rich in the ruins of the ancient Greek culture that formerly flourished there. Among our stops was Ephesus, once the site of the Temple of Artemis, one of the Seven Wonders of the Ancient World. There's nothing left of that glorious temple today—it was burned down by a disgruntled parishioner in 356 B.C., rebuilt by Alexander the Great, sacked by the Goths, and later stripped of its masonry to build the Byzantine cathedral of Hagia Sophia in Constantinople, so all that remains is an open field with a single column rising above a scattering of stonework. But in the small museum in the adjacent Turkish town of Seljuk are the two mysterious statues of Artemis that once were worshipped there: huge stone figures of a woman whose midsection is festooned with what seem to be dozens of breasts, though perhaps they are eggs. Breasts or eggs, no one is sure, but either way they are symbols of fertility, and it is apparent that the Artemis of Ephesus was a fertility goddess rather than the virginal huntress of classical Greek myth.

Artemis passed into Roman mythology as the goddess Diana, and continued to be worshipped there into the Christian era. We read in the Book of Acts, 19, that the Apostle Paul turned up there in the first century A.D. and denounced the cult of Diana and the famed statues thereof, saying, "They be no gods, which are made by hands." He called for the destruction of her shrine. The citizens of Ephesus, full of wrath at this, gathered and cried out with one voice, the Bible tells us, "Great is Diana of the Ephesians!" Eventually things quieted down, though, and Paul got out of town with his skin intact, and ultimately neither Diana nor Jesus emerged victorious from the fray, because today Ephesus is a very picturesque ruin and Allah is the god of the region where it was located.

Avram Davidson wrote a clever, charming, complex little story (did he ever write any other kind?) in 1958 called "Great is Diana," which makes oblique reference to the famed many-breasted statues of Ephesus. The Davidson story is mostly about breasts, rather than the cult of Diana/Artemis, but in any case I had long forgotten it in July of 1995, when, brimming with images from the previous year's Turkish trip, I set about to write a fantasy story that would explain what those strange statues were doing in Ephesus.

The immediate precipitating factor was a plaintive phone-call from Alice K. Turner, the fiction editor of *Playboy*, for whom I had written a great many stories over many years and with whom I had a remarkable editor-writer relationship that was for two decades a fascinating creative challenge for me. Alice called up to complain that her inventory of science-fiction stories had dwindled to zero, and wondered if I would mind writing one for her. I have attempted, since 1970 or so, to do no writing at all in the summer months, and here we were in the splendid California June of unending sunshine, and yet, and yet, how could I ignore such a request from Alice Turner? So I wrote her, on June 30, 1995, that I was halfway through the six-month holiday from writing that I had bestowed upon myself after a particularly grueling winter of work, but I was getting a bit restless with a daily life of swimming, gardening, and sitting on the porch reading, so perhaps I might just interrupt my *dolce far niente* and do a story for her.

And so I did, although things didn't work out quite as planned. Within ten days I had written "Diana of the Hundred Breasts," which I sent to her with a note saying, "Herewith is a report for you on What I Did On My

Summer Vacation In Turkey Last Year. The scenery is rendered reliably; I did make up a few of the details of the events, I have to confess."

But Alice didn't like the story. It was what she called an "I.R.S. Story", she said—stories that I would set in exotic places merely to prove, so she said, that my travel expenses were legitimately tax-deductible. Alice had rejected two or three of my foreign-based stories over the years, always with that same reason and always to my bewilderment, because I couldn't understand her objection to foreign-based stories, whether they were I.R.S.-connected or not. Also she didn't care much for the plot and she didn't think one of the characters was realistically rendered. And I think she was bothered by the fact that I had given her a fantasy story rather than the pure science-fiction tale that she had asked me for. (Though something in my excessively rational mind seems to recoil at the irrationality that lies at the heart of most fantasy themes, so that when I set out to write fantasy it usually turns out to have a science-fictional explanation, as can be seen here.)

Well, rejections happen. *Playboy* under Alice Turner was not only the highest-paying fiction market around, but also one of the toughest, and though I sold her plenty of stories over the years, I had to expect that once in a while, she would turn one down. I replied to her rejection note on July 31: "Well, of course I disagree, but what the hell. I'll sell it somewhere else and sell you something else next year."

Which I did. I shipped the story off to the new fantasy magazine *Realms of Fantasy*, edited by Shawna McCarthy, for whom I had written one of my favorite stories, "Sailing to Byzantium," when she had been editor of *Isaac Asimov's Science Fiction Magazine* ten years before. Shawna bought it instantly and published it in her February 1996 issue. I don't like having stories rejected any more than any other writer would, but in a long career it's bound to happen now and then to anybody, and I am quick on the rebound when it does.

A fantasy magazine published it, but is it fantasy or science fiction? I hardly think the distinction matters. But there's an alien in it, at any rate.

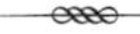

THE TWO FAMOUS MARBLE STATUES stand facing each other in a front room of the little museum in the scruffy Turkish town of Seljuk, which lies just north of the ruins of the once-great Greek and Roman city of Ephesus. There was a photograph of the bigger one in my guidebook, of course. But it hadn't prepared me—photos never really do—for the full bizarre impact of the actuality. The larger of the statues is about nine-feet tall, the other one about six. Archaeologists found both of them in the courtyard of a building of this ancient city where the goddess Diana was revered. They show—you must have seen a picture of one, some time or other—a serene, slender woman wearing an ornamental headdress that is all that remains of a huge, intricate crown. Her arms are outstretched and the lower half of her body is swathed in a tight cylindrical gown. From waist to ankles, that gown is decorated with rows of vividly carved images of bees and of cattle. But that's not where your eyes travel first, because the entire midsection of Diana of Ephesus is festooned with a grotesque triple ring of bulging pendulous breasts. Dozens of them, or several dozens. A great many.

"Perhaps they're actually eggs," said my brother Charlie the professor, standing just behind me. For the past eighteen months Charlie had been one of the leaders of the team of University of Pennsylvania archaeologists that has been digging lately at Ephesus. "Or fruits of some kind, apples, pears. Nobody's really sure. Globular fertility symbols, that's all we can say. But I think they're tits, myself. The tits of the Great Mother, with an abundance of milk for all. Enough tits to satisfy anybody's oral cravings, and then some."

"An abomination before the Lord," murmured our new companion Mr. Gladstone, the diligent Christian tourist, just about when I was expecting him to say something like that.

"Tits?" Charlie asked.

"These statues. They should be smashed in a thousand pieces and buried in the earth whence they came." He said it mildly, but he meant it.

"What a great loss to art that would be," said Charlie in his most pious way. "Anyway, the original statue from which these were copied fell from heaven. That's what the Bible says, right? Book of Acts. The image that Jupiter tossed down from the sky. It could be argued that Jupiter is simply one manifestation of Jehovah. Therefore this is a holy image. Wouldn't you say so, Mr. Gladstone?"

There was a cruel edge on Charlie's voice; but, then, Charlie is cruel. Charming, of course, and ferociously bright, but above all else, a smart-ass. He's three years older than I am, and three times as intelligent. You can imagine what my childhood was like. If I had ever taken his cruelties seriously, I suspect I would hate him; but the best defense against Charlie is never to take him seriously. I never have, nor anything much else, either. In that way Charlie and I are similar, I suppose. But only in that way. Mr. Gladstone refused to be drawn into Charlie's bantering defense of idolatry. Maybe he too had figured out how to handle Charlie, a lot quicker than I ever did.

"You are a cynic and a sophist, Dr. Walker," is all that he said. "There is no profit in disputing these matters with cynics. Or with sophists. Especially with sophists." And to me, five minutes later, as we rambled through a room full of mosaics and frescoes and little bronze statuettes: "Your brother is a sly and very clever man. But there's a hollowness about him that saddens me. I wish I could help him. I feel a great deal of pity for him, you know."

* * *

THAT ANYONE WOULD WANT TO feel pity for Charlie was a new concept to me. Envy, yes. Resentment, disapproval, animosity, even fear, perhaps. But pity? For the six-foot-three genius with the blond hair and blue eyes, the movie-star face, the seven-figure trust fund, the four-digit I.Q.? I am tall too, and when I reached 21, I came into money also, and I am neither stupid nor ugly; but it was always Charlie who got the archery trophy, the prom queen, the honor-roll scroll, the Phi Beta Kappa key. It was Charlie who always got anything and everything he wanted, effortlessly, sometimes bestowing his leftovers on me, but always in a patronizing way that thoroughly tainted them. I have sensed people pitying me, sometimes, because they look upon me as Charlie-minus, an inadequate simulacrum of the genuine article, a pallid secondary version of the extraordinary Charlie. In truth I think their compassion for me, if that's what it is, is misplaced: I don't see myself as all that goddamned pitiful. But Charlie? Pitying *Charlie*?

I was touring Greece and Turkey that spring, mostly the usual Aegean resorts, Mykonos and Corfu and Crete, Rhodes and Bodrum and Marmaris. I wander up and down the Mediterranean about half the year, generally, and, though I'm scarcely a scholar, I do of course look in on the various famous classical sites along my way. By now, I suppose, I've seen every ruined Roman and Greek temple and triumphal arch and ancient theater there is, from Volubilis and Thuburbo Majus in North Africa up through Sicily and Pompeii, and out to Spain and France on one side and Syria and Lebanon on the other. They all blur and run together in my mind, becoming a single generic site—fallen marble columns, weather beaten foundations, sand, little skittering lizards, blazing sun, swarthy men selling picture-postcards—but I keep on prowling them anyway. I don't quite know why.

There are no hotels remotely worthy of the name in or around the Ephesus ruins. But Charlie had tipped me off that I would find, about six miles down the road, a lavish new deluxe place high up on a lonely point overlooking the serene Aegean that catered mostly to groups of sun-worshipping Germans. It had an immense lobby with marble floors and panoramic windows, an enormous swimming pool, and an assortment of dining rooms that resounded day and night with the whoops and hollers of the beefy Deutschers, who never seemed to leave the hotel. Charlie drove out there to have dinner with me the night I arrived, and that was when we met Mr. Gladstone.

"Excuse me," he said, hovering beside our table, "but I couldn't help hearing you speaking in English. I don't speak German at all and, well, frankly, among all these foreigners I've been getting a little lonely for the mother tongue. Do you mind if I join you?"

"Well—" I said, not really eager for his company, because tonight was the first time I had seen my brother in a couple of years. But Charlie grandly waved him to a seat.

He was a grayish, cheerful man of about sixty, a small-town pastor from Ohio or Indiana or maybe Iowa, and he had been saving for something like twenty years to take an extensive tour of the Christian holy places of the Middle East. For the past three months he had been traveling with a little group of—pilgrims, I guess one could call them, six weeks bussing through Israel from Jerusalem to Beersheba, down to Mount Sinai, back up through the Galilee to Lebanon to see Sidon and Tyre, then out to Damascus, and so on and and so on, the full Two-Testament Special. His traveling companions had all flown home by now, but Mr. Gladstone had bravely arranged a special side trip just for himself to Turkey—to poky little Seljuk in particular—because his late wife had had a special interest in an important Christian site here. He had never traveled anywhere by himself before, not even in the States, and going it alone in Turkey was a bit of a stretch for him. But he felt he owed it to his wife's memory to make the trip, and so he was resolutely plugging along on his own here, having flown from Beirut to Izmir and then hired a car and driver to bring him down to Seljuk. He had arrived earlier this day.

"I didn't realize there was anything of special Christian interest around here," I said.

"The Cave of the Seven Sleepers of Ephesus," Mr. Gladstone explained. "My wife once wrote a little book for children about the Seven Sleepers. It was always her great hope to see their actual cave."

"The Seven Sleepers?"

He sketched the story for me quickly: the seven devout Christian boys who took refuge in a cave rather than offer sacrifices in the temple of the Roman gods, and who fell into a deep sleep and came forth two hundred years later to discover that Christianity had miraculously become the official religion of Rome while they were doing their Rip van Winkle act. What was supposedly their cave may still be seen just beyond the Roman stadium of Ephesus.

"There's also the Meryemana," Charlie said.

Mr. Gladstone gave him a polite blank smile. "Beg your pardon?"

"The house where the Virgin Mary lived in the last years of her life. Jesus told St. John the Apostle to look after her, and he brought her to Ephesus, so it's said. About a hundred years ago some Eastern Orthodox priests went looking for her house and found it, sure enough, about three miles outside town."

"Indeed."

"More likely it's sixth century Byzantine," said Charlie. "But the foundations are much older. The Orthodox Christians go there on pilgrimage there every summer. You really ought to see it." He smiled his warmest, most savage smile. "Ephesus has always been a center of mother-goddess worship, you know, and apparently it has continued to be one even in post-pagan times."

Mr. Gladstone's lips quirked ever so slightly. Though I assumed—correctly—that he was Protestant, even a Presbyterian was bound to be annoyed at hearing someone call the Virgin Mary a mother-goddess. But all he said was, "It would be interesting to see, yes."

Charlie wouldn't let up. "You will, of course, look in at the Seljuk Museum to see the predecessor goddess' statue, won't you? Diana, I mean. Diana of the Hundred Breasts. It's best to visit the museum before you begin your tour of the ruins, anyway. And the statues—there are two, actually—sum up the whole concept of the sacred female principle in a really spectacular way. The primordial mother, the great archetype. The celestial cow that nourishes the world. You need to see it, if you want truly to understand the bipolar sexual nature of the divine, eh, Mr. G?" He glanced toward me. "You too, Tim. The two of you, meet me in front of the museum at nine tomorrow, okay? Basic orientation lecture by Dr. Walker. Followed by a visit to ancient Ephesus, including the Cave of the Seven Sleepers. Perhaps the Meryemana afterward." Charlie flashed a dazzling grin. "Will you have some wine, Mr.Gladstone?"

"No, thank you," Mr. Gladstone said, quickly putting his hand over the empty glass in front of him.

* * *

After the museum, the next morning, we doubled back to the ruins of Ephesus proper. Mobs of tour groups were already there, milling around befuddledly as tour groups do, but Charlie zipped right around them to the best stuff. The ruins are in a marvelous state of preservation—a nearly intact Roman city of the first century A.D., the usual forum and temples and stadium and gymnasium and such, and of course the famous two-story library that the Turks feature on all those tourist posters.

We had the best of all possible guides. Charlie has a genuine passion for archaeology—it's the only thing, I suspect, that he really cares for, other than himself—and he pointed out a million details that we would otherwise have missed. With special relish he dwelled on the grotesqueries of the cult of Diana, telling us not only about the metaphorical significance of the goddess's multiplicity of breasts, but about the high priest who was always a eunuch—

"His title," said Charlie, "meant 'He who has been set free by God'"—and the staff of virgins who assisted him, and the special priests known as the Acrobatae, or "walkers on tip-toe," et cetera, et cetera. Mr. Gladstone showed signs of definite distaste as Charlie went on to speculate on some of the more flamboyant erotic aspects of pagan worship hereabouts, but he wouldn't stop. He never does, when he has a chance to display his erudition and simultaneously offend and unsettle someone.

Eventually it was mid-afternoon and the day had become really hot and we were only halfway through our tour of the ancient city, with the Cave of the Seven Sleepers still a mile or two in the distance. And clearly Mr. Gladstone was wilting. We decided to call it a day, and had a late lunch of kebabs and stewed eggplant at one of the innumerable and interchangeable little bistros in town. "We can go to the cave first thing tomorrow morning, when it's still cool," Charlie offered.

"Thank you. But I think I would prefer to visit it alone, if you don't mind. A private pilgrimage—for my late wife's sake, do you see? Something of a ceremonial observance."

"Certainly," Charlie intoned reverently. "I quite understand." I asked him if he would be coming out to the hotel again that evening for dinner with me. No, he said, he would be busy at the dig—the cool of the evening was a good time to work, without the distraction of gawking tourists—but we arranged to meet in the morning for breakfast and a little brotherly catching up on family news. I left him in town and drove back to the hotel with Mr. Gladstone.

"Your brother isn't a religious man, is he?" he said.

"I'm afraid that neither of us is, especially. It's the way we were raised."

"But he *really* isn't. You're merely indifferent; he is hostile."

"How can you tell?"

"Because," he said, "he was trying so hard to provoke me with those things he was saying about Diana of Ephesus. He makes no distinction between Christianity and paganism. All religions must be the same to him, mere silly cults. And so he thinks he can get at my beliefs somehow by portraying pagan worship as absurd and bizarre."

"He looks upon them all as cults, yes. But silly, no. In fact Charlie takes religion very seriously, though not exactly in the same way you do. He regards it as a conspiracy by the power elite to remain on top at the expense of the masses. And holy scriptures are just works of fiction dreamed up to perpetuate the authority of the priests and their bosses."

"He sees all religions that way, does he, without making distinctions?"

"Every one of them, yes. Always the same thing, throughout the whole of human history."

"The poor man," said Mr. Gladstone. "The poor empty-souled man. If only I could set him straight, somehow!"

There it was again: the compassion, the pity. For Charlie, of all people! Fascinating. Fascinating.

"I doubt that you'd succeed," I told him. "He's inherently a skeptical person. He's never been anything else. And he's a scientist, remember, a man who lives or dies by rational explanations. If it can't be explained, then it probably isn't real. He doesn't have a smidgeon of belief in anything he can't see and touch and measure."

"He is incapable of giving credence to the evidence of things not seen?"

"Excuse me?"

"'The substance of things hoped for, the evidence of things not seen.' Book of Hebrews, 11:1. It's St. Paul's definition of faith."

"Ah."

"St. Paul was here, you know. In this town, in Ephesus, on a missionary journey. Gods that are fashioned by human hands are no gods at all, he told the populace. Whereupon a certain Demetrius, a silversmith who earned his living making statuettes of the many-breasted goddess whose images we saw today in the museum, called his colleagues together and said, 'If this man has his way, the temple of the great goddess Diana will be destroyed and we will lose our livelihoods.' And when they heard these sayings, they were full of wrath, and cried out, saying, 'Great is Diana of the Ephesians.' And the whole city was filled with confusion.' That's the Book of Acts, 19:28. And there was such a huge uproar in town over the things that Paul was preaching that he found it prudent to depart very quickly for Macedonia."

"I see."

"But the temple of the goddess was destroyed anyway, eventually. And her statues were cast down and buried in the earth, and now are seen only in museums."

"And the people of Ephesus became Christians," I said. "And Moslems after that, it would seem."

He looked startled. My gratuitous little dig had clearly stung him. But then he smiled.

"I see that you are your brother's brother," he said.

* * *

I WAS UP LATE READING, and thinking about Charlie, and staring at the moonlight shimmering on the bay. About half past eleven, I hit the sack. Almost immediately my phone rang.

Charlie. "Are you alone, bro?"

"No," I said. "As a matter of fact, Mr. Gladstone and I are hunkering down getting ready to commit abominations before the lord."

"I thought maybe one of those horny Kraut ladies—"

"Cut it out. I'm alone, Charlie. And pretty sleepy. What is it?"

"Can you come down to the ruins? There's something I want to show you."

"Right now?"

"Now is a good time for this."

"I told you I was sleepy."

"It's something big, Tim. I need to show it to somebody, and you're the only person on this planet I even halfway trust."

"Something you discovered tonight?"

"Get in your car and come on down. I'll meet you by the Magnesian Gate. That's the back entrance. Go past the museum and turn right at the crossroads in town."

"Charlie—"

"Move your ass, bro. Please."

That "please," from Charlie, was something very unusual. In twenty minutes, I was at the gate. He was waiting there, swinging a huge flashlight. A tool-sack was slung over one shoulder. He looked wound up tight, as tense as I had ever seen him. Selecting a key from a chain that held at least thirty of them, he unlocked the gate and led me down a long straight avenue paved with worn blocks of stone. The moon was practically full and the ancient city was bathed in cool silvery light. He pointed out the buildings as we went by them: "The baths of Varius. The basilica. The necropolis. The temple of Isis." He droned the names in a singsong tone as though this were just one more guided tour. We turned to the right, onto another street that I recognized as the main one, where earlier that day I had seen the gate of Hercules, the temple of Hadrian, the library. "Here we are. Back of the brothel and the latrine."

We scrambled uphill perhaps fifty yards through gnarled scrubby underbrush until we came to a padlocked metal grate set in the ground in an otherwise empty area. Charlie produced the proper key and pulled back the grate. His flashlight beam revealed a rough earthen-walled tunnel, maybe five feet high, leading into the hillside. The air inside was hot and stale, with a sweet heavy odor of dry soil. After about twenty feet the tunnel forked. Crouching, we followed the right-hand fork, pushing our way through some bundles of dried leaves that seemed to have been put there to block its entrance.

"Look there," he said.

He shot the beam off to the left and I found myself staring at a place where the tunnel wall had been very carefully smoothed. An upright circular slab of rough-hewn marble perhaps a yard across was set into it there.

"What is it?" I asked him. "A gravestone? A commemorative plaque?"

"Some sort of door, more likely. Covering a funeral chamber, I would suspect. You see these?" He indicated three smaller circles of what looked like baked clay, mounted in a symmetrical way over the marble slab, arranged to form the angles of an equilateral triangle. They overlapped the edges of the slab as though sealing it into the wall. I went closer and saw inscriptions carved into the clay circles, an array of mysterious symbols and letters.

"What language is this? Not Greek. Hebrew, maybe?"

"No. I don't actually know what it is. Some unknown Anatolian script, or some peculiar form of Aramaic or Phoenician—I just can't say, Timmo. Maybe it's a nonsense script, even. Purely decorative sacred scribbles conveying spells to keep intruders away, maybe. You know, some kind of magical mumbo-jumbo. It might be anything."

"You found this tonight?"

"Three weeks ago. We've known this tunnel was here for a long time, but it was thought to be empty. I happened to be doing some sonar scanning overhead and I got an echo back from a previously uncharted branch, so I came down and took a look around. Nobody knows about it but me. And you."

Gingerly I ran my hand over the face of the marble slab. It was extraordinarily smooth, cool to the touch. I had the peculiar illusion that my fingertips were tingling, as though from a mild electrical charge.

"What are you going to do?" I asked.

"Open it."

"Now?"

"Now, bro. You and me."

"You can't do that!"

"I can't?"

"You're part of an expedition, Charlie. You can't just bust into a tomb, or whatever this is, on your own. It isn't proper procedure, is it? You need to have the other scientists here. And the Turkish antiquities officials—they'll string you up by the balls if they find out you've done a bit of secret free-lance excavating without notifying any local authorities."

"We break the seals. We look inside. If there's anything important in there, we check it out just to gratify our own curiosity and then we go away, and in the morning I discover it all over again and raise a big hullaballoo and we go through all of the proper procedures then. Listen, bro, there could be something big in there, don't you see? The grave of a high priest. The grave of some pre-historic king. The lost treasure of the Temple of Diana. The Ark of the Covenant. Anything. Anything. Whatever it is, I want to know. And I want to see it before anybody else does."

He was lit up with a passion so great that I could scarcely recognize him as my cool brother Charlie.

"How are you going to explain the broken seals?"

"Broken by some tomb-robber in antiquity," he said. "Who got frightened away before he could finish the job."

He had always been a law unto himself, my brother Charlie. I argued with him a little more, but I knew it would do no good. He had never been much of a team player. He wasn't going to have five or six wimpy colleagues and a bunch of Turkish antiquities officials staring over his shoulder while that sealed chamber was opened for the first time in two thousand years.

He drew a small battery-powered lamp from his sack and set it on the ground. Then he began to pull the implements of his trade out of the sack, the little chisels, the camel's-hair brushes, the diamond-bladed hacksaw.

"Why did you wait until I got here before you opened it?" I asked.

"Because I thought I might need help pulling that slab out of the wall, and who could I trust except you? Besides, I wanted an audience for the grand event."

"Of course."

"You know me, Timmo."

"So I do, bro. So I do."

He began very carefully to chisel off one of the clay seals.

It came away in two chunks. Setting it to one side, he went to work on the second one, and then the third. Then he dug his fingertips into the earthen wall at the edge of the slab and gave it an experimental tug.

"I do need you," he said. "Put your shoulder against the slab and steady it as I pry it with this crowbar. I don't want it just toppling out."

Bit by bit he wiggled it free. As it started to pivot and fall forward I leaned all my weight into it, and Charlie reached across me and caught it too, and together we were able to brace it as it left its aperture and guide it down carefully to the ground.

We stared into the blackest of black holes. Ancient musty air came roaring forth in a long dry whoosh. Charlie leaned forward and started to poke the flashlight into the opening.

But then he pulled back sharply and turned away, gasping as though he had inhaled a wisp of something noxious.

"Charlie?"

"Just a second." He waved his hand near his head a couple of times, the way you might do when brushing away a cobweb. "Just—a goddamn—second, Tim!" A convulsive shiver ran through him.

Automatically I moved toward him to see what the matter was and as I came up beside him in front of that dark opening I felt a sudden weird sensation, a jolt, a jab, and my head began to spin. And for a moment—just a moment—I seemed to hear a strange music, an eerie high-pitched wailing sound like the keening of elevator cables far, far away. In that crazy incomprehensible moment I imagined that I was standing at the rim of a deep ancient well, the oldest well of all, the well from which all creation flows, with strange shadowy things churning and throbbing down below, and from its depths rose a wild rush of perfumed air that dizzied and intoxicated me.

Then the moment passed and I was in my right mind again and I looked at Charlie and he looked at me.

"You felt it too, didn't you?" I said.

"Felt what?" he demanded fiercely. He seemed almost angry.

I searched for the words. But it was all fading, fading fast, and there was only Charlie with his face jammed into mine, angry Charlie, terrifying Charlie, practically daring me to claim that anything peculiar had happened.

"It was very odd, bro," I said finally. "Like a drug thing, almost."

"Oxygen deprivation, is all. A blast of old stale air."

"You think?"

"I know."

But he seemed uncharacteristically hesitant, even a little befuddled. He stood at an angle to the opening, head turned away, shoulders slumping, the flashlight dangling from his hand.

"Aren't you going to look inside?" I asked, after a bit.

"Give me a moment, Timmo."

"Charlie, are you all right?"

"Christ, yes! I breathed in a little dust, that's all." He knelt, rummaged in the tool sack, pulled out a canteen, took a deep drink. "Better," he said hoarsely. "Want some?" I took the canteen from him and he leaned into the opening again, flashing the beam around.

"What do you see?"

"Nothing. Not a fucking thing."

"They put up a marble slab and plaster it with inscribed seals and there's nothing at all behind it?"

"A hole," he said. "Maybe five feet deep, five feet high. A storage chamber of some kind, I would guess. Nothing in it. Absolutely fucking nothing, bro."

"Let me see."

"Don't you trust me?"

In fact I didn't, not very much. But I just shrugged; and he handed me the flashlight, and I peered into the hole. Charlie was right. The interior of the chamber was smooth and regular, but it was empty, not the slightest trace of anything.

"Shit," Charlie said. He shook his head somberly. "My very own Tutankh-amen tomb, only nothing's in it. Let's get the hell out of here."

Are you going to report this?"

"What for? I come in after hours, conduct illicit explorations, and all I have to show for my sins is an empty hole? What's the good of telling anybody that? Just for the sake of making myself look like an unethical son of a bitch? No, bro. None of this ever happened."

"But the seals—the inscriptions in an unknown script—"

"Not important. Let's go, Tim."

He still sounded angry, and not, I think, just because the little chamber behind the marble slab had been empty. Something had gotten to him just now, and gotten to him deeply. Had he heard the weird music too? Had he looked into that fathomless well? He hated all mystery, everything inexplicable. I think that was why he had become an archaeologist. Mysteries had a way of unhinging him. When I was maybe ten and he was thirteen, we had spent a rainy evening telling each other ghost stories, and finally we made one up together, something about spooks from another world who were haunting our attic, and our own story scared me so much that I began to cry. I imagined I heard strange creaks overhead. Charlie mocked me mercilessly, but it seemed to me that for a time he had looked a little nervous too, and when I said so he got very annoyed indeed; and then, bluffing all the way, I invited him to come up to the attic with me right then and there to see that it was safe, and he punched me in the chest and knocked me down. Later he denied the whole episode.

"I'm sorry I wasted your time tonight, keed," he said, as we hiked back up to our cars.

"That's okay. It just might have been something special."

"Just might have been, yeah."

He grinned and winked. He was himself again, old devil-may-care Charlie. "Sleep tight, bro. See you in the morning."

But I didn't sleep tight at all. I kept waking and hearing the wailing sound of far-off elevator cables, and my dreams were full of blurry strangenesses.

* * *

The next day I hung out at the hotel all day, breakfasting with Charlie—he didn't refer to the events of the night before at all—and lounging by the pool the rest of the time. I had some vague thought of hooking up with one of the German tourist ladies, I suppose, but no openings presented themselves, and I contented myself with watching the show. Even in puritanical Turkey, where the conservative politicians are trying to put women back into veils and ankle-length skirts, European women of all ages go casually topless at coastal resorts like this, and it was remarkable to see how much savoir-faire the Turkish poolside waiters displayed while taking bar orders from zaftig bare-breasted grandmothers from Hamburg or Munich and their stunning topless granddaughters.

Mr. Gladstone, who hadn't been around in the morning, turned up in late afternoon. I was in the lobby bar by then, working on my third or fourth post-lunch *raki*. He looked sweaty and tired and sunburned. I ordered a Coke for him.

"Busy day?"

"Very. The Cave of the Seven Sleepers was my first stop. A highly emotional experience, I have to say, not because of the cave itself, you understand, although the ancient ruined church there is quite interesting, but because—the associations—the memories of my dear wife that it summoned—"

"Of course."

"After that my driver took me out to the so-called House of the Virgin. Perhaps it's genuine, perhaps not, but either way it's a moving thing to see. The invisible presence of thousands of pilgrims hovers over it, the aura of centuries of faith." He smiled gently. "Do you know what I mean, Mr. Walker?"

"I think I do, yes."

"And in the afternoon I saw the Basilica of St. John, on Ayasuluk Hill."

I didn't know anything about that. He explained that it was the acropolis of the old Byzantine city—the steep hill just across the main highway from the center of the town of Seljuk. Legend had it that St. John the Apostle had been buried up there, and centuries later the Emperor Justinian built an enormous church on the site, which was, of course, a ruin now, but an impressive one.

"And you?" he said. "You visited with your brother?"

"In the morning, yes."

"A brilliant man, your brother. If only he could be happier, eh?"

"Oh, I think Charlie's happy, all right. He's had his own way every step of his life."

"Is that your definition of happiness? Having your own way?"

"It can be very helpful."

"And you haven't had your own way, is that it, Mr. Walker?"

"My life has been reasonably easy by most people's standards, I have to admit. I was smart enough to pick a wealthy great-grandfather. But compared with Charlie—he has an extraordinary mind, he's had a splendid scientific career, he's admired by all the members of his profession. I don't even have a profession, Mr. Gladstone. I just float around."

"You're young, Mr. Walker. You'll find something to do and someone to share your life with, and you'll settle down. But your brother—I wonder, Mr. Walker. Something vital is missing from his life. But he will never find it, because he is not willing to admit that it's missing."

"Religion, do you mean?"

"Not specifically, no. Belief, perhaps. Not religion, but belief. Do you follow me, Mr. Walker? One must believe in *something,* do you see? And your brother will not permit himself to do that." He gave me the gentle smile again. "Would you excuse me, now? I've had a rather strenuous day. I think a little nap, before supper—"

Since we were the only two Americans in the place, I invited him to join me again for dinner that night. He did most of the talking, reminiscing about his wife, telling me about his children—he had three, in their thirties—and describing some of the things he had seen in his tour of the Biblical places. I had never spent much time with anyone of his sort. A kindly man, an earnest man; and, I suspect, not quite as simple a man as a casual observer might think.

He went upstairs about half past eight. I returned to the bar and had a couple of raw Turkish brandies and thought hopeful thoughts about the stunning German granddaughters. Somewhere about ten, as I was considering going to bed, a waiter appeared and said, "You are Mr. Timothy Walker?"

"Yes."

"Your brother Charles is at the security gate and asks that you come out to meet him."

Mystified, I went rushing out into the courtyard. The hotel grounds are locked down every night and nobody is admitted except guests and the guests of guests. I saw the glare of headlights just beyond the gate. Charlie's car.

"What's up, bro?"

His eyes were wild. He gestured at me with furious impatience.

"In. In!" Almost before I closed the door he spun the car around and was zooming down the narrow, winding road back to Seljuk. He was hunched over the wheel in the most peculiar rigid way.

"Charlie?"

"Exactly what did you experience," he said tightly, "when we pulled that marble slab out of the wall?"

My reply was carefully vague.

"Tell me," he said. "Be very precise."

"I don't want you to laugh at me, Charlie."

"Just tell me."

I took a deep breath. "Well, then. I imagined that I heard far-off music. I had a kind of vision of—well, someplace weird and mysterious. I thought I smelled perfume. The whole thing lasted maybe half a second and then it was over."

He was silent a moment.

Then he said, in a strange little quiet way, "It was the same for me, bro."

"You denied it. I asked you, and you said no, Charlie."

"Well, I lied. It was the same for me." His voice had become very odd—thin, tight, quavering. Everything about him right now was tight. Something had to pop. The car was traveling at maybe eighty miles an hour on that little road and I feared for my life.

After a very long time he said, "Do you think there's any possibility, Tim, that we might have let something out of that hole in the ground when we broke those seals and pulled that slab out?"

I stared at him. "That's crazy, Charlie."

"I know it is. Just answer me: do you think we felt something moving past us as we opened that chamber?"

"Hey, we're too old to be telling each other spook stories, bro."

"I'm being serious."

"Bullshit you are," I said. "I hate it when you play with me like this."

"I'm not playing," Charlie said, and he turned around so that he was practically facing me for a moment. His face was twisted with strain. "Timmo, some goddamned thing that looks awfully much like Diana of Ephesus has been walking around in the ruins since sundown. Three people I know have seen her. Three very reliable people."

I couldn't believe that he was saying stuff like this. Not Charlie.

"Keep your eyes on the road, will you?" I told him. "You'll get us killed driving like that."

"Do you know how much it costs me to say these things? Do you know how lunatic it sounds to me? But she's real. She's there. She was sealed up in that hole, and we let her out. The foreman of the excavations has seen her, and Judy, the staff artist, and Mike Dornan, the ceramics guy."

"They're fucking with your head, Charlie. Or you're fucking with mine."

"No. No. No. No."

"Where are we going?" I asked.

"To look for her. To find out what the hell it is that those people think they saw. I've got to know, Tim. This time, I've absolutely got to know."

The desperation in Charlie's voice was something new in my experience of him. *I've absolutely got to know.* Why? Why? It was all too crazy. And dragging me out like this: why? To bear witness? To help him prove to himself that he actually was seeing the thing that he was seeing, if indeed he saw it? Or, maybe, to help him convince himself that there was nothing there to see? But he wasn't going to see anything. I was sure of that.

"Charlie," I said. "Oh, Charlie, Charlie, Charlie, this isn't happening, is it? Not really."

* * *

We pulled up outside the main gate of the ruins. A watchman was posted there, a Turk. He stepped quickly aside as Charlie went storming through into the site. I saw flashlights glowing in the distance, and then four or five American-looking people. Charlie's colleagues, the archaeologists.

"Well?" Charlie yelled. He sounded out of control.

A frizzy-haired woman of about forty came up from somewhere to our left. She looked as wild-eyed and agitated as Charlie. For the first time I began to think this might not be just some goofy practical joke.

"Heading east," the woman blurted. "Toward the stadium or maybe all the way out to the goddess sanctuary. Dick saw it too. And Edward thinks he did."

"Anybody get a photo?"

"Not that I know of," the woman said.

"Come on," Charlie said to me, and went running off at an angle to the direction we had just come. Frantically I chased after him. He was chugging uphill, into the thorny scrub covering the unexcavated areas of the city. By moonlight I saw isolated shattered pillars rising from the ground like broken teeth, and tumbledown columns that had been tossed around like so many toothpicks. As I came alongside him he said, "There's a little sanctuary of the Mother Goddess back there. Wouldn't that be the logical place that she'd want to go to?"

"For shit's sake, Charlie! What are you saying?"

He kept on running, giving me no answer. I fought my way up the hill through a tangle of brambles and canes that slashed at me like daggers, all the while wondering what the hell we were going to find on top. We were halfway up when shouts came to us from down the hill, people behind us waving and pointing. Charlie halted and listened, frowning. Then he swung around and started sprinting back down the hill. "She's gone outside the ruins," he called to me over his shoulder. "Through the fence, heading into town! Come on, Tim!"

I went running after him, scrambling downhill, then onward along the main entrance road and onto the main highway. I'm in good running shape, but Charlie was moving with a maniacal zeal that left me hard pressed to keep up with him. Twenty feet apart, we came pounding down the road past the museum and into town. All the dinky restaurants were open, even this late, and little knots of Turks had emerged from them to gather in the crossroads. Some were kneeling in prayer, hammering their heads against the pavement, and others were wildly gesticulating at one other in obvious shock and bewilderment. Charlie, without breaking stride, called out to them in guttural Turkish and got a whole babble of replies.

"Ayasuluk Hill," he said to me. "That's the direction she's going in."

We crossed the broad boulevard that divides the town in half. As we passed the bus station half a dozen men came running out of a side street in front of us, screaming as though they had just been disemboweled. You don't expect to hear adult male Turks screaming. They are a nation of tough people, by and large. These fellows went flying past us without halting, big men with thick black mustachios. Their eyes were wide and gleaming like beacons, their faces rigid and distended with shock and horror, as though twenty devils were coming after them.

"Charlie—"

"Look there," he said, in an utterly flat voice, and pointed into the darkness. Something—*something*—was moving away from us down that side street, something very tall and very strange. I saw a tapering conical body, a hint of weird appendages, a crackling blue-white aura. It seemed to be floating rather than walking, carried along by a serene but inexorable drifting motion almost as if its feet were several inches off the ground. Maybe they were. As we watched, the thing halted and peered into the open window of a house. There was a flash of blinding light, intense but short-lived. Then the front door popped open and a bunch of frantic Turks came boiling out like a pack of Keystone Cops, running in sixty directions at once, yelling and flinging their arms about as though trying to surrender.

One of them tripped and went sprawling down right at the creature's feet. He seemed unable to get up; he knelt there all bunched up, moaning and babbling, shielding his face with outspread hands. The thing paused and looked down, and seemed to reach its arms out in fluid gestures, and the blue-white glow spread for a moment like a mantle over the man. Then the light withdrew from him and the creature, gliding smoothly past the trembling fallen man, continued on its serene silent way toward the dark hill that loomed above the town.

"Come," Charlie said to me.

We went forward. The creature had disappeared up ahead, though we caught occasional glimpses of the blue-white light as it passed between the low little buildings of the town. We reached the man who had tripped; he had not arisen, but lay face down, shivering, covering his head with his hands. A low rumbling moan of fear came steadily from him. From in front of us, hoarse cries of terror drifted to us from here and there as this villager or that encountered the thing that was passing through their town, and now and again we could see that cool bright light, rising steadily above us until finally it was shining down from the upper levels of Ayasuluk Hill.

"You really want to go up there?" I asked him.

He didn't offer me an answer, nor did he stop moving forward. I wasn't about to turn back either, I realized. Willy-nilly I followed him to the end of the street, around a half-ruined mosque at the base of the hill, and up to a lofty metal gate tipped with spikes. Stoned on our own adrenaline, we swarmed up that gate like Crusaders attacking a Saracen fortress, went over the top, dropped down in the bushes on the far side. I was able to see, by the brilliant gleam of the full moon, the low walls of the destroyed Basilica of St. John just beyond, and, behind it, the massive Byzantine fortification that crowned the hill. Together we scrambled toward the summit.

"You go this way, Tim. I'll go the other and we'll meet on the far side."

"Right."

I didn't know what I was looking for. I just ran, leftward around the hill. Along the ramparts, into the church, down the empty aisles, out the gaping window-frames. Suddenly I caught a glimpse of something up ahead. Light, cool white light, an unearthly light very much like moonlight, only concentrated into a fiercely gleaming point hovering a couple of yards above the ground, thirty or forty feet in front of me.

"Charlie?" I called. My voice was no more than a hoarse gasp. I edged forward. The light was so intense now that I was afraid it might damage my eyes. But I continued to stare, as if the thing would disappear if I were to blink for even a millionth of a second.

I heard the wailing music again.

Soft, distant, eerie. Cables rubbing together in a dark shaft. This time it seemed to be turned outward, rising far beyond me, reaching into distant space or perhaps some even more distant dimension. Something calling, announcing its regained freedom, summoning—whom? *What?*

"Charlie?" I said. It was a barely audible croak. "Charlie?"

I noticed him now, edging up from the other side. I pointed at the source of the light. He nodded.

I moved closer. The light seemed to change, to grow momentarily less fierce. And then I was able to see her.

She wasn't exactly identical to the statues in the museum. Her face wasn't really a face, at least not a human one. She had beady eyes, faceted the way an insect's are. She had an extra set of arms, little dangling ones, coming out at her hips. And, though the famous breasts were there, at least fifty of them and maybe the hundred of legend, I don't think they were actual breasts because I don't think this creature was a mammal. More of a reptile, I would guess: leathery skin, more or less scaly the way a snake's is, and tiny dots of nostrils, and a black slithery tongue, jagged like a lightning bolt, that came shooting quickly out between her slitted slips again and again and again, as though checking on the humidity or the ambient temperature or some such thing.

I saw, and Charlie saw. For a fraction of a second I wanted to drop down on my knees and rub my forehead in the ground and give worship. And then I just wanted to run.

I said, "Charlie, I definitely think we ought to get the hell out of—"

"Cool it, bro," he said. He stepped forward. Walked right up to her, stared her in the face. I was terrified for him, seeing him get that close. She dwarfed him. He was like a doll in front of her. How had a thing this big managed to fit in that opening in the tunnel wall? How had those ancient Greeks ever managed to get her in there in the first place?

That dazzling light crackled and hissed around her like some sort of electrical discharge. And yet Charlie stood his ground, unflinching, rock-solid. The expression on my brother's face was a nearly incomprehensible mixture of anger and fear.

He jabbed his forefinger through the air at her.

"You," he said to her. It was almost a snarl. "Tell me what the hell you are."

They were maybe ten feet apart, the man and the—what? The goddess? The monster?

Charlie had to know.

"You speak English?" he demanded. "Turkish? Tell me. I'm the one who let you out of that hole. Tell me what you are. I want to know." Eye to eye, face to face. "Something from another planet, are you, maybe? Another dimension? An ancient race that used to live on the Earth before humans did?"

"Charlie," I whispered.

But he wouldn't let up. "Or maybe you're an actual, literal goddess," he said. His tone had turned softer, a mocking croon now. "Diana of Ephesus, is that who you are? Stepping right out of the pages of mythology in all your fantastic beauty? Well, do me some magic, goddess, if that's who you are. Do a miracle for me, just a little one." The angry edge was back in his voice. "Turn that tree into an elephant. Turn me into a sheep, if you can. What's the matter, Diana, you no spikka da English? All right. Why the hell should you? But how about Greek, then? Surely you can understand Greek."

"For Christ's sake, Charlie—"

He ignored me. It was as if I wasn't there. He was talking to her in Greek, now. I suppose it was Greek. It was harsh, thick-sounding, jaggedly rhythmic. His eyes were wild and his face was flushed with fury. I was afraid that she would hurl a thunderbolt of blue-white light at him, but no, no, she just stood there through all his whole harangue, as motionless as those statues of her in the little museum, listening patiently as my furious brother went on and on and on at her in the language of Homer and Sophocles.

He stopped, finally. Waited as if expecting her to respond.

No response came. I could hear the whistling sound of her slow steady breathing; occasionally there was some slight movement of her body; but that was all.

"Well, Diana?" Charlie said. "What do you have to say for yourself, Diana?"

Silence.

"You fraud!" Charlie cried, in a great and terrible voice. "You fake! Some goddess you are! You aren't real at all, and that's God's own truth. You aren't even here. You're nothing but a fucking hallucination. A projection of some kind. I bet I could walk up to you and put my hand right through you."

Still no reaction. Nothing. She just stood there, those faceted eyes glittering, that little tongue flickering. Saying nothing, offering him no help.

That was when he flipped out. Charlie seemed to puff up as if about to explode with rage, and went rushing toward her, arms raised, fists clenched in a wild gesture of attack. I wanted desperately to stop him, but my feet were frozen in place. I was certain that he was going to die. We both were.

"Damn you!" he roared, with something like a sob behind the fury. "Damn you, damn you, damn you!"

But before he could strike her, her aura flared up around her like a sheath, and for a moment the air was full of brilliant flares of cold flame that went whirling and whirling around her in a way that was too painful to watch. I caught a glimpse of Charlie staggering back from her, and I backed away myself, covering my face with my forearm, but even so the whirling lights came stabbing into my brain, forcing me to the ground. It seemed then that they all coalesced into a single searing point of white light, which rose like a dagger into the sky, climbing, climbing, becoming something almost like a comet, and—then—

Vanishing.

And then I blanked out.

It was just before dawn when I awakened. My eyes fluttered open almost hesitantly. The moon was gone, the first pink streaks of light beginning to appear. Charlie sat beside me. He was already awake. "Where is it?" I asked immediately.

"Gone, bro."

"Gone?"

He nodded. "Without a trace. If it ever was up here with us at all."

"What do you mean, if?"

"*If,* that's what I mean. Who the hell knows what was going on up here last night? Do you?"

"No."

"Well, neither do I. All I know is that it isn't going on anymore. There's nobody around but me and thee."

He was trying to sound like the old casual Charlie I knew, the man who had been everywhere and done everything and took it all in his stride. But there was a quality in his voice that I had never heard in it before, something entirely new.

"Gone?" I said, stupidly. "Really gone?"

"Really gone, yes. Vanished. You hear how quiet everything is?" Indeed the town, spread out below us, was silent except for the crowing of the first roosters and the far-off sound of a farm tractor starting up somewhere.

"Are you all right?" I asked him.

"Fine," he said. "Absolutely fine."

But he said it through clenched teeth. I couldn't bear to look at him. A thing had happened here that badly needed explanation, and no explanations were available, and I knew what that must be doing to him. I kept staring at the place where that eerie being had been, and I remembered that single shaft of light that had taken its place, and I felt a crushing sense of profound and terrible loss. Something strange and weirdly beautiful and utterly fantastic and inexplicable had been loose in the world for a little while, after centuries of—what? Imprisonment? Hibernation?—and now it was gone, and it would never return. It had known at once, I was sure, that this was no era for goddesses. Or whatever it was.

We sat side by side in silence for a minute or two.

"I think we ought to go back down now," I said finally.

"Right. Let's go back down," Charlie said.

And without saying another word as we descended, we made our way down the hill of Ayasuluk, the hill of St. John the Apostle, who was the man who wrote the Book of Revelations.

* * *

MR. GLADSTONE WAS HAVING BREAKFAST in the hotel coffee shop when Charlie and I came in. He saw at once that something was wrong and asked if he could help in any way, and after some hesitation we told him something of what had happened, and then we told him more, and then we told him the whole story right to the end.

He didn't laugh and he didn't make any sarcastic skeptical comments. He took it all quite seriously.

"Perhaps the Seal of Solomon was what was on that marble slab," he suggested. "The Turks would say some such thing, at any rate. King Solomon had power over the evil jinn, and locked them away in flasks and caves and tombs, and put his seal on them to keep them locked up. It's in the Koran."

"You've read the Koran?" I asked, surprised.

"I've read a lot of things," said Mr. Gladstone.

"The Seal of Solomon," Charlie said, scowling. He was trying hard to be his old self again, and almost succeeding. Almost. "Evil spirits. Magic. Oh, Jesus Christ!"

"Perhaps," said Mr. Gladstone.

"What?" Charlie said.

The little man from Ohio or Indiana or Iowa put his hand over Charlie's. "If only I could help you," he said. "But you've been undone, haven't you, by the evidence of things seen."

"You have the quote wrong," said Charlie. "'The substance of things hoped for, the evidence of things not seen.' Book of Hebrews, 11:1."

Mr. Gladstone was impressed. So was I.

"But this is different," he said to Charlie. "This time, you actually saw. You were, I think, a man who prided himself on believing in nothing at all. But now you can no longer even believe in your own disbelief." Charlie reddened. "Saw what? A goddess? Jesus! You think I believe that that was a goddess? A genuine immortal supernatural being of a higher order of existence? Or—what?—some kind of actual alien creature? You want me to believe it was an alien that had been locked up in there all that time? An alien from where? Mars? And who locked it up? Or was it one of King Solomon's jinn, maybe?"

"Does it really matter which it was?" Mr. Gladstone asked softly.

Charlie started to say something; but he choked it back. After a moment he stood. "Listen, I need to go now," he said. "Mr. Gladstone—Timmo—I'll catch up with you later, is that all right?"

And then he turned and stalked away. But before he left, I saw the look in his eyes.

His eyes. Oh, Charlie. Oh. Those eyes. Those frightened, empty eyes.

SUNRISE ON MERCURY

That curious ancient custom—now extinct, I think—of having writers construct stories around cover paintings, rather than having covers painted to illustrate scenes in stories that had already been written—brought "Sunrise on Mercury" into existence in the hyperactive November of 1956, when I was beginning to enter my most prolific years as a writer. In that vanished era, the pulp-magazine chains liked to print their covers four issues at once, which meant that there was usually no time to go through the process of buying a story, sending it out to an artist to be illustrated, making plates from the artist's painting, etc. Instead the artists thought up ideas for illustrations—a scene conceived for its qualities of vivid and dramatic visual excitement, but not necessarily embodying any sort of plausibility—and it went to press right away, while some reliable writer was hired to work it, by hook or by crook, into a story that could be published to accompany it. It's a measure of how quickly things had changed for me at this point that I was already being given such assignments, here in the second year of my career. But the editors had come to see that I could be depended on to utilize the illustration in some relatively plausible way and to turn my cover story in on time.

So Bob Lowndes, the editor of *Science Fiction Stories* and *Future Science Fiction*, would hand me proofs of two or three upcoming covers, and I would go home and write stories of five or six thousand words to accompany each one. The money wasn't much—a cent or maybe a cent and a half a word, cut-rate stuff even in those days—but it was a guaranteed sale, and so speedy was I at turning out the stories that even at $60 for 6,000 words, which is what I was paid for "Sunrise on Mercury," I did all right. (I could write a short story in a day, four of them a week with the fifth day reserved for visiting editorial offices to deliver stories and pick up new assignments, back then. $60 for a day's pay was nothing contemptible in 1956, when annual salaries in the mid-four-figure range were the norm.)

The cover that inspired this one, by Ed Emshwiller, showed the bleak landscape of Mercury with the sun rising ominously in the upper left-hand corner, a transparent plastic dome melting in Daliesque fashion in the upper right, and two harassed-looking men in spacesuits running for their lives below. Obviously something unexpected was going on, like sunrise happening a week ahead of schedule; so all I had to do was figure out a reason why that might occur, and I would have my sixty bucks. And so I conjured up a really alien life-form, as anything living on inhospitable Mercury would have to be, and wrote a story around it. The result, all things considered, wasn't half bad; and the story, which Lowndes used in the May 1957 *Science Fiction Stories*, has been frequently anthologized over the past fifty years.

Nine million miles to the sunward of Mercury, with the *Leverrier* swinging into the series of spirals that would bring it down on the solar system's smallest world, Second Astrogator Lon Curtis decided to end his life.

Curtis had been lounging in a webfoam cradle waiting for the landing to be effected; his job in the operation was over, at least until the *Leverrier*'s landing jacks touched Mercury's blistered surface. The ship's efficient sodium-coolant system negated the efforts of the swollen sun visible through the rear screen. For Curtis and his seven shipmates, no problems presented themselves; they had only to wait while the autopilot brought the ship down for man's second landing on Mercury.

Flight Commander Harry Ross was sitting near Curtis when he noticed the sudden momentary stiffening of the astrogator's jaws. Curtis abruptly reached for the control nozzle. From the spinnerets that had spun the webfoam came a quick green burst of dissolving fluorochrene; the cradle vanished. Curtis stood up.

"Going somewhere?" Ross asked.

Curtis's voice was harsh. "Just—just taking a walk."

Ross returned his attention to his microbook for a moment as Curtis walked away. There was the ratchety sound of a bulkhead dog being manipulated, and Ross felt a momentary chill as the cooler air of the superrefrigerated reactor compartment drifted in.

He punched a stud, turning the page. Then—

What the hell is he doing in the reactor compartment?

The autopilot would be controlling the fuel flow, handling it down to the milligram, in a way no human system could. The reactor was primed for the landing, the fuel was stoked, the compartment was dogged shut. No one—least of all a second astrogator—had any business going back there.

Ross had the foam cradle dissolved in an instant, and was on his feet a moment later. He dashed down the companionway and through the open bulkhead door into the coolness of the reactor compartment.

Curtis was standing by the converter door, toying with the release-tripper. As Ross approached, he saw the astrogator get the door open and put one foot into the chute that led downship to the nuclear pile.

"Curtis, you idiot! Get away from there! You'll kill us all!"

The astrogator turned, looked blankly at Ross for an instant, and drew up his other foot. Ross leaped.

He caught Curtis' booted foot in his hands, and despite a barrage of kicks from the astrogator's free boot, managed to drag Curtis off the chute. The astrogator tugged and pulled, attempting to break free. Ross saw the man's pale cheeks quivering. Curtis had cracked, but thoroughly.

Grunting, Ross yanked Curtis away from the yawning reactor chute and slammed the door shut. He dragged him out into the main section again and slapped him, hard.

"Why'd you want to do that? Don't you know what your mass would do to the ship if it got into the converter? You know the fuel intake's been calibrated already; 180 extra pounds and we'd arc right into the sun. What's wrong with you, Curtis?"

The astrogator fixed unshaking, unexpressive eyes on Ross. "I want to die," he said simply. "Why couldn't you let me die?"

He wanted to die.

Ross shrugged, feeling a cold tremor run down his back. There was no guarding against this disease. Just as aqualungers beneath the sea's surface suffered from *l'ivresse des grandes profondeurs*—rapture of the deeps—and knew no cure for the strange, depth-induced drunkenness that caused them to remove their breathing tubes fifty fathoms below, so did spacemen run the risk of this nameless malady, this inexplicable urge to self-destruction.

It struck anywhere. A repairman wielding a torch on a recalcitrant strut of an orbiting wheel might abruptly rip open his facemask and drink vacuum; a radioman rigging an antenna on the skin of his ship might suddenly cut his line, fire his directional pistol, and send himself drifting away. Or a second astrogator might decide to climb into the converter.

Psych Officer Spangler appeared, an expression of concern fixed on his smooth pink face. "Trouble?"

Ross nodded. "Curtis. Tried to jump into the fuel chute. He's got it, Doc."

Spangler rubbed his cheek and said: "They always pick the best times, dammit. It's swell having a psycho on a Mercury run."

"That's the way it is," Ross said wearily. "Better put him in stasis till we get home. I'd hate to have him running loose, looking for different ways of doing himself in."

"Why can't you let me die?" Curtis asked. His face was bleak. "Why'd you have to stop me?"

"Because, you lunatic, you'd have killed all the rest of us by your fool dive into the converter. Go walk out the airlock if you want to die—but don't take us with you."

Spangler glared warningly at him. "Harry—"

"Okay," Ross said. "Take him away."

The psychman led Curtis within. The astrogator would be given a tranquillizing injection and locked in an insoluble webfoam jacket for the rest of the journey. There was a chance he could be restored to sanity once they returned to Earth, but Ross knew that the astrogator would go straight for the nearest method of suicide the moment he was released aboard the ship.

Scowling, Ross turned away. A man spends his boyhood dreaming about space, he thought, spends four years at the Academy, and two more making dummy runs. Then he finally gets out where it counts and he cracks up. Curtis was an astrogation machine, not a normal human being; and he had just disqualified himself permanently from the only job he knew how to do.

Ross shivered, feeling chill despite the bloated bulk of the sun filling the rear screen. It could happen to anyone . . . even him. He thought of Curtis lying in a foam cradle somewhere in the back of the ship, blackly thinking over and over again, *I want to die,* while Doc Spangler muttered soothing things at him. A human being was really a frail form of life.

Death seemed to hang over the ship; the gloomy aura of Curtis's suicide-wish polluted the atmosphere.

Ross shook his head and punched down savagely on the signal to prepare for deceleration. Mercury's sharp globe bobbed up ahead. He spotted it through the front screen.

They were approaching the tiny planet middle-on. He could see the neat division now: the brightness of Sunside, that unapproachable inferno where zinc ran in rivers, and the icy blackness of Darkside, dull with its unlit plains of frozen CO2.

Down the heart of the planet ran the Twilight Belt, that narrow area of not-cold and not-heat where Sunside and Darkside met to provide a thin band of barely tolerable territory, a ring nine thousand miles in circumference and ten or twenty miles wide.

The *Leverrier* plunged planetward. Ross allowed his jangled nerves to grow calm. The ship was in the hands of the autopilot; the orbit, of course, was precomputed, and the analogue banks in the drive were serenely following the taped program, bringing the ship towards its destination smack in the middle of—

My God!

Ross went cold from head to toe. The precomputed tape had been fed to the analog banks—had been prepared by—had been entirely the work of—

Curtis.

A suicidal madman had worked out the *Leverrier*'s landing program.

Ross began to shake. How easy it would have been, he thought, for death-bent Curtis to work out an orbit that would plant the *Leverrier* in a smoking river of molten lead—or in the mortuary chill of Darkside.

His false security vanished. There was no trusting the automatic pilot; they'd have to risk a manual landing.

Ross jabbed down on the communicator button. "I want Brainerd," he said hoarsely.

The first astrogator appeared a few seconds later, peering in curiously. "What goes, Captain?"

"We've just carted your assistant Curtis off to the pokey. He tried to jump into the converter. Attempted suicide. I got to him in time. But in view of the circumstances, I think we'd better discard the tape you had him prepare and bring the ship down manually, yes?"

The first astrogator moistened his lips. "That sounds like a good idea."

"Damn right it is," Ross said, glowering.

* * *

As THE SHIP TOUCHED DOWN Ross thought, *Mercury is two hells in one.*

It was the cold, ice-bound kingdom of Dante's deepest pit—and it was also the brimstone empire of another conception. The two met, fire and frost, each hemisphere its own kind of hell.

He lifted his head and flicked a quick glance at the instrument panel above his deceleration cradle. The dials all checked: weight placement was proper, stability 100 per cent, external temperature a manageable 108 degrees F, indicating they had made their descent a little to the sunward of the Twilight Belt's exact middle. It had been a sound landing.

He snapped on the communicator. "Brainerd?"

"All okay, Captain."

"Manual landing?"

"I had to," the astrogator said. "I ran a quick check on Curtis' tape, and it was all cockeyed. The way he had us coming in, we'd have grazed Mercury's orbit by a whisker and kept on going straight into the sun. Nice?"

"Very sweet," Ross said. "But don't be too hard on the kid. He didn't want to go psycho. Good landing, anyway. We seem to be pretty close to the center of the Twilight Belt, and that's where I feel most comfortable."

He broke the contact and unwebbed himself. Over the shipwide circuit he called all hands fore, double pronto.

The men got there quickly enough—Brainerd first, then Doc Spangler, followed by Accumulator Tech Krinsky and the three other crewmen. Ross waited until the entire group had assembled.

They were looking around curiously for Curtis. Crisply, Ross told them, "Astrogator Curtis is going to miss this meeting. He's aft in the psycho bin. Luckily, we can shift without him on this tour."

He waited until the implications of that statement had sunk in. The men seemed to adjust to it well enough, he thought: momentary expressions of dismay, shock, even horror quickly faded from their faces.

"All right," he said. "Schedule calls for us to put in some thirty-two hours of extravehicular activity on Mercury. Brainerd, how does that check with our location?"

The astrogator frowned and made some mental calculations. "Current position is a trifle to the sunward edge of the Twilight Belt; but as I figure it, the sun won't be high enough to put the Fahrenheit much above 120 for at least a week. Our suits can handle that temperature with ease."

"Good. Llewellyn, you and Falbridge break out the radar inflaters and get the tower set up as far to the east as you can go without getting roasted. Take the crawler, but be sure to keep an eye on the thermometer. We've only got one heatsuit, and that's for Krinsky."

Llewellyn, a thin, sunken-eyed spaceman, shifted uneasily. "How far to the east do you suggest, sir?"

"The Twilight Belt covers about a quarter of Mercury's surface," Ross said. "You've got a strip forty-seven degrees wide to move around in—but I don't suggest you go much more than twenty-five miles or so. It starts getting hot after that. And keeps going up."

Ross turned to Krinsky. In many ways the accumulator tech was the expedition's key man: it was his job to check the readings on the pair of solar accumulators that had been left here by the first expedition. He was to measure the amount of stress created by solar energies here, so close to the source of radiation, study force-lines operating in the strange magnetic field of the little world, and reprime the accumulators for further testing by the next expedition.

Krinsky was a tall, powerfully built man, the sort of man who could stand up to the crushing weight of a heatsuit almost cheerfully. The heatsuit was necessary for prolonged work in the Sunside zone, where the accumulators were mounted—and even a giant like Krinsky could stand the strain for only a few hours at a time.

"When Llewellyn and Falbridge have the radar tower set up, Krinsky, get into your heatsuit and be ready to move. As soon as we've got the accumulator station located, Dominic will drive you as far east as possible and drop you off. The rest is up to you. Watch your step. We'll be telemetering your readings, but we'd like to have you back alive."

"Yes, sir."

"That's about it," Ross said. "Let's get rolling."

* * *

Ross's own job was purely administrative—and as the men of his crew moved busily about their allotted tasks, he realized unhappily that he himself was condemned to temporary idleness. His function was that of overseer; like the conductor of a symphony orchestra, he played no instrument himself and was on hand mostly to keep the group moving in harmony towards the finish.

Everyone was in motion. Now he had only to wait.

Llewellyn and Falbridge departed, riding the segmented, thermoresistant crawler that had traveled to Mercury in the belly of the *Leverrier*. Their job was simple: they were to erect the inflatable plastic radar tower out towards the sunward sector. The tower that the first expedition had left had long since librated into a Sunside zone and been liquefied; the plastic base and parabola, covered with a light reflective surface of aluminum, could hardly withstand the searing heat of Sunside.

Out there, it got up to 700 degrees when the sun was at its closest. The eccentricities of Mercury's orbit accounted for considerable temperature variations on Sunside, but the thermometer never showed lower than 300 degrees out there, even during aphelion. On Darkside, there was less of a temperature range; mostly the temperature hovered not far from absolute zero, and frozen drifts of heavy gases covered the surface of the land.

From where he stood, Ross could see neither Sunside nor Darkside. The Twilight Belt was nearly a thousand miles broad, and as the little planet dipped in its orbit the sun would first slide above the horizon, then slip back. For a twenty-mile strip through the heart of the Belt, the heat of Sunside and the cold of Darkside canceled out into a fairly stable, temperate climate; for five hundred miles on either side, the Twilight Belt gradually trickled towards the areas of extreme cold and raging heat.

It was a strange and forbidding planet. Humans could endure it for only a short time; it was worse than Mars, worse than the Moon. The sort of life capable of living permanently on Mercury was beyond Ross's powers of imagination. Standing outside the *Leverrier* in his spacesuit, he nudged the chin control that lowered a sheet of optical glass. He peered first towards Darkside, where he thought he saw a thin line of encroaching black—only illusion, he knew—and then towards Sunside.

In the distance, Llewellyn and Falbridge were erecting the spidery parabola that was the radar tower. He could see the clumsy shape outlined against the sky now—and behind it? A faint line of brightness rimming the bordering peaks? Illusion also, he knew. Brainerd had calculated that the sun's radiance would not be visible here for a week. And in a week's time they'd be back on Earth.

He turned to Krinsky. "The tower's nearly up. They'll be coming in with the crawler any minute. You'd better get ready to make your trip."

As the accumulator tech swung up the handholds and into the ship, Ross's thoughts turned to Curtis. The young astrogator had talked excitedly of seeing Mercury all the way out—and now that they were actually here, Curtis lay in a web of foam deep within the ship, moodily demanding the right to die.

Krinsky returned, now wearing the insulating bulk of the heatsuit over his standard rebreathing outfit. He looked more like a small tank than a man. "Is the crawler approaching, sir?"

"I'll check."

Ross adjusted the lensplate in his mask and narrowed his eyes. It seemed to him that the temperature had risen a little. Another illusion? He squinted into the distance.

His eyes picked out the radar tower far off towards Sunside. He gasped.

"Something the matter?" Krinsky asked.

"I'll say!" Ross squeezed his eyes tight shut and looked again. And—yes—the newly erected radar tower was drooping soggily and beginning to melt. He saw two tiny figures racing madly over the flat, pumice-covered ground to the silvery oblong that was the crawler. And—impossibly—the first glow of an unmistakable brightness was beginning to shimmer on the mountains behind the tower.

The sun was rising—a week ahead of schedule!

Ross ran back into the ship, followed by the lumbering figure of Krinsky. In the airlock, obliging mechanical hands descended to ease him out of his spacesuit; signaling to Krinsky to keep the heatsuit on, he dashed through into the main cabin.

"Brainerd? Brainerd! Where in hell are you?"

The senior astrogator appeared, looking puzzled. "What's up, Captain?"

"Look out the screen," Ross said in a strangled voice. "Look at the radar tower!"

"It's *melting,"* Brainerd said, astonished. "But that's—that's—"

"I know. It's impossible." Ross glanced at the instrument panel. External temperature had risen to 112 degrees—a jump of four degrees. And as he watched it glided up to 114°. It would take a heat of at least 500 degrees to melt the radar tower that way. Ross squinted at the screen and saw the crawler come swinging dizzily towards them: Llewellyn and Falbridge were still alive, then—though they probably had had a good cooking out there. The temperature outside the ship was up to 116 degrees. It would probably be near 200 degrees by the time the two men returned.

Angrily, Ross whirled to face the astrogator. "I thought you were bringing us down in the safety strip," he snapped. "Check your figures again and find out where the hell we *really* are. Then work out a blasting orbit, fast: That's the sun coming up over those hills."

* * *

The temperature had reached 120 degrees. The ship's cooling system would be able to keep things under control and comfortable until about 250 degrees; beyond that, there was danger of an overload. The crawler continued to draw near. It was probably hellish inside the little land car, Ross thought.

His mind weighed alternatives. If the external temperature went much over 250 degrees, he would run the risk of wrecking the ship's cooling system by waiting for the two in the crawler to arrive. There was some play in the system, but not much. He decided he'd give them until it hit 275 degrees to get back. If they didn't make it by then, he'd have to take off without them. It was foolish to try to save two lives at the risk of six. External temperature had hit 130 degrees. Its rate of increase was jumping rapidly.

The ship's crew knew what was going on now. Without the need of direct orders from Ross, they were readying the *Leverrier* for an emergency blastoff.

The crawler inched forward. The two men weren't much more than ten miles away now; and at an average speed of forty miles an hour they'd be back within fifteen minutes. Outside the temperature was 133 degrees. Long fingers of shimmering sunlight stretched towards them from the horizon.

Brainerd looked up from his calculation. "I can't work it. The damned figures don't come out."

"Huh?"

"I'm trying to compute our location—and I can't do the arithmetic. My head's all foggy."

What the hell. This was where a captain earned his pay, Ross thought. "Get out of the way," he said brusquely. "Let me do it."

He sat down at the desk and started figuring. He saw Brainerd's hasty notations scratched out everywhere. It was as if the astrogator had totally forgotten how to do his job.

Let's see, now. If we're—

He tapped out figures on the little calculator. But as he worked he saw that what he was doing made no sense. His mind felt bleary and strange; he couldn't seem to handle the elementary computations at all. Looking up, he said, "Tell Krinsky to get down there and make himself ready to help those men out of the crawler when they show up. They're probably half cooked."

Temperature 146 degrees. He looked down at the calculator. Damn: it shouldn't be that hard to do simple trigonometry, should it?

Doc Spangler appeared. "I cut Curtis free," he announced. "He isn't safe during takeoff in that cradle."

From within came a steady mutter. "Just let me die . . . just let me die . . ."

"Tell him he's likely to get his wish," Ross murmured. "If I can't manage to work out a blastoff orbit we're all going to fry right here."

"How come you're doing it? What's the matter with Brainerd?"

"Choked up. Couldn't make sense of his own figures. And come to think of it, I'm not doing so well myself."

Fingers of fog seemed to wrap around his mind. He glanced at the dial. Temperature 152 degrees outside. That gave the boys in the crawler 123 degrees to get back here . . . or was it 321 degrees? He was confused, utterly bewildered.

Doc Spangler looked peculiar too. The psych officer wore an odd frown. "I feel very lethargic suddenly," Spangler declared. "I know I really should get back to Curtis, but—"

The madman was keeping up a steady babble inside. The part of Ross's mind that still could think clearly realized that if left unattended Curtis was capable of doing almost anything.

Temperature 158 degrees.

The crawler seemed to be getting nearer. On the horizon the radar tower was melting into a crazy shambles.

There was a shriek. "Curtis!" Ross yelled, his mind hurriedly returning to awareness. He ran aft, with Spangler close behind.

Too late.

Curtis lay on the floor in a bloody puddle. He had found a pair of shears somewhere.

Spangler bent. "He's dead."

"Dead. Of course." Ross's brain felt totally clear now. At the moment of Curtis' death the fog had lifted. Leaving Spangler to attend to the body, he returned to the astrogation desk and glanced through the calculations he had been doing. Worthless. An idiotic mess.

With icy clarity he started again, and this time succeeded in determining their location. They had come down better than three hundred miles sunward of where they had thought they were landing. The instruments hadn't lied—but someone's eyes had. The orbit that Brainerd had so solemnly assured him was a "safe" one was actually almost as deadly as the one Curtis had computed.

He looked outside. The crawler had almost reached the ship. Temperature 167 degrees out there. There was plenty of time. They would make it with a few minutes to spare, thanks to the warning they had received from the melting radar tower.

But why had it happened? There was no answer to that.

* * *

GIGANTIC IN HIS HEATSUIT, KRINSKY brought Llewellyn and Falbridge aboard. They peeled out of their spacesuits and wobbled around unsteadily for a moment before they collapsed. They were as red as newly boiled lobsters.

"Heat prostration," Ross said. "Krinsky, get them into takeoff cradles. Dominic, you in your suit yet?"

The spaceman appeared at the airlock entrance and nodded.

"Good. Get down there and drive the crawler into the hold. We can't afford to leave it here. Double-quick, and then we're blasting off. Brainerd, that new orbit ready?"

"Yes, sir."

The thermometer grazed 200 degrees. The cooling system was beginning to suffer—but it would not have to endure much more agony. Within minutes the *Leverrier* was lifting from Mercury's surface—minutes ahead of the relentless advance of the sun. The ship swung into a parking orbit not far above the planet's surface.

As they hung there, catching their breaths, just one thing occupied Ross's mind: *why?* Why had Brainerd's orbit brought them down in a danger zone instead of the safety strip? Why had both he and Brainerd been unable to compute a blasting pattern, the simplest of elementary astrogation techniques? And why had Spangler's wits utterly failed him—just long enough to let the unhappy Curtis kill himself?

Ross could see the same question reflected on everyone's face: why?

He felt an itchy feeling at the base of his skull. And suddenly an image forced its way across his mind and he had the answer.

He saw a great pool of molten zinc, lying shimmering between two jagged crests somewhere on Sunside. It had been there thousands of years; it would be there thousands, perhaps millions, of years from now. Its surface quivered. The sun's brightness upon the pool was intolerable even to the mind's eye.

Radiation beat down on the pool of zinc—the sun's radiation, hard and unending. And then a new radiation, an electromagnetic emanation in a different part of the spectrum, carrying a meaningful message:

I want to die.

The pool of zinc stirred fretfully with sudden impulses of helpfulness.

The vision passed as quickly as it came. Stunned, Ross looked up. The expressions on the six faces surrounding him confirmed what he could guess.

"You all felt it too," he said.

Spangler nodded, then Krinsky and the rest of them.

"Yes," Krinsky said. "What the devil was it?"

Brainerd turned to Spangler. "Are we all nuts, Doc?"

The psych officer shrugged. "Mass hallucination . . . collective hypnosis . . . "

"No, Doc." Ross leaned forward. "You know it as well as I do. That thing was real. It's down there, out on Sunside."

"What do you mean?"

"I mean that wasn't any hallucination we had. That's something alive down there—or as close to alive as anything on Mercury can be." Ross's hands were shaking. He forced them to subside. "We've stumbled over something very big," he said.

Spangler stirred uneasily. "Harry—"

"No, I'm not out of my head! Don't you see—that thing down there, whatever it is, is sensitive to our thoughts! It picked up Curtis' godawful caterwauling the way a radar set grabs electromagnetic waves. His were the strongest thoughts coming through; so it acted on them and did its damnedest to help Curtis get what he wanted."

"You mean by fogging our minds and deluding us into thinking we were in safe territory, when actually we were right near sunrise territory?"

"But why would it go to all that trouble?" Krinsky objected. "If it wanted to help poor Curtis kill himself, why didn't it just fix things so we came down right *in* Sunside. We'd cook a lot quicker that way."

"Originally it did," Ross said. "It helped Curtis set up a landing orbit that would have dumped us into the sun. But then it realized that the rest of us *didn't* want to die. It picked up the conflicting mental emanations of Curtis and the rest of us, and arranged things so that he'd die and we wouldn't." He shivered. "Once Curtis was out of the way, it acted to help the surviving crew members reach safety. If you'll remember, we were all thinking and moving a lot quicker the instant Curtis was dead."

"Damned if that's not so," Spangler said. "But—"

"What I want to know is, do we go back down?" Krinsky asked. "If that thing is what you say it is, I'm not so sure I want to go within reach of it again. Who knows what it might make us do this time?"

"It wants to help us," Ross said stubbornly. "It's not hostile. You aren't afraid of it, are you, Krinsky? I was counting on you to go out in the heatsuit and try to find it."

"Not me!"

Ross scowled. "But this is the first intelligent life-form man has ever found in the solar system. We can't just run away and hide." To Brainerd he said, "Set up an orbit that'll take us back down again—and this time put us down where we won't melt."

"I can't do it, sir," Brainerd said flatly.

"Can't?"

"Won't. I think the safest thing is for us to return to Earth at once."

"I'm ordering you."

"I'm sorry, sir."

Ross looked at Spangler. Llewellyn. Falbridge. Right around the circle. Fear was evident on every face. He knew what each of the men was thinking.

I don't want to go back to Mercury.

Six of them. One of him. And the helpful thing below.

They had outnumbered Curtis seven to one—but Curtis' mind had radiated an unmixed death-wish. Ross knew he could never generate enough strength of thought to counteract the fear-driven thoughts of the other six.

Mutiny.

Somehow he did not care to speak the word aloud. Sometimes there were cases where a superior officer might legitimately be removed from command for the common good, and this might be one. of them, he knew. But yet—

The thought of fleeing without even pausing to examine the creature below was intolerable to him. But there was only one ship, and either he or the six others would have to be denied.

Yet the pool had contrived to satisfy both the man who wished to die and those who wished to stay alive. Now, six wanted to return—but must the voice of the seventh be ignored?

You're not being fair to me, Ross thought, directing his angry outburst towards the planet below. *I want to see you. I want to study you. Don't let them drag me back to Earth so soon.*

* * *

WHEN THE *LEVERRIER* RETURNED TO Earth a week later, the six survivors of the Second Mercury Expedition all were able to describe in detail how a fierce death-wish had overtaken Second Astrogator Curtis and driven him to suicide. But not one of them could recall what had happened to Flight Commander Ross, or why the heatsuit had been left behind on Mercury.

ALAREE

This little item dates from the early part of my career, and displays my growing professionalism. I wrote it in March of 1956—one of eight stories that I managed to produce that month, while still carrying a full class load in college. (They all sold!) Its theme is a good indication that I was trying to address the psychological preoccupations of the brilliant, cantankerous editor Horace Gold of *Galaxy*, John Campbell's most determined competitor, to whom I had not yet managed to sell a story. It's smoothly handled and I was sure that it would bring about a breakthrough for me there. But Gold had writers like Theodore Sturgeon and Fritz Leiber to deal with matters of this sort, and evidently didn't need my attempt at it. (Though he did start buying my work a few months later.) The story went bouncing around from magazine to magazine for over a year before an equally brilliant and equally cantankerous editor, the veteran Donald A. Wollheim, purchased it for the March 1958 issue of a short-lived and now wholly forgotten magazine called *Saturn Science Fiction* that he edited with his left hand while giving most of his attention to his highly successful and important paperback series, Ace Double Books.

When our ship left its carefully planned trajectory and started to wobble through space in dizzy circles, I knew we shouldn't have passed up that opportunity for an overhauling on Spica IV. My men and I were anxious to get back to Earth, and a hasty check had assured us that the *Aaron Burr* was in tiptop shape, so we had turned down the offer of an overhaul, which would have meant a month's delay, and set out straight for home.

As so often happens, what seemed like the most direct route home turned out to be the longest. We had spent far too much time on this survey trip already, and we were rejoicing in the prospect of an immediate return to Earth when the ship started turning cartwheels.

Willendorf, computerman first class, came to me looking sheepish, a few minutes after I'd noticed we were off course.

"What is it, Gus?" I asked.

"The feed network's oscillating, sir," he said, tugging at his unruly reddish-brown beard. "It won't stop, sir."

"Is Ketteridge working on it?"

"I've just called him," Willendorf said. His stolid face reflected acute embarrassment. Willendorf always took it personally whenever one of the cybers went haywire, as if it were his own fault. "You know what this means, don't you, sir?"

I grinned. "Take a look at this, Willendorf," I said, shoving the trajectory graphs towards him. I sketched out with my stylus the confused circles we had been traveling in all morning. "That's what your feed network's doing to us," I said, "and we'll keep on doing it until we get it fixed."

"What are you going to do, sir?"

I sensed his impatience with me. Willendorf was a good man, but his psych charts indicated a latent desire for officerhood. Deep down inside, he was sure he was at least as competent as I was to run this ship and probably a good deal more so.

"Send me Upper Navigating Technician Haley," I snapped. "We're going to have to find a planet in the neighborhood and put down for repairs."

It turned out there was an insignificant solar system in the vicinity, consisting of a small but hot white star and a single unexplored planet, Terra-size, a few hundred million miles out. After Haley and I had decided that that was the nearest port of refuge, I called a general meeting . . .

Quickly and positively I outlined our situation and explained what would have to be done. I sensed the immediate disappointment, but, gratifyingly, the reaction was followed by a general feeling of resigned pitching in. If we all worked, we'd get back to Earth, sooner or later. If we didn't, we'd spend the next century flip-flopping aimlessly in space.

After the meeting we set about the business of recovering control of the ship and putting it down for repairs. The feed network, luckily, gave up the ghost about ninety minutes later; it meant we had to stoke the fuel by hand, but at least it stopped that accursed oscillating.

We got the ship going, and Haley, navigating by feel in a way I never would have dreamed possible, brought us into the nearby solar system in hardly any time at all. Finally we swung into our landing orbit and made our looping way down to the surface of the little planet.

I studied my crew's faces carefully. We had spent a great deal of time together in space—much too much, really, for comfort—and an incident like this might very well snap them all if we didn't get going again soon enough. I could foresee disagreements, bickering, declaration of opinion where no opinion was called for.

I was relieved to discover that the planet's air was breathable. A rather high nitrogen concentration, to be sure—82 percent—but that left 17 percent for oxygen, plus some miscellaneous inerts, and it wouldn't be too rough on the lungs. I decreed a one-hour free break before beginning repairs.

Remaining aboard ship, I gloomily surveyed the scrambled feed network and tried to formulate a preliminary plan of action for getting the complex cybernetic instrument to function again, while my crew went outside to relax.

Ten minutes after I had opened the lock and let them out, I heard someone clanking around in the aft supplies cabin.

"Who's there?" I yelled.

"Me," grunted a heavy voice that could only be Willendorf's. "I'm looking for the thought-converter, sir."

I ran hastily through the corridor, flipped up the latch on the supplies cabin, and confronted him. "What do you want the converter for?" I snapped.

"Found an alien, sir," he said laconically.

My eyes widened. The survey chart said nothing about intelligent extraterrestrials in this limb of the galaxy, but then again this planet hadn't been explored yet.

I gestured towards the rear cabinet. "The converter helmets are in there," I said. "I'll be out in a little while. Make sure you follow technique in making contact."

"Of course, sir." Willendorf took the converter helmet and went out, leaving me standing there. I waited a few minutes, then climbed the catwalk to the air lock and peered out.

They were all clustered around a small alien being who looked weak and inconsequential in the midst of the circle. I smiled at the sight. The alien was roughly humanoid in shape, with the usual complement of arms and legs, and a pale-green complexion that blended well with the muted violet coloring of his world. He was wearing the thought-converter somewhat lopsidedly, and I saw a small green furry ear protruding from the left side. Willendorf was talking to him.

Then someone saw me standing at the open air lock, and I heard Haley yell to me, "Come on down, Chief!"

They were ringed around the alien in a tight circle. I shouldered my way into their midst. Willendorf turned to me.

"Meet Alaree, sir," he said. "Alaree, this is our commander."

"We are pleased to meet you," the alien said gravely. The converter automatically turned his thoughts into English, but maintained the trace of his oddly inflected accent. "You have been saying that you are from the skies."

"His grammar's pretty shaky," Willendorf interposed. "He keeps referring to any of us as 'you'—even you, who just got here."

"Odd," I said. "The converter's supposed to conform to the rules of grammar." I turned to the alien, who seemed perfectly at ease among us. "My name is Bryson," I said. "This is Willendorf, over here."

The alien wrinkled his soft-skinned forehead in momentary confusion. "We are Alaree," he said again.

"We? You and who else?"

"We and we else," Alaree said blandly. I stared at him for a moment, then gave up. The complexities of an alien mind are often too much for a mere Terran to fathom.

"You are welcome to our world," Alaree said after a few moments of silence.

"Thanks," I said. "Thanks."

I turned away, leaving the alien with my men. They had twenty-six minutes left of the break I'd given them, after which we would have to get back to the serious business of repairing the ship. Making friends with floppy-eared aliens was one thing, getting back to Earth was another.

* * *

The planet was a warm, friendly sort of place, with rolling fields and acres of pleasant-looking purple vegetation. We had landed in a clearing at the edge of a fair-sized copse. Great broad-beamed trees shot up all around us.

Alaree returned to visit us every day, until he became almost a mascot of the crew. I liked the little alien myself and spent some time with him, although I found his conversation generally incomprehensible. No doubt he had the same trouble with us. The converter had only limited efficiency, after all.

He was the only representative of his species who came. For all we knew, he was the only one of his kind on the whole planet. There was no sign of life elsewhere, and, although Willendorf led an unauthorized scouting party during some free time on the third day, he failed to find a village of any sort. Where Alaree went every night and how he had found us in the first place remained mysteries.

As for the feed network, progress was slow. Ketteridge, the technician in charge, had tracked down the foul-up and was trying to repair it without building a completely new network. Shortcuts again. He tinkered away for four days, setting up a tentative circuit, trying it out, watching it sputter and blow out, building another.

There was nothing I could do. But I sensed tension heightening among the crewmen. They were annoyed at themselves, at each other, at me, at everything.

On the fifth day, Ketteridge and Willendorf finally let their accumulated tenseness explode. They had been working together on the network, but they quarreled, and Ketteridge came storming into my cabin immediately afterward.

"Sir, I demand to be allowed to work on the network by myself. It's my speciality, and Willendorf's only snarling things up."

"Get me Willendorf," I said.

When Willendorf showed up I heard the whole story, decided quickly to let Ketteridge have his way—it was, after all, his specialty—and calmed Willendorf down. Then, reaching casually for some papers on my desk, I dismissed both of them. I knew they'd come to their senses in a day or so.

I spent most of the next day sitting placidly in the sun, while Ketteridge tinkered with the feed network some more. I watched the faces of the men. They were starting to smolder. They wanted to get home, and they weren't getting there. Besides, this was a fairly dull planet, and even the novelty of Alaree wore off after a while. The little alien had a way of hanging around men who were busy scraping fuel deposits out of the jet tubes, or something equally unpleasant, and bothering them with all sorts of questions.

The following morning I was lying blissfully on the grass near the ship, talking to Alaree. Ketteridge came to me, and by the tightness of his lips I knew he was in trouble.

I brushed some antlike blue insects off my trousers and rose to a sitting position, leaning against the tall, tough-barked tree behind me. "What's the matter, Ketteridge? How's the feed network?"

He glanced uneasily at Alaree for a moment before speaking. "I'm stuck, sir. I'll have to admit I was wrong. I can't fix it by myself."

I stood up and put my hand on his shoulder. "That's a noble thing to say, Ketteridge. It takes a big man to admit he's been a fool. Will you work with Willendorf now?"

"If he'll work with me, sir," Ketteridge said miserably.

"I think he will," I said. Ketteridge saluted and turned away, and I felt a burst of satisfaction. I'd met the crisis in the only way possible; if I had *ordered* them to cooperate, I would have gotten no place. The psychological situation no longer allowed for unbending military discipline.

After Ketteridge had gone, Alaree, who had been silent all this time, looked up at me in puzzlement. "We do not understand," he said.

"Not *we,*" I corrected. "*I.* You're only one person. *We* means many people."

"We are only one person?" Alaree said tentatively.

"No. *I* am only one person. Get it?"

He worried the thought around for a few moments; I could see his browless forehead contract in deep concentration.

"Look," I said. "I'm one person. Ketteridge is another person. Willendorf is another. Each one of them is an independent individual, an *I.*"

"And together you make *we?*" Alaree asked brightly.

"Yes and no," I said. "*We* is composed of many *I's*—but we still remain *I.*"

Again he sank deep in concentration, and then he smiled, scratched the ear that protruded from one side of the thought-helmet, and said, "*We* do not understand. But *I* do. Each of you is—is an *I.*"

"An individual," I said.

"An individual," he repeated. "A complete person. And together, to fly your ship, you must become a *we.*"

"But only temporarily," I said. "There still can be conflict between the parts. That's necessary, for progress. I can always think of the rest of them as *they.*"

"I . . . they," Alaree repeated slowly. "*They.*" He nodded. "It is difficult for me to grasp all this. I . . . think differently. But I am coming to understand, and I am worried."

That was a new idea. Alaree worried? Could be, I reflected. I had no way of knowing. I knew so little about Alaree—where on the planet he came from, what his tribal life was like, what sort of civilization he had, were all blanks.

“What kind of worries, Alaree?”

“You would not understand,” he said solemnly and would say no more.

Towards afternoon, as golden shadows started to slant through the closely packed trees, I returned to the ship. Willendorf and Ketteridge were aft, working over the feed network, and the whole crew had gathered around to watch and offer suggestions. Even Alaree was there, looking absurdly comical in his copper-alloy thought-converter helmet, standing on tiptoe and trying to see what was happening.

About an hour later, I spotted the alien sitting by himself beneath the long-limbed tree that towered over the ship. He was lost in thought. Evidently whatever his problem was, it was really eating him.

Towards evening, he made a decision. I had been watching him with a great deal of concern, wondering what was going on in that small but unfathomable mind. I saw him brighten, leap up suddenly, and cross the field, heading in my direction.

“Captain!”

“What is it, Alaree?”

He waddled up and stared gravely at me. “Your ship will be ready to leave soon. What was wrong is nearly right again.”

He paused, obviously uncertain of how to phrase his next statement, and I waited patiently. Finally he blurted out, “May I come back to your world with you?”

Automatically, the regulations flashed through my mind. I pride myself on my knowledge of the rules. And I knew this one.

* * *

> Article 101A
> No intelligent extraterrestrial life is to be transported from its own world to any civilized world under any reason whatsoever, without explicit beforehand clearance. The penalty for doing so is . . .

* * *

And it listed a fine of more money than was ever dreamed of in my philosophy.

I shook my head. “Can’t take you, Alaree. This is your world, and you belong here.”

A ripple of agony ran over his face. Suddenly he ceased to be the cheerful, roly-poly creature it was so impossible to take seriously, and became a very worried entity indeed. "You cannot understand," he said. "I no longer belong here."

* * *

NO MATTER HOW HARD HE pleaded, I remained adamant. And when to no one's surprise Ketteridge and Willendorf announced, a day later, that their pooled labors had succeeded in repairing the feed network, I had to tell Alaree that we were going to leave—without him.

He nodded stiffly, accepting the fact, and without a word stalked tragically away, into the purple tangle of foliage that surrounded our clearing.

He returned a while later, or so I thought. He was not wearing the thought-converter. That surprised me. Alaree knew the helmet was a valuable item, and he had been cautioned to take good care of it.

I sent a man inside to get another helmet for him. I put it on him—this time tucking that wayward ear underneath properly—and looked at him sternly. "Where's the other helmet, Alaree?"

"We do not have it," he said.

"*We?* No more I?"

"We," Alaree said. And as he spoke, the leaves parted and another alien—Alaree's very double—stepped out into the clearing.

Then I saw the helmet on the newcomer's head, and realized that he was no double. He was Alaree, and the other alien was the stranger!

"I see you're here already," the alien I knew as Alaree said to the other. They were standing about ten feet apart, staring coldly at each other. I glanced at both of them quickly. They might have been identical twins.

"We are here," the stranger said, "We have come to get you."

I took a step backward, sensing that some incomprehensible drama was being played out here among these aliens.

"What's going on, Alaree?" I asked.

"We are having difficulties," both of them said, as one.

Both of them.

I turned to the second alien. "What's your name?"

"Alaree," he said.

"Are you all named that?" I demanded.

"We are Alaree," Alaree Two said.

"They are Alaree," Alaree One said. "And *I* am Alaree. *I*."

At that moment there was a disturbance in the shrubbery, and half a dozen more aliens stepped through and confronted Alarees One and Two.

"We are Alaree," Alaree Two repeated exasperatingly. He made a sweeping gesture that embraced all seven of the aliens to my left, but pointedly excluded Alaree One at my right.

"Are we—you coming with we—us?" Alaree Two demanded. I heard the six others say something in approximately the same tone of voice, but since they weren't wearing converters, their words were only scrambled nonsense to me.

Alaree One looked at me in pain, then back at his seven fellows. I saw an expression of sheer terror in the small creature's eyes. He turned to me.

"I must go with them," he said softly. He was quivering with fear.

Without a further word, the eight marched silently away. I stood there, shaking my head in bewilderment.

We were scheduled to leave the next day. I said nothing to my crew about the bizarre incident of the evening before, but noted in my log that the native life of the planet would require careful study at some future time.

Blast-off was slated for 1100. As the crew moved efficiently through the ship, securing things, packing, preparing for departure, I sensed a general feeling of jubilation. They were happy to be on their way again, and I didn't blame them.

About half an hour before blast-off, Willendorf came to me. "Sir, Alaree's down below," he said. "He wants to come up and see you. He looks very troubled, sir."

I frowned. Probably the alien still wanted to go back with us. Well, it was cruel to deny the request, but I wasn't going to risk that fine. I intended to make that clear to him.

"Send him up," I said.

A moment later Alaree came stumbling into my cabin. Before he could speak I said, "I told you before—I can't take you off this planet, Alaree. I'm sorry about it."

He looked up pitiably and said, "You mustn't leave me!" He was trembling uncontrollably.

"What's wrong, Alaree?" I asked.

He stared intensely at me for a long moment, mastering himself, trying to arrange what he wanted to tell me into a coherent argument. Finally he said, "They would not take me back. I am alone."

"Who wouldn't take you back, Alaree?"

"They. Last night, Alaree came for me, to take me back. They are a *we*—an entity, a oneness. You cannot understand. When they saw what I had become, they cast me out."

I shook my head dizzily. "What do you mean?"

"You taught me . . . to become an *I,"* he said, moistening his lips. "Before, I was part of *we—they*. I learned your ways from you, and now there is no room for me here. They have cut me off. When the final break comes, I will not be able to stay on this world."

Sweat was pouring down his pale face, and he was breathing harder. "It will come any minute. They are gathering strength for it. But I am *I,"* he said triumphantly. He shook violently and gasped for breath.

I understood now. They were *all* Alaree. It was one planet-wide, self-aware corporate entity, composed of any number of individual cells. He had been one of them—but he had learned independence.

Then he had returned to the group—but he carried with him the seeds of individualism, the deadly, contagious germ we Terrans spread everywhere. Individualism would be fatal to such a group mind; it was cutting him loose to save itself. Just as diseased cells must be excised for the good of the entire body, Alaree was inexorably being cut off from his fellows lest he destroy the bond that made them one.

I watched him as he sobbed weakly on my acceleration cradle. "They . . . are . . . cutting . . . me . . . loose . . . *now!"*

He writhed horribly for a brief moment, and then relaxed and sat up on the edge of the cradle. "It is over," he said calmly. "I am fully independent."

I saw a stark *aloneness* reflected in his eyes, and behind that a gentle indictment of me for having done this to him. This world, I realized, was no place for Earthmen. What had happened was our fault—mine more than anyone else's.

"Will you take me with you?" he asked again. "If I stay here, Alaree will kill me."

I scowled wretchedly for a moment, fighting a brief battle within myself, and then I looked up. There was only one thing to do—and I was sure, once I explained on Earth, that I would not suffer for it.

I took his hand. It was cold and limp; whatever he had just been through, it must have been hell. "Yes," I said softly. "You can come with us."

And so Alaree joined the crew of the *Aaron Burr.* I told them about it just before blast-off, and they welcomed him aboard in traditional manner.

We gave the sad-eyed little alien a cabin near the cargo hold, and he established himself quite comfortably. He had no personal possessions—"It is not *their* custom." he said—and promised that he'd keep the cabin clean.

He had brought with him a rough-edged, violet fruit that he said was his staple food. I turned it over to Kechnie for synthesizing, and we blasted off.

Alaree was right at home aboard the *Burr.* He spent much time with me—asking questions.

"Tell me about Earth," Alaree would ask. The alien wanted desperately to know what sort of a world he was going to.

He would listen gravely while I explained. I told him of cities and wars and spaceships, and he nodded sagely, trying to fit the concepts into a mind only newly liberated from the gestalt. I knew he could comprehend only a fraction of what I was saying, but I enjoyed telling him. It made me feel as if Earth were coming closer that much faster, simply to talk about it.

And he went around begging everyone, "Tell me about Earth." They enjoyed telling him, too—for a while.

Then it began to get a little tiresome. We had grown accustomed to Alaree's presence on the ship, flopping around the corridors doing whatever menial job he had been assigned to. But—although I had told the men why I had brought him with us, and though we all pitied the poor lonely creature and admired his struggle to survive as an individual entity—we were slowly coming to the realization that Alaree was something of a nuisance aboard ship.

Especially later, when he began to change.

Willendorf noticed it first, twelve days out from Alaree's planet. "Alaree's been acting pretty strange these days, sir," he told me.

"What's wrong?" I asked.

"Haven't you spotted it, sir? He's been moping around like a lost soul—very quiet and withdrawn, like."

"Is he eating well?"

Willendorf chuckled loudly. "I'll say he is! Kechnie made up some synthetics based on the piece of fruit he brought with him, and he's been stuffing himself wildly. He's gained ten pounds since he came on ship. No, it's not lack of food!"

"I guess not," I said. "Keep an eye on him, will you? I feel responsible for his being here, and I want him to come through the voyage in good health."

After that, I began to observe Alaree more closely myself, and I detected the change in his personality too. He was no longer the cheerful, childlike being who delighted in pouring out questions in endless profusion. Now he was moody, silent, always brooding, and hard to approach.

On the sixteenth day out—and by now I was worried seriously about him—a new manifestation appeared. I was in the hallway, heading from my cabin to the chartroom, when Alaree stepped out of an alcove. He reached up, grasped my uniform lapel, and, maintaining his silence, drew my head down and stared pleadingly into my eyes.

Too astonished to say anything, I returned his gaze for nearly thirty seconds. I peered into his transparent pupils, wondering what he was up to. After a good while had passed, he released me, and I saw something like a tear trickle down his cheek.

"What's the trouble, Alaree?"

He shook his head mournfully and shuffled away.

I got reports from the crewmen that day and next that he had been doing this regularly for the past eighteen hours—waylaying crewmen, staring long and deep at them as if trying to express some unspeakable sadness, and walking away. He had approached almost everyone on the ship.

I wondered now how wise it had been to allow an extraterrestrial, no matter how friendly, to enter the ship. There was no telling what this latest action meant.

I started to form a theory. I suspected what he was aiming at, and the realization chilled me. But once I reached my conclusion, there was nothing I could do but wait for confirmation.

On the nineteenth day, Alaree again met me in the corridor. This time our encounter was more brief. He plucked me by the sleeve, shook his head sadly and shrugged his shoulders, and walked away.

That night, he took to his cabin, and by morning he was dead. He had apparently died peacefully in his sleep.

* * *

"I GUESS WE'LL NEVER UNDERSTAND him, poor fellow," Willendorf said, after we had committed the body to space. "You think he had too much to eat, sir?"

"No," I said. "It wasn't that. He was lonely, that's all. He didn't belong here, among us."

"But you said he had broken away from that group-mind," Willendorf objected.

I shook my head. "Not really. That group-mind arose out of some deep psychological and physiological needs of those people. You can't just declare your independence and be able to exist as an individual from then on if you're part of that group-entity. Alaree had grasped the concept intellectually, to some extent, but he wasn't suited for life away from the corporate mind, no matter how much he wanted to be."

"He couldn't stand alone?"

"Not after his people had evolved that gestalt setup. He learned independence from us," I said. "But he couldn't live with us, really. He needed to be part of a whole. He found out his mistake after he came aboard and tried to remedy things."

I saw Willendorf pale. "What do you mean, sir?"

"You know what I mean. When he came up to us and stared soulfully into our eyes. *He was trying to form a new gestalt—out of us!* Somehow he was trying to link us together, the way his people had been linked."

"He couldn't do it, though," Willendorf said fervently.

"Of course not. Human beings don't have whatever need it is that forced those people to merge. He found that out, after a while, when he failed to get anywhere with us."

"He just couldn't do it," Willendorf repeated.

"No. And then he ran out of strength," I said somberly, feeling the heavy weight of my guilt. "He was like an organ removed from a living body. It can exist for a little while by itself, but not indefinitely. He failed to find a new source of life—and he died." I stared bitterly at my fingertips.

"What do we call it in my medical report?" asked Ship Surgeon Thomas, who had been silent up till then. "How can we explain what he died from?"

"Call it—*malnutrition,*" I said.

THE SOUL-PAINTER AND THE SHAPESHIFTER

The very active year of 1981, though it was a year in which I wrote only short stories, was colored for me in many ways by the publication the year before of the big novel *Lord Valentine's Castle*, which had marked my return to writing after the four-year retirement period. The book got a lot of attention, and not simply because it demonstrated that I hadn't really given up writing after all. It flirted for a little while with the best-seller lists; it gained me a Hugo nomination; and, as I looked at it a year or so after having written it, I realized that Majipoor, the giant world that I had created for it, was one of my most fully realized science-fictional inventions, and did not deserve to be abandoned after a single visit.

So I began to prowl through the 14,000-year history of Majipoor that I had put together for *Lord Valentine's Castle*, looking for episodes that deserved stories in their own right. When Underwood-Miller, a small press publisher then doing a great deal of high-quality work, asked me for an original novella, I responded in October of 1980 with a long Majipoor story, "The Desert of Stolen Dreams," set about a thousand years before the novel. A few months later, George Scithers, then the editor of *Isaac Asimov's Science Fiction Magazine*, suggested I do a Majipoor story for him, and I responded with another novella, "A Thief in Ni-Moya." At that point I realized that I had now written about one-third of the material I would need for a collection of new Majipoor tales, and, since the huge planet abounded in potential story material, I set to work in earnest in the spring and summer of 1981 to bring that book into being.

Story followed story quickly: one in April, one in May, one in June, three in July, one in August, and the tenth and last in September. I assembled them into a sort of pseudo-novel for him under the title of *Majipoor Chronicles*, which would appear in 1982 under the imprint of Arbor House, a relatively new publishing company for which I had begun writing.

The *Majipoor* stories depict among other things, the relationships between the various intelligent species that had come from all over the galaxy to take up residence on that vast, all but infinite planet. Here is one of them. *OMNI* published it in its November, 1981 issue.

It has become an addiction. Hissune's mind is opening now in all directions, and the Register of Souls is the key to an infinite world of new understanding. When one dwells in the Labyrinth one develops a peculiar sense of the world as vague and unreal, mere names rather than concrete places: only the dark and hermetic Labyrinth has substance, and all else is vapor. But Hissune has journeyed by proxy to every continent now, he has tasted strange foods and seen weird landscapes, he has experienced extremes of heat and cold, and in all that he has come to acquire a comprehension of the complexity of the world that, he suspects, very few others have had. Now he goes back again and again. No longer does he have to bother with forged credentials; he is so regular a user of the archives that a nod is sufficient to get him within, and then he has all the million yesterdays of Majipoor at his disposal. Often he stays with a capsule for only a moment or two, until he has determined that it contains nothing that will move him farther along the road to knowledge. Sometimes of a morning he will call up and dismiss eight, ten, a dozen records in rapid succession. True enough, he knows, that every being's soul contains a universe; but not all universes are equally interesting, and that which he might learn from the innermost depths of one who spent his life sweeping the streets of Piliplok or murmuring prayers in the entourage of the Lady of the Isle does not seem immediately useful to him, when he considers other possibilities. So he summons capsules and rejects them and summons again, dipping here and there into Majipoor's past, and keeps at it until he finds himself in contact with a mind that promises real revelation. Even Coronals and Pontifexes can be bores, he has discovered. But there are always wondrous unexpected finds—a man who fell in love with a Metamorph, for example—

IT WAS A SURFEIT OF perfection that drove the soul-painter Therion Nismile from the crystalline cities of Castle Mount to the dark forests of the western continent. All his life he had lived amid the wonders of the Mount, traveling through the Fifty Cities according to the demands of his career, exchanging one sort of splendor for another every few years. Dundilmir was his native city—his first canvases were scenes of the Fiery Valley, tempestuous and passionate with the ragged energies of youth—and then he dwelled some years in marvelous Canzilaine of the talking statues, and afterward in Stee the awesome, whose outskirts were three days' journey across, and in golden Halanx at the very fringes of the Castle, and for five years at the Castle itself, where he painted at the court of the Coronal Lord Thraym. His paintings were prized for their calm elegance and their perfection of form, which mirrored the flawlessness of the Fifty Cities to the ultimate degree. But the beauty of such places numbs the soul, after a time, and paralyzes the artistic instincts. When Nismile reached his fortieth year he found himself beginning to identify perfection with stagnation; he loathed his own most famous works; his spirit began to cry out for upheaval, unpredictability, transformation.

The moment of crisis overtook him in the gardens of Tolingar Barrier, that miraculous park on the plain between Dundilmir and Stipool. The Coronal had asked him for a suite of paintings of the gardens, to decorate a pergola under construction on the Castle's rim. Obligingly Nismile made the long journey down the slopes of the enormous mountain, toured the forty miles of park, chose the sites where he meant to work, set up his first canvas at Kazkas Promontory, where the contours of the garden swept outward in great green symmetrical pulsating scrolls. He had loved this place when he was a boy. On all of Majipoor there was no site more serene, more orderly, for the Tolingar gardens were composed of plants bred to maintain themselves in transcendental tidiness. No gardener's shears touched these shrubs and trees; they grew of their own accord in graceful balance, regulated their own spacing and rate of replacement, suppressed all weeds in their environs, and controlled their proportions so that the original design remained forever unbreached. When they shed their leaves or found it needful to drop an entire dead bough, enzymes within dissolved the cast-off matter quickly into useful compost. Lord Havilbove, more than a hundred years ago, had been the founder of this garden; his successors Lord Kanaba and Lord Sirruth had continued and extended the program of genetic modification that governed it; and under the present Coronal Lord Thraym its plan was wholly fulfilled, so that now it would remain eternally perfect, eternally balanced. It was that perfection which Nismile had come to capture.

He faced his blank canvas, drew breath deep down into his lungs, and readied himself for entering the trance state. In a moment his soul, leaping from his dreaming mind, would in a single instant imprint the unique intensity of his vision of this scene on the psychosensitive fabric. He glanced one last time at the gentle hills, the artful shrubbery, the delicately angled leaves—and a wave of rebellious fury crashed against him, and he quivered and shook and nearly fell. This immobile landscape, this static, sterile beauty, this impeccable and matchless garden, had no need of him; it was itself as unchanging as a painting, and as lifeless, frozen in its own faultless rhythms to the end of tie. How ghastly! How hateful! Nismile swayed and pressed his hands to his pounding skull. He heard the soft surprised grunts of his companions, and when he opened his eyes he saw them all staring in horror and embarrassment at the blackened and bubbling canvas. "Cover it!" he cried, and turned away. Everyone was in motion at once; and in the center of the group Nismile stood statue-still. When he could speak again he said quietly, "Tell Lord Thraym I will be unable to fulfill his commission."

And so that day in Dundilmir he purchased what he needed and began his long journey to the lowlands, and out into the broad hot flood-plain of the Iyann River, and by riverboat interminably along the sluggish Iyann to the western port of Alaisor; and at Alaisor he boarded, after a wait of weeks, a ship bound for Numinor on the Isle of Sleep, where he tarried a month. Then he found passage on a pilgrim-ship sailing to Piliplok on the wild continent of Zimroel. Zimroel, he was sure, would not oppress him with elegance and perfection. It had only eight or nine cities, which in fact were probably little more than frontier towns. The entire interior of the continent was wilderness, into which Lord Stiamot had driven the aboriginal Metamorphs after their final defeat four thousand years ago. A man wearied of civilization might be able to restore his soul in such surroundings.

Nismile expected Piliplok to be a mudhole, but to his surprise it turned out to be an ancient and enormous city, laid out according to a maddeningly rigid mathematical plan. It was ugly but not in any refreshing way, and he moved on by riverboat up the Zimr. He journeyed past great Ni-moya, which was famous even to inhabitants of the other continent, and did not stop there; but at a town called Verf he impulsively left the boat and set forth in a hired wagon into the forests to the south. When he had traveled so deep into the wilderness that he could see no trace of civilization, he halted and built a cabin beside a swift dark stream. It was three years since he had left Castle Mount. Through all his journey he had been alone and had spoken to others only when necessary, and he had not painted at all.

Here Nismile felt himself beginning to heal. Everything in this place was unfamiliar and wonderful. On Castle Mount, where the climate was artificially controlled, an endless sweet springtime reigned, the unreal air was clear and pure, and rainfall came at predictable intervals. But now he was in a moist and humid rain-forest, where the soil was spongy and yielding, clouds and tongues of fog drifted by often, showers were frequent, and the vegetation was a chaotic, tangled anarchy, as far removed as he could imagine from the symmetries of Tolingar Barrier. He wore little clothing, learned by trial and error what roots and berries and shoots were safe to eat, and devised a wickerwork weir to help him catch the slender crimson fish that flashed like skyrockets through the stream. He walked for hours through the dense jungle, savoring not only its strange beauty but also the tense pleasure of wondering if he could find his way back to his cabin. Often he sang, in a loud erratic voice; he had never sung on Castle Mount. Occasionally he started to prepare a canvas, but always he put it away unused. He composed nonsensical poems, voluptuous strings of syllables, and chanted them to an audience of slender towering trees and incomprehensibly intertwined vines. Sometimes he wondered how it was going at the court of Lord Thraym, whether the Coronal had hired a new artist yet to paint the decorations for the pergola, and if the halatingas were blooming now along the road to High Morpin. But such thoughts came rarely to him.

He lost track of time. Four or five or perhaps six weeks—how could he tell?—went by before he saw his first Metamorph.

The encounter took place in a marshy meadow two miles upstream from his cabin. Nismile had gone there to gather the succulent scarlet bulbs of mud-lilies, which he had learned to mash and roast into a sort of bread. They grew deep, and he dug them by working his arm into the muck to the shoulder and groping about with his cheek pressed to the ground. He came up muddy-faced and slippery, clutching a dripping handful, and was startled to find a figure calmly watching him from a distance of a dozen yards.

He had never seen a Metamorph. The native beings of Majipoor were perpetually exiled from the capital continent, Alhanroel, where Nismile had spent all his years. But he had an idea of how they looked, and he felt sure this must be one: an enormously tall, fragile, sallow skinned being, sharp-faced, with inward-sloping eyes and barely perceptible nose and stringy, rubbery hair of a pale greenish hue. It wore only a leather loin-harness and a short sharp dirk of some polished black wood was strapped to its hip. In eerie dignity the Metamorph stood balanced with one frail long leg twisted around the shin of the other. It seemed both sinister and gentle, menacing and comic. Nismile chose not to be alarmed.

"Hello," he said. "Do you mind if I gather bulbs here?"

The Metamorph was silent.

"I have, the cabin down the stream. I'm Therion Nismile. I used to be a soul-painter, when I lived on Castle Mount."

The Metamorph regarded him solemnly. A flicker of unreadable expression crossed its face. Then it turned and slipped gracefully into the jungle, vanishing almost at once.

Nismile shrugged. He dug down for more mud-lily bulbs.

A week or two later he met another Metamorph, or perhaps the same one, this time while he was stripping bark from a vine to make rope for a bilantoon-trap. Once more the aborigine was wordless, materializing quietly like an apparition in front of Nismile and contemplating him from the same unsettling one-legged stance. A second time Nismile tried to draw the creature into conversation, but at his first words it drifted off, ghostlike. "Wait!" Nismile called. "I'd like to talk with you. I—" But he was alone.

A few days afterward he was collecting firewood when he became aware yet again that he was being studied. At once he said to the Metamorph, "I've caught a bilantoon and I'm about to roast it. There's more meat than I need. Will you share my dinner?" The Metamorph smiled—he took that enigmatic flicker for a smile, though it could have been anything—and as if by way of replying underwent a sudden astonishing shift, turning itself into a mirror image of Nismile, stocky and muscular, with dark penetrating eyes and shoulder-length black hair. Nismile blinked wildly and trembled; then, recovering, he smiled, deciding to take the mimicry as some form of communication, and said, "Marvelous! I can't begin to see how you people do it!" He beckoned. "Come. It'll take an hour and a half to cook the bilantoon, and we can talk until then. You understand our language, don't you? Don't you?" It was bizarre beyond measure, this speaking to a duplicate of himself. "Say something, eh? Tell me: is there a Metamorph village somewhere nearby? *Piurivar,*" he corrected, remembering the Metamorphs' name for themselves. "Eh? A lot of Piurivars hereabouts, in the jungle?" Nismile gestured again. "Walk with me to my cabin and we'll get the fire going. You don't have any wine, do you? That's the only thing I miss, I think, some good strong wine, the heavy stuff they make in Muldemar. Won't taste that ever again, I guess, but there's wine in Zimroel, isn't there? Eh? Will you say something?" But the Metamorph responded only with a grimace, perhaps intended as a grin, that twisted the Nismile-face into something harsh and strange; then it resumed its own form between one instant and the next and with calm floating strides went walking away.

Nismile hoped for a time that it would return with a flask of wine, but he did not see it again. Curious creatures, he thought. Were they angry that he was camped in their territory? Were they keeping him under surveillance out of fear that he was the vanguard of a wave of human settlers? Oddly, he felt himself in no danger. Metamorphs were generally considered to be malevolent; certainly they were disquieting beings, alien and unfathomable. Plenty of tales were told of Metamorph raids on outlying human settlements, and no doubt the Shapeshifter folk harbored bitter hatred for those who had come to their world and dispossessed them and driven them into these jungles; but yet Nismile knew himself to be a man of good will, who had never done harm to others and wanted only to be left to live his life, and he fancied that some subtle sense would lead the Metamorphs to realize that he was not their enemy. He wished he could become their friend. He was growing hungry for conversation after all this time of solitude, and it might be challenging and rewarding to exchange ideas with these strange folk; he might even paint one. He had been thinking again lately of returning to his art, of experiencing once more that moment of creative ecstasy as his soul leaped the gap to the psychosensitive canvas and inscribed on it those images that he alone could fashion. Surely he was different now from the increasingly unhappy man he had been on Castle Mount, and that difference must show itself in his work. During the next few days he rehearsed speeches designed to win the confidence of the Metamorphs, to overcome that strange shyness of theirs, that delicacy of bearing which blocked any sort of contact. In time, he thought, they would grow used to him, they would begin to speak, to accept his invitation to eat with him, and then perhaps they would pose—

But in the days that followed he saw no more Metamorphs. He roamed the forest, peering hopefully into thickets and down mistswept lanes of trees, and found no one. He decided that he had been too forward with them and had frightened them away—so much for the malevolence of the monstrous Metamorphs!—and after a while he ceased to expect further contact with them. That was disturbing. He had not missed companionship when none seemed likely, but the knowledge that there were intelligent beings somewhere in the area kindled an awareness of loneliness in him that was not easy to bear.

One damp and warm day several weeks after his last Metamorph encounter Nismile was swimming in the cool deep pond formed by a natural dam of boulders half a mile below his cabin when he saw a pale slim figure moving quickly through a dense bower of blue-leaved bushes by the shore. He scrambled out of the water, barking his knees on the rocks. "Wait!" he shouted. "Please—don't be afraid—don't go—"The figure disappeared, but Nismile, thrashing frantically through the underbrush, caught sight of it again in a few minutes , learning casually now against an enormous tree with vivid red bark.

Nismile stopped short, amazed, for the other was no Metamorph but a human woman.

She was slender and young and naked, with thick auburn hair, narrow shoulders, small high breasts, bright playful eyes. She seemed altogether unafraid of him, a forest-sprite who had obviously enjoyed leading him on this little chase. As he stood gaping at her she looked him over unhurriedly, and with an outburst of clear tinkling laughter said, "You're all scratched and torn! Can't you run in the forest any better than that?"

"I didn't want you to get away."

"Oh, I wasn't going to go far. You know, I was watching you for a long time before you noticed me. You're the man from the cabin, right?"

"Yes. And you—where do you live?"

"Here and there," she said airily.

He stared at her in wonder. Her beauty delighted him, her shamelessness astounded him. She might almost be an hallucination, he thought. Where had she come from? What was a human being, naked and alone, doing in this primordial jungle?

Human?

Of course not, Nismile realized, with the sudden sharp grief of a child who has been given some coveted treasure in a dream, only to awaken aglow and perceive the sad reality. Remembering how effortlessly the Metamorph had mimicked him, Nismile comprehended the dismal probability: this was some prank, some masquerade. He studied her intently, seeking a sign of Metamorph identity, a flickering of the projection, a trace of knife-sharp cheekbones and sloping eyes behind the cheerfully impudent face . She was convincingly human in every degree. But yet—how implausible to meet one of his own kind here, how much more likely that she was a Shapeshifter, a deceiver—

He did not want to believe that. He resolved to meet the possibility of deception with a conscious act of faith, in the hope that that would make her be what she seemed to be.

"What's your name?" he asked.

"Sarise. And yours?"

"Nismile. Where *do* you live?"

"In the forest."

"Then there's a human settlement not far from here?"

She shrugged. "I live by myself." She came toward him—he felt his muscles growing taut as she moved closer, and something churning in his stomach, and his skin seemed to be blazing—and touched her fingers lightly to the cuts the vines had made on his arms and chest.

"Don't those scratches bother you?"

"They're beginning to. I should wash them."

"Yes. Let's go back to the pool. I know a better way than the one you took. Follow me!"

She parted the fronds of a thick clump of ferns and revealed a narrow, well-worn trail. Gracefully she sprinted off, and he ran behind her, delighted by the ease of her movements, the play of muscles in her back and buttocks. He plunged into the pool a moment after her and they splashed about. The chilly water soothed the stinging of the cuts. When they climbed out, he yearned to draw her to him and enclose her in his arms, but he did not dare. They sprawled on the mossy bank.

There was mischief in her eyes.

He said, "My cabin isn't far."

"I know."

"Would you like to go there?"

"Some other time, Nismile."

"All right. Some other time."

"Where do you come from?" she asked.

"I was born on Castle Mount. Do you know where that is? I was a soul-painter at the Coronal's court. Do you know what soul-painting is? It's done with the mind and a sensitive canvas, and—I could show you. I could paint you, Sarise. I take a close look at something, I seize its essence with my deepest consciousness, and then I go into a kind of trance, almost a waking dream, and I transform what I've seen into something of my own and hurl it on the canvas, I capture the truth of it in one quick blaze of transference—" He paused. "I could show you best by making a painting of you."

She scarcely seemed to have heard him.

"Would you like to touch me, Nismile?"

"Yes. Very much."

The thick turquoise moss was like a carpet. She rolled toward him and his hand hovered above her body, and then he hesitated, for he was certain still that she was a Metamorph playing some perverse Shapeshifter game with him, and a heritage of thousands of years of dread and loathing surfaced in him, and he was terrified of touching her and discovering that her skin had the clammy repugnant texture that he imagined Metamorph skin to have, or that she would shift and turn into a creature of alien form the moment she was in his arms. Her eyes were closed, her lips were parted, her tongue flickered between them like a serpent's: she was waiting. In terror he forced his hand down to her breast. But her flesh was warm and yielding and it felt very much the way the flesh of a young human woman should feel, as well as he could recall after these years of solitude. With a soft little cry she pressed herself into his embrace. For a dismaying instant the grotesque image of a Metamorph rose in his mind, angular and long-limbed and noseless, but he shoved the thought away fiercely and gave himself up entirely to her lithe and vigorous body.

For a long time afterward they lay still, side by side, hands clasped, saying nothing. Even when a light rainshower came they did not move, but simply allowed the quick sharp sprinkle to wash the sweat from their skins. He opened his eyes eventually and found her watching him with keen curiosity.

"I want to paint you," he said.

"No."

"Not now. Tomorrow. You'll come to my cabin, and—"

"No."

"I haven't tried to paint in years. It's important to me to begin again. And I want very much to paint you."

"I want very much not to be painted," she said.

"Please."

"No," she said gently. She rolled away and stood up. "Paint the jungle. Paint the pool. Don't paint me, all right, Nismile? All right?"

He made an unhappy gesture of acceptance.

She said, "I have to leave now."

"Will you tell me where you live?"

"I already have. Here and there. In the forest. Why do you ask these questions?"

"I want to be able to find you again. If you disappear, how will I know where to look?"

"I know where to find you," she said. "That's enough."

"Will you come to me tomorrow? To my cabin?"

"I think I will."

He took her hand and drew her toward him. But now she was hesitant, remote. The mysteries of her throbbed in his mind. She had told him nothing, really, but her name. He found it too difficult to believe that she, like he, was a solitary of the jungle, wandering as the whim came; but he doubted that he could have failed to detect, in all these weeks, the existence of a human village nearby.

The most likely explanation still was that she was a Shapeshifter, embarked for who knew what reason on an adventure with a human. Much as he resisted that idea, he was too rational to reject it completely. But she *looked* human, she *felt* human, she *acted* human. How good were these Metamorphs at their transformations? He was tempted to ask her outright whether his suspicions were correct, but that was foolishness; she had answered nothing else, and surely she would not answer that. He kept his questions to himself. She pulled her hand gently free of his grasp and smiled and made the shape of a kiss with her lips, and stepped toward the fern-bordered trail and was gone.

Nismile waited at his cabin all the next day. She did not come. It scarcely surprised him. Their meeting had been a dream, a fantasy, an interlude beyond time and space. He did not expect ever to see her again. Toward evening he drew a canvas from the pack he had brought with him and set it up, thinking he might paint the view from his cabin as twilight purpled the forest air; he studied the landscape a long while, testing the verticals of the slender trees against the heavy horizontal of a thick sprawling yellow-berried bush, and eventually shook his head and put his canvas away. Nothing about this landscape needed to be captured by art. In the morning, he thought, he would hike upstream past the meadow to a place where fleshy red succulents sprouted like rubbery spikes from a deep cleft in a great rock: a more promising scene, perhaps.

But in the morning he found excuses for delaying his departure, and by noon it seemed too late to go. He worked in his little garden plot instead—he had begun transplanting some of the shrubs whose fruits or greens he ate—and that occupied him for hours. In late afternoon a milky fog settled over the forest. He went in; and a few minutes later there was a knock at the door.

"I had given up hope," he told her.

Sarise's forehead and brows were beaded with moisture. The fog, he thought, or maybe she had been dancing along the path. "I promised I'd come," she said softly.

"Yesterday."

"This is yesterday," she said, laughing, and drew a flask from her robe. "You like wine? I found some of this. I had to go a long distance to get it. Yesterday."

It was a young gray wine, the kind that tickles the tongue with its sparkle. The flask had no label, but he supposed it to be some Zimroel wine, unknown on Castle Mount. They drank it all, he more than she—she filled his cup again and again—and when it was gone they lurched outside to make love on the cool damp ground beside the stream, and fell into a doze afterward , she waking him in some small hour of the night and leading him to his bed. They spent the rest of the night pressed close to one another, and in the morning she showed no desire to leave. They went to the pool to begin the day with a swim; they embraced again on the turquoise moss; then she guided him to the gigantic red-barked tree where he had first seen her, and pointed out to him a colossal yellow fruit, three or four yards across, that had fallen from one of its enormous branches. Nismile looked at it doubtfully. It had split open, and its interior was a scarlet custardy stuff, studded with huge gleaming black seeds. "Dwikka," she said. "It will make us drunk."· She stripped off her robe and used it to wrap great chunks of the dwikka-fruit, which they carried back to his cabin and spent all morning eating. They sang and laughed most of the afternoon. For dinner they grilled some fish from Nismile's weir, and later, as they lay arm in arm watching the night descend, she asked him a thousand questions about his past life, his painting, his boyhood, his travels, about Castle Mount, the Fifty Cities, the Six Rivers, the royal court of Lord Thraym, the royal Castle of uncountable rooms. The questions came from her in a torrent, the newest one rushing forth almost before he had dealt with the last. Her curiosity was inexhaustible. It served, also, to stifle his; for although there was much he yearned to know about her—everything—he had no chance to as it, and just as well, for he doubted she would give him answers.

"What will we do tomorrow?" she asked, finally.

So they became lovers. For the first few days they did little but eat and swim and embrace and devour the intoxicating fruit of the dwikka tree. He ceased to fear, as he had at the beginning, that she would disappear as suddenly as she had come to him. Her flood of questions subsided, after a time, but even so he chose not to take his turn, preferring to leave her mysteries unpierced.

He could not shake his obsession with the idea that she was a Metamorph. The thought chilled him—that her beauty was a lie, that behind it she was alien and grotesque—especially when he ran his hands over the cool sweet smoothness of her thighs or breasts. He had constantly to fight away his suspicions. But they would not leave him. There were no human outposts in this part of Zimroel and it was too implausible that this girl—for that was all she was, a girl—had elected, as he had, to take up a hermit's life here. Far more likely, Nismile thought, that she was native to this place, one of the unknown number of Shapeshifters who slipped like phantoms through these humid groves. When she slept he sometimes watched her by faint starlight to see if she began to lose human form. Always she remained as she was; and even so, he suspected her.

And yet, and yet, it was not in the nature of Metamorphs to seek human company or to show warmth toward them. To most people of Majipoor the Metamorphs were ghosts of a former era, revenants, unreal, legendary. Why would one seek him out in his seclusion, offer itself to him in so convincing a counterfeit of love, strive with such zeal to brighten his days and enliven his nights? In a moment of paranoia he imagined Sarise reverting in the darkness to her true shape and rising above him as he slept to plunge a gleaming dirk into his throat: revenge for the crimes of his ancestors. But what folly such fantasies were! If the Metamorphs here wanted to murder him, they had no need of such elaborate charades.

It was almost as absurd to believe that she was a Metamorph as to believe that she was not.

To put these matters from his mind he resolved to take up his art again. On an unusually clear and sunny day he set out with Sarise for the rock of the red succulents, carrying a raw canvas. She watched, fascinated, as he prepared everything.

"You do the painting entirely with your mind?" she asked.

"Entirely. I fix the scene in my soul, I transform and rearrange and heighten, and then—you'll see."

"It's all right if I watch? I won't spoil it?"

"Of course not."

"But if someone else's mind gets into the painting—"

"It can't happen. The canvases are tuned to me." He squinted, made frames with his fingers, moved a few feet this way and that. His throat was dry and his hands were quivering. So many years since last he had done this: would he still have the gift? And the technique? He aligned the canvas and touched it in a preliminary way with his mind. The scene was a good one, vivid, bizarre, the color contrasts powerful ones, the compositional aspects challenging, that massive rock, those weird meaty red plants, the tiny yellow floral bracts at their tips, the forest-dappled sunlight—yes, yes, it would work, it would amply serve as the vehicle through which he could convey the texture of this dense tangled jungle, this place of shapeshifting—

He closed his eyes. He entered trance. He hurled the picture to the canvas.

Sarise uttered a small surprised cry.

Nismile felt sweat break out all over; he staggered and fought for breath; after a moment he regained control and looked toward the canvas.

"How beautiful!" Sarise murmured.

But he was shaken by what he saw. Those dizzying diagonals—the blurred and streaked colors—the heavy greasy sky, hanging in sullen loops from the horizon—it looked nothing like the scene he had tried to capture, and, far more troublesome, nothing like the work of Therion Nismile. It was a dark and anguished painting, corrupted by unintended discords.

"You don't like it?" she asked.

"It isn't what I had in mind."

"Even so—how wonderful, to make the picture come out on the canvas like that—and such a lovely thing—"

"You think it's lovely?"

"Yes, of course! Don't you?"

He stared at her. This? Lovely? Was she flattering him, or merely ignorant of prevailing tastes, or did she genuinely admire what he had done? This strange tormented painting, this somber and alien work—

Alien.

"You don't like it," she said, not a question this time.

"I haven't painted in almost four years. Maybe I need to go about it slowly, to get the way of it right again—"

"I spoiled your painting," Sarise said.

"You? Don't be silly."

"My mind got mixed into it. My way of seeing things."

"I told you that the canvases are tuned to me alone. I could be in the midst of a thousand people and nothing of them would affect the painting."

"But perhaps I distracted you, I swerved your mind somehow."

"Nonsense."

"I'll go for a walk. Paint another one while I'm gone."

"No, Sarise. This one is splendid. The more I look at it, the more pleased I am. Come: let's go home, let's swim and eat some dwikka and make love. Yes?"

He took the canvas from its mount and rolled it. But what she had said affected him more than he would admit. Some kind of strangeness *had* entered the painting, no doubt of it. What if she had managed somehow to taint it, her hidden Metamorph soul radiating its essence into his spirit, coloring the impulses of his mind with an alien hue—

They walked downstream in silence. When they reached the meadow of the mud-lilies where Nismile had seen his first Metamorph, he heard himself blurt, "Sarise, I have to ask you something."

"Yes?"

He could not halt himself . "You aren't human, are you? You're really a Metamorph, right?"

She stared at him wide-eyed, color rising in her cheeks.

"Are you serious?"

He nodded.

"Me a Metamorph?" She laughed, not very convincingly. "What a wild idea!"

"Answer me, Sarise. Look into my eyes and answer me."

"It's too foolish, Therion."

"Please. Answer me."

"You want me to prove I'm human? How could I?"

"I want you to tell me that you're human. Or that you're something else."

"I'm human," she said. "Can I believe that? "

"I don't know. Can you? I've given you your answer." Her eyes flashed with mirth. "Don't I feel human? Don't I act human? Do I seem like an imitation?"

"Perhaps I'm unable to tell the difference."

"Why do you think I'm a Metamorph?"

"Because only Metamorphs live in this jungle," he said. "It seems—logical. Even though—despite—" He faltered. "Look, I've had my answer. It was a stupid question and I'd like to drop the subject. All right?"

"How strange you are! You must be angry with me. You do think I spoiled your painting."

"That's not so."

"You're a very poor liar, Therion."

"All right. *Something* spoiled my painting. I don't know what. It wasn't the painting I intended."

"Paint another one, then."

"I will. Let me paint you, Sarise."

"I told you I didn't want to be painted."

"I need to. I need to see what's in my own soul, and the only way I can know—"

"Paint the dwikka-tree, Therion. Paint the cabin."

"Why not paint you?"

"The idea makes me uncomfortable."

"You aren't giving me a real answer. What is there about being painted that—"

"Please, Therion."

"Are you afraid I'll see you on the canvas in a way that you won't like? Is that it? That I'll get a different answer to my questions when I paint you?"

"Please."

"Let me paint you."

"No."

"Give me a reason, then."

"I can't," she said.

"Then you can't refuse." He drew a canvas from his pack. "Here, in the meadow, now. Go on, Sarise. Stand beside the stream. It'll take only a moment—"

"No, Therion."

"If you love me, Sarise, you'll let me paint you."

It was a clumsy bit of blackmail, and it shamed him to have attempted it; and angered her, for he saw a harsh glitter in her eyes that he had never seen before. They confronted each other for a long tense moment.

Then she said in a cold flat voice, " Not here, Therion. At the cabin. I'll let you paint me there, if you insist."

Neither of them spoke the rest of the way home.

He was tempted to forget the whole thing. It seemed to him that he had imposed his will by force, that he had committed a sort of rape, and he almost wished he could retreat from the position he had won.

But there would never now be any going back to the old easy harmony between them; and he had to have the answers he needed. Uneasily he set about preparing a canvas.

"Where shall I stand?" she asked.

"Anywhere. By the stream. By the cabin."

In a slouching slack-limbed way she moved toward the cabin. He nodded and dispiritedly began the final steps before entering trance. Sarise glowered at him. Tears were welling in her eyes.

"I love you," he cried abruptly, and went down into trance, and the last thing he saw before he closed his eyes was Sarise altering her pose, coming out of her moody slouch, squaring her shoulders, eyes suddenly bright, smile flashing.

When he opened his eyes the painting was done and Sarise was staring timidly at him from the cabin door.

"How is it?" she asked.

"Come. See for yourself."

She walked to his side. They examined the picture together, and after a moment Nismile slipped his arm around her shoulder. She shivered and moved closer to him.

The painting showed a woman with human eyes and Metamorph mouth and nose, against a jagged and chaotic background of clashing reds and oranges and pinks.

She said quietly, "Now do you know what you wanted to know?"

"Was it you in the meadow? And the other two times?"

"Yes."

"Why?"

"You interested me, Therion. I wanted to know all about you. I had never seen anything like you."

"I still don't believe it," he whispered.

She pointed toward the painting. "Believe it, Therion."

"No. No."

"You have your answer now."

"I *know* you're human. The painting lies."

"No, Therion."

"Prove it for me. Change for me. Change now." He released her and stepped a short way back. "Do it. Change for me."

She looked at him sadly. Then, without perceptible transition, she turned herself into a replica of him, as she had done once before: the final proof, the unanswerable answer. A muscle quivered wildly in his cheek. He watched her unblinkingly and she changed again, this time into something terrifying and monstrous, a nightmarish gray pockmarked balloon of a thing with flabby skin and eyes like saucers and a hooked black beak; and from that she went to the Metamorph form, taller than he, hollow-chested and featureless, and then she was Sarise once more, cascades of auburn hair, delicate hands, firm strong thighs.

"No," he said. "Not that one. No more counterfeits."

She became the Metamorph again.

He nodded. "Yes. That's better. Stay that way. It's more beautiful."

"Beautiful, Therion ?"

"I find you beautiful. Like this. As you really are. Deception is always ugly."

He reached for her hand. It had six fingers, very long and narrow, without fingernails or visible joints. Her skin was silky and faintly glossy, and it felt not at all as he had expected. He ran his hands lightly over her slim, practically fleshless body. She was altogether motionless.

"I should go now," she said at last.

"Stay with me. Live here with me."

"Even now?"

"Even now. In your true form."

"You still want me?"

"Very much," he said. " Will you stay?"

She said, "When I first came to you, it was to watch you, to study you, to play with you, perhaps even to mock and hurt you. You are the enemy, Therion. Your kind must always be the enemy. But as we began to live together I saw there was no reason to hate you. Not *you,* you as a special individual, do you understand?"

It was the voice of Sarise coming from those alien lips. How strange, he thought, how much like a dream.

She said, "I began to want to be with you. To make the game go on forever, do you follow? But the game had to end. And yet I still want to be with you."

"Then stay, Sarise."

"Only if you truly want me."

"I've told you that."

"I don't horrify you?"

"No."

"Paint me again, Therion. Show me with a painting. Show me love on the canvas, Therion, and then I'll stay."

* * *

He painted her day after day, until he had used every canvas, and hung them all about the interior of the cabin, Sarise and the dwikka-tree, Sarise in the meadow, Sarise against the milky fog of evening, Sarise at twilight, green against purple. There was no way he could prepare more canvases, although he tried. It did not really matter. They began to go on long voyages of exploration together, down one stream and another, into distant parts of the forest, and she showed him new trees and flowers, and the creatures of the jungle, the toothy lizards and the burrowing golden worms and the sinister ponderous amorfibots sleeping away their days in muddy lakes. They said little to one another; the time for answering questions was over and words were no longer needed.

Day slipped into day, week into week, and in this land of no seasons it was difficult to measure the passing of time. Perhaps a month went by, perhaps six. They encountered nobody else. The jungle was full of Metamorphs, she told him, but they were keeping their distance, and she hoped they would leave them alone forever.

One afternoon of steady drizzle he went out to check his traps, and when he returned an hour later he knew at once something was wrong. As he approached the cabin four Metamorphs emerged. He felt sure that one was Sarise, but he could not tell which one. "Wait!" he cried, as they moved past him. He ran after them. "What do you want with her? Let her go! Sarise? Sarise? Who are they? What do they want?"

For just an instant one of the Metamorphs flickered and he saw the girl with the auburn hair, but only for an instant; then there were four Metamorphs again, gliding like ghosts toward the depths of the jungle. The rain grew more intense, and a heavy fog-bank drifted in, cutting off all visibility. Nismile paused at the edge of the clearing, straining desperately for sounds over the patter of the rain and the loud throb of the stream. He imagined he heard weeping; he thought he heard a cry of pain, but it might have been any other sort of forest-sound. There was no hope of following the Metamorphs into that impenetrable zone of thick white mist.

He never saw Sarise again, nor any other Metamorph. For a while he hoped he would come upon Shapeshifters in the forest and be slain by them with their little polished dirks, for the loneliness was intolerable now. But that did not happen, and when it became obvious that he was living in a sort of quarantine, cut off not only from

Sarise—if she was still alive—but from the entire society of the Metamorph folk, he found himself unable any longer to dwell in the clearing beside the stream. He rolled up his paintings of Sarise and carefully dismantled his cabin and began the long and perilous journey back to civilization. It was a week before his fiftieth birthday when he reached the borders of Castle Mount. In his absence, he discovered, Lord Thraym had become Pontifex and the new Coronal was Lord Vildivar, a man of little sympathy with the arts. Nismile rented a studio on the riverbank at Stee and began to paint again. He worked only from memory: dark and disturbing scenes of jungle life, often showing Metamorphs lurking in the middle distance. It was not the sort of work likely to be popular on the cheerful and airy world of Majipoor, and Nismile found few buyers at first. But in time his paintings caught the fancy of the Duke of Qurain, who had begun to weary of sunny serenity and perfect proportion. Under the duke's patronage Nismile's work grew fashionable, and in the later years of his life there was a ready market for everything he produced.

He was widely imitated, through never successfully, and he was the subject of many critical essays and biographical studies. "Your paintings are so turbulent and strange," one scholar said to him. "Have you devised some method of working from dreams?"

"I work only from memory," said Nismile.

"From painful memory, I would be so bold as to venture."

"Not at all," answered Nismile. "All my work is intended to help me recapture a time of joy, a time of love, the happiest and most precious moment of my life." He stared past the questioner into distant mists, thick and soft as wool, that swirled through clumps of tall slender trees bound by a tangled network of vines.

TO THE DARK STAR

The spring of 1966 was a busy time for me, even as it went in that very busy decade. I had just finished expanding a short story called "Hopper" into a novel for Doubleday; I was getting started on a vast non-fiction account of the quest for El Dorado for Bobbs-Merrill; I was sketching out the novella of distant prehistoric times that would become "Hawksbill Station" for Galaxy and later to be expanded into a novel. In the middle of all this, I somehow found time to write a story for Joseph Elder, who had been my agent for a while, but was about to begin his brief but distinguished editorial career. Joe was planning a book called *The Farthest Reaches*, original stories of galactic exploration, and in April 1966 I gave him "To the Dark Star"—one of the first explorations in science-fictional terms of the black hole concept. Black holes are old stuff by now—there was a photograph of one on the front page of my newspaper this very morning—but I was working on the cutting edge of science fiction when I wrote about one here, more than fifty years ago.

We came to the dark star, the microcephalon and the adapted girl and I, and our struggle began. A poorly assorted lot we were, to begin with. The microcephalon hailed from Quendar IV, where they grow people with greasy gray skins, looming shoulders, and virtually no heads at all. He—it—was wholly alien, at least. The girl was not, and so I hated her.

She came from a world in the Procyon system, where the air was more or less Earth-type, but the gravity was double ours. There were other differences, too. She was thick through the shoulders, thick through the waist, a block of flesh. The genetic surgeons had begun with human raw material, but they had transformed it into something nearly as alien as the microcephalon. Nearly.

We were a scientific team, so they said. Sent out to observe the last moments of a dying star. A great interstellar effort. Pick three specialists at random, put them in a ship, hurl them halfway across the universe to observe what man had never observed before. A fine idea. Noble. Inspiring. We knew our subject well. We were ideal.

But we felt no urge to cooperate, because we hated one another.

The adapted girl—Miranda—was at the controls the day that the dark star actually came into sight. She spent hours studying it before she deigned to let us know that we were at our destination. Then she buzzed us out of our quarters.

I entered the scanning room. Miranda's muscular bulk overflowed the glossy chair before the main screen. The microcephalon stood beside her, a squat figure on a tripodlike arrangement of bony legs, the great shoulders hunched and virtually concealing the tiny cupola of the head. There was no real reason why any organism's brain *had* to be in its skull, and not safely tucked away in the thorax; but I had never grown accustomed to the sight of the creature. I fear I have little tolerance for aliens.

"Look," Miranda said, and the screen glowed.

The dark star hung in dead center, at a distance of perhaps eight light-days—as close as we dared to come. It was not quite dead, and not quite dark. I stared in awe. It was a huge thing, some four solar masses, the imposing remnant of a gigantic star. On the screen there glowed what looked like an enormous lava field. Islands of ash and slag the size of worlds drifted in a sea of molten and glowing magma. A dull red illumination burnished the screen. Black against crimson, the ruined star still throbbed with ancient power. In the depths of that monstrous slagheap compressed nuclei groaned and gasped. Once the radiance of this star had lit a solar system; but I did not dare think of the billions of years that had passed since then, nor of the possible civilizations that had hailed the source of light and warmth before the catastrophe.

Miranda said, “I’ve picked up the thermals already. The surface temperature averages about nine hundred degrees. There’s no chance of landing.”

I scowled at her. “What good is the *average* temperature? Get a specific. One of those islands—”

“The ash masses are radiating at two hundred and fifty degrees. The interstices go from one thousand degrees on up. Everything works out to a mean of nine hundred degrees, and you’d melt in an instant if you went down there. You’re welcome to go, brother. With my blessing.”

“I didn’t say—”

“You implied that there’d be a safe place to land on that fireball,” Miranda snapped. Her voice was a basso boom; there was plenty of resonance space in that vast chest of hers. “You snidely cast doubt on my ability to—”

“We will use the crawler to make our inspection,” said the microcephalon in its reasonable way. “There never was any plan to make a physical landing on the star.”

Miranda subsided. I stared in awe at the sight that filled our screen.

A star takes a long time to die, and the relict I viewed impressed me with its colossal age. It had blazed for billions of years, until the hydrogen that was its fuel had at last been exhausted, and its thermonuclear furnace started to splutter and go out. A star has defenses against growing cold; as its fuel supply dwindles, it begins to contract, raising its density and converting gravitational potential energy into thermal energy. It takes on new life; now a white dwarf, with a density of tons per cubic inch, it burns in a stable way until at last it grows dark.

We have studied white dwarfs for centuries, and we know their secrets—so we think. A cup of matter from a white dwarf now orbits the observatory on Pluto for our further illumination.

But the star on our screen was different.

It had once been a large star—greater than the Chandrasekhar limit, 1.2 solar masses. Thus it was not content to shrink step by step to the status of a white dwarf. The stellar core grew so dense that catastrophe came before stability; when it had converted all its hydrogen to iron-56, it fell into catastrophic collapse and went supernova. A shock wave ran through the core, converting the kinetic energy of collapse into heat. Neutrinos spewed outward; the envelope of the star reached temperatures upwards of 200 billion degrees; thermal energy became intense radiation, streaming away from the agonized star and shedding the luminosity of a galaxy for a brief, fitful moment.

What we beheld now was the core left behind by the supernova explosion. Even after that awesome fury, what was intact was of great mass. The shattered hulk had been cooling for eons, cooling toward the final death. For a small star, that death would be the simple death of coldness: the ultimate burnout, the black dwarf drifting through the void like a hideous mound of ash, lightless, without warmth. But this, our stellar core, was still beyond the Chandrasekhar limit. A special death was reserved for it, a weird and improbable death.

And that was why we had come to watch it perish, the microcephalon and the adapted girl and I.

I parked our small vessel in an orbit that gave the dark star plenty of room. Miranda busied herself with her measurements and computations. The microcephalon had more abstruse things to do. The work was well divided; we each had our chore. The expense of sending a ship so great a distance had necessarily limited the size of the expedition. Three of us: a representative of the basic human stock, a representative of the adapted colonists, a representative of the race of microcephalons, the Quendar people, the only other intelligent beings in the known universe.

Three dedicated scientists. And therefore three who would live in serene harmony during the course of the work, since as everyone knows scientists have no emotions and think only of their professional mysteries. As everyone knows.

I said to Miranda, "Where are the figures for radial oscillation?"

She replied, "See my report. It'll be published early next year in—"

"Damn you, are you doing that deliberately? I need those figures now!"

"Give me your totals on the mass-density curve, then."

"They aren't ready. All I've got is raw data."

"That's a lie! The computer's been running for days! I've seen it," she boomed at me.

I was ready to leap at her throat. It would have been a mighty battle; her 300-pound body was not trained for personal combat as mine was, but she had all the advantages of strength and size. Could I club her in some vital place before she broke me in half? I weighed my options.

Then the microcephalon appeared and made peace once more with a few feathersoft words.

Only the alien among us seemed to conform at all to the stereotype of that emotionless abstraction, "the scientist." It was not true, of course; for all we could tell, the microcephalon seethed with jealousies and lusts and angers, but we had no clue to their outward manifestation. Its voice was flat as a vocoder transmission. The creature moved peacefully among us, the mediator between Miranda and me. I despised it for its mask of tranquility. I suspected, too, that the microcephalon loathed the two of us for our willingness to vent our emotions, and took a sadistic pleasure from asserting superiority by calming us.

We returned to our research. We still had some time before the last collapse of the dark star.

It had cooled nearly to death. Now there was still some thermonuclear activity within that bizarre core, enough to keep the star too warm for an actual landing. It was radiating primarily in the optical band of the spectrum, and by stellar standards its temperature was nil, but for us it would be like prowling the heart of a live volcano.

Finding the star had been a chore. Its luminosity was so low that it could not be detected optically at a greater distance than a light-month or so; it had been spotted by a satellite-borne X-ray telescope that had detected the emanations of the degenerate neutron gas of the core. Now we gathered round and performed our functions of measurement. We recorded things like neutron drip and electron capture. We computed the time remaining before the final collapse. Where necessary, we collaborated; most of the time we went our separate ways. The tension aboard ship was nasty. Miranda went out of her way to provoke me. And, though I like to think I was beyond and above her beastliness, I have to confess that I matched her, obstruction for obstruction. Our alien companion never made any overt attempt to annoy us; but indirect aggression can be maddening in close quarters, and the microcephalon's benign indifference to us was as potent a force for dissonance as Miranda's outright shrewishness or my own deliberately mulish responses.

The star hung in our viewscreen, bubbling with vitality that belied its dying state. The islands of slag, thousands of miles in diameter, broke free and drifted at random on the sea of inner flame. Now and then spouting eruptions of stripped particles came heaving up out of the core. Our figures showed that the final collapse was drawing near, and that meant that an awkward choice was upon us. Someone was going to have to monitor the last moments of the dark star. The risks were high. It could be fatal.

None of us mentioned the ultimate responsibility.

We moved toward the climax of our work. Miranda continued to annoy me in every way, sheerly for the devilishness of it. How I hated her! We had begun this voyage coolly, with nothing dividing us but professional jealousy. But the months of proximity had turned our quarrel into a personal feud. The mere sight of her maddened me, and I'm sure she reacted the same way. She devoted her energies to an immature attempt to trouble me. Lately she took to walking around the ship in the nude, I suspect trying to stir some spark of sexual feeling in me that she could douse with a blunt, mocking refusal. The trouble was that I could feel no desire whatever for a grotesque adapted creature like Miranda, a mound of muscle and bone twice my size. The sight of her massive udders and monumental buttocks stirred nothing in me but disgust.

The witch! Was it desire she was trying to kindle by exposing herself that way, or loathing? Either way, she had me. She must have known that.

In our third month in orbit around the dark star, the microcephalon announced, "The coordinates show an approach to the Schwarzschild radius. It is time to send our vehicle to the surface of the star."

"Which one of us rides monitor?" I asked.

Miranda's beefy hand shot out at me. "You do."

"I think you're better equipped to make the observations," I told her sweetly.

"Thank you, no."

"We must draw lots," said the microcephalon.

"Unfair," said Miranda. She glared at me. "He'll do something to rig the odds. I couldn't trust him."

"How else can we choose?" the alien asked.

"We can vote," I suggested. "I nominate Miranda."

"I nominate him," she snapped.

The microcephalon put his ropy tentacles across the tiny nodule of skull between his shoulders. "Since I do not choose to nominate myself," he said mildly, "it falls to me to make a deciding choice between the two of you. I refuse the responsibility. Another method must be found."

We let the matter drop for the moment. We still had a few more days before the critical time was at hand.

With all my heart I wished Miranda into the monitor capsule. It would mean at best her death, at worst a sober muting of her abrasive personality, if she were the one who sat in vicariously on the throes of the dark star. I was willing to stop at nothing to give her that remarkable and demolishing experience.

What was going to happen to our star may sound strange to a layman; but the theory had been outlined by Einstein and Schwarzschild a thousand years ago, and had been confirmed many times, though never until our expedition had it been observed at close range. When matter reaches a sufficiently high density, it can force the local curvature of space to close around itself, forming a pocket isolated from the rest of the universe. A collapsing supernova core creates just such a Schwarzschild singularity. After it has cooled to near-zero temperature, a core of the proper Chandrasekhar mass undergoes a violent collapse to zero volume, simultaneously attaining an infinite density.

In a way, it swallows itself and vanishes from this universe—for how would the fabric of the continuum tolerate a point of infinite density and zero volume?

Such collapses are rare. Most stars come to a state of cold equilibrium and remain there. We were on the threshold of a singularity, and we were in a position to put an observer vehicle right on the surface of the cold star, sending back an exact description of the events up until the final moment when the collapsing core broke through the walls of the universe and disappeared.

Someone had to ride gain on the equipment, though. Which meant, in effect, vicariously participating in the death of the star. We had learned in other cases that it becomes difficult for the monitor to distinguish between reality and effect; he accepts the sensory percepts from the distant pickup as his own experience. A kind of psychic backlash results; often an unwary brain is burned out entirely.

What impact would the direct experience of being crushed out of existence in a singularity have on a monitoring observer?

I was eager to find out. But not with myself as the sacrificial victim.

I cast about for some way to get Miranda into that capsule. She, of course, was doing the same for me. It was she who made her move first, by attempting to drug me into compliance.

What drug she used, I have no idea. Her people are fond of the nonaddictive hallucinogens, which help them break the monotony of their stark, oversized world. Somehow Miranda interfered with the programming of my food supply and introduced one of her pet alkaloids. I began to feel the effects an hour after I had eaten. I walked to the screen to study the surging mass of the dark star—much changed from its appearance of only a few months before—and as I looked, the image in the screen began to swirl and melt, and tongues of flame did an eerie dance along the horizons of the star.

I clung to the rail. Sweat broke from my pores. Was the ship liquefying? The floor heaved and buckled beneath me. I looked at the back of my hand and saw continents of ash set in a grouting of fiery magma.

Miranda stood behind me. "Come with me to the capsule," she murmured. "The monitor's ready for launching now. You'll find it wonderful to see the last moments."

Lurching after her, I padded through the strangely altered ship. Miranda's adapted form was even more alien than usual; her musculature rippled and flowed, her golden hair held all the colors of the spectrum, her flesh was oddly puckered and cratered, with wiry filaments emerging from the skin. I felt quite calm about entering the capsule. She slid back the hatch, revealing the gleaming console of the panel within and I began to enter, and then suddenly the hallucination deepened and I saw in the darkness of the capsule a devil beyond all imagination.

I dropped to the floor and lay there twitching.

Miranda seized me. To her I was no more than a doll. She lifted me, began to thrust me into the capsule. Perspiration soaked me. Reality returned. I slipped from her grasp and wriggled away, rolling toward the bulkhead. Like a beast of primordial forests she came ponderously after me.

"No," I said. "I won't go."

She halted. Her face twisted in anger, and she turned away from me in defeat. I lay panting and quivering until my mind was purged of phantoms. It had been close.

It was my turn a short while later. Fight force with force, I told myself. I could not risk more of Miranda's treachery. Time was running short.

From our surgical kit I took a hypnoprobe used for anesthesia, and rigged it in a series with one of Miranda's telescope antennae. Programming it for induction of docility, I left it to go to work on her. When she made her observations, the hypnoprobe would purr its siren song of sinister coaxing, and—perhaps—Miranda would bend to my wishes.

It did not work.

I watched her going to her telescopes. I saw her broad-beamed form settling in place. In my mind I heard the hypnoprobe's gentle whisper, as I knew it must sound to Miranda. It was telling her to relax, to obey. "The capsule . . . get into the capsule . . . you will monitor the crawler . . . you . . . you . . . you will do it."

I waited for her to arise and move like a sleepwalker to the waiting capsule. Her tawny body was motionless. Muscles rippled beneath that obscenely bare flesh. The probe had her! Yes! It was getting to her!

She clawed at the telescope as though it were a steel-tipped wasp drilling her brain. The barrel recoiled, and she pushed herself away from it, whirling around. Her eyes glowed with rage. Her enormous body reared up before me. She seemed half berserk. The probe had had some effect on her; I could see her dizzied strides, and knew that she was awry. But it had not been potent enough. Something within that adapted brain of hers gave her the strength to fight off the murky shroud of hypnotism.

"You did that!" she roared. "You gimmicked the telescope, didn't you?"

"I don't know what you mean, Miranda."

"Liar! Fraud! Sneak!"

"Calm down. You're rocking us out of orbit."

"I'll rock all I want! What was that thing that had its fingers in my brain? You put it there? What was it, the hypnoprobe you used?"

"Yes," I admitted coolly. "And what was it you put into my food? Which hallucinogen?"

"It didn't work."

"Neither did my hypnoprobe. Miranda, someone's got to get into that capsule. In a few hours we'll be at the critical point. We don't dare come back without the essential observations. Make the sacrifice."

"For *you?*"

"For science," I said.

I got the horselaugh I deserved. Then Miranda strode toward me. She had recovered her coordination in full, now, and it seemed as though she were planning to thrust me into the capsule by main force. Her ponderous arms enfolded me. The stink of her thickened hide made me retch. I felt ribs creaking within me. I hammered at her body, searching for pressure points that would drop her in a felled heap. We punished each other cruelly, grunting back and forth across the cabin. It was a fierce contest of skill against mass. She would not fall, and I would not crush.

The toneless buzz of the microcephalon said, "Release each other. The collapsing star is nearing its Schwarzschild radius. We must act now."

Miranda's arms slipped away from me. I stepped back, glowering at her, to suck breath into my battered body. Livid bruises were appearing on her skin. We had come to a mutual awareness of mutual strength; but the capsule still was empty. Hatred hovered like a globe of ball lightning between us. The gray, greasy alien creature stood to one side.

I would not care to guess which one of us had the idea first, Miranda or I. But we moved swiftly. The microcephalon scarcely murmured a word of protest as we hustled it down the passage and into the room that held the capsule. Miranda was smiling. I felt relief. She held the alien tight while I opened the hatch, and then she thrust it through. We dogged the hatch together.

"Launch the crawler," she said

I nodded and went to the controls. Like a dart from a blowgun the crawler housing was expelled from our ship and journeyed under high acceleration to the surface of the dark star. It contained a compact vehicle with sturdy jointed legs, controlled by remote pickup from the observation capsule aboard ship. As the observer moved arms and feet within the control harnesses, servo relays actuated the hydraulic pistons in the crawler, eight light-days away. It moved in parallel response, clambering over the slag-heaps of a solar surface that no organic life could endure.

The microcephalon operated the crawler with skill. We watched through the shielded video pickups, getting a close-range view of that inferno. Even a cold sun is more terrifyingly hot than any planet of man.

The signals coming from the star altered with each moment, as the full force of the red-shift gripped the fading light. Something unutterably strange was taking place down there; and the mind of our microcephalon was rooted to the scene. Tidal gravitational forces lashed the star. The crawler was lifted, heaved, compressed, subjected to strains that slowly ripped it apart. The alien witnessed it all, and dictated an account of what he saw, slowly, methodically, without a flicker of fear.

The singularity approached. The tidal forces aspired toward infinity. The microcephalon sounded bewildered at last as it attempted to describe the topological phenomena that no eye had seen before. Infinite density, zero volume—how did the mind comprehend it? The crawler was contorted into an inconceivable shape; and yet its sensors obstinately continued to relay data, filtered through the mind of the microcephalon and into our computer banks.

Then came silence. Our screens went dead. The unthinkable had at last occurred, and the dark star had passed within the radius of singularity. It had collapsed into oblivion, taking with it the crawler. To the alien in the observation capsule aboard our ship, it was as though he too had vanished into the pocket of hyperspace that passed all understanding.

I looked toward the heavens. The dark star was gone. Our detectors picked up the outpouring of energy that marked its annihilation. We were buffeted briefly on the wave of force that ripped outward from the place where the star had been, and then all was calm.

Miranda and I exchanged glances.

"Let the microcephalon out," I said.

She opened the hatch. The alien sat quite calmly at the control console. It did not speak. Miranda assisted it from the capsule. Its eyes were expressionless; but they had never shown anything, anyway.

* * *

We are on our way back to the worlds of our galaxy, now. The mission has been accomplished. We have relayed priceless and unique data.

The microcephalon has not spoken since we removed it from the capsule. I do not believe it will speak again.

Miranda and I perform our chores in harmony. The hostility between us is gone. We are partners in crime, now edgy with guilt that we do not admit to one another. We tend our shipmate with loving care.

Someone had to make the observations, after all. There were no volunteers. The situation called for force, or the deadlock would never have been broken.

But Miranda and I hated each other, you say? Why, then, should we cooperate?

We both are humans, Miranda and I. The microcephalon is not. In the end. That made the difference. In the last analysis, Miranda and I decided that we humans must stick together. There are ties that bind.

We speed on toward civilization.

She smiles at me. I do not find her hateful now. The microcephalon is silent.

BEAUTY IN THE NIGHT

The Alien Years, which I look upon as one of the most successful novels I wrote in the latter part of my career, had a curious composite history. Between 1983 and 1986 I had written a number of unrelated stories in which the Earth is invaded by virtually omnipotent alien beings. The first of these was "Against Babylon," which I wrote late in 1983 for *OMNI* (which took two years to publish it). Then came 1985's "Hannibal's Elephants," also for *Omni* (published in 1988), and 1986's "The Pardoner's Tale," written for *Playboy* and published in 1987. These stories were in no way intended as a series, and in fact were contradictory and incompatible in most details beyond the basic concept of an invaded Earth. But over time it dawned on me that the seeds of a major novel lay in these relatively light-hearted tales of interplanetary conquest.

In 1995 I offered the book to HarperCollins, my publisher at that time, and wrote it in the winter of 1996-97. "Against Babylon," virtually in its entirety, became the opening chapter. A small piece of "Hannibal's Elephants" was incorporated into one of the early sequences. Then I used nearly all of "The Pardoner's Tale" in the latter part of the book. In each case I altered the names of characters to make them fit the overall story I had devised for the novel.

It was all done so smoothly that very few people—not even my own bibliographer—noticed that I had tucked two and a half short stories a decade old into the lengthy new novel. And to make life even more difficult for bibliographers, I then proceeded to carve three new stories out of the text of the book and sell them as individual items to the glossy, high-paying new science fiction magazine *Science Fiction Age*, which Scott Edelman was editing.

They needed a little bending and polishing around the edges to turn into properly rounded short stories, of course. But the process of extraction and revision turned out to be a success. The best of the three, I think, was the first, "Beauty in the Night." Scott used it in his September 1997 issue, and it was chosen the following year not only for Gardner Dozois's annual *Year's Best Science Fiction* anthology but also for David Hartwell's similar collection, *Year's Best SF*. It has gone on to various other sorts of publication, both in the United States and abroad, since then.

The other two—"On the Inside" (*Science Fiction Age*, November 1997) and the novella "The Colonel in Autumn" (*Science Fiction Age*, March 1998)—have had successful independent afterlives as well. But "Beauty in the Night" strikes me as the strongest of the extracted segments of *The Alien Years*, a fitting representative of my work in the second half of the 1990s, and a good example of my fundamental belief that alien life-forms are . . . well, alien.

One: Nine Years from Now

He was a Christmas child, was Khalid—Khalid the Entity-Killer, the first to raise his hand against the alien invaders who had conquered Earth in a single day, sweeping aside all resistance as though we were no more than ants to them. Khalid Haleem Burke, that was his name, English on his father's side, Pakistani on his mother's, born on Christmas Day amidst his mother's pain and shame and his family's grief. Christmas child though he was, nevertheless he was not going to be the new Savior of mankind, however neat a coincidence that might have been. But he would live, though his mother had not, and in the fullness of time he would do his little part, strike his little blow, against the awesome beings who had with such contemptuous ease taken possession of the world into which he had been born.

* * *

To be born at Christmastime can be an awkward thing for mother and child, who even at the best of times must contend with the risks inherent in the general overcrowding and understaffing of hospitals at that time of year. But prevailing hospital conditions were not an issue for the mother of the child of uncertain parentage and dim prospects who was about to come into the world in unhappy and disagreeable circumstances in an unheated upstairs storeroom of a modest Pakistani restaurant grandly named Khan's Mogul Palace in Salisbury, England, very early in the morning of this third Christmas since the advent of the conquering Entities from the stars.

Salisbury is a pleasant little city that lies to the south and west of London and is the principal town of the county of Wiltshire. It is noted particularly for its relatively unspoiled medieval charm, for its graceful and imposing thirteenth-century cathedral, and for the presence, eight miles away, of the celebrated prehistoric megalithic monument known as Stonehenge.

Which, in the darkness before the dawn of that Christmas day, was undergoing one of the most remarkable events in its long history; and, despite the earliness (or lateness) of the hour, a goodly number of Salisbury's inhabitants had turned out to witness the spectacular goings-on.

But not Haleem Khan, the owner of Khan's Mogul Palace, nor his wife Aissha, both of them asleep in their beds. Neither of them had any interest in the pagan monument that was Stonehenge, let alone the strange thing that was happening to it now. And certainly not Haleem's daughter Yasmeena Khan, who was seventeen years old and cold and frightened, and who was lying half naked on the bare floor of the upstairs storeroom of her father's restaurant, hidden between a huge sack of raw lentils and an even larger sack of flour, writhing in terrible pain as shame and illicit motherhood came sweeping down on her like the avenging sword of angry Allah.

She had sinned. She knew that. Her father, her plump, reticent, overworked, mortally weary, and in fact already dying father, had several times in the past year warned her of sin and its consequences, speaking with as much force as she had ever seen him muster; and yet she had chosen to take the risk. Just three times, three different boys, only one time each, all three of them English and white.

Andy. Eddie. Richie.

Names that blazed like bonfires in the neural pathways of her soul.

Her mother—no, not really her mother; her true mother had died when Yasmeena was three; this was Aissha, her father's second wife, the robust and stolid woman who had raised her, had held the family and the restaurant together all these years—had given her warnings too, but they had been couched in entirely different terms.

"You are a woman now, Yasmeena, and a woman is permitted to allow herself some pleasure in life," Aissha had told her. "But you must be careful." Not a word about sin, just taking care not to get into trouble.

Well, Yasmeena had been careful, or thought she had, but evidently not careful enough. Therefore she had failed Aissha. And failed her sad quiet father too, because she had certainly sinned despite all his warnings to remain virtuous, and Allah now would punish her for that. Was punishing her already. Punishing her terribly.

She had been very late discovering she was pregnant. She had not expected to be. Yasmeena wanted to believe that she was still too young for bearing babies, because her breasts were so small and her hips were so narrow, almost like a boy's. And each of those three times when she had done It with a boy—impulsively, furtively, half reluctantly, once in a musty cellar and once in a ruined omnibus and once right here in this very storeroom—she had taken precautions afterward, diligently swallowing the pills she had secretly bought from the smirking Hindu woman at the shop in Winchester, two tiny green pills in the morning and the big yellow one at night, five days in a row.

The pills were so nauseating that they *had* to work. But they hadn't. She should never have trusted pills provided by a Hindu, Yasmeena would tell herself a thousand times over; but by then it was too late.

The first sign had come only about four months before. Her breasts suddenly began to fill out. That had pleased her, at first. She had always been so scrawny; but now it seemed that her body was developing at last. Boys liked breasts. You could see their eyes quickly flicking down to check out your chest, though they seemed to think you didn't notice it when they did. All three of her lovers had put their hands into her blouse to feel hers, such as they were; and at least one—Eddie, the second—had actually been disappointed at what he found there. He had said so, just like that: "Is that *all*?"

But now her breasts were growing fuller and heavier every week, and they started to ache a little, and the dark nipples began to stand out oddly from the smooth little circles in which they were set. So Yasmeena began to feel fear; and when her bleeding did not come on time, she feared even more. But her bleeding had *never* come on time. Once last year it had been almost a whole month late, and she an absolute pure virgin then.

Still, there were the breasts; and then her hips seemed to be getting wider. Yasmeena said nothing, went about her business, chatted pleasantly with the customers, who liked her because she was slender and pretty and polite, and pretended all was well. Again and again at night her hand would slide down her flat boyish belly, anxiously searching for hidden life lurking beneath the taut skin. She felt nothing.

But something was there, all right, and by early October it was making the faintest of bulges, only a tiny knot pushing upward below her navel, but a little bigger every day. Yasmeena began wearing her blouses untucked, to hide the new fullness of her breasts and the burgeoning rondure of her belly. She opened the seams of her trousers and punched two new holes in her belt. It became harder for her to do her work, to carry the heavy trays of food all evening long and to put in the hours afterward washing the dishes, but she forced herself to be strong. There was no one else to do the job. Her father took the orders and Aissha did the cooking and Yasmeena served the meals and cleaned up after the restaurant closed. Her brother Khalid was gone, killed defending Aissha from a mob of white men during the riots that had broken out after the Entities came, and her sister Leila was too small, only five, no use in the restaurant.

No one at home commented on the new way Yasmeena was dressing. Perhaps they thought it was the current fashion. Life was very strange, in these early years of the Conquest.

Her father scarcely glanced at anyone these days; preoccupied with his failing restaurant and his failing health, he went about bowed over, coughing all the time, murmuring prayers endlessly under his breath. He was forty years old and looked sixty. Khan's Mogul Palace was nearly empty, night after night, even on the weekends. People did not travel any more, now that the Entities were here. No rich foreigners came from distant parts of the world to spend the night at Salisbury before going on to visit Stonehenge. The inns and hotels closed; so did most of the restaurants, though a few, like Khan's, struggled on because their proprietors had no other way of earning a living. But the last thing on Haleem Khan's mind was his daughter's changing figure.

As for her stepmother, Yasmeena imagined that she saw her giving her sidewise looks now and again, and worried over that. But Aissha said nothing. So there was probably no suspicion. Aissha was not the sort to keep silent, if she suspected something.

The Christmas season drew near. Now Yasmeena's swollen legs were as heavy as dead logs and her breasts were hard as boulders and she felt sick all the time. It was not going to be long, now. She could no longer hide from the truth. But she had no plan. If her brother Khalid were here, he would know what to do. Khalid was gone, though. She would simply have to let things happen and trust that Allah, when He was through punishing her, would forgive her and be merciful.

Christmas Eve, there were four tables of customers. That was a surprise, to be so busy on a night when most English people had dinner at home. Midway through the evening Yasmeena thought she would fall down in the middle of the room and send her tray, laden with chicken biriani and mutton vindaloo and boti kebabs and schooners of lager, spewing across the floor. She steadied herself then; but an hour later she did fall; or, rather, sagged to her knees, in the hallway between the kitchen and the garbage bin where no one could see her.

She crouched there, dizzy, sweating, gasping, nauseated, feeling her bowels quaking and strange spasms running down the front of her body and into her thighs; and after a time she rose and continued on with her tray toward the bin.

It will be this very night, she thought.

And for the thousandth time that week she ran through the little calculation in her mind: *December 24 minus nine months is March 24, therefore it is Richie Burke, the father. At least he was the one who gave me pleasure also.*

Andy, he had been the first. Yasmeena couldn't remember his last name. Pale and freckled and very thin, with a beguiling smile, and on a humid summer night just after her sixteenth birthday when the restaurant was closed because her father was in hospital for a few days with the beginning of his trouble, Andy invited her dancing and treated her to a couple of pints of brown ale and then, late in the evening, told her of a special party at a friend's house that he was invited to, only there turned out to be no party, just a shabby stale-smelling cellar room and an old spavined couch, and Andy's busy hands roaming the front of her blouse and then going between her legs and her trousers coming off and then, quick, *quick*!, the long hard narrow reddened thing emerging from him and sliding into her, done and done and done in just a couple of moments, a gasp from him and a shudder and his head buried against her cheek and that was that, all over and done with. She had thought it was supposed to hurt, the first time, but she had felt almost nothing at all, neither pain nor anything that might have been delight. The next time Yasmeena saw him in the street Andy grinned and turned crimson and winked at her, but said nothing to her, and they had never exchanged a word since.

Then Eddie Glossop, in the autumn, the one who had found her breasts insufficient and told her so. Big broad-shouldered Eddie, who worked for the meat merchant and who had an air of great worldliness about him. He was old, almost twenty-five. Yasmeena went with him because she knew there was supposed to be pleasure in it and she had not had it from Andy. But there was none from Eddie either, just a lot of huffing and puffing as he lay sprawled on top of her in the aisle of that burned-out omnibus by the side of the road that went toward Shaftesbury. He was much bigger down there than Andy, and it hurt when he went in, and she was glad that this had not been her first time. But she wished she had not done it at all.

And then Richie Burke, in this very storeroom on an oddly warm night in March, with everyone asleep in the family apartments downstairs at the back of the restaurant. She tiptoeing up the stairs, and Richie clambering up the drainpipe and through the window, tall, lithe, graceful Richie who played the guitar so well and sang and told everyone that some day he was going to be a general in the war against the Entities and wipe them from the face of the Earth. A wonderful lover, Richie. Yasmeena kept her blouse on because Eddie had made her uneasy about her breasts. Richie caressed her and stroked her for what seemed like hours, though she was terrified that they would be discovered and wanted him to get on with it; and when he entered her, it was like an oiled shaft of smooth metal gliding into her, moving so easily, easily, easily, one gentle thrust after another, on and on and on until marvelous palpitations began to happen inside her and then she erupted with pleasure, moaning so loud that Richie had to put his hand over her mouth to keep her from waking everyone up.

That was the time the baby had been made. There could be no doubt of that. All the next day she dreamed of marrying Richie and spending the rest of the nights of her life in his arms. But at the end of that week Richie disappeared from Salisbury—some said he had gone off to join a secret underground army that was going to launch guerrilla warfare against the Entities—and no one had heard from him again.

Andy. Eddie. Richie.

* * *

AND HERE SHE WAS ON the floor of the storeroom again, with her trousers off and the shiny swollen hump of her belly sending messages of agony and shame through her body. Her only covering was a threadbare blanket that reeked of spilled cooking oil. Her water had burst about midnight. That was when she had crept up the stairs to wait in terror for the great disaster of her life to finish happening. The contractions were coming closer and closer together, like little earthquakes within her. Now the time had to be two, three, maybe four in the morning. How long would it be? Another hour? Six? Twelve?

Relent and call Aissha to help her?

No. No. She didn't dare.

Earlier in the night voices had drifted up from the streets to her. The sound of footsteps. That was strange, shouting and running in the street, this late. The Christmas revelry didn't usually go on through the night like this. It was hard to understand what they were saying; but then out of the confusion there came, with sudden clarity:

"The aliens! They're pulling down Stonehenge, taking it apart!"

"Get your wagon, Charlie, we'll go and see!"

Pulling down Stonehenge. Strange. Strange. Why would they do that? Yasmeena wondered. But the pain was becoming too great for her to be able to give much thought to Stonehenge just now, or to the Entities who had somehow overthrown the invincible white men in the twinkling of an eye and now ruled the world, or to anything else except what was happening within her, the flames dancing through her brain, the ripplings of her belly, the implacable downward movement of—of—

Something.

"Praise be to Allah, Lord of the Universe, the Compassionate, the Merci-ful," she murmured timidly. "There is no god but Allah, and Mohammed is His prophet."

And again: "Praise be to Allah, Lord of the Universe."

And again.

And again.

The pain was terrible. She was splitting wide open.

"Abraham, Isaac, Ishmael!" That *something* had begun to move in a spiral through her now, like a corkscrew driving a hot track in her flesh. "Mohammed! Mohammed! Mohammed! There is no god but Allah!" The words burst from her with no timidity at all, now. Let Mohammed and Allah save her, if they really existed. What good were they, if they would not save her, she so innocent and ignorant, her life barely begun? And then, as a spear of fire gutted her and her pelvic bones seemed to crack apart, she let loose a torrent of other names, Moses, Solomon, Jesus, Mary, and even the forbidden Hindu names, Shiva, Krishna, Shakti, Kali, anyone at all who would help her through this, anyone, anyone, anyone, anyone—

She screamed three times, short, sharp, piercing screams.

She felt a terrible inner wrenching and the baby came spurting out of her with astonishing swiftness. A gushing Ganges of blood followed it, a red river that spilled out over her thighs and would not stop flowing.

Yasmeena knew at once that she was going to die.

Something wrong had happened. Everything would come out of her insides and she would die. That was absolutely clear to her. Already, just moments after the birth, an eerie new calmness was enfolding her. She had no energy left now for further screaming, or even to look after the baby. It was somewhere down between her spread thighs, that was all she knew. She lay back, drowning in a rising pool of blood and sweat. She raised her arms toward the ceiling and brought them down again to clutch her throbbing breasts, stiff now with milk. She called now upon no more holy names. She could hardly remember her own.

She sobbed quietly. She trembled. She tried not to move, because that would surely make the bleeding even worse.

An hour went by, or a week, or a year.

Then an anguished voice high above her in the dark:

"What? Yasmeena? Oh, my god, my god, my god! Your father will perish!"

Aissha, it was. Bending to her, engulfing her. The strong arm raising her head, lifting it against the warm motherly bosom, holding her tight.

"Can you hear me, Yasmeena? Oh, Yasmeena! My god, my god!" And then an ululation of grief rising from her stepmother's throat like some hot volcanic geyser bursting from the ground. "Yasmeena! Yasmeena!"

"The baby?" Yasmeena said, in the tiniest of voices.

"Yes! Here! Here! Can you see?"

Yasmeena saw nothing but a red haze.

"A boy?" she asked, very faintly.

"A boy, yes."

In the blur of her dimming vision, she thought she saw something small and pinkish-brown, smeared with scarlet, resting in her stepmother's hands. Thought she could hear him crying, even.

"Do you want to hold him?"

"No. No." Yasmeena understood clearly that she was going. The last of her strength had left her. She was moored now to the world by a mere thread.

"He is strong and beautiful," said Aissha. "A splendid boy."

"Then I am very happy." Yasmeena fought for one last fragment of energy. "His name—is—Khalid. Khalid Haleem Burke."

"Burke?"

"Yes. Khalid Haleem Burke."

"Is that the father's name, Yasmeena? Burke?"

"Burke. Richie Burke." With her final sliver of strength she spelled the name.

"Tell me where he lives, this Richie Burke. I will get him. This is shameful, giving birth by yourself, alone in the dark, in this awful room! Why did you never say anything? Why did you hide it from me? I would have helped. I would—"

* * *

But Yasmeena Khan was already dead. The first shaft of morning light now came through the grimy window of the upstairs storeroom. Christmas Day had begun.

Eight miles away, at Stonehenge, the Entities had finished their night's work. Three of the towering alien creatures had supervised while a human work crew, using hand-held pistol-like devices that emitted a bright violet glow, had uprooted every single one of the ancient stone slabs of the celebrated megalithic monument on windswept Salisbury Plain as though they were so many jackstraws. And had rearranged them so that what had been the outer circle of immense sandstone blocks now had become two parallel rows running from north to south; the lesser inner ring of blue slabs had been moved about to form an equilateral triangle; and the sixteen-foot-long block of sandstone at the center of the formation that people called the Altar Stone had been raised to an upright position at the center.

A crowd of perhaps two thousand people from the adjacent towns had watched through the night from a judicious distance as this inexplicable project was being carried out. Some were infuriated; some were saddened; some were indifferent; some were fascinated. Many had theories about what was going on, and one theory was as good as another, no better, no worse

Two: Sixteen Years from Now

You could still see the ghostly lettering over the front door of the former restaurant, if you knew what to look for, the pale greenish outlines of the words that once had been painted there in bright gold: Khan's Mogul Palace. The old swinging sign that had dangled above the door was still lying out back, too, in a clutter of cracked basins and discarded stewpots and broken crockery.

But the restaurant itself was gone, long gone, a victim of the Great Plague that the Entities had casually loosed upon the world as a warning to its conquered people, after an attempt had been made at an attack on an Entity encampment. Half the population of Earth had died so that the Entities could teach the other half not to harbor further rebellious thoughts. Poor sad Haleem Khan himself was gone too, the ever-weary little brown-skinned man who in ten years had somehow saved five thousand pounds from his salary as a dishwasher at the Lion and Unicorn Hotel and had used that, back when England had a queen and Elizabeth was her name, as the seed money for the unpretentious little restaurant that was going to rescue him and his family from utter hopeless poverty. Four days after the Plague had hit Salisbury, Haleem was dead. But if the Plague hadn't killed him, the tuberculosis that he was already harboring probably would have done the job soon enough. Or else simply the shock and disgrace and grief of his daughter Yasmeena's ghastly death in childbirth two weeks earlier, at Christmastime, in an upstairs room of the restaurant, while bringing into the world the bastard child of the long-legged English boy, Richie Burke, the future traitor, the future quisling.

Haleem's other daughter, the little girl Leila, had died in the Plague also, three months after her father and two days before what would have been her sixth birthday. As for Yasmeena's older brother, Khalid, he was already two years gone by then. That was during the time that now was known as the Troubles. A gang of long-haired yobs had set forth late one Saturday afternoon in fine English wrath, determined to vent their resentment over the conquest of the Earth by doing a lively spot of Paki-bashing in the town streets, and they had encountered Khalid escorting Aissha home from the market. They had made remarks; he had replied hotly; and they beat him to death.

Which left, of all the family, only Aissha, Haleem's hardy and tireless second wife. She came down with the Plague, too, but she was one of the lucky ones, one of those who managed to fend the affliction off and survive—for whatever that was worth—into the new and transformed and diminished world. But she could hardly run the restaurant alone, and in any case, with three quarters of the population of Salisbury dead in the Plague, there was no longer much need for a Pakistani restaurant there.

Aissha found other things to do. She went on living in a couple of rooms of the now gradually decaying building that had housed the restaurant, and supported herself, in this era when national currencies had ceased to mean much and strange new sorts of money circulated in the land, by a variety of improvised means. She did housecleaning and laundry for those people who still had need of such services. She cooked meals for elderly folks too feeble to cook for themselves. Now and then, when her number came up in the labor lottery, she put in time at a factory that the Entities had established just outside town, weaving little strands of colored wire together to make incomprehensibly complex mechanisms whose nature and purpose were never disclosed to her.

And when there was no such work of any of those kinds available, Aissha would make herself available to the lorry drivers who passed through Salisbury, spreading her powerful muscular thighs in return for meal certificates or corporate scrip or barter units or whichever other of the new versions of money they would pay her in. That was not something she would have chosen to do, if she had had her choices. But she would not have chosen to have the invasion of the Entities, for that matter, nor her husband's early death and Leila's and Khalid's, nor Yasmeena's miserable lonely ordeal in the upstairs room, but she had not been consulted about any of those things, either. Aissha needed to eat in order to survive; and so she sold herself, when she had to, to the lorry-drivers, and that was that.

As for why survival mattered, why she bothered at all to care about surviving in a world that had lost all meaning and just about all hope, it was in part because survival for the sake of survival was in her genes, and—mostly—because she wasn't alone in the world. Out of the wreckage of her family she had been left with a child to look after—her grandchild, her dead stepdaughter's baby, Khalid Haleem Burke, the child of shame. Khalid Haleem Burke had survived the Plague too. It was one of the ugly little ironies of the epidemic that the Entities had released upon the world that children who were less than six months old generally did not contract it. Which created a huge population of healthy but parentless babes.

He was healthy, all right, was Khalid Haleem Burke. Through every deprivation of those dreary years, the food shortages and the fuel shortages and the little outbreaks of diseases that once had been thought to be nearly extinct, he grew taller and straighter and stronger all the time. He had his mother's wiry strength and his father's long legs and dancer's grace. And he was lovely to behold. His skin was tawny golden-brown, his eyes were a glittering blue-green, and his hair, glossy and thick and curly, was a wonderful bronze color, a magnificent Eurasian hue. Amidst all the sadness and loss of Aissha's life, he was the one glorious beacon that lit the darkness for her.

There were no real schools, not any more. Aissha taught little Khalid herself, as best she could. She hadn't had much schooling herself, but she could read and write, and showed him how, and begged or borrowed books for him wherever she might. She found a woman who understood arithmetic, and scrubbed her floors for her in return for Khalid's lessons. There was an old man at the south end of town who had the Koran by heart, and Aissha, though she was not a strongly religious woman herself, sent Khalid to him once a week for instruction in Islam. The boy was, after all, half Moslem. Aissha felt no responsibility for the Christian part of him, but she did not want to let him go into the world unaware that there was—somewhere, *somewhere!*—a god known as Allah, a god of justice and compassion and mercy, to whom obedience was owed, and that he would, like all people, ultimately come to stand before that god upon the Day of Judgment.

* * *

"AND THE ENTITIES?" KHALID ASKED her. He was six, then. "Will they be judged by Allah too?"

"The Entities are not people. They are jinn."

"Did Allah make them?"

"Allah made all things in heaven and on Earth. He made us out of potter's clay and the jinn out of smokeless fire."

"But the Entities have brought evil upon us. Why would Allah make evil things, if He is a merciful god?"

"The Entities," Aissha said uncomfortably, aware that wiser heads than hers had grappled in vain with that question, "*do* evil. But they are not evil themselves. They are merely the instruments of Allah."

"Who has sent them to us to do evil," said Khalid. "What kind of god is that, who sends evil among His own people, Aissha?"

She was getting beyond her depth in this conversation, but she was patient with him. "No one understands Allah's ways, Khalid. He is the One God and we are nothing before him. If He had reason to send the Entities to us, they were good reasons, and we have no right to question them." *And also to send sickness,* she thought, *and hunger, and death, and the English boys who killed your uncle Khalid in the street, and even the English boy who put you into your mother's belly and then ran away. Allah sent all of those into the world, too.* But then she reminded herself that if Richie Burke had not crept secretly into this house to sleep with Yasmeena, this beautiful child would not be standing here before her at this moment. And so good sometimes could come forth from evil. Who were we to demand reasons from Allah? Perhaps even the Entities had been sent here, ultimately, for our own good.

Perhaps.

* * *

Of Khalid's father, there was no news all this while. He was supposed to have run off to join the army that was fighting the Entities; but Aissha had never heard that there was any such army, anywhere in the world.

Then, not long after Khalid's seventh birthday, when he returned in mid-afternoon from his Thursday Koran lesson at the house of old Iskander Mustafa Ali, he found an unknown white man sitting in the room with his grandmother, a man with a great untidy mass of light-colored curling hair and a lean, angular, almost fleshless face with two cold, harsh blue-green eyes looking out from it as though out of a mask. His skin was so white that Khalid wondered whether he had any blood in his body. It was almost like chalk. The strange white man was sitting in his grandmother's own armchair, and his grandmother was looking very edgy and strange, a way Khalid had never seen her look before, with glistening beads of sweat along her forehead and her lips clamped together in a tight thin line.

The white man said, leaning back in the chair and crossing his legs, which were the longest legs Khalid had ever seen, "Do you know who I am, boy?"

"How would he know?" his grandmother said.

The white man looked toward Aissha and said, "Let me do this, if you don't mind." And then, to Khalid: "Come over here, boy. Stand in front of me. Well, now, aren't we the little beauty? What's your name, boy?"

"Khalid."

"Khalid. Who named you that?"

"My mother. She's dead now. It was my uncle's name. He's dead too."

"Devil of a lot of people are dead who used to be alive, all right. Well, Khalid, my name is Richie."

"Richie," Khalid said, in a very small voice, because he had already begun to understand this conversation.

"Richie, yes. Have you ever heard of a person named Richie? Richie *Burke*."

"My—father." In an even smaller voice.

"Right you are! The grand prize for that lad! Not only handsome but smart, too! Well, what would one expect, eh?—Here I be, boy, your long-lost father! Come here and give your long-lost father a kiss."

Khalid glanced uncertainly toward Aissha. Her face was still shiny with sweat, and very pale. She looked sick. After a moment she nodded, a tiny nod.

He took half a step forward and the man who was his father caught him by the wrist and gathered him roughly in, pulling him inward and pressing him up against him, not for an actual kiss but for what was only a rubbing of cheeks. The grinding contact with that hard, stubbly cheek was painful for Khalid.

"There, boy. I've come back, do you see? I've been away seven worm-eaten miserable years, but now I'm back, and I'm going to live with you and be your father. You can call me 'Dad.'"

Khalid stared, stunned.

"Go on. Do it. Say, 'I'm so very glad that you've come back, Dad.'"

"Dad," Khalid said uneasily.

"The rest of it too, if you please."

"I'm so very glad—" He halted.

"That I've come back."

"That you've come back—"

"*Dad.*"

Khalid hesitated. "Dad," he said.

"There's a good boy! It'll come easier to you after a while. Tell me, did you ever think about me while you were growing up, boy?"

Khalid glanced toward Aissha again. She nodded surreptitiously.

Huskily he said, "Now and then, yes."

"Only now and then? That's all?"

"Well, hardly anybody has a father. But sometimes I met someone who did, and then I thought of you. I wondered where you were.

Aissha said you were off fighting the Entities. Is that where you were, Dad? Did you fight them? Did you kill any of them?"

"Don't ask stupid questions. Tell me, boy: do you go by the name of Burke or Khan?"

"Burke. Khalid Haleem Burke."

"Call me '*sir*' when you're not calling me '*Dad*.' Say, 'Khalid Haleem Burke, sir.'"

"Khalid Haleem Burke, sir. Dad."

"One or the other. Not both." Richie Burke rose from the chair, unfolding himself as though in sections, up and up and up. He was enormously tall, very thin. His slenderness accentuated his great height. Khalid, though tall for his age, felt dwarfed beside him. The thought came to him that this man was not his father at all, not even a man, but some sort of demon, rather, a jinni, a jinni that had been let out of its bottle, as in the story that Iskander Mustafa Ali had told him. He kept that thought to himself. "Good," Richie Burke said. "Khalid Haleem Burke. I like that. Son should have his father's name. But not the Khalid Haleem part. From now on your name is—ah—Kendall. Ken for short."

"Khalid was my—"

"—uncle's name, yes. Well, your uncle is dead. Practically everybody is dead, Kenny. Kendall Burke, good English name. Kendall *Hamilton* Burke, same initials, even, only English. Is that all right, boy? What a pretty one you are, Kenny! I'll teach you a thing or two, I will. I'll make a man out of you."

* * *

Here I be, boy, your long-lost father!

Khalid had never known what it meant to have a father, nor ever given the idea much examination. He had never known hatred before, either, because Aissha was a fundamentally calm, stable, accepting person, too steady in her soul to waste time or valuable energy hating anything, and Khalid had taken after her in that. But Richie Burke, who taught Khalid what it meant to have a father, made him aware of what it was like to hate, also.

Richie moved into the bedroom that had been Aissha's, sending Aissha off to sleep in what had once had been Yasmeena's room. It had long since gone to rack and ruin, but they cleaned it up, some, chasing the spiders out and taping oilcloth over the missing window-panes and nailing down a couple of floor-boards that had popped up out of their proper places. She carried her clothes-cabinet in there by herself, and set up on it the framed photographs of her dead family that she had kept in her former bedroom, and draped two of her old saris that she never wore any more over the bleak places on the wall where the paint had flaked away.

It was stranger than strange, having Richie living with them. It was a total upheaval, a dismaying invasion by an alien life-form, in some ways as shocking in its impact as the arrival of the Entities had been.

He was gone most of the day. He worked in the nearby town of Winchester, driving back and forth in a small brown pre-Conquest automobile. Winchester was a place where Khalid had never been, though his mother had, to purchase the pills that were meant to abort him. Khalid had never been far from Salisbury, not even to Stonehenge, which now was a center of Entity activity anyway, and not a tourist sight. Few people in Salisbury traveled anywhere these days. Not many had automobiles, because of the difficulty of obtaining petrol, but Richie never seemed to have any problem about that.

Sometimes Khalid wondered what sort of work his father did in Winchester; but he asked about it only once. The words were barely out of his mouth when his father's long arm came snaking around and struck him across the face, splitting his lower lip and sending a dribble of blood down his chin.

Khalid staggered back, astounded. No one had ever hit him before. It had not occurred to him that anyone would.

"You must never ask that again!" his father said, looming mountain-high above him. His cold eyes were even colder, now, in his fury. "What I do in Winchester is no business of yours, nor anyone else's, do you hear me, boy? It is my own private affair. My own—private—affair."

Khalid rubbed his cut lip and peered at his father in bewilderment. The pain of the slap had not been so great; but the surprise of it, the shock—that was still reverberating through his consciousness. And went on reverberating for a long while thereafter.

He never asked about his father's work again, no. But he was hit again, more than once, indeed with fair regularity. Hitting was Richie's way of expressing irritation. And it was difficult to predict what sort of thing might irritate him. Any sort of intrusion on his father's privacy, though, seemed to do it. Once, while talking with his father in his bedroom, telling him about a bloody fight between two boys that he had witnessed in town, Khalid unthinkingly put his hand on the guitar that Richie always kept leaning against his wall beside his bed, giving it only a single strum, something that he had occasionally wanted to do for months; and instantly, hardly before the twanging note had died away, Richie unleashed his arm and knocked Khalid back against the wall. "You keep your filthy fingers off that instrument, boy!" Richie said; and after that Khalid did. Another time Richie struck him for leafing through a book he had left on the kitchen table, that had pictures of naked women in it; and another time, it was for staring too long at Richie as he stood before the mirror in the morning, shaving. So Khalid learned to keep his distance from his father; but still he found himself getting slapped for this reason and that, and sometimes for no reason at all. The blows were rarely as hard as the first one had been, and never ever created in him that same sense of shock. But they were blows, all the same. He stored them all up in some secret receptacle of his soul.

Occasionally Richie hit Aissha, too—when dinner was late, or when she put mutton curry on the table too often, or when it seemed to him that she had contradicted him about something. That was more of a shock to Khalid than getting slapped himself, that anyone should dare to lift his hand to Aissha.

The first time it happened, which occurred while they were eating dinner, a big carving knife was lying on the table near Khalid, and he might well have reached for it had Aissha not, in the midst of her own fury and humiliation and pain, sent Khalid a message with her furious blazing eyes that he absolutely was not to do any such thing. And so he controlled himself, then and any time afterward when Richie hit her. It was a skill that Khalid had, controlling himself—one that in some circuitous way he must have inherited from the ever-patient, all-enduring grandparents whom he had never known and the long line of oppressed Asian peasants from whom they descended. Living with Richie in the house gave Khalid daily opportunity to develop that skill to a fine art.

Richie did not seem to have many friends, at least not friends who visited the house. Khalid knew of only three.

There was a man named Arch who sometimes came, an older man with greasy ringlets of hair that fell from a big bald spot on the top of his head. He always brought a bottle of whiskey, and he and Richie would sit in Richie's room with the door closed, talking in low tones or singing raucous songs. Khalid would find the empty whiskey bottle the following morning, lying on the hallway floor. He kept them, setting them up in a row amidst the restaurant debris behind the house, though he did not know why.

The only other man who came was Syd, who had a flat nose and amazingly thick fingers, and gave off such a bad smell that Khalid was able to detect it in the house the next day. Once, when Syd was there, Richie emerged from his room and called to Aissha, and she went in there and shut the door behind her and was still in there when Khalid went to sleep. He never asked her about that, what had gone on while she was in Richie's room. Some instinct told him that he would rather not know.

There was also a woman: Wendy, her name was, tall and gaunt and very plain, with a long face like a horse's and very bad skin, and stringy tangles of reddish hair. She came once in a while for dinner, and Richie always specified that Aissha was to prepare an English dinner that night, lamb or roast beef, none of your spicy Paki curries tonight, if you please. After they ate, Richie and Wendy would go into Richie's room and not emerge again that evening, and the sounds of the guitar would be heard, and laughter, and then low cries and moans and grunts.

One time in the middle of the night when Wendy was there, Khalid got up to go to the bathroom just at the time she did, and encountered her in the hallway, stark naked in the moonlight, a long white ghostly figure. He had never seen a woman naked until this moment, not a real one, only the pictures in Richie's magazine; but he looked up at her calmly, with that deep abiding steadiness in the face of any sort of surprise that he had mastered so well since the advent of Richie. Coolly he surveyed her, his eyes rising from the long thin legs that went up and up and up from the floor and halting for a moment at the curious triangular thatch of woolly hair at the base of her flat belly, and from there his gaze mounted to the round little breasts set high and far apart on her chest, and at last came to her face, which, in the moonlight had unexpectedly taken on a sort of handsomeness if not actual comeliness, though before this Wendy had always seemed to him to be tremendously ugly. She didn't seem displeased at being seen like this. She smiled and winked at him, and ran her hand almost coquettishly through her straggly hair, and blew him a kiss as she drifted on past him toward the bathroom. It was the only time that anyone associated with Richie had ever been nice to him: had even appeared to notice him at all.

But life with Richie was not entirely horrid. There were some good aspects.

One of them was simply being close to so much strength and energy: what Khalid might have called *virility*, if he had known there was any such word. He had spent all his short life thus far among people who kept their heads down and went soldiering along obediently, people like patient plodding Aissha, who took what came to her and never complained, and shriveled old Iskander Mustafa Ali, who understood that Allah determined all things and one had no choice but to comply, and the quiet, tight-lipped English people of Salisbury, who had lived through the Conquest, and the Great Silence when the aliens had turned off all the electrical power in the world, and the Troubles, and the Plague, and who were prepared to be very, very English about whatever horror was coming next.

Richie was different, though. Richie hadn't a shred of passivity in him. "We shape our lives the way we want them to be, boy," Richie would say again and again. "We write our own scripts. It's all nothing but a bloody television show, don't you see that, Kenny-boy?"

That was a startling novelty to Khalid: that you might actually have any control over your own destiny, that you could say "no" to this and "yes" to that and "not right now" to this other thing, and that if there was something you wanted, you could simply reach out and take it. There was nothing Khalid wanted. But the *idea* that he might even have it, if only he could figure out what it was, was fascinating to him.

Then, too, for all of Richie's roughness of manner, his quickness to curse you or kick out at you or slap you when he had had a little too much to drink, he did have an affectionate side, even a charming one. He often sat with them and played his guitar, and taught them the words of songs, and encouraged them to sing along with them, though Khalid had no idea what the songs were about and Aissha did not seem to know either. It was fun, all the same, the singing; and Khalid had known very little fun. Richie was immensely proud of Khalid's good looks and agile, athletic grace, also, and would praise him for them, something which no one had ever done before, not even Aissha. Even though Khalid understood in some way that Richie was only praising himself, really, he was grateful even so.

Richie took him out behind the building and showed him how to throw and catch a ball. How to kick one, too, a different kind of ball. And sometimes there were cricket matches in a field at the edge of town; and when Richie played in these, which he occasionally did, he brought Khalid along to watch. Later, at home, he showed Richie how to hold the bat, how to guard a wicket.

Then there were the drives in the car. These were rare, a great privilege. But sometimes, of a sunny Sunday, Richie would say, "Let's take the old flivver for a spin, eh, Kenny, lad?" And off they would go into the green countryside, usually no special destination in mind, only driving up and down the quiet lanes, Khalid gawking in wonder at this new world beyond the town. It made his head whirl in a good way, as he came to understand that the world actually did go on and on past the boundaries of Salisbury, and was full of marvels and splendors.

So, though at no point did he stop hating Richie, he could see at least some mitigating benefits that had come from his presence in their home. Not many. Some.

Three: Nineteen Years from Now

Once Richie took him to Stonehenge. Or as near to it as it was possible now for humans to go. It was the year Khalid turned ten: a special birthday treat.

"Do you see it out there in the plain, boy? Those big stones? Built by a bunch of ignorant prehistoric buggers who painted themselves blue and danced widdershins in the night. Do you know what 'widdershins' means, boy? No, neither do I. But they did it, whatever it was. Danced around naked with their thingummies jiggling around, and then at midnight they'd sacrifice a virgin on the big altar stone. Long, long ago. Thousands of years. Come on, let's get out and have a look."

Khalid stared. Huge gray slabs, set out in two facing rows flanking smaller slabs of blue stone set in a three-cornered pattern, and a big stone standing upright in the middle. And some other stones lying sideways on top of a few of the gray ones. A transparent curtain of flickering reddish-green light surrounded the whole thing, rising from hidden vents in the ground to nearly twice the height of a man. Why would anyone have wanted to build such a thing? It all seemed like a tremendous waste of time.

"Of course, you understand this isn't what it looked like back then. When the Entities came, they changed the whole business around from what it always was, buggered it all up. Got laborers out here to move every single stone. And they put in the gaudy lighting effects, too. Never used to be lights, certainly not that kind. You walk through those lights, you die, just like a mosquito flying through a candle flame. Those stones there, they were set in a circle originally, and those blue ones there—hey, now, lad, look what we have! You ever see an Entity before, Ken?"

Actually, Khalid had: twice. But never this close. The first one had been right in the middle of the town at noontime. It had been standing outside the entrance of the cathedral cool as you please, as though it happened to be in the mood to go to church: a giant purple thing with orange spots and big yellow eyes. But Aissha had put her hand over his face before he could get a good look, and had pulled him quickly down the street that led away from the cathedral, dragging him along as fast as he was able to could go. Khalid had been about five then. He dreamed of the Entity for months thereafter.

The second time, a year later, he had been with friends, playing within sight of the main highway, when a strange vehicle came down the road, an Entity car that floated on air instead of riding on wheels, and two Entities were standing in it, looking right out at them for a moment as they went floating by. Khalid saw only the tops of their heads that time: their great eyes again, and a sort of a curving beak below, and a great V-shaped slash of a mouth, like a frog's. He was fascinated by them. Repelled, too, because they were so bizarre, these strange alien beings, these enemies of mankind, and he knew he was supposed to loathe and disdain them. But fascinated. Fascinated. He wished he had been able to see them better.

Now, though, he had a clear view of the creatures, three of them. They had emerged from what looked like a door that was set right in the ground, out on the far side of the ancient monument, and were strolling casually among the great stones like lords or ladies inspecting their estate, paying no heed whatever to the tall man and the small boy standing beside the car parked just outside the fiery barrier. It amazed Khalid, watching them teeter around on the little ropy legs that supported their immense tubular bodies, that they were able to keep their balance, that they didn't simply topple forward and fall with a crash.

It amazed him, too, how beautiful they were. He had suspected that from his earlier glances, but now their glory fell upon him with full impact.

The luminous golden-orange spots on the glassy, gleaming purple skin—like fire, those spots were. And the huge eyes, so bright, so keen: you could read the strength of their minds in them, the power of their souls. Their gaze engulfed you in a flood of light. Even the air about the Entities partook of their beauty, glowing with a liquid turquoise radiance.

"There they be, boy. Our lords and masters. You ever see anything so bloody hideous?"

"Hideous?"

"They ain't pretty, isn't that right?"

Khalid made a noncommittal noise. Richie was in a good mood; he always was, on these Sunday excursions. But Khalid knew only too well the penalty for contradicting him in anything. So he looked upon the Entities in silence, lost in wonder, awed by the glory of these strange gigantic creatures, never voicing a syllable of his admiration for their elegance and majesty.

Expansively Richie said, "You heard correctly, you know, when they told you that when I left Salisbury just before you were born, it was to go off and join an army that meant to fight them. There was nothing I wanted more than to kill Entities, nothing. Christ Eternal, boy, did I ever hate those creepy bastards! Coming in like they did, taking our world away quick as you please. But I got to my senses pretty fast, let me tell you. I listened to the plans the underground army people had for throwing off the Entity yoke, and I had to laugh. I had to *laugh*! I could see right away that there wasn't a hope in hell of it. This was even before they put the Great Plague upon us, you understand. I knew. I damn well knew, I did. They're as powerful as gods. You want to fight against a bunch of gods, lots of luck to you. So I quit the underground then and there. I still hate the bastards, mind you, make no mistake about that, but I know it's foolish even to dream about overthrowing them. You just have to fashion your accommodation with them, that's all there is. You just have to make your peace within yourself and let them have their way. Because anything else is a fool's own folly."

Khalid listened. What Richie was saying made sense. Khalid understood about not wanting to fight against gods. He understood also how it was possible to hate someone and yet go on unprotestingly living with him.

"Is it all right, letting them see us like this?" he asked. "Aissha says that sometimes when they see you, they reach out from their chests with the tongues that they have there and snatch you up, and they take you inside their buildings and do horrible things to you there."

Richie laughed harshly. "It's been known to happen. But they won't touch Richie Burke, lad, and they won't touch the son of Richie Burke at Richie Burke's side. I guarantee you that. We're absolutely safe."

Khalid did not ask why that should be. He hoped it was true, that was all.

Two days afterward, while he was coming back from the market with a packet of lamb for dinner, he was set upon by two boys and a girl, all of them about his age or a year or two older, whom he knew only in the vaguest way. They formed themselves into a loose ring just beyond his reach and began to chant in a high-pitched, nasal way: "*Quisling, quisling, your father is a quisling!*"

"What's that you call him?"

"Quisling."

"He is not."

"He is! He is! *Quisling, quisling, your father is a quisling!*"

Khalid had no idea what a quisling was. But no one was going to call his father names. Much as he hated Richie, he knew he could not allow that. It was something Richie had taught him: *Defend yourself against scorn, boy, at all times.* He meant against those who might be rude to Khalid because he was part Pakistani; but Khalid had experienced very little of that. Was a quisling someone who was English but had had a child with a Pakistani woman? Perhaps that was it. Why would these children care, though? Why would anyone?

"*Quisling, quisling—*"

Khalid threw down his package and lunged at the closest boy, who darted away. He caught the girl by the arm, but he would not hit a girl, and so he simply shoved her into the other boy, who went spinning up against the side of the market building. Khalid pounced on him there, holding him close to the wall with one hand and furiously hitting him with the other.

His two companions seemed unwilling to intervene. But they went on chanting, from a safe distance, more nasally than ever.

"*Quis-ling, quis-ling, your fa-ther is a quis-ling!*"

"Stop that!" Khalid cried. "You have no right!" He punctuated his words with blows. The boy he was holding was bleeding, now, his nose, the side of his mouth. He looked terrified.

"*Quis-ling, quis-ling—*"

They would not stop, and neither would Khalid. But then he felt a hand seizing him by the back of his neck, a big adult hand, and he was yanked backward and thrust against the market wall himself. A vast meaty man, a navvy, from the looks of him, loomed over Khalid. "What do you think you're doing, you dirty Paki garbage? You'll kill the boy!"

"He said my father was a quisling!"

"Well, then, he probably is. Get on with you, now, boy! Get on with you!"

He gave Khalid one last hard shove, and spat and walked away. Khalid looked sullenly around for his three tormentors, but they had run off already. They had taken the packet of lamb with them, too.

That night, while Aissha was improvising something for dinner out of yesterday's rice and some elderly chicken, Khalid asked her what a quisling was. She spun around on him as though he had cursed Allah to her ears. Her face all ablaze with a ferocity he had not seen in it before, she said, "Never use that word in this house, Khalid. Never! Never!" And that was all the explanation she would give. Khalid had to learn, on his own, what a quisling was; and when he did, which was soon thereafter, he understood why his father had been unafraid, that day at Stonehenge when they stood outside that curtain of light and looked upon the Entities who were strolling among the giant stones. And also why those three children had mocked him in the street. *You just have to fashion your accommodation with them, that's all there is.* Yes. Yes. Yes. To fashion your accommodation.

Four: Twenty Years from Now

It was after the time that Richie beat Aissha so severely, and then did worse than that—violated her, raped her—that Khalid definitely decided that he was going to kill an Entity.

Not kill Richie. Kill an Entity.

It was a turning point in Khalid's relationship with his father, and indeed in Khalid's whole life, and in the life of any number of other citizens of Salisbury, Wiltshire, England, that time when Richie hurt Aissha so. Richie had been treating Aissha badly all along, of course. He treated *everyone* badly. He had moved into her house and had taken possession of it as though it were his own. He regarded her as a servant, there purely to do his bidding, and woe betide her if she failed to meet his expectations. She cooked; she cleaned the house; Khalid understood now that sometimes, at his whim, Richie would make her come into his bedroom to amuse him or his friend Syd or both of them together. And there was never a word of complaint out of her. She did as he wished; she showed no sign of anger or even resentment; she had given herself over entirely to the will of Allah. Khalid, who had not yet managed to find any convincing evidence of Allah's existence, had not. But he had learned the art of accepting the unacceptable from Aissha. He knew better than to try to change what was unchangeable. So he lived with his hatred of Richie, and that was merely a fact of daily existence, like the fact that rain did not fall upward.

Now, though, Richie had gone too far.

Coming home plainly drunk, red-faced, enraged over something, muttering to himself. Greeting Aissha with a growling curse, Khalid with a stinging slap. No apparent reason for either. Demanding his dinner early. Getting it, not liking what he got. Aissha offering mild explanations of why beef had not been available today. Richie shouting that beef bloody well *should* have been available to the household of Richie Burke.

So far, just normal Richie behavior when Richie was having a bad day. Even sweeping the serving-bowl of curried mutton off the table, sending it shattering, thick oily brown sauce splattering everywhere, fell within the normal Richie range.

But then, Aissha saying softly, despondently, looking down at what had been her prettiest remaining sari now spotted in twenty places, "You have stained my clothing." And Richie going over the top. Erupting. Berserk. Wrath out of all measure to the offense, if offense there had been.

Leaping at her, bellowing, shaking her, slapping her. Punching her, even. In the face. In the chest. Seizing the sari at her midriff, ripping it away, tearing it in shreds, crumpling them and hurling them at her. Aissha backing away from him, trembling, eyes bright with fear, dabbing at the blood that seeped from her cut lower lip with one hand, spreading the other one out to cover herself at the thighs.

Khalid staring, not knowing what to do, horrified, furious.

Richie yelling. "I'll stain you, I will! I'll give you a sodding stain!" Grabbing her by the wrist, pulling away what remained of her clothing, stripping her all but naked right there in the dining room. Khalid covering his face. His own grandmother, forty years old, decent, respectable, naked before him: how could he look? And yet how could he tolerate what was happening? Richie dragging her out of the room, now, toward his bedroom, not troubling even to close the door. Hurling her down on his bed, falling on top of her. Grunting like a pig, a pig, a pig, a pig.

I must not permit this.

Khalid's breast surged with hatred: a cold hatred, almost dispassionate. The man was inhuman, a jinni. Some jinn were harmless, some were evil; but Richie was surely of the evil kind, a demon.

His father. An evil jinni.

But what did that make him? What? What? What? What?

Khalid found himself going into the room after them, against all prohibitions, despite all risks. Seeing Richie plunked between Aissha's legs, his shirt pulled up, his trousers pulled down, his bare buttocks pumping in the air. And Aissha staring upward past Richie's shoulder at the frozen Khalid in the doorway, her face a rigid mask of horror and shame: gesturing to him, making a repeated brushing movement of her hand through the air, wordlessly telling him to go away, to get out of the room, not to watch, not to intervene in any way.

He ran from the house and crouched cowering amid the rubble in the rear yard, the old stewpots and broken jugs and his own collection of Arch's empty whiskey bottles. When he returned, an hour later, Richie was in his room, chopping malevolently at the strings of his guitar, singing some droning tune in a low, boozy voice. Aissha was dressed again, moving about in a slow, downcast way, cleaning up the mess in the dining room. Sobbing softly. Saying nothing, not even looking at Khalid as he entered. A sticking-plaster on her lip. Her cheeks looked puffy and bruised. There seemed to be a wall around her. She was sealed away inside herself, sealed from all the world, even from him.

"I will kill him," Khalid said quietly to her.

"No. That you will not do." Aissha's voice was deep and remote, a voice from the bottom of the sea.

She gave him a little to eat, a cold chapati and some of yesterday's rice, and sent him to his room. He lay awake for hours, listening to the sounds of the house, Richie's endless drunken droning song, Aissha's barely audible sobs. In the morning nobody said anything about anything.

* * *

KHALID UNDERSTOOD THAT IT WAS impossible for him to kill his own father, however much he hated him. But Richie had to be punished for what he had done. And so, to punish him, Khalid was going to kill an Entity.

The Entities were a different matter. They were fair game.

For some time now, on his better days, Richie had been taking Khalid along with him as he drove through the countryside, doing his quisling tasks, gathering information that the Entities wanted to know and turning it over to them by some process that Khalid could not even begin to understand, and by this time Khalid had seen Entities on so many different occasions that he had grown quite accustomed to being in their presence.

And had no fear of them. To most people, apparently, Entities were scary things, ghastly alien monsters, evil, strange; but to Khalid they still were, as they always had been, creatures of enormous beauty. Beautiful the way a god would be beautiful. How could you be frightened by anything so beautiful? How could you be frightened of a god?

They didn't ever appear to notice him at all. Richie would go up to one of them and stand before it, and some kind of transaction would take place. While that was going on, Khalid simply stood to one side, looking at the Entity, studying it, lost in admiration of its beauty. Richie offered no explanations of these meetings and Khalid never asked.

The Entities grew more beautiful in his eyes every time he saw one. They were beautiful beyond belief. He could almost have worshipped them. It seemed to him that Richie felt the same way about them: that he was caught in their spell, that he would gladly fall down before them and bow his forehead to the ground.

And so.

I will kill one of them, Khalid thought.

Because they are so beautiful. Because my father, who works for them, must love them almost as much as he loves himself, and I will kill the thing he loves. He says he hates them, but I think it is not so: I think he loves them, and that is why he works for them. Or else he loves them and hates them both. He may feel the same way about himself. But I see the light that comes into his eyes when he looks upon them.

So I will kill one, yes. Because by killing one of them I will be killing some part of *him*. And maybe there will be some other value in my doing it, besides.

* * *

FIVE: TWENTY-TWO YEARS FROM NOW

Richie Burke said, "Look at this goddamned thing, will you, Ken? Isn't it the goddamnedest fantastic piece of shit anyone ever imagined?"

They were in what had once been the main dining room of the old defunct restaurant. It was early afternoon. Aissha was elsewhere, Khalid had no idea where. His father was holding something that seemed something like a rifle, or perhaps a highly streamlined shotgun, but it was like no rifle or shotgun he had ever seen. It was a long, slender tube of greenish-blue metal with a broad flaring muzzle and what might have been some type of gunsight mounted midway down the barrel and a curious sort of computerized trigger arrangement on the stock. A one-of-a-kind sort of thing, custom made, a home inventor's pride and joy.

"Is it a weapon, would you say?"

"A weapon? A weapon? What the bloody hell do you *think* it is, boy? It's a fucking Entity-killing gun! Which I confiscated this very day from a nest of conspirators over Warminster way. The whole batch of them are under lock and key this very minute, thank you very much, and I've brought Exhibit A home for safe keeping. Have a good look, lad. Ever seen anything so diabolical?"

Khalid realized that Richie was actually going to let him handle it. He took it with enormous care, letting it rest on both his outstretched palms. The barrel was cool and very smooth, the gun lighter than he had expected it to be.

"How does it work, then?"

"Pick it up. Sight along it. You know how it's done. Just like an ordinary gunsight."

Khalid put it to his shoulder, right there in the room. Aimed at the fireplace. Peered along the barrel.

A few inches of the fireplace were visible in the crosshairs, in the most minute detail. Keen magnification, wonderful optics. Touch the right stud, now, and the whole side of the house would be blown out, was that it? Khalid ran his hand along the butt.

"There's a safety on it," Richie said. "The little red button. There. That. Mind you don't hit it by accident. What we have here, boy, is nothing less than a rocket-powered grenade gun. A bomb-throwing machine, virtually. You wouldn't believe it, because it's so skinny, but what it hurls is a very graceful little projectile that will explode with almost incredible force and cause an extraordinary amount of damage, altogether extraordinary. I know because I tried it. It was amazing, seeing what that thing could do."

"Is it loaded now?"

"Oh, yes, yes, you bet your little brown rump it is! Loaded and ready! An absolutely diabolical Entity-killing machine, the product of months and months of loving work by a little band of desperados with marvelous mechanical skills. As stupid as they come, though, for all their skills. Here, boy, let me have that thing before you set it off somehow."

Khalid handed it over.

"Why stupid?" he asked. "It seems very well made."

"I *said* they were skillful. This is a goddamned triumph of miniaturization, this little cannon. But what makes them think they could kill an Entity at all? Don't they imagine anyone's ever tried? Can't be done, Ken, boy. Nobody ever has, nobody ever will."

Unable to take his eyes from the gun, Khalid said obligingly, "And why is that, sir?"

"Because they're bloody unkillable!"

"Even with something like this? Almost incredible force, you said, sir. An extraordinary amount of damage."

"It would fucking well blow an Entity to smithereens, it would, if you could ever hit one with it. Ah, but the trick is to succeed in firing your shot, boy! Which cannot be done. Even as you're taking your aim, they're reading your bloody mind, that's what they do. They know exactly what you're up to, because they look into our minds the way we would look into a book. They pick up all your nasty little unfriendly thoughts about them. And then—bam!—they give you the bloody Push, the thing they do to people with their minds, you know, and you're done for, piff paff poof. We've heard of four cases, at least. Attempted Entity assassination. Trying to take a shot as an Entity went by. Found the bodies, the weapons, just so much trash by the roadside." Richie ran his hands up and down the gun, fondling it almost lovingly. "—This gun here, it's got an unusually great range, terrific sight, will fire upon the target from an enormous distance. Still wouldn't work, I wager you. They can do their telepathy on you from three hundred yards away. Maybe five hundred. Who knows, maybe a thousand. Still, a damned good thing that we broke this ring up in time. Just in case they could have pulled it off somehow."

"It would be bad if an Entity was killed, is that it?" Khalid asked.

Richie guffawed. "Bad? Bad? It would be a bloody catastrophe. You know what they did, the one time anybody managed to damage them in any way? No, how in hell would you know? It was right around the moment you were getting born. Some buggerly American idiots launched a laser attack from space on an Entity building. Maybe killed a few, maybe didn't, but the Entities paid us back by letting loose a plague on us that wiped out damn near every other person there was in the world. Right here in Salisbury they were keeling over like flies. Had it myself. Thought I'd die. Damned well hoped I *would*, I felt so bad. Then I arose from my bed of pain and threw it off. But we don't want to risk bringing down another plague, do we, now? Or any other sort of miserable punishment that they might choose to inflict. Because they certainly will inflict one. One thing that has been clear from the beginning is that our masters will take no shit from us, no, lad, not one solitary molecule of shit."

He crossed the room and unfastened the door of the cabinet that had held Khan's Mogul Palace's meager stock of wine in the long-gone era when this building had been a licensed restaurant. Thrusting the weapon inside, Richie said, "This is where it's going to spend the night. You will make no reference to its presence when Aissha gets back. I'm expecting Arch to come here tonight, and you will make no reference to it to him, either. It is a top secret item, do you hear me? I show it to you because I love you, boy, and because I want you to know that your father has saved the world this day from a terrible disaster, but I don't want a shred of what I have shared with you just now to reach the ears of another human being. Or another inhuman being for that matter. Is that clear, boy? Is it?"

"I will not say a word," said Khalid.

* * *

AND SAID NONE. BUT THOUGHT quite a few.

All during the evening, as Arch and Richie made their methodical way through Arch's latest bottle of rare pre-Conquest whiskey, salvaged from some vast horde found by the greatest of good luck in a Southampton storehouse, Khalid clutched to his own bosom the knowledge that there was, right there in that cabinet, a device that was capable of blowing the head off an Entity, if only one could manage to get within firing range without announcing one's lethal intentions.

Was there a way of achieving that? Khalid had no idea.

But perhaps the range of this device was greater than the range of the Entities' mind-reading capacities. Or perhaps not. Was it worth the gamble? Perhaps it was. Or perhaps not.

Aissha went to her room soon after dinner, once she and Khalid had cleared away the dinner dishes. She said little these days, kept mainly to herself, drifted through her life like a sleepwalker. Richie had not laid a violent hand on her again, since that savage evening several years back, but Khalid understood that she still harbored the pain of his humiliation of her, that in some ways she had never really recovered from what Richie had done to her that night. Nor had Khalid.

He hovered in the hall, listening to the sounds from his father's room until he felt certain that Arch and Richie had succeeded in drinking themselves into their customary stupor. Ear to the door: silence. A faint snore or two, maybe.

He forced himself to wait another ten minutes. Still quiet in there. Delicately he pushed the door, already slightly ajar, another few inches open. Peered cautiously within.

Richie slumped head down at the table, clutching in one hand a glass that still had a little whiskey in it, cradling his guitar between his chest and knee with the other. Arch on the floor opposite him, head dangling to one side, eyes closed, limbs sprawled every which way. Snoring, both of them. Snoring. Snoring. Snoring.

Good. Let them sleep very soundly.

Khalid took the Entity-killing gun now from the cabinet. Caressed its satiny barrel. It was an elegant thing, this weapon. He admired its design. He had an artist's eye for form and texture and color, did Khalid: some fugitive gene out of forgotten antiquity miraculously surfacing in him after a dormancy of centuries, the eye of a Gandharan sculptor, of a Rajput architect, a Gujerati miniaturist coming to the fore in him after passing through all those generations of the peasantry. Lately he had begun doing little sketches, making some carvings. Hiding everything away so that Richie would not find it. That was the sort of thing that might offend Richie, his taking up such piffling pastimes. Sports, drinking, driving around: those were proper amusements for a man.

On one of his good days last year Richie had brought a bicycle home for him: a startling gift, for bicycles were rarities nowadays, none having been available, let alone manufactured, in England in ages. Where Richie had obtained it, from whom, with what brutality, Khalid did not like to think. But he loved his bike. Rode long hours through the countryside on it, every chance he had. It was his freedom; it was his wings. He went outside now, carrying the grenade gun, and carefully strapped it to the bicycle's basket.

He had waited nearly three years for this moment to make itself possible.

Nearly every night nowadays, Khalid knew, one could usually see Entities traveling about on the road between Salisbury and Stonehenge, one or two of them at a time, riding in those cars of theirs that floated a little way above the ground on cushions of air. Stonehenge was a major center of Entity activities nowadays and there were more and more of them in the vicinity all the time. Perhaps there would be one out there this night, he thought. It was worth the chance: he would not get a second opportunity with this captured gun that his father had brought home.

About halfway out to Stonehenge there was a place on the plain where he could have a good view of the road from a little copse several hundred yards away. Khalid had no illusion that hiding in the copse would protect him from the mind-searching capacities the Entities were said to have. If they could detect him at all, the fact that he was standing in the shadow of a leafy tree would not make the slightest difference. But it was a place to wait, on this bright moonlit night. It was a place where he could feel alone, unwatched.

He went to it. He waited there.

He listened to night-noises. An owl; the rustling of the breeze through the trees; some small nocturnal animal scrabbling in the underbrush.

He was utterly calm.

Khalid had studied calmness all his life, with his grandmother Aissha as his tutor. From his earliest days he had watched her stolid acceptance of poverty, of shame, of hunger, of loss, of all kinds of pain. He had seen her handling the intrusion of Richie Burke into her household and her life with philosophical detachment, with stoic patience. To her it was all the will of Allah, not to be questioned.

Allah was less real to Khalid than He was to Aissha, but Khalid had drawn from her her infinite patience and tranquility, at least, if not her faith in God. Perhaps he might find his way to God later on. At any rate, he had long ago learned from Aissha that yielding to anguish was useless, that inner peace was the only key to endurance, that everything must be done calmly, unemotionally, because the alternative was a life of unending chaos and suffering. And so he had come to understand from her that it was possible even to hate someone in a calm, unemotional way. And had contrived thus to live calmly, day by day, with the father whom he loathed.

For the Entities he felt no loathing at all. Far from it. He had never known a world without them, the vanished world where humans had been masters of their own destinies. The Entities, for him, were an innate aspect of life, simply *there*, as were hills and trees, the moon, or the owl who roved the night above him now, cruising for squirrels or rabbits. And they were very beautiful to behold, like the moon, like an owl moving silently overhead, like a massive chestnut tree.

He waited, and the hours passed, and in his calm way he began to realize that he might not get his chance tonight, for he knew he needed to be home and in his bed before Richie awakened and could find him and the weapon gone. Another hour, two at most, that was all he could risk out here.

Then he saw turquoise light on the highway, and knew that an Entity vehicle was approaching, coming from the direction of Salisbury. It pulled into view a moment later, carrying two of the creatures standing serenely upright, side by side, in their strange wagon that floated on a cushion of air.

Khalid beheld it in wonder and awe. And once again marveled, as ever, at the elegance of these Entities, their grace, their luminescent splendor.

How beautiful you are! Oh, yes. Yes.

They moved past him on their curious cart as though traveling on a river of light, and it seemed to him, dispassionately studying the one on the side closer to him, that what he beheld here was surely a jinni of the jinn: Allah's creature, a thing made of smokeless fire, a separate creation. Which none the less must in the end stand before Allah in judgment, even as we.

How beautiful. How beautiful.

I love you.

He loved it, yes. For its crystalline beauty. A jinni? No, it was a higher sort of being than that; it was an angel. It was a being of pure light—of cool clear fire, without smoke. He was lost in rapt admiration of its angelic perfection.

Loving it, admiring it, even worshipping it, Khalid calmly lifted the grenade gun to his shoulder, calmly aimed, calmly stared through the gun-sight. Saw the Entity, distant as it was, transfixed perfectly in the crosshairs. Calmly he released the safety, as Richie had inadvertently showed him how to do. Calmly put his finger to the firing stud.

His soul was filled all the while with love for the beautiful creature before him as—calmly, calmly, calmly—he pressed the stud. He heard a whooshing sound and felt the weapon kicking back against his shoulder with astonishing force, sending him thudding into a tree behind him and for a moment knocking the breath from him; and an instant later the left side of the beautiful creature's head exploded into a cascading fountain of flame, a shower of radiant fragments. A greenish-red mist of what must be alien blood appeared and went spreading outward into the air.

The stricken Entity swayed and fell backward, dropping out of sight on the floor of the wagon.

In that same moment the second Entity, the one that was riding on the far side, underwent so tremendous a convulsion that Khalid wondered if he had managed to kill it, too, with that single shot. It stumbled forward, then back, and crashed against the railing of the wagon with such violence that Khalid imagined he could hear the thump. Its great tubular body writhed and shook, and seemed even to change color, the purple hue deepening almost to black for an instant and the orange spots becoming a fiery red. At so great a distance it was hard to be sure, but Khalid thought, also, that its leathery hide was rippling and puckering as if in a demonstration of almost unendurable pain.

It must be feeling the agony of its companion's death, he realized. Watching the Entity lurch around blindly on the platform of the wagon in what had to be terrible pain, Khalid's soul flooded with compassion for the creature, and sorrow, and love. It was unthinkable to fire again. He had never had any intention of killing more than one; but in any case he knew that he was no more capable of firing a shot at this stricken survivor now than he would be of firing at Aissha.

During all this time the wagon had been moving silently onward as though nothing had happened; and in a moment more it turned the bend in the road and was gone from Khalid's sight, down the road that led toward Stonehenge.

He stood for a while watching the place where the vehicle had been when he had fired the fatal shot. There was nothing there now, no sign that anything had occurred. *Had* anything occurred? Khalid felt neither satisfaction nor grief nor fear nor, really, any emotion of any other sort. His mind was all but blank. He made a point of keeping it that way, knowing he was as good as dead if he relaxed his control even for a fraction of a second.

Strapping the gun to the bicycle basket again, he pedaled quietly back toward home. It was well past midnight; there was no one at all on the road. At the house, all was as it had been; Arch's car parked in front, the front lights still on, Richie and Arch snoring away in Richie's room.

Only now, safely home, did Khalid at last allow himself the luxury of letting the jubilant thought cross his mind, just for a moment, that had been flickering at the threshold of his consciousness for an hour:

Got you, Richie! Got you, you bastard!

He returned the grenade gun to the cabinet and went to bed, and was asleep almost instantly, and slept soundly until the first bird-song of dawn.

* * *

In the tremendous uproar that swept Salisbury the next day, with Entity vehicles everywhere and platoons of the glossy balloon-like aliens that everybody called Spooks going from house to house, it was Khalid himself who provided the key clue to the mystery of the assassination that had occurred in the night.

"You know, I think it might have been my father who did it," he said almost casually, in town, outside the market, to a boy named Thomas whom he knew in a glancing sort of way. "He came home yesterday with a strange sort of big gun. Said it was for killing Entities with, and put it away in a cabinet in our front room."

Thomas would not believe that Khalid's father was capable of such a gigantic act of heroism as assassinating an Entity. No, no, no, Khalid argued eagerly, in a tone of utter and sublime disingenuousness: he did it, I know he did it, he's always talked of wanting to kill one of them one of these days, and now he has.

He has?

Always his greatest dream, yes, indeed.

Well, then—

Yes. Khalid moved along. So did Thomas. Khalid took care to go nowhere near the house all that morning. The last person he wanted to see was Richie. But he was safe in that regard. By noon Thomas evidently had spread the tale of Khalid Burke's wild boast about the town with great effectiveness, because word came traveling through the streets around that time that a detachment of Spooks had gone to Khalid's house and had taken Richie Burke away.

"What about my grandmother?" Khalid asked. "She wasn't arrested too, was she?"

"No, it was just him," he was told. "Billy Cavendish saw them taking him, and he was all by himself. Yelling and screaming, he was, the whole time, like a man being hauled away to be hanged."

Khalid never saw his father again.

During the course of the general reprisals that followed the killing, the entire population of Salisbury and five adjacent towns was rounded up and transported to walled detention camps near Portsmouth. A good many of the deportees were executed within the next few days, seemingly by random selection, no pattern being evident in the choosing of those who were put to death. At the beginning of the following week the survivors were sent on from Portsmouth to other places, some of them quite remote, in various parts of the world.

Khalid was not among those executed. He was merely sent very far away.

He felt no guilt over having survived the death-lottery while others around him were being slain for his murderous act. He had trained himself since childhood to feel very little indeed, even while aiming a rifle at one of Earth's beautiful and magnificent masters. Besides, what affair was it of his, that some of these people were dying and he was allowed to live? Everyone died, some sooner, some later. Aissha would have said that what was happening was the will of Allah. Khalid more simply put it that the Entities did as they pleased, always, and knew that it was folly to ponder their motives.

Aissha was not available to discuss these matters with. He was separated from her before reaching Portsmouth and Khalid never saw her again, either. From that day on it was necessary for him to make his way in the world on his own.

He was not quite thirteen years old. Often, in the years ahead, he would look back at the time when he had slain the Entity; but he would think of it only as the time when he had rid himself of Richie Burke, for whom he had had such hatred. For the Entities he had no hatred at all, and when his mind returned to that event by the roadside on the way to Stonehenge, to the alien being centered in the crosshairs of his weapon, he would think only of the marvelous color and form of the two star-born creatures in the floating wagon, of that passing moment of beauty in the night.

ABOUT THE AUTHOR

ROBERT SILVERBERG IS ONE OF science fiction's most beloved writers, and the author of such contemporary classics as *Dying Inside, Downward to the Earth, Lord Valentine's Castle,* and *At Winter's End.* He is a former president of the Science Fiction and Fantasy Writers of America and the winner of five Nebula Awards and five Hugo Awards. In 2005, the Science Fiction and Fantasy Writers of America presented him with the Grand Master Award.

RECENT AND FORTHCOMING BOOKS FROM THREE ROOMS PRESS

FICTION

Meagan Brothers
Weird Girl and What's His Name

Ron Dakron
Hello Devilfish!

Michael T. Fournier
Hidden Wheel
Swing State

William Least Heat-Moon
Celestial Mechanics

Aimee Herman
Everything Grows

Eamon Loingsigh
Light of the Diddicoy
Exile on Bridge Street

John Marshall
The Greenfather

Aram Saroyan
Still Night in L.A.

Richard Vetere
The Writers Afterlife
Champagne and Cocaine

Julia Watts
Quiver

MEMOIR & BIOGRAPHY

Nassrine Azimi and
Michel Wasserman
Last Boat to Yokohama: The Life and Legacy of Beate Sirota Gordon
(English & Persian editions)

William S. Burroughs & Allen Ginsberg
Don't Hide the Madness: William S. Burroughs in Conversation with Allen Ginsberg edited by Steven Taylor

James Carr
BAD: The Autobiography of James Carr

Richard Katrovas
Raising Girls in Bohemia: Meditations of an American Father; A Memoir in Essays

Judith Malina
Full Moon Stages: Personal Notes from 50 Years of The Living Theatre

Phil Marcade
Punk Avenue: Inside the New York City Underground, 1972-1982

Alvin Orloff
Disasterama! Adventures in the Queer Underground 1977–1997

Stephen Spotte
My Watery Self: Memoirs of a Marine Scientist

PHOTOGRAPHY-MEMOIR

Mike Watt
On & Off Bass

SHORT STORY ANTHOLOGIES

SINGLE AUTHOR

The Alien Archives: Stories
by Robert Silverberg

First-Person Singularities: Stories
by Robert Silverberg
with an introduction by John Scalzi

Tales from the Eternal Café: Stories
by Janet Hamill, with an introduction by Patti Smith

Time and Time Again: Sixteen Trips in Time
by Robert Silverberg

MULTI-AUTHOR

Crime + Music: Twenty Stories of Music-Themed Noir
edited by Jim Fusilli

Dark City Lights: New York Stories
edited by Lawrence Block

Florida Happens: Bouchercon 2018 Anthology
edited by Greg Herren

Have a NYC I, II & III: New York Short Stories;
edited by Peter Carlaftes & Kat Georges

Songs of My Selfie: An Anthology of Millennial Stories
edited by Constance Renfrow

The Obama Inheritance: 15 Stories of Conspiracy Noir
edited by Gary Phillips

This Way to the End Times: Classic and New Stories of the Apocalypse
edited by Robert Silverberg

MIXED MEDIA

John S. Paul
Sign Language: A Painter's Notebook (photography, poetry and prose)

FILM & PLAYS

Israel Horovitz
My Old Lady: Complete Stage Play and Screenplay with an Essay on Adaptation

Peter Carlaftes
Triumph For Rent (3 Plays)
Teatrophy (3 More Plays)

Kat Georges
Three Somebodies: Plays about Notorious Dissidents

HUMOR

Peter Carlaftes
A Year on Facebook

DADA

Maintenant: A Journal of Contemporary Dada Writing & Art (Annual, since 2008)

TRANSLATIONS

Thomas Bernhard
On Earth and in Hell
(poems of Thomas Bernhard with English translations by Peter Waugh)

Patrizia Gattaceca
Isula d'Anima / Soul Island
(poems by the author in Corsican with English translations)

César Vallejo | Gerard Malanga
Malanga Chasing Vallejo
(selected poems of César Vallejo with English translations and additional notes by Gerard Malanga)

George Wallace
EOS: Abductor of Men
(selected poems in Greek & English)

ESSAY COLLECTION

Womentality: Thirteen Empowering Stories by Everyday Women Who Said Goodbye to the Workplace and Hello to Their Lives
edited by Erin Wildermuth

POETRY COLLECTIONS

Hala Alyan
Atrium

Peter Carlaftes
DrunkYard Dog
I Fold with the Hand I Was Dealt

Thomas Fucaloro
It Starts from the Belly and Blooms

Inheriting Craziness is Like a Soft Halo of Light

Kat Georges
Our Lady of the Hunger

Robert Gibbons
Close to the Tree

Israel Horovitz
Heaven and Other Poems

David Lawton
Sharp Blue Stream

Jane LeCroy
Signature Play

Philip Meersman
This is Belgian Chocolate

Jane Ormerod
Recreational Vehicles on Fire
Welcome to the Museum of Cattle

Lisa Panepinto
On This Borrowed Bike

George Wallace
Poppin' Johnny

Three Rooms Press | New York, NY | Current Catalog: www.threeroomspress.com
Three Rooms Press books are distributed by PGW/Ingram: www.pgw.com